The Burning

The Burning

a novel

THOMAS LEGENDRE

Little, Brown and Company
New York • Boston

Little, Brown and Company
Hachette Book Group USA
1271 Avenue of the Americas, New York, NY 10020
Visit our Web site at www.HachetteBookGroupUSA.com

First U.S. Edition: June 2006

The characters and events in this book are fictitious. Any similarity to real persons, living or dead, is coincidental and not intended by the author.

Originally published in the U.K. in March 2006 by Little, Brown

Library of Congress Cataloging-in-Publication Data

Legendre, Thomas.
    The burning : a novel / Thomas Legendre. — 1st U.S. ed.
        p.   cm.
    ISBN-10: 0-316-15380-X
    ISBN-13: 978-0-316-15380-5
        1. Gambling — Nevada — Las Vegas — Fiction.   2. Economists — Fiction.   I. Title.

    PR6112.E42B87 2006
    823'.92 — dc22   2006040819

10 9 8 7 6 5 4 3 2 1

Q-FF

Book design by Meryl Sussman Levavi

Printed in the United States of America

For Allyson

In a different way than in the past, man will have to return to the idea that his existence is a free gift of the sun.

— Nicholas Georgescu-Roegen,
The Entropy Law and the Economic Process

The Burning

Sure, it was Vegas, but he wanted to step outside. He walked over to the sliding doors and parted them wide open, tasting the heat as it swelled over him — a tang in his mouth that took him by surprise, like the flavor of someone you've just kissed. He leaned on the railing. The metal glowed against his forearms, branding his skin. He smiled. This was what he wanted. The surfaces near him radiating. A fever in all the concrete and pavement. Everything touched with fire. He took a deep breath, but then his chest seized up and he started coughing with his head dropped below his shoulders, seasick-tourist pose. Yes, this is what he wanted. This is humanity on the aggregate scale. This is what you want, this is what you get.

By the time he looked up again his eyes were weak and watery and he had to work his gaze slowly outward: The railings. The stucco. The guitar angled toward heaven with its pulsing red fret and sky-blue body, its golden lights flaring over the parking lot. There were palm trees stretching their necks above the great pink plains of the rooftops, construction cranes in the distance with warning lights blinking at their extremities. Another casino was visible — a mock-up of the New York skyline featuring a Brooklyn Bridge, an Empire State, and a Statue of Liberty all clustered together and out of proportion like a scene inside a paperweight. He coughed again. The sun had disappeared, but the horizon still glowed like a hearth. He tried to restore the place to naked desert in his mind but didn't know what sort of plants or animals to resurrect. What things lived in the mountains over there? Fading now. Parched, barren, sharp-edged. He was in the Mojave Desert, he was in Las Vegas, and his lungs were burning with exhaust and the churned-up dust of construction, the city doing its usual heavy breathing. But he didn't know that. His name was Logan Smith and he had just earned a Ph.D. in Economics at the University of Pennsylvania and he wasn't going to sleep in his hotel room tonight. But he didn't know that either.

"It screams, doesn't it," a voice said behind him. "It makes you want to do everything."

Logan glanced back. Deck had emerged from the bathroom freshly showered and shaved, his hair spiked gently with a dab of gel as if it just happened to turn out that way.

"Why do I suspect," Logan said, thinking it was going to be funny until he was halfway through the sentence, "that your everything is different from mine?"

"Blame Prentis. He needs love and attention tonight." Deck came over to the railing and gripped it with both hands, like he was testing its strength. "And why don't you join us. The marginal utility of your first purchase always exceeds the price. Give it a try, Dr. Smith."

This was the joke, already wearing thin, since graduation last week. But Deck liked to get mileage out of his wit. He was angular, finely muscled, a slight stoop to his shoulders that came, it could be said, from adapting himself to the company of smaller people. His mouth went slightly crooked whenever he spoke, like he was telling you a wry and delicious secret.

"I've been socking away cash for the past six months," he said. "Slowly, you know, so I didn't really feel the drain. This is all free."

"I can't see any casinos besides that New York thing."

"The Strip is that way," he said, jerking a thumb over his shoulder. "And anyway, forget the other casinos. You want to know the best one? You're standing on it. This is the place. I won't even mention the ladies across the street. A thirty-second walk. Throw away your car keys."

"So why did we rent a car?"

"Try it, you'll like it."

Logan shifted his gaze back toward New York. A few hours ago he had made the mistake of confessing that he had never been to a strip club. Now it was like having a salesman in his living room. "Really, Deck. Why the car? That was a five-minute drive from the airport, and half of it was traffic lights."

Deck touched his wrist to his forehead, blotting the first signs of perspiration. "Insurance," he said. "We want to be perfectly flexible. You never know what you might want to do."

"Or what Prentis might want to do." Logan squared his shoulders and felt a dewy moisture inside his shirt. It felt good. Of course, part of the enjoyment, he had to admit, came from seeing Deck refuse to acknowledge how much the open doors bothered him. As if it would be too much of a confession.

"You see the growth figures for this place?" Deck asked. "Fastest-growing city in the country. I'd love to see how much per capita GDP this place carries on its back. Feel the blood pumping. Low unemployment, high wages, a cost of living index smaller than your shoe size. The price of a house . . ." He trailed off when he saw Logan reaching into his pocket again for that slip of paper. "You don't have to memorize it, for Christ's sake."

Logan frowned at the numbers. "You're sure this is legal? I see myself being dragged outside and thrown into a car with a bunch of mobster-types for a little ride in the desert, if you know what I mean."

"Please, Dr. Smith. That's the old Vegas. It's all clean and corporate now."

Logan scrubbed a hand through his hair — dark, woolly, prone to Afro if he let it grow more than a couple of inches. It resisted all attempts at alteration. Even Emma, his most recent girlfriend and an amateur hairdresser to boot, had failed to make a change that didn't clash with his broad nose, his permanent tan — which, she and Logan had agreed, was the obvious result of a tryst or two buried with one of Mom's ancestors back in South Carolina. Not that either of his parents would acknowledge it. They claimed it was a rogue Italian gene. Logan, on the other hand, simply wondered if love — or, at the very least, consent — had been a factor in the equation.

He folded the scrap of paper and stuffed it into his pocket. "So if I follow the Basic Strategy, it maximizes my chances of winning."

"It's the cruise control of blackjack. Set it on the table next to you. Or burn it and ask the dealer when to hit, split, double, whatever. He'll tell you the same thing. What you have there is a strategy based on the mathematical probabilities. It's the odds. It's the law."

"But what if I don't —"

The door opened and slammed shut behind them. "Love well, whip well, as Ben Franklin would say. You won't believe what the cocktail waitresses are wearing."

This was Prentis Blewster: loud-mouthed, blunt-nosed, his face half-lit with the expression of someone who laughs loudest at his own jokes. He sold weather derivatives to companies interested in hedging against climate risk, which meant that he traded and leveraged options that were worth a certain amount of money to ski resorts for below-average snowfall and to ice cream stores for rainy summers. He and his co-workers were the only people in the East Coast financial markets who kept copies of the *Farmer's Almanac* in their desks. It should be emphasized, however, that what he sold wasn't insurance. This was high-voltage stuff. Or at least as high-voltage as you could get in Philadelphia.

He came up behind them and draped his arms over their shoulders. "I'm thinking about the time zones and realizing it's way past dinnertime."

Logan resisted a burlesque impulse to shrug off Prentis's arm before he turned and went to his duffel bag. There was a minute or two of coordination — a change of shoes, an inventory of his wallet — before he was ready. As he followed Deck into the hallway, though, he remembered the jug of spring-water he had bought at a convenience store on the way to the hotel. It was still sitting on the front seat of the car. Heating up, probably. He went back into the room and grabbed the key from the bedside table. He'd bring the jug up to the room after dinner. He had heard things about the tapwater in Vegas. Faulty treatment systems. Traces of gasoline and excrement in the pipeline from Lake Mead.

The sliding doors were still open. The air outside was simmering, the traffic thrumming. The guitar pulsing brightly in the dusk. He crossed the room and lingered there for a moment, gazing at the city's costume jewelry. This happened, he thought, every single night. He closed the doors and glanced at a framed photo of Jimi Hendrix over the bed — the Monterrey shot of him kneeling in front of his burning guitar, squirting lighter fluid on the flames. It would be funny to sleep under that.

Deck and Prentis were already a few strides ahead of him in the hallway, joking about the cymbals shading the light fixtures, the g-clefs and quarter notes patterned in the carpet. Logan caught up with them at the elevator. There were a couple of ashtrays next to the doors with the casino's logo stamped into the powdery white sand, utterly pristine and odorless, as if the last thing that belonged there was a cigarette.

Prentis ran a finger through it. "It's like sugar."

Deck smiled and looked over at Logan for a moment of simpatico, but was met with a subtle frown instead. Oh come on, Deck thought. Give it a rest. Did he really expect anyone to believe he didn't want to go to a strip club? Deck would have to spell it out during dinner: This wasn't real. It didn't mean anything. Nobody back in Philadelphia would ever find out about this. They were just three anonymous guys in Vegas for a couple of days, and whatever happened here, stayed here. It was no accident, for example, that Deck didn't spend much time with Prentis in Philadelphia. He recognized a social liability when he saw one. But a liability in one place can be an asset in another. In Vegas, the guy was a spark plug. He got the engine running. It was easy enough to break away whenever you felt like it, especially if women were involved. You simply apologized for your friend's bad behavior and it made you look even better than you would have looked alone.

The elevator doors opened to a pumping, keyboard-sweetened melody that synchronized the movements of everyone who heard it. A processed voice singing about love. They stepped into an interior of fake leopard skin and smoked glass.

Deck arched an eyebrow. "Elevator music."

"You know what Freud said about elevators, boys."

"You've read Freud?" Logan didn't want to sound like a snob, but this was too much.

"My mom's a shrink. Don't ever tell me your dreams."

The elevator lurched to a halt. The music stopped. The lights went out. They tried to look at each other to gauge their reactions, but it was like floating in some lonely corner of the universe where light simply didn't exist.

"I'm patient," Prentis said. "But let me tell you this happened to me once in Chicago and it turned into a night of ill-will."

"Was that the time—"

"Trapped with a ladyfriend, yes, indeed. I politely suggested we do the transaction right there instead of in my room. Oh, the words that came out of that mouth."

OK, Logan had made a mistake and it went like this: A couple of days after defending his dissertation he had wandered into Taps, the local grad-student hangout, to shake off his post-partum depression and set his lack of job prospects in the proper perspective, at which point he ran into Deck, who had also defended his dissertation and was flying to Vegas, he said, for two nights of celebration. Was Logan interested? Cheap flight. Free hotel room. Extra bed. Or at least floor space. It had seemed like the sort of silly and extreme thing he needed. But he hadn't known about Prentis.

"You ever hear from Eastfield?" Deck's voice.

"Um, no." It seemed like a strange time to bring up the job search.

"Don't feel bad. A.E.A. was a funeral this year. Nobody got second interviews."

Logan turned toward Deck—or, rather, where he thought Deck was standing. "How about you?"

There was a pause. "Two interviews next week. Eastfield and Dalton. Sorry."

"I didn't know you applied to Eastfield."

"They came to me. They're looking for someone in Micro and Econometrics."

Of course they were. Everyone was. Deck's dissertation had examined the effects of point-of-sale ATM purchases on individual consumption functions, using data derived from 126 subjects who, for some reason, didn't mind having their checking accounts scrutinized. His analysis was clear-cut, convincing, and, Logan thought, entirely predictable. It combined relevant econometric models with a measure of innovation just large enough to create the impression of originality without the threat of its actual repercussions. Members of Deck's committee had smiled at several points during his defense. The handshakes afterward had been vigorous.

The air was getting stale. Logan closed his eyes for a moment. When he opened them again he couldn't see any difference.

Prentis's voice rose up suddenly. "Hey, what's your dissertation about?"

Logan knew this was meant for him. "Adam Smith."

"Who's that, your uncle?"

"He was the one who wrote—"

"Yeah, yeah, I know. I was joking."

"The topic isn't just Adam Smith," Deck said, apparently on Logan's behalf, "but a careful examination of Smith's argument in *The Wealth of Nations* to expose an inconsistency in his theory of self-interest. You know that line about the butcher and the baker."

"And the candlestick maker?" Prentis barked out a laugh. "Is that grad school or pre-school?"

"'It is not,'" Logan recited, "'from the benevolence of the butcher, the brewer, or the baker, that we expect our dinner, but from their regard to their own self-interest.'"

Deck slipped into a pseudo-English accent. "Dr. Smith performs a rigorous analysis of the text to show that Uncle Adam didn't, in fact, believe self-interest excluded benevolence, as the previous quote suggests. Uncle Adam was sloppy in that one section, you see. But that's the section everyone reads. His words have been taken out of context and misused ever since." He resumed his normal voice. "How's that?"

"Bravo," Logan said.

"So he . . ." Prentis seemed to be struggling with a thought. "So he's saying that Smith was wrong?"

"I don't actually say he was wrong. I say he was inconsistent and contradictory. A lot of current economic theory has been derived from Smith as if his points about self-interest are perfectly cogent. But they're not. Most of the text indicates that benevolence is the guiding principle of people's behavior and that self-interest has only a limited role in social and economic relations."

"Uh-huh."

"And, besides, what Smith means by 'self-interest' is entirely different from what we mean when we use the word today."

"So you're saying—"

"He's saying," Deck said, jumping in again, "that the very foundation of economics is flawed. But it's all between the lines. You should read it. It rocks."

Just then everything came back to life—lights, music, elevator—and they jolted with the sudden movement. The feeling after an outage of having not only power, but senses restored. A new song came from the speakers.

"Yow! We're back, boys, and I like what I see." Prentis did a swing of the hips, Elvis-style, and pointed at the smoked glass, where they all stood reflected. "We look like real citizens."

Logan blinked and tried to follow Prentis's thought. If by "real citizens" he meant the Three Stooges, then he was probably right. Deck went for an urbane look with a bright blue shirt and pleated charcoal pants, while Prentis wore the middle-manager-on-vacation uniform of collared shirt, jeans, and sneakers. Logan, by contrast, had chosen an earth-toned shirt from Morocco that Emma had given to him for his birthday last year. The truth was that he rarely risked shopping for his own clothing. The failures were too frequent and deep. Instead he let the women of his life dress him and he accepted their taste without question. If you arranged his closet in chronological order you'd see the taste of each successive girlfriend displayed in the strata, like the Earth's history in layers of rock. He was that easy. He was the kind of guy who stayed in touch with his ex-girlfriends. There were e-mails, postcards, occasional phone calls to inform of engagements and pregnancies. They had found men with solid careers. He understood the need.

The elevator opened to the main floor, where the music was louder and more momentous, magnified in the wider space. There were ringing slot machines. Knots of people around tables. Players cheering rabidly at one of the craps games.

"Sorry about that, gentlemen." A security agent reached out and held the doors open for them. He stood sideways to let them pass, but with his barrel chest, his beefy neck, his arms like telephone poles, it didn't make much difference. The body of a Polynesian idol, Logan thought. He was wearing an earpiece attached to a spiral cord that disappeared under his black sportcoat. "This one's been givin' us trouble all week."

They made their way over to a display case where one of Elton John's rhinestone outfits stood empty and suspended, as if worn by a ghost. Logan laughed. Jeremy Bentham in his glass case. The greatest pleasure for the greatest number. Welcome to the Panopticon.

Prentis rubbed his hands together. "Let's do a lap before dinner, boys."

Viewed from above, the casino looked like a wheel with a raised hub and outer-rim. There was a circular bar at the center, a sunken mid-section that held all the blackjack and roulette and craps tables, and a promenade along the perimeter where Prentis, Deck, and Logan were walking now, past the slot machines, the glass-shelved gift shops, the themed restaurants, the sports-book with multiplexed screens like the facets of an insect's eye showing baseball and basketball and horse racing and hockey, a computerized board overhead displaying the odds like a train schedule. There were too many things to look at. Rock paraphernalia everywhere. A dead drummer's kit perched over a roulette table. Autographed guitars. A chandelier composed of saxophones. Prentis was talking the whole time, apparently itemizing his budget for the evening. Logan tried to tune it out. If he went straight to the blackjack tables after dinner, they'd get the hint.

Deck leaned toward him. "All right," he said into Logan's ear. "I know he's not exactly your blood-brother, but try to detente this one. Ride it out."

Deck waited for a reply and was disappointed when he didn't get one. He liked to think of himself as the kind of guy who could smooth out the wrinkles between his friends. Especially when those friends were from the East Coast. Let's be objective here. As an expatriate from southern California— and a relatively blond one at that—he had enjoyed a certain cachet at Penn, slowing his voice to half-speed and giving a big sunny smile whenever he wanted some extra latitude. Beach boy. Easy rider of life's waves. People seemed to imagine him surfing through his teens and then graduating magna cum laude—although the truth, it should be noted, was a more painful experience involving violin lessons while his friends played baseball in the street. One of those paper-cuts of childhood. He didn't tell anyone about it, of course, just like he didn't tell anyone his full name was Dechert. But that was another issue. What mattered at the moment was this: the flux, the flow, the exchange. The process taking place all around him. This was a service economy in high gear. This was humanity on the aggregate scale. Here was supply. Here was demand. For every price there is a quantity, for every quantity a price. Call him sentimental, but he sensed a beauty in the working of all these linked utility functions, these multi-rowed matrices of want and satisfaction. He understood it in ways that most people didn't: Happiness equals consumption divided by desire.

He looked over at Logan. Logan looked over at him. For a moment it seemed like they were going to say something to each other, but then one of the slot machines erupted near them and a young woman started screaming.

A red strobe began to flash with a shrill and steady bell like an old-fashioned bank alarm. They watched the proceedings for a minute or two—the man with the clipboard, the security guard, the spruced-up handyman checking the machine—until they got bored and followed Prentis into a fifties-style diner, where they gave their order to a waitress in pink polyester and discussed the odds of hitting a jackpot.

They hadn't noticed her during their lap around the casino. Coarse, heavy, cherrywood hair. Thickly freckled skin. A slight curl to her upper lip. Green eyes the color of oxidized metal. A smoky voice. Because she smoked, off and on. Mostly on. Her name was Dallas Cole and she wore a black corduroy vest over a green satin blouse that matched her eyes totally by coincidence, to be perfectly honest, as she stood at her blackjack table with the cards fanned, her hands resting on the felt. The required body language. This was what, Tuesday? And she loathed this first dead hour when she came on duty at the beginning of the week, basically waiting for people to finish dinner and sharpen up the dream of winning. It was usually like this: a spaced-out feeling as she stood there trying to forget all the dirty dishes piled in the sink or her failure, yet again, to make an appointment at the auto shop to fix either the odometer or gas gauge, take your pick, because she needed at least one of them to end this procedure of stopping at the pump whenever the tank felt low. And when she said "feel" she didn't mean the weight differential, which was what Felix thought, but actual nerve readings, like do I feel like cereal or pancakes this morning. The constant use of intuition was exhausting.

She glanced back at Felix, who seemed to be ignoring her this evening. Never date a floor man. Who you work with. Who's married. Never mind what he does for you in bed. She had ended the affair several times, relapsed several times, and then finally called it quits nearly a month ago. But the aftershocks still took her by surprise. The sharp glances or lack thereof, the veiled comments when he supervised her shuffle. Like she had done something evil. Like how dare she be dissatisfied with the terms of their relationship, which consisted of sexual skirmishes in her apartment whenever he could slip away from his precious Lauren or Laura or whatever her name was. No evidence of him in Dallas's life except his extra toothbrush, which she now used to scrub detergent into stained clothing. They had hidden it from the other employees as well as the wife. Exhausting. She couldn't live that way. She wasn't that sort of person. Once in a while she'd call his house and hang up when his wife answered, and then she'd sit there afterward, thinking, this isn't who I am. She was wide open and straightforward, a blackjack dealer with a half-completed degree at UNLV and she needed to get back to it soon. She hadn't been registered as a full-time student for a few years. Make that five. And don't forget that vacant era between high school and college when she had worked housekeeping at the Pyramid, waiting for the true path of her life to reveal itself. She had wasted a lot of time. Last week she had noticed tiny crinkles along her upper lip and then conducted a full-body inspection in front of the mirror, the results of which were not entirely satisfactory. She wasn't old but she wasn't young either, is what she was thinking these days.

She liked the song playing on the system. Plain and basic. Guitar, bass, drums. A hard, clean voice.

A few people strolled by and eyed her hesitantly, afraid to make the commitment just yet. She smiled. Take a seat so we can enjoy ourselves. Really. Nothing was better than a full table and nothing was worse than an empty one. But they continued toward the craps game. Of course. They wanted high octane.

"Are you open?" a man asked.

She looked him over. He had either the beginnings of a tan or the remains of one. Close-cropped hair, bluish-gray eyes. Strong jaw. Broad nose. Dallas always went for that exclusive offer known as the face. Who could explain it. Her desires didn't have clear-cut definitions, so don't even try. His shirt had an odd design, a burnt-earth color that she liked. A man who knew how to dress.

"Sit down," she said.

"Is this legal?" He held up a square of paper. "I'm asking now so I don't get shot in the kneecaps and thrown off Hoover Dam."

"That only happens if you count cards. Basic Strategy is kosher."

She gathered up the cards, shuffled, squared them against the shoe, and then pushed the whole thing toward him with the cutter resting on top. He took the cutter and examined it for a moment, like a child wondering what to do with this piece of plastic, and she stopped herself from making a smart comment because she didn't want to risk driving him away. Besides, if Felix heard her he'd be on the phone to management before she even reached the end of the sentence. So she gently told him what to do, and he inserted the cutter, and she finished shuffling and then loaded the cards into the shoe.

He pulled a few bills from his pocket and held them out to her.

"On the table," she told him, tapping the felt with her index finger.

He set them down. She spread them diagonally, called the amount to

Felix, and counted out the chips, half in blues, half in reds, all marked with the casino's logo on one side and famous musicians on the other, the edges filigreed with lyrics about money. She lifted the paddle and poked his cash into the drop box and said good luck. Then she dealt. He ended up with a ten and a six. She had a queen showing.

He glanced at his scrap of paper.

"You're supposed to hit."

"So it says. All right."

"Make the sign."

"The sign?"

"For the camera."

He looked up at the tinted hemispheres in the ceiling. "You mean the Eye in the Sky?"

"I mean the camera. Like this." She tapped the felt with her index finger. "That means 'Hit me.'"

He did it. She hit him with an eight and he busted.

"Do I get to see yours?"

She turned over her other card even though she wasn't supposed to, technically, because it slowed down the game. But sometimes she did it in the interest of customer relations and management gave her space on the issue. One of the reasons she liked working here.

She flipped it over. A nine. "See? You would have lost."

"I did lose."

"You know what I mean."

Logan was wondering exactly what she meant when he heard a female voice behind him.

"Drink?"

He swiveled on his stool to find a waitress wearing a low-cut leather vest and leopard-skin shorts and black stockings. For an instant he forgot what he was going to say. The sudden cleavage, the profound contour of her hips. By the time he had recovered and asked for a bourbon and ginger ale, he realized she had seen his expression on a thousand other faces before. A bright but hard demeanor about her. Of course, the outfit was ridiculous, like most things that attracted men. But here was the truth: it worked. His mind seemed to have very little say in the matter. He turned back toward the dealer.

His next hand was already dealt. He ignored it. "Dallas," he said, looking at her nametag. "That's—"

"If you make any jokes involving the state of Texas I will basically deal you bad cards all night, and not because I want to. It generates negative energy."

He glanced down at his cards. "Seventeen. What am I supposed to do with that?"

"Always stand on seventeen."

"Right."

"Make the sign."

"Which is?"

She made a no-more gesture with her palm facing down. He imitated it. Then she flipped over her card. Nineteen.

"If I say your name is beautiful, and if I say it suits you perfectly — and if I say it because I'm motivated by honesty rather than a desire for better cards — does that mean I'll get better cards as a karmic reward?"

She smiled as she cleared away his spot. He placed another chip on it. His hands were large but with unusually slender wrists. Cracked skin at the knuckles. Short nails. No wedding ring. No rings at all. Not even a watch. Sometimes she could read a guy by looking at his hands, but this one was a question mark.

"I already distrust this Basic Strategy. I'm supposed to hold on a twelve?"

"Because I'm showing a six. The general assumption is any card you can't see is a ten. I have a sixteen, is what you're thinking. I'll have to hit and then I'll bust."

He made the hold sign. She flipped her card over. A five. She took another hit, and there it was, a ten — but one card later than she said it would be. She ended up with twenty-one.

"Bad example," she said.

"An exception to the law," he said.

"Right. You're learning." She cleared away his spot. She waited. "You need to put another bet out there."

"You're fast."

"I have to get the hands out at a certain rate."

"Even if we're talking?"

"You have to play to stay."

He hit again and lost again. During the next deal she caught him looking at her face, a more-than-inquisitive glance she experienced sometimes and enjoyed, to be perfectly honest, as long as it was from the neck up. She kept cool, though, directing her smile toward his cards, a king and a queen.

"Guess what you're supposed to do now?"

He made the hold sign.

She flipped over a ten to go with her eight already showing. "See?" she said, paying him. "Easy go, easy come."

He nearly laughed. It was a reversal of the old saying his father had used a couple of months earlier — "easy come, easy go" — to explain the sudden loss of his family's accumulated wealth. The truth, if it must be told, was that Logan had grown up in a section of Philadelphia known as Society Hill, buffered from life's shocks by private schools and a summer home in Maine. This was a little-known fact. You had to work your way through several child-hood stories before you realized his house was a three-story Colonial with fanlights and flowerboxes, his street lined with oaks gently heaving up the brick sidewalks. Instead of an alley outside his bedroom window, there was a court with benches and cherry blossoms, a garage whose door flipped up like the lid of a breadbox. But it all belonged to somebody else now. His parents refused to tell him why. As far as he could tell, power of attorney had been abused, funds had been liquidated, and a former accountant was now living abundantly in the Caribbean. Both the Philadelphia and Maine houses, along with everything in them, had been auctioned off to pay some mysterious debts while his parents resettled in a rented apartment. Unlike Sarah, his younger sister, who had taken up windsurfing in Maui and could scarcely be bothered to send an e-mail every couple of months, Logan lay awake at night worrying. Sure, his parents could take care of themselves. But he wanted to send them some extra money as soon as he found a job. He wanted to help out. In the meantime, though, he was arguing with them — not about where the money had gone, but about their refusal to discuss where the money had gone. On this subject they held to the WASP code of silence. You might as well ask them about their sex lives.

It followed, then, that Logan might have done his degree differently if he had known the family fortune was going to evaporate overnight. This is all speculation, of course, but maybe he wouldn't have avoided the math so much. Maybe he wouldn't have slipped through graduate school on subsistence-level econometrics and focused so exclusively on historical texts, spending his time tracing, say, the influence of Mandeville's *Fable of the Bees* on Adam Smith's theory of rational self-interest. It was a pleasure to write papers without having to whip up coefficients or variables to prove every little thing. And it was a strategy that served him well until the very end, when he looked up from the final draft of his dissertation and found himself marooned on Humanities Island. There he was, sitting under a lone coconut tree in his ragged clothing, scanning the horizon for a decent job — a horizon limited by a dissertation that implicitly criticized the ideology of the economics profession. Not many ships wanted to bring a saboteur on board. What else could he do? The only bright spot had been a short article — a simplified extract from his dissertation, to be accurate — published a few months earlier in *Revenue,* a glossy monolith whose cadre of editors rarely allowed non–Nobel contenders to join its eminent debates. But the promise suggested by the publication simply hadn't materialized into anything substantial. He had even glanced once or twice toward the private sector, but knew from all his unfettered hours at the Penn library that the object of his passion was obscure, his pace slow, his attention span too easily disrupted by ringing phones and pointless meetings to qualify him for most offices in the civilized world. He wanted a job where he could work on one project at a time, with self-imposed deadlines and spontaneous breaks. He wanted a job with guaranteed vacations and holidays. And although it would be ridiculous to say he wanted a low salary, the clear evidence is that he was prepared to accept it, even in light of his parents' financial troubles. He could live with a thin wallet.

In other words, he wanted to teach. He had led discussion sections for a couple of professors and then taught a few courses on his own during his final year, hashing out the material with students who, it seemed to him, showed a raw interest in it. He liked to focus on an issue without becoming microscopic, taking time to explore, experiment, speculate, try this or that idea on for size. He could trot out Galbraith's Dependence Effect, for example, just to see how the class would react to the sacrilegious notion that economic production doesn't satisfy a predetermined demand, but instead creates the very wants that it claims to satisfy. Logan enjoyed working through the material with his students. He enjoyed discussing some of the forgotten texts and acknowledging that although some of the arguments had been disproved outright, others picked at and slowly stripped of their meat over the years, a few insights remained. Never mind, as Deck said one blurry night at Taps, that the guy couldn't find his way out of an aggregate supply function if you drew him a map. Logan liked to scour the theoretical junkyards for old parts and stockpile them in his backyard, so to speak, just in case the right engine came along. And he wasn't as mathematically inept as everyone thought. He simply drew different conclusions. A case in point:

"How many decks are in that shoe?" he asked.

"Six."

"OK. Six decks. A lot of the cards are worth ten, mainly because of the face cards, but there are also a lot of —"

"You should split those."

He looked down at his cards, a pair of eights. After she explained the procedure, he put another chip next to his original bet and waited as she separated the cards, then played them as two different hands. Sixes and sevens came out. Bust, bust.

"Which supports," he said, gesturing at the ruins, "the point I was going to make."

"About those non-ten cards."

"I'm supposed to assume any undealt card is a ten, but the odds of that actually being the case are probably about thirty percent."

"What do you do for a living?"

"There isn't any room for luck in this Basic Strategy."

"Luck is math, to be perfectly honest. There's a higher chance of drawing a ten than any other single card. You're not the kind of guy who puts on a shirt and tie every day, is what I'm thinking."

"Fifteen. I should . . ."

"Hit it."

"But you have a nine showing."

"Exactly."

"I have a bad feeling about this. If I get anything higher than a six—"

"Hit it."

Her smile was dissipating. OK, he thought. All right. He sighed in mock obedience and, averting his face, touched his pinky to the felt as if it might summon a lower card.

When he looked again his bet was gone and some kind of supervisor was standing next to her. Logan's immediate thought was that he had done something wrong. The guy had bulked-out shoulders and a mild glower in his eye, his hands clasped in front of him like a Secret Service agent.

"You should have a comp card," the guy said.

"A what?"

"Comp card. It entitles you to benefits."

"Benefits," Logan repeated. It was like trying to understand a custom in a foreign country where the letters are backward and the money seems to be fake. He glanced at the guy's nametag. Felix.

"A free meal. A free room, maybe. Depending on how much you gamble."

Logan hesitated. Technically speaking, this was an invitation, but it felt like the exact opposite. The expression was all hard lines and surfaces. The eyes of a playground bully, the face of an ex–frat boy.

"He doesn't want it," Dallas finally said.

Felix swiveled his head toward her. "I believe the man can speak for himself. I'm offering," he said, turning back to Logan, "because if you stay at this table you're going to need all the help you can get."

Dallas paused in mid-deal. Her body stiffened. "Playing with fire," she said. "You know that?"

He smiled. "I'm not playing with fire. I'm working with it."

A shrill guitar solo was coming from the speakers. Logan glanced at the cards in front of him and made the hit sign without even thinking. Dallas dealt him another card. A nine to go with his twelve. Twenty-one. He looked at Felix. "I wouldn't want to belong to a club that would have me as a member. Thanks anyway."

Felix didn't move. He stood there, motionless, until one of the other dealers called his name.

"I have to confess," Logan said, after Felix was safely out of range, "that I stole that line from the Marx Brothers."

She didn't reply.

"Bonus points if you can tell me which brother."

She shrugged.

"Multiple choice. A: Harpo. B: Groucho. C: Zeppo. D: Karlo, with a K."

A smile rose to her face as she figured out the joke. "Karlo Marx."

"Author of the *Communisto Manifesto,*" he said in his best Italian accent. "With Frederico Engelli. Full of great recipes, but not very well organized. I really don't want to hit that, do I?"

She finished laughing before she answered. "I'm teaching you how to play. Listen to me. Follow the odds."

He shrugged helplessly. An arm sheathed in diaphanous black netting appeared in front of him and set a drink on the table, complete with napkin and plastic stirring rod. One of Vegas's legendary free cocktails. But it was good luck to tip the waitress, wasn't it? Logan had heard that somewhere. Probably from a waitress. He picked up a chip and placed it on her tray and resisted the urge to follow her with his eyes as she walked away.

He turned back to Dallas. "I'm an economist," he said.

She lowered her chin and looked at him. Her hair shifted and caught the light differently, taking on a certain weight, a certain substance. "And you don't trust the odds," she said. "What would your co-workers say?"

"What co-workers?"

She was about to say something else when another dealer came up behind her and tapped her on the shoulder. Break time. She cleared her hands by clapping them softly and then opening them with her fingers spread. Part of the procedure.

"You're not going anywhere," she said, stepping away from the table. "I'm still teaching you. You're staying right there."

Logan promised he wouldn't move. The new dealer was a soft-spoken man with a goatee and a mild German accent by the name of Weiss. He dealt gently but ruthlessly. Logan faced him alone. A few prospective players hovered at the edges and watched the carnage for a while before moving on. But even as he remained alone at the table, he felt the crowd—the general flux—increasing around him. The music grew louder. The slots became more hysterical in their ringing. The waitress came around again and replaced his empty glass with a full one, accepting his tip with a smile that, he realized, was designed for the same purpose as her outfit.

The game was bleeding him with a surprising steadiness. All the images in his mind had involved sweat and adrenaline, fortunes decided in split-seconds. This was like paying rent. But it was all right. The alternative was to wander the casino by himself and potentially get caught in Deck and Prentis's dragnet when they returned from the strip club. So he nodded along to the music. He gulped his free drink. And he continued losing. His goal was to survive until Dallas returned.

Dallas finished her salad in the employee dining room and pushed the empty plate away. She put up her feet on the chair next to her and lit a cigarette although she had basically quit last week. The truth was that she had discovered an extra pack in her purse and she was thinking why not finish it off. It was all right to backslide once in a while. Besides, the sweet tang of smoke in her lungs was life as she knew it. This was her. Breathing, existing. Sharpened and concentrated. This was her chest expanding and contracting with the bittersweet sensation of herself. There was no other way to explain it.

Her thoughts kept coming back to Logan. He might not be there when she returned. Nothing she could do about that. But it would be a cold table without him. A bad night, to be perfectly honest. Of course, even the best-case scenario ended with him getting on a plane back to the real world and Dallas sitting alone in her apartment with nothing to show for it except another mark on her headboard. So forget it, then. She had learned an important lesson with Felix. Recognize a dead end when you see one.

She looked at the clock and took a final drag from her cigarette before standing up, the smoke still roiling in her lungs. Heading past the vending machines, the serving line, the employee restrooms, she reached the hallway and followed it out to the main floor. The music returned. The ringing slots. The smoke and energy. She was sick of it and crazy for it at the same time, like give me more of what I hate.

When she saw Logan at her table she realized, almost matter-of-factly, that he wanted her in some deep and inexplicable way. The knowledge took hold slowly, spreading outward from the center of her chest, brightening every nerve. Yes. She smiled at him. He smiled back and gestured at his dwindling chips. She was overcome with an urge to pick his locks. It was the only way to know him. She started dealing again. What she missed these days was the notion of sex as a means instead of an end in itself, to be perfectly honest. Her more recent lovers had enjoyed her as if she were some kind of intramural sport. Yes. That was the problem. That was exactly the problem.

OK. So here she was, dealing. A few of the other spots were occupied and she had to give everyone equal attention, getting out the hands quickly and efficiently because it was prime time now. She coached Logan whenever she could. She knew this game. She knew what was good for him.

When it was time to shuffle again she called it out, according to procedure, and Felix came over and made a show of scrutinizing her every move. Strip, cut, riffle, cut again, all the way to the end. Like she'd mess it up. She placed the cutter on top of the cards and slid the whole thing toward Logan.

"Cut 'em thin to win," she said.

Logan cleared his mind, narrowed his eyes, and pretended to bless the cards before he inserted the cutter. Then he winked at Felix just for the hell of it. Felix turned his back on him. Logan smiled. Dallas smiled. They smiled together. This was a feeling he liked, smiling with her, a blood-luscious glow in his veins from the mixed drinks. He began asking a few harmless questions about her life, just to see what he could learn, and discovered she had grown up about five miles away from where he was sitting. The old Las Vegas, she said. Casinos packed along Fremont Street. The entire city visible from Red Rock Park. Wherever that was. He wanted to see it. He thought about asking her to take him there tomorrow, but stopped short. Felix was either an ex- or soon-to-be-ex-boyfriend, and he was still hovering. Besides, Logan didn't want to poison the game.

"Insurance?" she asked.

"What's that?"

"I have an ace showing, right? If you give me an amount equal to half your bet, you're protected from my potential blackjack."

Logan was trying to pay attention to her words, but the silken contours of her neck, her tender throat, were difficult to ignore. He wondered what her skin tasted like.

"I don't know," he finally said. "You tell me. Do I want insurance?"

"No," she said.

"No," he repeated, shaking his head.

She put her two cards together with the ace on top and slid them over to the peeper. "It's a girl," she said, flipping over the second card, a queen, for blackjack.

He gripped his heart as if he had been shot. "Medic!"

"Stop it," she said, trying not to laugh.

The other players eventually picked up and left. He was alone again. The next time the waitress came around he ordered springwater. This was the end. Two chips left. He propped his chin on his hand and set the next-to-last chip out there. His cards came out. A six and a five. Her card was a three.

"Double down," Dallas said.

"Assuming it's a ten in that shoe." He had played similar hands a couple of times already. The problem with doubling was that he could have only one more card. A high card would be heaven, a low card hell. He searched her eyes for a moment. She seemed to want more from him than just a decision on the cards.

"Last chance," she said.

He sighed. He obeyed. He placed his last chip next to his original bet and tapped the felt. She gave him another card. A two. Of course. She played out her hand until she ended up with twenty. That was it. He stood up.

"Where are you going?"

"I'm done."

"No you're not."

"What am I going to play with, pennies?"

"Those bills in your left pocket."

He looked down at it with an expression of exaggerated shock. "Are you psychic?"

"It's a requirement of the job."

"This," he said, patting his pocket, "is what I'm planning to spend on meals during the next couple of days."

She stood with her hands resting on the table, the most recent cards in the discard pile and the chips in the rack. She could see him thinking about it. She cleared her hands and gathered her hair into a ponytail, held it for a moment, and then shook it out again. She started talking, persuading him to stay. She knew how. It was all about the fluctuations, the necessity of riding out the losses to reach the hot streaks, because the game favored the player with deep pockets, which was the spic-and-span truth.

"Besides," she added, "they're going to raise the minimum bet soon. But if you're already playing, you're grandfathered. Keep your bets small when you're losing, big when you're winning."

He drew his watch out of his pocket, a cheap digital model with half the wristband missing. "When do they raise the minimum?"

She eyed the people milling around them. "Soon."

"I mean what time?"

She shook her head. "Time doesn't matter. It's all about the crowd."

"Supply and demand," he said, more to himself than her. He took out his remaining cash and held it in his palm for a moment. Tomorrow night's gambling money. He could feel Dallas's gaze on him. He couldn't imagine surviving another night in Las Vegas with nothing to spend. But he couldn't imagine leaving this table either. One of his favorite songs began to play.

He tossed the bills onto the table.

"You're making me happy," she said.

He didn't know what to say to that. He really didn't. So he smiled. He obeyed her instructions and resumed his losing streak. But the decline, he had to admit, was much milder now, alleviated by some positive trends in which the cards did what they were supposed to do. Other players sat down next to him. When all seven spots were occupied Felix came over, removed the minimum-bet sign, and replaced it with a new one listing a higher amount. Logan looked around. The casino had reached critical mass. Every table occupied, every dealer busy. People were clogging the lanes between the tables now, spilling down the stairway from the center bar. There were men in sportcoats and designer pants, women in fringes and sequins. Velvet dresses, satin skirts. High heels, low necklines. This is it, he thought.

Weiss showed up again and tapped Dallas for a break. She cleared her hands and said she'd be back soon. She looked at Logan when she said it.

"Weiss has a halo of good luck," a woman next to Logan said. He looked at her — a brown-eyed blonde with frosted lips and hair styled in layers for a tossed, carefree look. "Can you see it?" she asked.

He shrugged and said he could see halos and horns on everyone, as a matter of fact, and she laughed and touched him on the ribs as if he had made the most supremely funny comment in the world. His eyes wandered down the length of her body. A short red dress with a slit up the side. Trim thighs. Calves like scissor-blades trying to cut something, it seemed to him, whenever she crossed and recrossed her legs, which she did repeatedly, as if they didn't quite fit together properly. This isn't happening, he thought. She doesn't really want me. Unless—

"Mother-in-law," a guy sitting next to Logan said. He was wearing a turned-back baseball cap.

"What?"

"That. Seventeen."

"Why is seventeen a 'mother-in-law'?"

"You want to hit her, but you can't." He scooped up his chips and left.

At the far end of the table a young guy wearing a tank top began to shout "bang" every time the dealer busted. His name, he said, was Spoons. The two women sitting next to him, mousy-looking twins from San Jose who shared an ashtray and gave each other high-fives to celebrate the rare blackjack, began to join in. Bang-bang. Logan warded off a few more comments from the blonde and, during the next shuffle, turned the opposite way and struck up a conversation with the man who had replaced the mother-in-law beater— an ex–football player, judging by the freakish mass of him, his limbs evidently stiffened with the injuries of a hard career. His head, when he turned it, swiveled like a tank turret. But the voice was mild and sweet, the perfect narrator of children's stories.

Dallas returned. Everyone welcomed her. There was a little give-and-take between her and Logan, but it was too difficult now with the table crowded, the cards and chips flying at a faster rate.

"I don't know about you," the blonde said, nudging Logan again, "but I'm sick of treading water. I want some net worth."

Logan wondered if there was a way to switch seats without causing a spectacle. Maybe the player at the far end—a man who was either Japanese or American of Japanese descent—would trade with him. He wore a wrinkled white shirt, a tie loosened and skewed away from his collar with the top button undone, stubble along the upper lip and chin. A hard day at the office. Or maybe a hard day at the office in Tokyo.

Logan looked at his next hand. Nineteen. He glanced at the other spots and saw face cards, a couple of aces paired with nines. Everyone held. Dallas flipped over an ace to go with her ten. A collective groan.

The Japanese man cleared his throat and announced, in perfect English, "The art of losing isn't hard to master."

Logan felt his buzz tapering off and ordered another drink. If there was one thing he would accomplish tonight, it would be this state of light but constant inebriation. As the waitress whisked away his empty bottle of springwater he remembered the jug sitting in the car. He had been so focused on getting away from Prentis and Deck after dinner that he had forgotten to take it up to the room. Later, he thought. After I lose everything. He looked at Dallas and made a show of counting his chips.

"You're a brave man," she said. "But if you trust me and stay with the Basic Strategy, your luck will change."

"I've heard that before," Spoons said. "I want to see you go bang on this hand."

Logan heard a voice behind him. "What's this?"

He turned. The voice belonged to a giant — another football player, he guessed — hovering over his friend's shoulder. This one was black and completely bald, a gold stud gleaming in one of his earlobes. He reached down and fingered his friend's chips. "You was up, what, six hundred when I saw you last? You was building Rome."

"Burning, more like."

"In twenty minutes?"

"A severed femoral artery empties faster than you can imagine."

"Come again?"

"I'll catch you at the roulette table."

The man stepped back as if he had been insulted. "Craps," he said. "You want to find me, craps is where I'm at." He detached himself from the table and moved off, clearing a lane through the crowd. There was a teetering, drunken reel to the place now, the bump-and-grind of a large party. The music was inching up louder to overcome the noise. Logan saw a few men in Hawaiian shirts carrying blow-up dolls, a group of women in pink dresses surrounding a bride.

"What's a femoral artery?" he asked, turning back to the man sitting next to him.

The man pointed down toward his crotch. "It's in your thigh. My PT told me about it one day. Cut it and you die in, like, ten minutes."

"What's a PT?"

"Physical therapist. She's waiting for you."

He looked at Dallas. He looked at his cards. Thirteen. He tapped the felt.

"Are you sure?" Dallas asked. Her face-up card was a five.

"I guess I'm supposed to stay."

"Stay and pray."

"But I'm feeling contrary."

"Stay and pray," she repeated.

"You want to know what I think?" the blonde next to him said. "I think you should go with your gut. Use the Force, Luke."

The music paused for a moment as one song ended and another began. Logan took a breath. He made the hold sign. The blonde played next, shaking her head and tsk-tsking as she drew an eight. "That would have been yours," she said needlessly. After she and the Japanese man had finished playing out their hands, Dallas turned over a seven to go with her five. Then she drew an eight. Twenty. She avoided his eyes as she swept away his bet.

Just then the blonde placed a hand on his thigh and leaned in close. "I know a better way to spend money," she said. "Come on."

Logan's face reddened. He managed to shake his head and say thanks anyway as he stood up. Excusing himself, he headed toward the bathroom, bumping and nudging his way through the crowd, catching the stray edges of conversations that merged into a medley he almost enjoyed. People were lined up outside one of the restaurants. Men cheering ferociously at the sportsbook. He reached an open section and then finally the restroom with the ranged urinals, the relative silence, the vacant stare at the tile just a few inches from his face. Somebody was vomiting in one of the stalls. He imagined himself back in Philadelphia, circling potential jobs in the newspaper. He could wait tables. He could load shipping containers, sweep floors. It wouldn't bring in much money, but it would build character, as his father would say. And maybe, he thought, some physique along with it. He could use it. Everyone around him seemed bigger and stronger.

Dallas watched the blonde gather up her chips and leave. This sort of thing didn't surprise her anymore. Occasionally one of these freelance prostitutes slipped under the radar and roamed the floor for a while, sniffing at the men for cash. They avoided the high-stakes tables because that's where security was sharpest. Dallas should have notified Felix, technically speaking, but she wouldn't talk to him now if the casino was on fire, to be perfectly honest. Besides, this case was kind of borderline. She hadn't heard what the blonde had said to Logan. What did management expect? Dallas was a blackjack dealer. She wasn't a psychic. The blonde could be an over-friendly divorcee from Ohio trying to feel good about herself again. Dallas was the sort of woman who gave other women the benefit of the doubt.

Another woman took the blonde's place — an older one with graying, up-swept hair and reading glasses who kept consulting her husband as if he might walk away and leave her there unless his services were desperately needed.

Logan returned. He won some, lost some. At one point he hit a winning streak and, just as he was beginning to feel prosperous, lost a couple of hands and realized the cards had turned on him again. His pile shrank. It kept shrinking until he was down to one chip. He set it out there.

He drew a ten and a two. Dallas had a nine showing.

"Ouch," a voice behind him said. It was Deck. "I don't mean to rub salt, Dr. Smith, but I see evidence of reckless betting."

"On the contrary. The road of Basic Strategy led me here."

"Is that your last chip?"

"The end." He watched one of the San Jose twins split a pair of aces and work her way up to nineteen on the first hand.

"You missed quite a show," Deck said, his voice coming in low, so no-body else could hear.

"I'll live."

"Oh no. You haven't really lived until you've seen the marquee perform-ance across the street. This is a woman with her own zip code."

"Then I'll send her a postcard." He watched the football player add a two to the pair of deuces he already had. Then a three. One of those absurd hands when all the low cards come out of the shoe. "Where's Prentis?"

"Funny you should ask. My advice is to wait awhile before going up to the room."

Logan twisted around on his stool. "You don't mean—"

"He's taking care of some important business. Totally by accident. She was on her way out, we were on our way in. He'll be a new man afterward. A decent guy. Detente, Dr. Smith. Give him a chance. It's your turn."

Logan turned toward the table again and found Dallas waiting for him to make a sign. Basic Strategy said hit, so he asked for one. A ten. Bust.

"Bad luck," Deck said. "Come on, I'll buy you a drink."

Deck waited for Logan to stand up from the table, but it didn't happen. And as he looked at the dealer, he realized why. Some chemistry there. Of course, her body was up to specs. And he had to admit that the hair was sexy too. A ravishing little curl to that upper lip. But she was one of those women who always wanted it her way. Deck could spot the type. It was all about her. She'd get you into her bedroom and cover you with rapid-fire kisses that were supposed to be exciting. One of those gobblers who drove him up the wall.

Logan, sucker that he was, stood up and reached into his pocket and pulled out more cash.

"I thought that was the end," Deck said.

"It was. It is. This is food money."

Deck looked at the other players for a reaction and saw a lot of raised eyebrows. Amusement all around. And the dealer—surprise, surprise—was trying to conceal her pleasure. Logan was making a fool of himself.

"I recommend a hiatus," he said. "A drink at the center bar. Let's go to the sportsbook and sit in those recliners like true nobility. I'll place a baseball bet in your honor."

"Thanks, but I'm staying here."

"Slow down, Dr. Smith. Think. This isn't rational behavior. This is an upward-sloping demand curve."

Logan smiled. The Beatles were playing on the sound system. "Helter skelter," he said along with Paul McCartney, stuffing the Basic Strategy sheet into Deck's shirt pocket.

Deck watched him for another minute before he turned and stalked off. He didn't care how much anyone at Penn praised Logan's insight or unconventional thinking. Look at him now, emptying his wallet for a few more minutes of footsie with the blackjack dealer. The guy was a fool. That article in *Revenue,* for example, had been a fluke or possibly even an accident, especially when Deck's submissions—far better ones, to be sure—had been greeted with the standard-issue no thanks. How did Logan do that? A flash of the national exposure that Deck secretly craved. Not that Logan had done anything with it. He wouldn't know what to do with national exposure if you handed it to him on a silver platter. But anyway Deck put it behind him the way he jettisoned most of life's minor disappointments and headed toward the sportsbook to enjoy some solo time, maybe recline with a drink or two, place a couple of bets on tomorrow's games. He'd relax and contemplate the odds for the World Series, which was so far away from this point in the season that the numbers were objects of wonder, like the light from distant stars.

Upstairs, under a framed photo of Jimi Hendrix, Prentis looked down at the woman giving him a blowjob and wished he had a little bit of cocaine to snort off her hipbones—not so much for the rush as for the novelty of it, something to tell his friends. He liked this one. A disheveled blonde in a short red dress. Eager. She knew how to use her fingers and mouth. He told her to stand up, then turned her around and bent her forward, lifting up her dress with a tantalizing gentleness before he yanked down her underwear and took her from behind, his all-time favorite position.

The woman had already reached back to make sure the condom was still in place before she let him stick it inside her. Cherry flavored. The taste lingering like cough syrup in her mouth. She kept her hands planted on the bed, her eyes on the clock through her tousled hair, reminding herself to pick up some toilet paper on the way home. Her gaze swept over the room one last time to make sure she hadn't missed anything worth stealing. And then the digits changed to thirty. Finally. She eased a hand up between her legs and started caressing his balls, which made him come immediately. The funny thing was how surprised and grateful they were afterward, like you did it for their pleasure.

Logan eyed his cards, a king and a queen. "Split," he said, setting out another chip.

Dallas smiled faintly and searched his face for the joke.

"Split," he said again.

"I'm confused."

"So am I. I don't know why I'm doing this."

"Then don't," Spoons said. "It's like you're sawing off your own legs or something."

With the word "saw" Logan heard the New Jersey accent and suddenly noticed the gold chain around the guy's neck. Of course. There is no escape. He could survive a plane crash in Africa and someone from Cherry Hill would come bushwhacking through the jungle to rescue him. The waitress appeared at his side and he ordered another drink, then looked at Dallas again. "Split, please."

Dallas showed him an expression of kind indulgence as she dealt a card to go with his queen. An ace. Blackjack. Cheers rose up from the table. Then she dealt a card to go with his king. Another ace. More cheers, applause, laughter.

"The universe trembles," she said as she paid him.

He didn't say a word. A delicious warmth was washing through him, a sudden sensitivity to the warp and stress of the air, the ringing of the slots. With his next hand he doubled on a sixteen and drew a five. After that he held on a twelve when Dallas was showing a ten and smiled when she busted. He split a pair of nines, doubled on each one, and ended up with a pair of nineteens, which beat Dallas's eighteen just fine, thank you. He was playing contrary to Basic Strategy at almost every turn and winning at almost every turn. His pile grew. He raised the amounts of his bets in accordance with Dallas's earlier instructions, but she didn't seem to be rooting for him anymore. A stiff expression had replaced her smile. He couldn't stop, though. He was drawing perfect cards and having a ripple effect on the other players' hands, like a single drummer upsetting the rhythm of an orchestra. And they were all winning. This new rhythm, he decided, was better than the old.

"New rules," the football player announced. "We're splitting face cards. We're hitting anything higher than thirteen."

"Twelve," one of the San Jose twins said. "Let's make it twelve."

"Is this a rebellion?" Dallas asked. "Am I the evil dictator?" She had changed up the shuffle, but it didn't seem to be helping. And Felix, the bastard, was letting her fry out here. In this kind of situation he was supposed to pull her off the table and substitute Weiss or somebody else — and he would do it, but not until the ripples had worked their way up to the shift manager. There would be a video review. She'd have to explain the coincidence, suddenly dealing supernatural cards to this guy she had been flirting with all night. She glanced back at Felix, who was pretending not to notice.

She looked at Logan, who was smiling.

"Hit me," he said. He had eighteen.

"No, no, no."

"Hit me hard," he said. "I want to feel it. I want it to hurt."

He wanted a hit? All right, she thought. She'd smack him right off his stool. She dealt him a card. A three. Goddamn it.

The football player gave Logan a pat on the back and nearly sent him face down into his pile of chips. Everyone was laughing and cheering. It sounded like a craps table now.

The waitress delivered another drink. Logan triple-tipped her.

The Japanese man spoke softly as he played out his hand. "The protocol, I believe, is to tip the dealer when you're winning."

Logan nodded. Yes. Absolutely. He grabbed a handful of chips and leaned across the table and stacked them in front of Dallas, knowing as he did it that even with this winning streak it was too much, more than he spent in a month, but he couldn't turn back, he couldn't change his behavior, he had tried to play it safe and steady, just like everything else in his life, but he wasn't that kind of gambler and so maybe he wasn't that kind of person either.

She pointed at his spot. "Put them in front of your bet."

"Why?"

"I want you to play a hand for me."

"You mean, play two hands?"

"The same hand for both of us. If you win, I win."

"But you think I'm going to lose."

She replied with a green gaze that was gorgeous and terrible. He picked up the chips and stacked them in front of his own bet. "I get it," he said. "You're the kind of woman who wants nothing if she can't have everything."

She stopped right in the middle of her deal and shot him a look. Logan's pulse slammed inside him. That's it, he thought. He had gone too far. He had broken some kind of taboo and a couple of security agents were going to snatch him right off his stool any minute now. But she continued dealing and nobody came.

"I find it fascinating when someone tells me what I want," she said to Spoons because he was sitting at first base and she basically had to keep getting the hands out at the specified rate no matter what. She dealt to the twins and the football player.

"I'm sorry," Logan said, when she finally came around to him.

"Are you holding or hitting?"

He had a pair of tens. "I feel like I stepped on a landmine."

"I need to see a signal from you."

"Not until you accept my apology."

She took a deep breath, although it didn't do a damn thing for her, to be perfectly honest. "All right. Fine. I accept."

"Do you want me to stay or hit?"

"You know what you should do."

"I'm not asking what I should do. I'm asking what you want me to do."

"I'm just the dealer," she said.

"And I'm just the player."

Neither of them said anything for a minute.

"Hold or hit?" she asked again.

"Split," he finally said, setting two more stacks of chips out there, one next to his bet, another next to hers.

"You don't have to double the tip. You can choose which one—"

"Hit me."

She dealt him a two to go with the first ten, but he didn't see it. He refused to take his eyes away from hers.

"Double," he said.

"Look at your cards before you say that."

"I prefer not to." With his fingers he found the necessary chips and moved them into position.

"What you're saying is, you really want me to hit you."

"Yes. Hit me. Hit me hard."

The next card was a four. They moved on to his next hand and he did the same thing, doubling his bet after receiving a four he didn't even see, and drew another two. When it was done he looked down and saw that he had four large bets, two for himself and two for Dallas—his entire stock of money—riding on a pair of sixteens. It was all over. He'd have to go electronic if he wanted to continue. And why not? He could follow this trend to its natural conclusion. He could go to the ATM and drain his savings account, tap into his credit cards and bleed his future of whatever possibilities it contained. There would be a certain pleasure in the death.

Dallas dealt to the gray-haired woman at Logan's side and the Japanese man at the end. Then she played out her own hand. She started with twelve and kept adding cards—small ones that came so fast Logan didn't have time to add them up. The cutter came out before she finished. She slid it into the discard pile. She drew again. She finally stopped. Logan gazed at the staggered results. The hearts and clubs. The numbers. His mind was fumbling with them but nothing was happening.

"Bang!"

Cheers went up all around him and the football player slapped him on the back again. The ruckus of a celebration. They whistled and clapped as Dallas stacked chips in front of him, doubling all the piles. He reached out and raked it in like a cowboy in a saloon. When it was over he looked at Dallas. She was shuffling with great care, stripping the cards and feeding the small piles together, squaring the edges against the side of the shoe.

"I don't know how much you make," he said, "but I'm willing to bet, no pun intended, that I doubled your wages for the night."

"You're right about that. You don't know how much I make."

Just then a new dealer came up behind Dallas and tapped her on the shoulder. Her shift was over. She cleared her hands. Logan opened his mouth to say something, anything, but nothing happened. He couldn't find any words. He sat there dumbly as she turned and walked away.

The parking lot had a hellish aspect. Rows of dead-eyed cars. The odor of baked asphalt and rubber. The psychedelic pulse of the guitar, tinting his clothing as he walked. The jug of water was waiting for him in the rental car. Sure, it was probably warm, but he had seen an ice machine near their room. But then again, the ice was made from tapwater, wasn't it? He heard a jet somewhere overhead. He looked up. The stars were invisible, the constellations pleading weakly beyond the city's glare. One row over, a woman in a flowery silk blouse stepped out of a pickup truck and left the door open as she staggered away, barefoot, with her shoes in her hands. A man in a panama hat sat behind the wheel smoking a cigar. Logan almost didn't recognize the rental when he saw it. He pulled out his key.

"No way," a voice said. "You're not driving."

By the time he spotted Dallas she was only a few car lengths away, walking toward him in her green blouse, the vest folded up and clenched in her hand. Her hair was tied back.

"Call me Missy the Mormon, but you've had too many drinks."

"Missy the Mormon?"

"In case you didn't notice, there's a whole fleet of cabs at the main entrance, waiting for people just like you."

"You don't understand." He nodded toward the car, the jug on the seat. "I'm thirsty."

"Thirsty." She shot her hip out and leveled her eyes at him. "You mean you're primed. You're buzzed but not quite drunk enough. Right? It would be nice to go finish the job at some cheap bar, is what you're thinking. Assuming you don't kill anyone in the process." She shook her head. "You don't want to drive. What you want is a cab."

"I find it fascinating when someone tells me what I want."

That stopped her. Her expression shifted, found the edges of some kind of anger, but then dissolved again. She lowered her eyes. In the light of the guitar he noticed a few strands of hair trailing down over her ears and for a moment she seemed utterly unaware of herself and even more beautiful because of it. She started fussing with the vest in her hand. "You won a lot of money."

"Five dollars."

She raised her eyes to him. "What?"

"I counted up my chips," he said, patting his pocket. "I have enough to pay off a nasty credit card balance that's been dogging me for the last few months. Plus five dollars."

Another jet passed overhead. A door slammed somewhere. An engine started.

"We pool our tokes," she said.

"Your what?"

"Our tips. We call them tokes. At the end of each shift all the money is pooled and divided equally among the dealers. It's included in our paycheck. We pay taxes on it."

"A Communist casino," he said. "Karlo Marx would be pleased."

She smiled faintly, shifted her weight to her other hip. Her legs looked long and lean.

"Actually," he added, "that's not true. Marx wouldn't be pleased, because the employees don't own the means of production and the surplus value is way off the scale."

"You're not getting in that car," she said.

"Oh yeah? Then what am I doing out here in Hades?"

"You're coming home with me. I have a couch. I'll bring you back tomorrow morning."

Logan experienced a flash of surprise and was about to offer the token protest when his glance wandered to the hotel's blazing windows. The shared room. The remains of Prentis's appetites. He didn't want to spend the night there. And he didn't need to. He was a couch-sleeper, a cat-napper, a half-clothed passout pro. He'd hang upside down in Dallas's closet if necessary.

He followed her to her car. He went around to the passenger side and waited. Then he realized she was looking at him across the roof.

"You're not really going to sleep on the couch. You know that, right?"

He felt a smile rise to his face.

"Fair warning," she said. "I'm trouble."

He shrugged. "Who isn't?"

She waited another moment, then opened her door and slid behind the wheel and reached across the seat and let him in. He descended into a world of fast-food wrappers and stale coffee cups. An overstuffed ashtray. The dashboard was cracked, the radio knobs missing. He lifted himself up and tugged out a wire hanger and let it drop to the floor and almost said something about the real trouble being here in the car, but caught himself. He needed to guard his words. This woman's pressure points were discovered accidentally, and with serious consequences. He knew that now. The air-conditioning didn't seem to work, so he rolled down the window and stuck his arm into the hot night as they drove past the strip malls and discount hotels, the electric temples running full blast — light and heat everywhere, it seemed, a world of colored fire.

chapter 2

Eighteen months later, in Arizona, he woke to a phone trilling way out there in the kitchen and he was up and running toward it before he even knew why. He was naked. How about that. He crossed cold tile in the living room, avoiding all the hard angles and symmetries in the low reefs of furniture until he slammed his shin against an overturned chair. He stumbled over some scattered couch cushions and finally came limping into the kitchen. The cordless phone was somewhere among the coffee spills, the bagel stubs, the knife puttied with cream cheese and placed like a gauntlet in the middle of the counter. Dallas had left a mess to show him it wasn't over. He found the phone under a sprawled newspaper.

"Logan," Silverson's voice said, "apologies for calling you at home, but I do want to ask a favor before you come on campus this morning."

Logan leaned forward with his elbows on the counter and felt its surface like a shock against his stomach. Here was the first mistake of the day—rearing up from a dream and rushing to the phone as if it no longer had the usual consequences. The refrigerator hummed next to him. The windows showed a backyard of bougainvillea, firethorn shrubs, citrus trees with trunks painted white to ward off the summer sun. Palm fronds and rotten fruit littered the lawn. Leaves and twigs floating, suspended, in the heavy water of their swimming pool. Sunlight dissipating the morning chill. It was January.

"As you know, Mr. Moore is going to arrive on Monday. And as you know, we had originally planned for him to stay at a hotel, but . . . well, I do agree with the search committee that it is important to impress each applicant with our warmth. And since you and Mr. Moore are former colleagues, it is my hope . . ."

Logan let the mouthpiece drop below his chin and waited for the formal phrasings, the old-world ovations to come to a close. When your department chair clings to his British citizenship despite two decades in the American

Southwest, you don't reply until you hear that final downswing at the end of the sentence. He touched his neck where Dallas had bitten it and wondered if it looked as bad as it felt. He glanced down at the cherried abrasions on his knees. Remarkable.

"Logan? Are you there?"

"Yes. I have room for Deck — I mean, Mr. Moore — here at my house."

"Wonderful. It will only be for a few days. The interview is Tuesday and the informal discussions on Wednesday."

"I thought the search committee wanted to get it done in one day."

"Under normal circumstances. But Mr. Moore is the leading candidate. They want to be thorough."

"Of course."

"Oh, and Logan?"

He braced himself. "Yes?"

"I'm afraid the fall curriculum may not be favorable to your request."

"May not or will not?"

There was a pause. "We've been over this. You know the constraints. We can hardly fill one section of History of Economic Thought per year, let alone an extra course devoted to classical theory."

"Not just classical theory. Smith's formulations of classical theory as it relates to contemporary practice. This is relevant, Max. This is cutting-edge."

"Nevertheless. We have other requirements at this time. We need you for Macroeconomics, which as you know is the —"

Backbone of the curriculum, Logan lip-synched, as Silverson spoke the words. Of course. He thanked Silverson for letting him know and assured him that, really, it was no problem putting Deck up for a few nights. Logan hit the disconnect button and slid the phone away from him and pressed both fists against the counter. Intro to Macro. The neoclassical fairy tale. He couldn't really blame Silverson for avoiding a fight when he was on the verge of retirement. But it was Logan's last chance to make a change before Dr. Novak took over as chair and officially began to reorganize the Economics department into the new Economics Institute, the full details of which had yet to be disclosed. Logan already suspected that his voice would be heard even less than it was now. What was he going to do? Maybe he should have negotiated with Silverson, offered to pick up Deck at the airport in exchange for the new course approval, even though Deck was the last person he wanted to see. He looked around and tried to imagine what Deck would make of this household, with its troubled inner-city and crumbling infrastructure. He touched the tender spot on his neck again. Their marriage couldn't handle a visitor right now — although, in the short run, he had to admit, a guest would put Dallas on good behavior. He could use the ceasefire.

On his way back to the bedroom he set the chair upright and tossed the cushions back on the couch. Dallas's torn blouse was under the coffee table. He picked it up, examined the rip, held it to his nose for the faint ochre of her body. He couldn't remember exactly how the argument had reached critical mass, how they had ended up nearly naked in the middle of the living room, Dallas scratching and biting and finally pulling him down to the floor and wrapping her legs around him until they were fucking right there on the tile, Logan calling her names that surprised him, words he hadn't even known were in his mind. It was the best sex they had had in months. They had trudged to bed afterward, exhausted, silent. They had slept without touching.

He gathered up the clothing and carried it to the bedroom and began sorting it out on the bed. A sour smell in the sheets. Dallas's indented pillow. He hadn't heard her alarm go off that morning. Hey, wait a minute.

He reached across the bed and punched down her pillow and made a noise when he saw the numbers on her clock. Half an hour. He started moving. He pulled drawers, yanked hangers, frisked yesterday's pants for his wallet. He went to the bathroom to shave and found it filled with the stale remains of Dallas's shower. Door closed, fan off. Sabotage. As if she had known it would screw him up. He wiped the mirror and cursed at the sight of his neck, returned to his closet for a collared shirt.

Backing out of the driveway, he saw Puffy and hit the brakes just in time. He opened the door and leaned out.

"Not now," he said to the cat.

Puffy meowed a pretty-please. This was the neighborhood stray — affectionate, mellow, his dusty-auburn coat thickened from spending winter nights outside. Logan wanted to adopt him, but Dallas repeatedly vetoed the proposal because, she said, Logan was allergic. It didn't matter that Logan was willing to put up with the sneezes. She didn't want to live with some teary-eyed nose-blower. She wasn't a nurse, for crying out loud. And she didn't like cats, period. She shooed Puffy away from their yard and forbade Logan to encourage him in any way. Hence the packets of cat food stashed behind the lawnmower in the garage. Logan got out of his car and went there now, grabbed a packet, and took it over to the side of the house, the usual rendezvous point, where Puffy rubbed himself indulgently against Logan's leg as he tore the seal. Logan dumped the food on the ground and ran his palm over Puffy's silk-soft hair, his bowed head gobbling quietly.

"You didn't get this from me. All right?"

He headed back to his car, almost forgetting to hit the button for the garage door before peeling away.

The one-night stand in Vegas had been intense and beautiful and strange, but their cross-country addresses had prevented any real discussion of meeting again. They hadn't even bothered to exchange phone numbers afterward. Later that summer, however, a call had come to Logan's committee chair at Penn from an old colleague at Arizona State University culling the ranks for someone who could teach not only Macro but History of Economic Thought because the person slated for the position had pulled out at the last minute and, three days later, after a salvo of faxed credentials and a hasty phone interview, Logan was on the highway with his car packed so tight he could feel the door latches straining. The goodbyes to his family and friends had been sudden, spare, triaged down to the essential notes. Silas, his best friend, had seen him off with a hug. Logan didn't feel it until he reached the steamy flats of Ohio and found himself among the barns, the ragged crops, the threshers rusting peacefully in the fields, finally lowering his window to the sound of insects only to realize tears were spilling from his eyes. Although he hadn't expected to find a job near home, he hadn't prepared himself for this loss either. He thought of turning around. Maybe he hadn't searched the East Coast thoroughly enough. Maybe there was a hidden prep school or an undiscovered college near Philadelphia.

He kept going. He crossed the river near St. Louis and endured the purgatory of Missouri and Oklahoma, an endless blank sky egging him on through the Texas panhandle and the plains of New Mexico. Then the high desert of Arizona. Broad and bare and lonely. Flagstaff's green peaks materializing slowly on the horizon. He couldn't drive fast enough. The gas pedal such a paltry thing. The highway rising, pines springing up around him. Hey, he thought. Look at this. Cool air, friendly sunshine. He was going to be all right. He'd meet people. He'd make a new life.

But then he turned south. Elevation signs registered his descent on a highway cut against the flanks of ribbed canyons, volcanic rock with scree and boulders the color of dried blood, basins of empty air at his side. Heat swelled up around him. Evergreens dwindled and gave way to clusters of prickly pear, thorny shrubs, trees with fish-bone branches and wispy leaves. The soil changed to a pale gold as he rode over humped hills, dipped into gulches, crossed bridges over sandy washes. On the horizon he saw mountains massed like thunderheads and a few solitary peaks with flat tops and misshapen crowns. During a long, swerving descent, he spotted his first saguaro, then legions of them studding the slopes, arms angled every which way, the heat beyond all measure now, swirling through the car because — get this — he didn't have air-conditioning. The sweat coming from his glands made him realize that all other secretions had been superficial, cosmetic. This was real. This was the very juice of his body. He almost pulled over. He almost walked into the desert with his head lifted and arms raised, seeking the rapture of heat death.

The land finally flattened. Cacti gave way to tractors, grinning billboards, pretty pink roofs. A full hour of concrete and diesel before he reached Tempe, indistinguishable from Phoenix and half a dozen other cities that had spread and melted together over the years to create the Valley of the Sun. Despite Vegas, he had been hoping for adobe houses and the composure of old Mexico. Instead he found L.A.'s retarded little brother with its clogged pores and bad breath, its teenage ambition. At that point he didn't know that subdivisions were consuming the Sonoran Desert at the rate of one acre per hour, but he woke every morning dehydrated, mummified, diminished by a steady loss he couldn't quite name.

And something else. All the wrong people were friendly to him in all the wrong ways. He introduced himself to colleagues who nodded vacantly and drifted away, but at the supermarket encountered cashiers who insisted on discussing the pros and cons of instant rice. He nearly went catatonic in his apartment trying to prepare for his courses. White walls, pale carpet, futon. His books suffocating in their cardboard boxes. A silent phone indicating that even the telemarketers didn't know who he was. And then one day he lay back on his futon — salty-skinned, heat-stunned, the cake-batter walls doing little to shield him from the blinding fire of afternoon — and picked up the phone for movie times. But instead he surprised himself by dialing Nevada information. Las Vegas. Last name, Cole. First name, Dallas.

"Still splitting face cards?" she asked, preempting the small talk, the gentle maneuvers he had expected for their attitudes to fall into place.

"If you deal 'em, I'll split 'em."

"How long are you in town?"

"I'm not in town," he said, and then surprised himself with an ad-lib. "Not yet. My flight arrives on Friday."

"Where are you staying?"

He almost named the hotel where they had met, but he didn't want to push his luck. "Actually, I haven't figured that out. I'll probably call for a reservation at the —"

"Don't bother. You can stay at my place."

"Are you sure?"

"It's basically why you called, right?"

Even as his face flooded with heat, he knew this was what he had been hoping for—but even so, he wanted to make sure she didn't misunderstand him. "I don't live in Philadelphia anymore," he said, blundering into an explanation. "I mean, I have a job in Phoenix. Arizona State University."

"When did this happen?"

"A couple of weeks ago."

There was a pause on the other end of the line. "Are you calling me because you're bored, or because you really want to see me again?"

"I'm calling because I've been thinking about you ever since I crossed the Mississippi."

"You're in Phoenix with no friends and nothing to do, is what I'm thinking."

"True. But that doesn't change how I feel about you." He adjusted the pillow behind his head and stretched out his legs. He liked this open negotiation. He had wasted his adult years, it suddenly seemed to him, on relationships with East Coast women who expected him to decode their faint and contradictory signals, to know what they wanted even when they didn't know it themselves.

A long pause. She seemed to be making a decision. "What time is your flight?" she asked.

"I don't know. I mean, I don't have one yet. I lied."

"Are you serious?"

"I figured you'd be more likely to see me if you thought I was coming to town anyway."

She laughed. "That's good. That's really good. I was going to tell you to take a cab, but just for that I'll meet you at the airport."

The flight to Vegas was short and cheap, and she was waiting for him exactly where she'd said she would be. She was only slightly different than he remembered—her hair richer and deeper, a more slinky join in the hips. Better than he remembered. They walked briskly to her car, like two people late for a business meeting, and then shoved their way through rush-hour traffic on the wide avenues before finally arriving at her apartment. She lived on the second floor. Logan watched the firm curves of her ass as he followed her up the stairs and, after he crossed the threshold, kicked the door shut and pressed her up against the wall before she could even drop her purse. This, it should be noted, was a move that contradicted all his previous experience—again, with East Coast women—in which such passionate gambles had rarely paid off.

Dallas responded by threading her fingers into his hair and biting his neck. She tried to unbutton his shirt, but he knelt on the floor and began kissing her stomach, gripping her waist to feel the rich slope of it, the hourglass forces at work in her body. Eventually they staggered over to her bedroom, where the blinds were already drawn, sunlight trellised against the wall. Air ducts whispering. A car alarm whining in the parking lot outside. The last of their clothes came off and he discovered a tender spot on the upper reaches of her thigh that, over the next several months, he couldn't get enough of, like a peach that never lost its flavor.

He saw her almost every weekend after that, escaping from his colorless routine at the university. Sometimes she greeted him with silky surprises under her clothing, or else high heels and tight skirts, stockings and garters. And she began to guide him into new territory. Touch me here. Nibble me there. Try *this*. Move your cock like *that*. He enjoyed following directions. It took the pressure off. He didn't have to guess at her pleasure or worry about counterfeit sighs and groans. In fact, he felt so free that he began to improvise, adding fingers to one thing, spontaneous movements to another, new angles and cadences that had never occurred to him before. For the first time in his life he saw a woman have a second and then a third orgasm — great seizures that sent her flying into space and then tumbling back again, avidly roaming his body afterward until she triggered his own pulses, his own intensities. Lying there afterward, he expected her to make a remark about it, but she simply gave him the usual compliments. This, apparently, was the nature of her love.

They took showers together, lathering each other up with spice-scented soaps. They gave each other backrubs and drank champagne in bed. They saw movies. They went to bars. They saw live music at a venue connected to the casino where she worked but avoided the casino itself — and, in fact, all casinos — because, she said, she needed a break from that atmosphere, and for dinner they went to mid-range restaurants where the servers, former coworkers of hers, slipped them free desserts and drinks. In the afternoons they snacked on wine and cheese from a specialty shop Logan noticed one day in the strip mall near her apartment. They talked about colors and comedy, dreams and politicians, countries they had never visited and why they wanted to go there some day. To Logan's relief they didn't dwell on their families or their histories or even their jobs. The essential corners and angles of their personalities were revealed, he felt, by discussing things outside their lives.

Sometimes he pretended to sleep late just to hear her singing in the shower. The lunar sadness of her voice. Why hadn't anyone drafted her into a band? Why wasn't she spending her nights poised at a microphone, setting fire to every heart in the audience? All those famous rock and blues and jazz bands coming through town. It surprised him, but she said Vegas was a watering-hole for some of the best music in the world. A little-known fact. Logan agreed, surrendering himself to her judgment. Brought up with the proper lessons and recitals, and then having a music snob for a college room-mate, he knew what he was supposed to like. But the truth was that he simply didn't have an ear for it. Why this and not that, which sounded nearly the same? To his embarrassment, he sometimes liked the "overproduced, candy-ass crap" that his friends derided. But Dallas never made snide comments. She simply described what she liked — the way so-and-so played the piano to emphasize it was a percussion instrument, for example. She could spot developments and recapitulations, tune changes, call-responses in the tiniest quiver of a melody.

"There's something we need to say to each other before you leave tomorrow," she said one night. They were at their favorite hangout, deliberately being silly by dancing to a slow song on the jukebox while everyone else hunkered in the booths or played video poker at the consoles built into the bar.

"Before I leave tomorrow?"

"Make that, before you come back next weekend. Before we take this thing any farther."

Further, he thought, but didn't say. She didn't like it when he corrected her.

"Because I feel a certain way about you, and I need to know if you feel that way too."

He nodded. They were swaying slowly, his hands on her hips, her arms wrapped loosely around his neck. Her body was warm and slightly sweaty. The chemistry of her late-night skin. Hair storming around her face. As they revolved he saw fragments of the bar passing behind her, a television flaring in the corner, an elbow raised for a tequila shot. "I do feel that way," he said.

"Then we need to say it."

"I think we're already saying it."

"We're saying it like people afraid of saying it, is what I'm thinking."

He understood, then, that she simply wanted him to come out with it first. "I love you," he said.

She stopped moving. Their arms were still around each other, but they were motionless now, the song surging in its final chorus. "Are you saying it because you think it's what I want, or because—"

He ran his hands up through her kinky hair and took hold of her face and gazed into those tropical green eyes of hers. "I love you, I love you, I love you."

She winced ecstatically, digging her fingernails into his shoulders. "I love you, too," she said. "Thank fucking God."

They went home and nearly wrecked her bed. The next day she cried when she dropped him off at the airport. As the weeks went by they would call each other's answering machines and leave erotic messages along with affirmations of love, which he saved and played over and over again like a greatest hits album. He would relive their greatest moments while masturbating in the shower. He'd think of her lace-top stockings during faculty meetings and see her name in the text of books he read, hallucinate her voice into songs on the radio, and it seemed absurd to him that she wasn't a star of some kind, that other men weren't following her home from the supermarket and leaving their grandmothers' engagement rings on her doorstep simply to get her attention. The sex and affection and rich fatty food wasn't satisfying his love but feeding it, intensifying his urge for the things that made his waist thicker and his Mondays lethargic and wan. But he needed to get work done at the university, so he made a point of eating more sensibly and going to bed earlier during the week even as it revolted him, even as the hallways of the Economics building took on a monastic glow in his eyes and the chilled rooms reeked of marble and incense. With Dallas waiting for him every weekend it was easier to bear the limited curriculum, the straightlaced committees that demanded his participation and then ignored it, his colleagues' tendency to view him as a rookie who would wise up to the commandments of the free market after a couple of years. Dallas carried him through the dumb-ass days. She gave a sense of balance to his life. But by November he was tired of traveling every weekend and he finally lured her to Phoenix, which she hadn't visited, she said, in basically ten years, and she pronounced the city habitable before she boarded the plane again on Sunday night. She visited twice more before she found a job at a casino on one of the nearby reservations, although the benefits didn't include health insurance. Somehow the topic came up that she'd qualify for the ASU plan if she were Logan's spouse, and they were married a month later by a justice of the peace in Phoenix because neither of them had connections to local religion and because the Vegas chapels were like fast food, in Logan's opinion, delicious and convenient but bad for the heart.

Let's face it, he thought as he hit the main thoroughfare — a six-lane autobahn named, no joke, Rural Road — they had experienced certain cycles in their marriage. There had been prosperous periods followed by recessions. Sex fluctuated along with the usual factors. But last night? Last night didn't qualify as a reversal of fortune or even a recovery from a long downturn. They had entered a whole new paradigm, and he didn't know what to make of it. He didn't know how to feel.

He drove past the banked strip malls, the fast-food restaurants, the steady retail blur, his engine wheezing and shuddering every time he pressed the gas pedal. His car was on the brink of collapse, yet it looked like a grand prix candidate next to Dallas's. A few weeks ago he had spent an entire afternoon restraining her from a so-called inventory blowout at one of the local dealerships. She was fed up with driving a jalopy. Fair enough, he had said, but there were other priorities right now. Mortgage payments. Furniture payments. And although he didn't like to acknowledge it, he was, in fact, siphoning some money into high-risk-but-socially-responsible investments via an old friend in Philadelphia. More on this later.

He grabbed his sunglasses and put them on. For the past year he had been worrying about money and now he'd have to start worrying about sex — and sex, like money, tended to drag everything else along with it. Never mind that this was supposed to be the quiet season for him to work on his book. Of course, it was entirely possible — and this wasn't Logan's thought, but it needs to be said anyway — that he and Dallas were having problems precisely because he was devoting so much energy to his research. He had already spent weeks probing various economic theories for a few hollow spots he could punch through and connect into some sort of escape tunnel, as if all his ideas would be lurking behind everyone else's. But he hadn't found anything. In fact, he was beginning to think he simply wasn't smart enough to fulfill his own ambition despite the time he had set aside for it. He had agreed to teach extra courses the previous summer and fall in exchange for a lighter load this spring. Nothing on his plate this semester except History of Economic Thought. Oh, and a couple of graduate students working on dissertations that no one else wanted to touch. And a textbook selection committee. And a presentation for the A.E.A. conference, which was not only taking place in Tempe this year, but scheduled to include a visit from the chairman of the President's Council of Economic Advisers. Logan was supposed to participate in a panel discussion about "economic modeling for the future," or some such thing, and he needed to have a work in progress as a point of reference. He had already published two articles since arriving at ASU, but neither of them was appropriate. The first, a subtle examination of Chapter 5 of *The Wealth of Nations*, clarified Smith's Labor Theory of Value by grafting onto it principles from various chapters in Book One, while the second article, comparing Smith's ideas about growth to similar ideas by Adam Ferguson, a figure of the Scottish Enlightenment, was a masterpiece of irrelevance. And although the article in *Revenue* had been the keystone of his curriculum vitae when he had applied for the job at ASU, it was no longer recent enough to count as a sign of progress. As a competitor in the publish-or-perish race, he needed to come up with a full-length book to keep him in the running. He needed to make another lap around the tenure track. The tenure track that Deck, no doubt, would hit at a sprinter's pace as soon as he was hired. No. Don't even think about it now.

Logan cut the wheel and headed down a side street. Rural Road. Beware of places named after abstract concepts. Grand Avenue's malnourished storefronts were bad enough, but in the desert he and Dallas had discovered an old hag of a mining town called Superior, a retirement community named Young, and a narcoleptic sinkhole that proudly identified itself as Surprise. Someone having fun with Plato's concept of pure forms — which he would have to explain in, let's see, ten minutes or so. He turned one way and then another, jagging around a park with some palm trees and a cluster of ramadas shading concrete picnic tables. There was a jungle gym, a shining slide. The serenity of an empty swingset.

He came to the parking garage and stopped at the automatic gate. As he was rooting through the glove compartment for his passcard, he happened to glance at his old copy of *The Wealth of Nations* on the floor. Worn edges, swelled binding, pages missing in action. His grad-school teddy bear. He couldn't put it on his shelf, but he couldn't throw it away either. He found the passcard, inserted it into the slot. Checkpoint Charlie admitted him. He was going to work.

Dallas couldn't stand it. So the place was basically a bargain-basement casino, not much better than a video arcade, and she had known that when she had accepted the job, but the waitress was this ex-stripper who shouted down the aisles instead of walking over and simply asking people if they wanted cocktails. Like some peanut vendor at a ballgame. What kind of service was that? The management had no finesse, no sense of grandeur. They had made a decision a long time ago to cater to the local coin-junkies, the assorted misfits playing hooky from their jobs, and let's not even mention Mr. and Mrs. Camcorder from Cleveland out here for the winter in their mobile homes. All of whom were card-carrying members of what you call the no-frills crowd. Dallas understood that. She also understood that it was no fun, and that her only hope was the promotion to poker dealer they had promised her eons ago.

She had filled all the auxiliary boxes and now she was making her rounds past the slots — the hunched backs of the players, the padded stools, the smoking, the drinking, the ding-ding-ding. She was wearing her moneybags, her tickets, her radio. She was a person who made change. Which meant she liquefied Social Security checks and welfare payments, to be perfectly honest, and used her radio to notify the shift manager of every stray movement she made. I'm going here, I'm going there, I'm doing this, I'm doing that. She stopped and leaned against the center display, a planter filled with fake plants and an iron statuette of an eagle rising from a lake or river with a fish in its talons. Brass rails, neutral walls, televisions mounted overhead with their sports and weather. Subsistence-level music came from the speakers. OK, here she was. She exhaled through her teeth. She was fighting off an almost blinding ache for a cigarette.

This wasn't the life she had imagined for herself. At first it had been wonderful — the escape from unpaid bills and second-string friends, the vindication of knowing the next time Felix dialed her number it would be disconnected. After Logan suggested the move to Phoenix she had told Lucinda, the one friend worth telling, that she was getting married to a high-powered economist who taught at ASU, knowing the news would filter slowly through town until it reached Felix and then percolated up to the management of the casino where she was no longer allowed to work. She wanted everyone to know — indirectly, of course — that she was moving on to bigger and better things. And it seemed only fitting that Logan, who unknowingly had caused her to be put on probation, should also be her savior when the probation ended badly.

It had gone something like this: Several months after Logan's winning streak, a cheat had been caught at her table — a bland, white-collar-type sitting at first base with a miniature camera up his sleeve, viewing the cards as she slid them out of the shoe and sending the images, it was later learned, to a van in the parking lot where they were voice-relayed to the money-man at third base. Whatever. Dallas didn't care at first. But then she was taken into a room for a video review and her shuffle, her technique, her demeanor that evening were considered suspicious. She had laughed and bantered too much. She had dealt the cards too slowly — maybe, the head of security suggested, so the cheat could get a better shot of them? There were meetings with gaming enforcement agents and inspectors with the Nevada State Gaming Commission. Lawyers became involved. Charges were filed. Did she know cheating was a felony in Nevada? Did she know she could be found guilty of conspiracy to commit a fraudulent gaming act, possession or use of a cheating device, unlawful use of a calculating device, burglary, and a bunch of other trumped-up allegations nobody had ever heard of? After a few weeks, though, the charges were dropped for lack of evidence. But that didn't stop the casino from firing her. And it didn't prevent her name from appearing on the blacklist. She couldn't get a job in Vegas now unless she faked her own death and returned with a brand-new face.

She had hidden the whole thing from Logan. The legal threats and unemployment had been bad enough, in her opinion, without having them pollute her weekends, because whenever Logan showed up she felt divine. Now, don't get her wrong. She wasn't looking for goddess-status or anything like that, but she had encouraged his worship by, paradoxically, showing him exactly what she liked in the bedroom. He was obviously impressed by her straightforwardness, so she gave it full rein. At the time she figured, what the hell. She wasn't the sort of woman who expected her lovers to be psychic. And besides, you don't get what you want by waiting for it to happen to you. You make it happen. So she instructed him accordingly until, like that first night at the blackjack table, she lost control of the lesson and found herself having multiple orgasms — which, despite Felix's robust acrobatics, she had never experienced before. Fortunately, Logan was so amazed by the whole thing that he didn't notice her own astonishment. At that point she realized she had a high-stakes relationship on her hands. She went on her best behavior. And she steered him clear of the casinos, not only because of her persona non grata situation, but because she didn't want him to disappear into any of the games — which, let's face it, had almost happened that first night even though she was the one dealing to him.

An old lady with a wide-brimmed sun hat and walking stick came over and handed Dallas a ten. She clicked out the quarters, dumped them into the woman's hand. Go nuts, grandma. This was Dallas's life now. Low stakes. She had actually enjoyed it for a while, the way you enjoyed stepping into a cool, empty church in the middle of the day. The refreshing space. The tranquility. It was great for about twenty minutes. She had thought about going back to school, but here it was, the beginning of another semester at ASU without her name on the roster. She could feel the launch window passing, the extra energy required not only to sign up but catch up. Logan brought home the new catalog every semester and encouraged her to try a course or two, even full time if she wanted, because, he said, she could quit her job and they could survive without the money, and she appreciated it, she really did, but she simply couldn't find the desire. Let's call it a motivational issue. At UNLV she had swallowed aspirin and antacids by the handful during final exams. She wasn't the sort of person who could retain book knowledge. Besides, she wasn't a fool about her age. With her next birthday the digits would click over into a whole new terrible decade shared with women seeking second marriages and ways to hide the crow's feet around their eyes. Occasionally she discovered a sign or two — nothing too visible, really, but a subtle loss in the texture of her face, a shift in the set of her bones — that signaled the end of her gravity-free twenties. She was fighting a losing battle with her body-type, is what she was thinking, and eventually she would have to surrender to that true self crouched deep down inside her. It had happened to her mother. And look at the pathetic life her mother had now.

The radio squawked. She picked it up and replied. Yeah, yeah, she was about to head over to that section. She stepped away from the planter and realized her blouse was sticking to the spot on her lower back where she had scraped against the tile last night. She gently peeled the fabric away from the wound. Too bad she had forgotten to bandage it that morning. And don't even ask about the pain between her legs, because she had never been so saddle-sore her entire life. Maybe it was a new style of sex she had invented last night — halfway between a fight and a fuck. She nearly laughed. Call it what you want, but it had been the truest expression of feeling between them in the past few months. Here was the problem: What Logan took as equilibrium she took as complacency. She hadn't been able to wring any passion out of him lately unless it involved a crisis of some kind.

She was striding through the casino now, down a vacant aisle where the machines were begging for attention with their bright lights and chimes. Logan was slowly disappearing into his worries, into his work, into odd rhythms of thought that nobody, in her opinion, could ever comprehend. And meanwhile, what was she getting? The leftovers. As if moving to Phoenix and taking a marriage vow had given him permission to take her for granted. No, she thought. No. That wasn't going to happen. He wasn't going to —

A hand fell on her shoulder. She turned. An old man, out of breath, was waving a twenty in her face as if he had been chasing her for miles. She took the bill from him. She clicked out his change. And as he toddled back to his machine she stood there for a minute, wondering if she had made a mistake.

Logan turned toward the chalkboard and realized, a second too late, that he had seen Dallas among his students. A silken heat rose to his face. He pivoted again and searched the upper slopes of the lecture hall until he located her.

No. Not her. There was a basic resemblance, exaggerated by the tank top the student was wearing, but her complexion was paler than Dallas's, with a wilder, slightly artificial shade of cherrywood in her hair. He let out a breath and jiggled the chalk in his hand, trying to remember what he had been saying. There was a long, spacious silence. An empty ache in his stomach. His mouth brassy with instant coffee. The faces out there began to flicker with sudden attention, sensing tragedy in the air, the possibility of something about to go wrong. But it had already gone wrong — at home, and at school. He had checked his mailbox this morning and discovered what the topic of last week's special meeting had been: The bold new direction of the Economics Institute.

Plato, he finally said, as a citizen of ancient Greece, took slavery for granted and defended it vigorously as a necessary condition of the ideal state. In fact, Plato believed that a healthy society was a stratified one in which only the lower classes — mostly farmers and artisans — would be allowed to pursue profit and material wealth, as long as they were excluded from positions of power. Members of the ruling class, by contrast, would not be allowed to hold money. The rulers wouldn't be any more jealous of the lower class for making money than the lower class would be of the rulers for wielding power. Power and money would be two different things. The overarching goal of this society was human improvement.

These were the prefabricated sentences, laboratory-tested, reliable, that he used to establish some of the key differences between the ancient world and this one, with apologies for the simplifications and distortions. As he continued with the usual inventory of Plato's and Aristotle's contributions — their distinction between use value and exchange value, their descriptions of money's various functions, their observations about the division of labor two millennia before Adam Smith — he tried not to feel the weight of the room around him. Windowless. Fluorescent lit. Bluish walls and upholstered seats rising toward a bunker where a film projector sat, unused, behind a peephole. It had the acoustic tile and canned air of institutional buildings everywhere. The podium had a gleaming pine finish, but it wobbled whenever he touched it, making a thudding sound against the hollow floor of the stage.

The Dallas lookalike kicked off her shoes and drew up her legs, folding them beneath her. Like someone watching TV at home. She wasn't taking notes. Bare midriff, exposed bra straps. The sexual radiation was casual, almost careless. If he couldn't control his eyes, his thoughts, his desires — the message seemed to be — then it was his problem. Maybe that was her point. Maybe that was Dallas's point.

Plato and Aristotle lived in an era when the household was the center of production. It was a pre-industrial world. A world of agriculture. Think of the Southern plantations before the Civil War and you get the general idea. Activities now conducted in the free market rarely took place outside the domestic sphere. In fact, the word "economics" is derived from the Greek word for "household." The household, quite simply, was a microcosm for society as a whole. By analyzing a single household, you could understand the entire . . .

He trailed off. The living room, the kitchen, the backyard. Their torn clothing. He remembered the names he had called her on the floor last night and his legs began to shimmy a little and he had to take a step forward to steady himself, his knees a little watery, not quite solid.

A heavy silence. The faces seemed sober in the pale light, concerned for his welfare. He appreciated that. He really did. He opened his mouth.

"A chemist, a physicist, and an economist," he said, "are marooned on a desert island with a crate full of canned food but nothing to open the cans with. The chemist considers the situation carefully and suggests lighting a fire under the cans to increase their internal pressure and blow them open. The physicist, on the other hand, finds a sharp rock and recommends using it as a wedge to open the cans. But the economist offers a more elegant solution. 'First of all,' he says, 'let's assume we have a can opener . . .'"

He turned his back on the laughter and went to the chalkboard, where he drew a standard graph: price on the vertical axis, quantity on the horizontal, a downward-sloping demand curve intersecting an upward-sloping supply curve. This was the first thing students saw in Econ 101. Everyone knew it. It was like $E=mc^2$.

"This is a platonic graph. A pure form. An ideal. Why do I say this? Good question. Let's start by listing the assumptions behind this model."

He scanned the faces, the noncommittal expressions. Something was different and he realized it was their attention—crystallized, palpable, no longer full of the fidgets and daydreams he usually sensed out there. He waited.

A hand went up. It belonged to a student with dark hair, flames tattooed down the underside of his arm. "Perfect Information," he said.

"Yes. Perfect Information." Logan spread his arms in an expansive gesture. "The assumption that all producers and consumers have accurate, complete information about not only the commodity they're exchanging, but all the alternatives as well. It also means that the concerned parties know the opportunity costs of using resources for other things. Translation? Omniscience. It means you know the price of a banana in Flagstaff. It means you know the price of bananas in every grocery store in the world. Name another assumption."

Someone stirred in the front row. A twiggy, ginger-haired woman wearing a ripped T-shirt and cut-off shorts. "Rational Behavior?" she offered.

"Rational Behavior. The assumption that producers and consumers make decisions that are most effective in helping them achieve clear-cut, conscious objectives. The objectives themselves, however, are considered neither rational nor irrational. Raise your hand if that's you."

A hand appeared somewhere in the mid-section and a neighbor immediately swatted it down. A few of them laughed. Logan smiled. He paced slowly across the stage, toward a thermostat mounted and caged on the far wall, the control pad untouchable, the temperature set too high during winter, too low during summer. The aggregate attention span of the class — a simple mean determined by taking the total of all interest and dividing it by the number of students — was holding steady, but he feared the inevitable downturn.

"My favorite," he said, "is known as *ceteris paribus,* which economists translate as 'all other things unchanged.' According to this assumption, the effect of price is isolated from the effect of all other factors that influence the quantities of supply and demand. Forget taste, forget mood, forget the rude person behind the counter who gives you the evil eye whenever you ask him to go easy on the cream cheese. In fact, forget everything. The only thing that matters, according to this model, is the price."

The Dallas lookalike — whose name, by the way, was Erin — set her feet on the floor and leaned forward. Maybe it was the way he paced the stage. An agitated air about him. Focused, but not quite in control. Maybe it was this unscripted behavior.

"Plato believed that both knowledge and the objects of knowledge are immutable. He believed that physical reality is an invalid source of enlightenment because the objects around us are constantly in flux. Shadows on the wall. The only way to gain knowledge is to transcend the information provided by the senses in order to discover the unchanging objects outside the cave." He gestured at the chalkboard. "Pure forms. Ideals. A direct vision of the sun, which for Plato represented the source of all knowledge."

He turned and looked at it. Price, quantity. Intersecting supply and demand. The notation of human desire. This is what you want, this is what you get.

He leaned against the podium and nearly lost his balance as it wobbled under his weight. The class laughed. He laughed. It was all right. He'd appear onstage with a unicycle and some juggling pins if it would get the point across. How else was he going to bridge the gap? He was, after all, feeling somewhat old these days — an emotional rather than a physical sensation caused by all the changes he saw in his students, the styles and slangs slowly shifting out of phase with his. They seemed to be going tribal lately. There were tattoos, piercings, wild hair, as if they were yearning for another continent, or maybe this one before ships showed up loaded with smallpox and guns.

"Does this make sense?" he asked.

Heads nodded, voices murmured yes.

"OK," he said. "All right."

Not that this was a lesson he wanted any of his colleagues to know about. Not that he knew what he was doing anymore. Not that it would change anything in his career, or his marriage, or his life.

Dallas stopped at her favorite machine. She had discovered it — that is, noticed it — maybe three weeks ago in this corner where the light was dimmer, the foot-traffic not as heavy. You didn't get bumped by half-drunk idiots. You didn't know time was passing because nothing around you changed. And for reasons more mysterious than the pyramids of Egypt, management let employees play the slots without hassle.

She reached back and unwound the elastic cord from her ponytail and shook out her hair. She stood there for another minute. Her shift was over and if she had any sense she'd go to the payroll window to cash up her tokes, almost all of which were quarters, and drive home so she could make some sort of goodwill gesture to let Logan know everything was basically all right. She glanced at her watch. He wouldn't be home for a couple of hours, though, would he?

She pulled out the stool and sat down. The beauty of Bonus Poker, quite frankly, was the odds, along with the payoff for hitting a Royal. She chucked quarters into the slot and immediately came up with four Queens. She smiled. A sign of things to come.

There were side effects for every job you had. As a blackjack dealer she had been taught to clear her hands automatically whenever she touched part of her own body. The soft clap, the fingers spread to demonstrate that she had neither added nor removed anything from her person, so to speak. Which was fine. But she had absorbed it so deeply, had let it become such a part of herself, that she continued doing it in public places. In the supermarket she would clear her hands after stuffing lettuce into a bag. In clothing stores she'd do it after touching a couple of dresses on the rack. People in Vegas, wise about casino life, had understood. People in Phoenix had looked at her like she was a sociopath playing patty-cake with an imaginary friend. Fortunately, the habit had worn off a few months after moving in with Logan. Now it was her radio reflexes. She said "Copy" to people on the phone. And, of course, she still said "Good luck" at the end of every transaction. You can take the girl out of the casino, but you can't take the casino out of the —

"Is this seat taken?"

Dallas looked over at him. Mid-thirties, she guessed. Sandy-haired and tall, with a thickness to his limbs offset by a delicate face, like a construction worker turned model. In pre-Logan days she would have given him an opening, but now she simply said no and turned back to her screen.

"Why thank you," he said, as if she had kindly offered him a seat.

She played piano-style, hands hovering over the panel with her fingers hitting the hold buttons simultaneously, then shifting to the draws and deals with a tempo so steady you could almost tap your foot to it. As a little girl she had taken piano lessons until her father disappeared one day and her mother sold the piano before he could return to pick it up. The circumstances of the whole episode — that is, the affair with his secretary — had been revealed to her much later, long after she had stopped expecting Dad to show up for his visitations on time, if at all. Now all she had were illegible memories of notes and chords and keys. Sharp, flat. Major, minor. There had been an exercise book and a metronome and a teacher named Mrs. Bloomington, if memory serves, who had scolded Dallas for failing to practice until Dallas shut her up one day by playing a tune, flipping the pages of the score at the right places to give Mrs. Bloomington the impression that she knew how to read it when in fact she was simply recalling the notes exactly as Mrs. Bloomington had played them ten minutes earlier. During her brief stint at UNLV she had signed up for an Introduction to Music course to satisfy one of the general requirements and come out of it with a B simply by attending the classes and listening to what the teacher played. She never even bought the textbook, let alone the recordings she was supposed to study. And although she missed the majority of the rote stuff on the exams — the names of the composers, the epochs, the types of instruments — she aced the listening sections. Her teacher wrote a note at the bottom of her final exam asking to see her during his office hours. She didn't bother. What was he going to do, accuse her of cheating? Offer congratulations for winning Name That Tune? In either case, it was worthless. She wanted a vocation with a more tangible payoff, thank you very much. Besides, it was tough enough simply to survive the studying and morning-afters of student life. How many times had she puzzled over the vast prairie of an open book? How many times had she walked back to her dorm room at 5 a.m. with her arms folded against the chill of an empty world, her heels clacking on the pavement?

The machine kept teasing her with hands that were one card short of a straight, forcing her to take the longshot or go for a pair of face cards, the lowest payoff. She fidgeted, stretched her neck, fidgeted again. Slow, aromatic coils of cigarette smoke were wafting across her face. Her blood pleading for a small taste. It had been over six months since her last cigarette.

She turned to her neighbor. "Mind if I bum one?"

"Nothing would please me more," he said, fishing a pack from his shirt pocket. Then he chuckled. "Well, almost nothing."

She selected one, placed it between her lips, and was just about to ask for a flame when one appeared in front of her. The expensive silver lighter of someone who's made the commitment. She leaned into it, got the cigarette going, then tilted her head back and exhaled a cloud. She nodded thanks. She went on playing. And with the smoke inside her she began to gain clarity, serenity, definition. Elevated into sharper being. It was an experience that people who warned of cancer couldn't understand.

Her neighbor started in with the questions. Did she know what to do with a couple of eights and a queen. Why was the payoff for four of a kind higher for cards above five than for cards below. A full house was hard to get so why was the payoff so small. She glanced at him once and gave him an I-don't-know sharp enough to drop an elephant, but he wouldn't stop. She wasn't the type of woman who responded to Southern charm, or whatever it was the guy was trying. Although she had to admit a certain pleasure in the attention. And he wasn't bad-looking. But it was simply out of the question. She gathered a section of her hair and drew it over her shoulder to block his view of her face, one of her standard defenses.

He wondered why the payoff for three of a kind was the same for jacks or better as it was for jacks or below when there was no payoff for a pair below jacks.

She flipped her hair back over her shoulder. "Look," she said, holding up her hand. "This is a wedding ring. This means I'm having sex with somebody else tonight."

He didn't say anything. He sat there with a cigarette burning in the corner of his mouth, his face screwed into a Popeye squint as if what she said hurt real bad. This was the part where she was supposed to regret her harsh words and be nice to him. She had seen it happen a zillion times at her old table in Vegas. How many women screwed men because they felt sorry for them, is what she wanted to know.

She turned back to her screen and continued playing. He lingered for another minute or two and then cashed out, the clink-clink-clink of the coins in the hopper a welcome sound to her ears. In her peripheral vision she saw him rise from his seat and move on.

She sat back for a moment. She took a succulent drag off the cigarette, almost down to the filter already, and let the smoke do its thing. She wasn't vain or anything like that, but she knew she was attractive by the sheer quantity of men who approached her. Numbers don't lie. And to her credit, she had been acting like a porcupine ever since she had moved to Phoenix, willing to focus on Logan as long as it was vice versa. Because, well, when she had been seeing Logan but still living in Vegas there had been one or two relapses with Felix. Make that three. Blame it on the mystery of her multiple orgasms, which she needed to verify as the product of Logan's attention rather than her own sexual development. No, wait. Well, all right — yes, it was the orgasm riddle, which she really wanted to solve. But it was also the comfort of a known quantity. It was like a meal at her favorite diner, where she could slump in the booth and wear her frumpy sweatshirt and stub out her cigarettes in the saucers, after months of filet mignon and champagne.

Yet the guilt afterward had been like one of those illnesses you get in exotic countries, with chills and lethargy and mortal fear. She wouldn't ever do it again. She loved Logan. She really loved him. She simply wanted him to appreciate everything she had given up.

Logan drank from a plastic cup full of lemonade and scanned the crowd. His colleagues were at the far end of the room, gathered into formations that revealed the alliances and ententes, the cold wars of the Economics department. There were Pang and Deadmarsh and Niman. There were Bertuzzi and Hardy. There was Max Silverson with his vest and pocket watch, his neutral tie, his running shoes. And there, most important of all, was Tibor Novak — a.k.a. Dr. No, scheduled to lead the new Economics Institute into the badlands of econometrics and statistical techniques. According to the memo Logan had received that morning, private funding would be used not only for research, but for actual courses and scholarships and "administrative functions." Whatever that meant. Logan suspected he would know what it meant if he had simply attended the special meeting last week, but he had played hooky to be with Dallas on her day off.

Dr. No believed that all trade was, by definition, free trade, that the rising tide of development lifted all boats, and that problems such as poverty and pollution were aggravated, rather than solved, by social programs because they distorted the incentives of the free market. He was middle-aged, slim, vigorous. His hair was thick and prematurely white, his eyes metallic gray. He had been the youngest-ever member of the President's Council of Economic Advisers and then the youngest-ever chairman before moving into academia. He was renowned for his rhetorical skills. According to legend, the floors of conference rooms across the country were still slick with the blood of his vanquished opponents. And so Logan usually avoided him. Especially today. He hadn't spoken to anyone in the department since the phone conversation with Silverson that morning. He wanted to cool off.

He went over to the hors d'oeuvres and started gobbling. A few hours ago, in his office, he had tried to eat a sandwich while looking at last quarter's figures — the GDP and the CPI and all the other VIPs of economic growth — only to feel his stomach tighten up. Now he was hungry again. He glanced at the clock on the wall. Too late for lunch, too early for dinner. No matter. He roved over the trays and shallow dishes, the mandalas of cheese and crackers. The vegetables, the sour cream.

He didn't know why he was here. Nobody seemed to know. A new university president had taken the reins last year and this was his first major announcement. A former CEO of a mid-size corporation, he approached his job like a retiree trying his hand at watercolors or wood carving. Logan, like most people, expected something momentous today. This was one of those rooms reserved for administrative blue bloods and their guests, the chiefs of staff whose salaries were inversely proportional to the amount of contact they had with students. He looked around as he munched. Faux-crystal lamps. Generic landscape paintings. Royal red draperies stretching from ceiling to floor, concealing not windows but plain walls. The tables were covered with crisp, bullet-proof linen, the chairs molded for the sort of heavy-duty sitting required to endure long speeches. The pseudo-ballroom look you saw in hotel convention rooms. And was that the faint odor of carpet glue? He poured himself another cup of lemonade. When he looked up, Dr. No was coming toward the hors d'oeuvres table.

Logan moved away and found himself navigating the edges of other conversations, other concerns. He heard comments about courses and committees, covert politics, ghosts in the departmental machines. Someone mentioned the weather. He stopped. Just for the hell of it he introduced himself to a man who turned out to be a climatologist studying air samples in Phoenix. His name was Trubowitz and he wagged his head a little as he talked, emphasizing certain points. Carbon dioxide concentrations, he said, were 50 percent higher in Phoenix than elsewhere over the desert, which had ramifications not only for local weather, but for the growth of urban plants and fire-hazard weeds. The dome of carbon dioxide over the city could, in effect, be used to model Earth's future climate.

"Think of this place," Trubowitz said, with an expansive gesture, "as a laboratory to study the greenhouse effect. I would have been happy with a 10 percent difference. But 50! I mean, stop the presses." He laughed. "All right. I know it's gruesome, and I'm the first one to admit it, but there are mornings when CO_2 concentrations in Phoenix are up to 550 parts per million. And I love it. You're wondering why. I'll tell you why. The average concentration around the world is about 365." He looked hard into Logan's eyes. "OK? It was about 280 before the Industrial Revolution. The average world concentration won't equal what we have here until about the middle of the next century, at which point your favorite ski resort is probably going to be a water park." He threw up his hands. "Stop the presses."

Logan altered his expression and made a sign as if he had spotted someone across the room, then excused himself and worked his way farther through the crowd. He struck up a conversation with an environmental biologist studying rats that had developed an immunity to the most deadly pesticide on the market, consuming five times the lethal dosage, she said, before being eaten by foxes, owls, raccoons, hawks, and coyotes, who of course were dying promptly. Logan moved on and talked to an atmospheric chemist fresh off the plane from eastern China, where a haze of suspended sulfur and soot particles was preventing sunlight from reaching farmland and reducing crop production by almost 30 percent. He spoke to a marine biologist on loan from one of the coastal universities who was studying the numerous oceanic dead zones created by fertilizer and sewage runoff. He met a geologist who informed him about the peculiar salts in the canals and rivers of central Arizona—which, he claimed, caused the bad taste in the water. It's perfectly safe, he said. Just don't drink it if you're pregnant.

Logan found a chair and sat down, feeling hollow and slightly shaky, sugared-up with lemonade. To the vast number of incomes dependent on environmental degradation, he'd have to add the vast number of incomes dependent on studying it. He rubbed his eyes. He couldn't bring himself to join the Econ pack. Maybe they wouldn't notice his absence. Maybe they wouldn't care.

A woman sat down next to him and pulled off one of her high-heeled shoes. "Who makes such a thing?" She held it up like the skull of Yorick. "I've owned this piece of merchandise for three months and already a nail comes poking into my foot. Where's the integrity? Where's the quality control?"

Logan was about to offer an answer when he realized she hadn't looked at him and, in fact, probably didn't know he was listening. He looked her over—short-sleeved blouse, dark pants, a pair of steel-rimmed glasses perched slightly forward on her nose. Her hair nearly reached her shoulders and had the tannic color of old photographs.

She sighed melodramatically, then wedged the shoe between her knees and leaned forward, pressing the insole with her thumb. She grunted and pressed harder. Tendons surfaced on her arm. Her elbow trembled.

"Pull it out," Logan said.

She slumped forward and let out a breath. "Then the heel falls off and I walk like Captain Cook. No thank you."

Logan held out his hand.

She looked at him for a moment, sizing him up. Then she passed it over. He stood, flipped up the cloth on the table nearest him, and pressed the insole against the corner, gripping the table with his other hand so it wouldn't move.

"Test it," he said, handing it back to her.

She slipped it onto her foot and stood. "Yes," she said. "Thank you."

"I think Captain Cook was the guy who discovered Hawaii, and I think he had two normal legs."

She sat down again. "You knew what I meant."

"I did?"

"You imagined a pirate with a peg leg."

He nodded slowly. "And an eyepatch."

"Hobbling around on the deck of a ship, seeking whales."

"I see your point."

She extended her leg and examined the shoe as if she were trying it on for the first time, then set it down again. "My yoga instructor says I should throw away my high heels, but then my whole wardrobe would be thrown out of joint."

"Because they're complements."

"Excuse me?"

"Commodities used in conjunction with each other are called complements. Like hot dogs and hot dog rolls. Since your shoes have to match your outfits, you can't simply throw away all your high-heeled shoes and wear flats instead. It's a type of —" He stopped himself when he saw the look of faint amusement spreading across her face. "Sorry. I'm an economist."

"The dismal science."

"You're familiar with it."

"I took an introductory course many years ago in college, but I remember virtually nothing. During my senior year, though, I read a fascinating book that criticized the entire epistemology, so to speak, of mainstream economics."

"Who was the author?"

She frowned. "I'll remember in a minute or two. It wasn't very flattering to your profession, I'm afraid. It was for a course about paradigm shifts in which my teacher wanted to illustrate the major differences between hard science and social science. The author of the book argued, if I remember correctly, that orthodox economic theory ignores some basic physical realities."

"That sounds like Galbraith."

She shook her head.

"Marx?"

"Please," she said, wrinkling her nose. "This author was named . . ." She tilted her head back and gazed at the ceiling. "Georgescu."

"Never heard of him."

"Exactly. That was my teacher's point." She ruffled her hair back. There were a few jewels riveted to the outer rim of her ear, a star hanging from her lobe. Logan wondered how much pain had been involved in that process.

"Say the name again."

"Georgescu. G-e-o-r-g-e-s-c-u."

"You must have a photographic memory."

"Not photographic. Precise. My colleagues are always impressed when I remember the page number for a formula."

"You're a mathematician."

"An astrophysicist. And now I feel we can't keep speaking without introducing ourselves." She held out her hand. "Keris Aguilar."

"Logan Smith."

They shook hands.

"Aguilar," he said. "Spanish, right?"

She shrugged. "Spanish, Lebanese, Slavic, Swedish, and many others. I'm a walking casserole. A mutt. When I reach the part of the questionnaire asking for ethnicity, I check every box. It helped with college scholarships when I was younger, but not, I'm afraid, with research grants these days."

"And your research is?"

"Cosmic background radiation." She crossed her legs and clasped her hands over her knee. "Next summer we're launching a satellite to detect microwave photons and examine temperature patterns in three million separate regions of space. Ripples, if you will, of the Big Bang. I'll skip the tedious details except to say that if all goes well, the satellite will provide enough data to help us determine the geometric shape of the universe."

"I didn't know that infinity could have a shape."

"That's just it. I have a problem, Logan, with an infinite universe. Consider the implications. An infinite universe means that eventually you'll find a place where the atoms are arranged exactly as they are in this room, and thus an infinite number of Logan Smiths and Keris Aguilars are having this same conversation an infinite number of times. Does this make sense to you?"

There was a shift in the general sound. He glanced toward the doorway and saw the president — pleated, tailor-cut, groomed to the follicle — speaking with a few upper-echelon administrators. "No," he said, looking at Keris again. "It doesn't make sense."

"Exactly. Because you sense the truth. We live in a finite universe. Moreover, this finite universe is such a place where, if you travel far enough, eventually you'll end up where you started."

Logan frowned. "How —"

She held up a finger. "We look into space with our telescopes and see hundreds of billions of galaxies. Correct? But what if it's an illusion? What if the universe is actually a vast hall of mirrors? Some of those galaxies might be images of our own galaxy eons ago. Perhaps we're seeing light from a very young version of the Milky Way that has been traveling for thirteen billion years, making a complete loop around a finite universe."

"So you're saying there are only a few galaxies?"

59

"I'm saying that it's possible for the universe to contain mirages. Multiple images of a much smaller number of galaxies. If so, then I can go to the astronomers down the hall and say, 'That galaxy over there at redshift three, that's the Milky Way. And that one over there at redshift four, that's also the Milky Way, but earlier.' I can say these images are the result of light taking different routes through the universe at different points in the Milky Way's history."

Logan sat back. "But how . . ." He trailed off. He didn't know how to phrase the question, never mind follow her line of thought.

"You feel that space is simple and flat. Correct?"

Logan nodded.

"We believed the Earth was flat until we sailed around it."

"Yes, but . . ."

"Close your eyes for a moment."

Logan shut his eyes and tried not to smile. This was something, he supposed, that people did at self-help seminars, visualizing the world they wanted to live in. He was aware of the conversations boiling around him, people milling through the rows of chairs, searching for seats. The speech or presentation or whatever it was called was going to begin in a few minutes.

"Imagine a simple piece of paper. This is 'flat' space as we perceive it. If we roll up this piece of paper into a tube, it would still seem flat to a tiny creature living on the surface. Correct? Now let's take this even further. Bend the tube around and glue the two ends together so it's shaped like a doughnut. You're living on the surface of this doughnut, Logan, or this bagel, whichever delicacy you prefer, but it's so large, and you're so small, that to you it seems to be an infinitely long, flat plane. The only way to recognize the curvature is to travel all the way around and return to your starting point. Or perhaps identify light rays that have already made the journey."

He opened his eyes and looked at her. She was still sitting with her legs crossed, hands folded on her lap. The frames of her glasses, he realized, were perched slightly crooked on the bridge of her nose. He resisted an urge to reach out and straighten them.

"You can tell that from a satellite?"

"Of course. The detectors will search for repeated temperature patterns in the cosmic microwave background, and after about six months, we'll have enough—"

A deliberate cough came over the sound system. The president was standing at the podium, adjusting the goose-necked microphone as the room began to pressurize — voices dying off, heads turning forward, a couple of last-minute arrivals struggling toward empty seats. Logan spotted the Economics faculty sitting about six rows ahead and off to the right. A minor infraction of social protocol on his part. Maybe, he thought, he'd spend the rest of his life committing misdemeanors.

The president gave his greetings, his salutations, his standard what-a-long-strange-trip-it's-been description of his various challenges since assuming the helm sixteen months ago. Logan stopped listening almost immediately. He wondered if the universe really had a shape. He wondered if it really mattered. Maybe we'd make it to the next planet or two if we were lucky, but in essence the human race was Earth-bound. It was strictly local. So what if the other galaxies turned out to be baby pictures of our own? It wouldn't change the way we lived. It would simply alter the mood. The universe would seem less . . . well, less celestial. He glanced at Keris. Her eyes were closed and she was breathing deeply through her nose with a subtle, resonant sound that reminded him of distant wind. A meditation of some kind. She was a person whose research, he thought, squared perfectly with her desire. He faced forward again and touched the tender spot on his neck — which, he now realized, Dallas had done not only to inflict pain, but also to mark him in an obvious location. To make him see it every time he looked in the mirror. She had clawed at his body as if she had been trying to break him open, to dig something out of him. But what? What did she want? The shape of his universe? He was just beginning to understand the shape of hers. The density of her hips, the storms and tremors inside her, the tropical moisture between her legs.

"Which is why," the president said, "after much consultation with the Board of Regents, along with Mr. Wellington and Mr. Sanchez and many others who made valuable contributions to the proposal, we have allowed Dr. Novak to implement this pilot program next fall."

Logan blinked. Pilot program. Novak. Wait a minute.

"This public-private partnership, sponsored in part by PrimeBank and the Midnight Corporation, heralds a more streamlined, responsive approach to our administration. Envision, if you will, a confederation of institutes operating under the rubric of the university. Institutes no longer bound by the strict procedures and regulations of a command-and-control departmental system. Institutes with their own separate tuition brackets and funding structures, completely at liberty to adjust or 'upsize' their curriculum along with, of course, the size and composition of their own faculty — operating as 'cells,' if you will, within the organism of the university instead of cogs in a bureaucratic machine."

Logan was overcome by a blank sensation. Public-private partnership. During the last year or so, there had been numerous meetings about creating a "grant-writing system," as Dr. No phrased it, to relieve individual faculty members of the task, which he considered an inefficient use of time and resources. The focus of the meetings had gradually drifted toward partnerships with a few of the larger corporations in the country. But this went beyond anything he had heard about. Logan pressed his index fingers to his eyelids and listened to the rest of the speech, the rhetorical tide slowly receding to expose Dr. No's involvement in the project from its very inception. The project itself still seemed exceedingly vague. How far could you take it? There were entry-level undergraduates to consider, inter-disciplinary issues that would be exacerbated by the—

Applause. Logan raised his head. The president stepped aside and turned the podium over to Dr. No, who in turn issued many thanks for the assistance and indulgence he had received. He spoke for a while about decisions facing the new Economics Institute. He spoke about fresh approaches to old problems. He spoke about adventure and discovery. Logan watched him — the white hair, the finely chiseled face that most people would have described as venerable — while he made his remarks, smiling occasionally to signal a joke or a self-deprecating comment. He got away with his egotism by constantly mocking it. The Economics Institute, he said, would be a marriage between the public and private. At that point Logan wanted to stand up like the person at the back of the church to say why the wedding should not take place.

"The funny thing," Dr. No said, "is how spontaneously and naturally this program developed. As I recall, John, we were sitting in the back of your car. I was asking for money and getting nowhere" — he paused to let some laughter subside — "and you joked about fattening up the funding lines with a little bit of private money, at which point we just looked at each other." His gaze narrowed appreciatively, recalling the full intensity of the moment. "That was when we realized we had a real project on our hands."

Logan looked over at Keris. Her eyes were still closed, her deep breathing still in progress, visualizing the shape of the universe. Its contours. Its demand curves. They were probably the same thing.

As the thought struck him, he nearly rose from his chair. That was it. That was why it mattered. What's out there is in here too. Run a lap around the galaxy and find yourself at the beginning of the race again with the starter's pistol raised for the Big Bang. Watch the explosion, the separation. Witness price divided from quantity, desire from satisfaction, reality cut into sight and sound. This is the truth of the universe. This is you at the end of the equation.

chapter 3

Call him silly, call him sentimental, but Deck fantasized about returning to the West Coast someday to accept a position at Berkeley or Stanford—you know, one of those citadels where you could still claim California without having your own history staring you in the face every day. He wouldn't go back to Orange County. In fact, he wanted someone to offer him a job there just so he could turn it down. He needed a buffer between youth and adulthood. He needed some distance for the prestige to glow. Look at him now, daydreaming at thirty-three thousand feet: He sat by the window with his arms folded, his head angled toward the endless eye-ache of sky. Clouds streamed below. He had his tray, his drink, his salted nuts. The most recent issue of *Revenue* stuffed into the pouch in front of him. The pilot was announcing the weather in Philadelphia, as if nobody knew what it would be during the first week of February.

The position at ASU was beginning to look like a good springboard. There were resources, connections. His work would feed into the proper conduits and bring him the recognition he deserved, because say what you want about Eastfield's student-to-teacher ratio, it was simply out of the loop. He wanted to plug in again. It was his fault for not understanding the ramifications of working in New Hampshire. A few insiders had warned him about what kind of world it would be—small, white, tight—but he had fallen for the big-fish-in-a-small-pond allure, and now, eighteen months later, he wanted out. So he was getting out. He had made the decision, strangely enough, last October when he was leaving the Econ building one day and ran into another instructor who remarked on the beautiful weather. Deck had started to laugh at the obvious joke and then caught himself when he saw the instructor's reaction. He had looked around at the wilting grass, the naked trees, the landscape so clearly settling into its yearly coma, and thought *this* was a nice day? Keep in mind Deck had grown up playing baseball through the winter and body-surfing at Newport Beach almost every

New Year's Day — wearing a wetsuit, of course, but still. His colleagues' attitude toward the climate was an index of deeper issues. They knew little of the world and therefore were easily pleased.

A bell sounded. A female voice came over the speakers. It was time to sit up, drink up, batten down the hatches. One of the attendants came crashing down the aisle with her cart and then, afterward, with everything locked away, the plane began to descend. There was a gentle tilt into the full exposure of the morning, lozenges of sunlight drifting across the cabin, illuminating the opposite wall and the faces of some of the other passengers. He felt a great uplift, a pureness of being released from weather and human concern with the Earth burning luminously below him. He loved flying. It was like being everywhere and nowhere at once.

As the plane continued to drop he recognized the configurations of the old world — the clotted houses and treetops, the tangled streets. He knew exactly where he was. There was I-95. There was the broad swerve of the Delaware River. The landscape scrolled beneath him until downtown Philadelphia came into view. The bare girders of the Walt Whitman Bridge. A rusted ship plowing toward the sea. For just a moment the sun caught the glass flanks of the skyscrapers and ignited the terraces, the towers, the metal-edged armor. The Delaware and Schuylkill rivers shining like varicose veins. He could see the Ben Franklin Parkway on the other side of town, askew from the rest of the grid and losing itself in Fairmount Park. The art museum's Greco-Roman pillars and dome, the corrugations of the cement steps. And there was the baseball stadium almost directly below him. Not that he wanted to go back to Penn or anything, but there were certain things he missed. Cheesesteaks. Phillies games. They had eased his East Coast claustrophobia, given him the proper down time between dissertation chapters.

His work on individual consumption functions had been lauded and encouraged by a few key people, but he had let it go because he had sensed trouble down the road — the kind of trouble that only someone with his level of intimacy with the data could sense. In other words, the innovation wasn't going to be as great as his preliminary research suggested. Sturdy enough for a dissertation, but not for a book. He had wanted to show that point-of-sale ATM transactions, when isolated from other expenditures, would result in step-shaped consumption functions with a series of zero-slope or nearly horizontal plateaus bridging the traditional upward-sloping sections. But as he expanded the scope of his field study, the evidence began to resist him, the plateaus suggested by the original sample size disappearing with alarming speed and finality. Consumers, it turned out, weren't using their debit cards any differently than they were using their checkbooks or cash. So he scuttled the whole thing. If anyone asked, he said it was on the back-burner for a while, until he modified the equations. He knew how to downsize his problems when it was necessary.

The plane swung down toward the airport and passed over a bunch of refineries with their smoking ribcages, their crowns of fire. Hard to believe this was Logan's hometown. And hard to believe Logan was living in Arizona too. Deck had to laugh at that one. Mr. Colonial Heritage striding into the saloon and playing poker with the cowboys. He was probably stuck in that dead-end niche of his, trying to make himself useful to the department. He couldn't work with empirical data. That was his weakness. Although his colleagues and associates — including, most notably, the editors of *Revenue* — hadn't made the connection between Logan's topic and its convenient lack of formulas, Deck knew an evasion when he saw one. Throw some real figures at the guy and he'd duck every time. And, all right, sure, Logan could handle himself in the classroom, and he could write better than most people, but those skills were secondary. They were minor. Logan belonged in the minor leagues. At first Deck had been worried about working at the same university, but this recent insight had eased his anxiety. It would all be fine as long as Logan stayed out of his way.

The wheels hit the tarmac. The plane rocked and swayed a little as the retros blasted, and then they coasted for a while with the flight attendant singsonging the usual cautions and welcomes. They pulled into the gate. People jumped up and began struggling at the overhead bins, switching on their handhelds to see what they had missed in the last ninety minutes. Deck didn't move. He had a phone in his pocket, but he kept it under control. He took things at his speed, in his order. He smiled. Although most of his classmates had pegged him as the kind of guy to go for the private sector after finishing his degree, he had avoided it. He didn't want to consult. He didn't want to analyze emerging markets for the This 'N' That Corporation. He didn't want to do foreign currency forecasts behind a desk somewhere. He wanted to be the man in the crowd nobody recognizes but everyone senses — the one who explains the turning of the wheels, who determines what the wheels are, who whispers into the ears of presidents and policy-makers. Those were the calls he wanted on his phone. Not some customer or employer expecting you to hustle. No way.

He stood. He stretched. There was plenty of time to make his connecting flight to Phoenix. In fact, there was enough time to find a corner at the gate and spread out with the figures for his latest project, which, if all went according to plan, he was going to present at the conference next month for maximum effect. Talk about luck. Not only was ASU hosting it this year, but there would be an appearance by the chairman of the President's Council of Economic Advisers — which, it should be noted, was a job Deck wouldn't mind having for himself someday.

He eased into the aisle. Five weeks from now he'd be flying west again with a finished article in his briefcase. He'd be ready to make a name for himself. In the meantime, he'd have to be patient with both the macro and the micro — that is, not only the overarching plan, but the daily bump and grind of getting there. And here was a perfect example: An old man in front of him, pulling a four-footed cane from the overhead. It looked like a miniature coffee table attached to a pole. Deck reached up and grabbed one of the butt-ends, guiding it to the floor so it didn't put out anybody's eye. The old man didn't even realize it. Deck smiled faintly. He continued on — slowly, of course, giving the old man plenty of space, glancing out the portals now and then to bide his time. A few earmuffed workers were out there maneuvering their rigs and conveyers up to the aircraft, connecting it to its feeding tubes. The unrecognized work. Deck knew exactly how they felt.

Logan stood in his study, a.k.a. the guest bedroom, with the window open and the door closed, shoving folders into his bookbag. The room was small but comfortable, with a large desk, a bedside table that doubled as a printer stand, a closet for his archives, and some built-in shelves. He slid the last folder into his bag and tried to shut the flap, but it was overstuffed. Forget it. He set it on his desk next to his laptop and turned to the shelves. He selected Smith, Marx, Keynes. He examined the cracked spines. Enough for now. He could come back for more if necessary. Deck was staying for just a few days and, besides, it wasn't like the room would be hermetically sealed. He stuffed the books into the sideflaps of his computer case. Maybe it would be good for him to work on campus this week. No domestic distractions.

He went to the window with his mug of coffee and inhaled the scent of dew, moist soil, fruit hanging from the citrus trees in the backyard. He listened to the pipes humming inside the wall. Dallas's voice reaching him faintly through the length of the house. She was singing again, cutting into the low registers of a deep and sultry tune he couldn't identify. An old song, maybe. Something from a 1940s noir where the hero orders a double scotch while the femme fatale sings into a toaster-sized microphone, a twenty-piece band terraced behind her.

She was taking a long shower this morning, which meant she was shaving her legs. It was her day off and he couldn't help wondering what she had planned. After going to the movies yesterday, they had spent the rest of the afternoon pillaging the stores on Mill Avenue and, although Logan hadn't bought anything, Dallas had ended up with a few slinky dresses that she had modeled for him afterward — slit-hipped, backless, fitted tightly to her shape. When he saw them on her he almost forgot about the bill.

The water stopped. Logan gathered up his stuff and carried it out to his car in the garage, then came back for his mug. He looked the room over. The bed was made, the closet door open. Empty hangers awaiting Deck's shirts. He lifted the printer off the table and set it on the floor. Then he closed the window and went to the kitchen.

"I'll cook," Dallas said, leaning against the counter in her blue silk robe. Her hair hung in long, damp lengths. She was peeling a banana.

"You'll cook?"

"Tonight," she said. "Dinner. I'll run to the supermarket and do a Julia Child imitation for your friend."

"He's not exactly my friend." Logan walked past her and placed his mug in the sink.

"I know. You haven't seen him since Penn and you're worried."

He turned. "I am?"

"You've been hiding in your study. Pacing." She broke off the top of the banana with her fingers and popped it into her mouth. Her robe was tied loosely, the slack neckline revealing the upper halves of her breasts. Ever since that episode in the living room last week she had started wearing silk chemises to bed at night and this blue robe in the morning. A few days ago he had tried the door to the bathroom while she was showering and found it locked. Like he wasn't allowed to see her plainly naked anymore.

"Since when do you eat bananas?"

"Since I started buying them. Potassium, dear husband. Potassium. You may hate those women's magazines, but there's some knowledge in there."

"Did I say that? Did I say those magazines are bad?"

She broke off another piece. "I'll buy some beer, too, in case your friend likes that sort of thing. As far as hard alcohol goes, we already have enough to drown an elephant, to be perfectly honest, so I'm not worried. What time are you picking him up?"

"Deck doesn't get picked up. He rents cars."

"So I guess you'll be here when he arrives."

"Of course."

"And when will that be?"

Logan faced her across the kitchen. She was still leaning against the counter, her jaw working slowly. He watched the soft pulse of her throat as she swallowed. Those delicate hollows and dells. A couple of nights ago his lips had migrated down her neck and along the slope of her breasts until her hands had come up and stopped him. She was tired, she had said. She was working the next morning.

"You want to know when I'll be coming home this afternoon?"

She popped the rest of the banana into her mouth and nodded, eyebrows raised slightly, like he was the one acting strangely.

"Five," he said. "Maybe earlier. It depends, I guess, on how much work I get done today. Really, I could come home at any time. Is that a problem?"

She wiped the corners of her mouth with an index finger. She tossed the banana peel toward the garbage can and didn't seem to care that it missed. She came across the kitchen toward him.

"This project," Logan found himself saying as she eased herself up against him, "isn't going to be easy. I mean, Silverson won't even let me teach a course on the material, which is indicative, I think, of how the book will be received if I don't state my case convincingly enough. And with the conference next month the pressure is only going to get worse. I need to be working on something that I can mention during the panel discussion. I need a rough draft. Or at the very least an outline."

She didn't reply. Daylight filled the kitchen, giving her eyes extra facets and depths, a fierce emerald tint. She wrapped her hand around the back of his head and brought his face down to hers for a long, hot kiss. Damp shower-musk. The flavor of banana and, underneath it, a faint taste of tobacco in her mouth. She had started smoking again and was trying to hide it. Her glands gave off the odor. Her breath confessed to it every night as she slept, revealing the deep, dark secret of her lungs.

Not that he didn't enjoy the kiss, the feel of her body through the silk. His hands traveled down her waist and found the plump curve of her backside. The slippery play of the robe against her skin. He began to get an erection.

She stepped away and readjusted her robe. "Sorry," she said. "I know it's getting late. You should go to work."

He stood there swaying a little, engorged with pressures and pulses that refused to subside. He couldn't think of anything to say. He looked at the clock. Then he looked at her again. One thing was clear: She wasn't going to let him get away with a quickie. No twenty-minute session in the bedroom this morning. No way. He'd have to choose between her and work.

She crossed the kitchen and opened the refrigerator and stood there for a moment in the cold light, surveying all the packages and containers. Her robe annealed to her body. The points of her breasts outlined in metallic, sheeny blue. She grabbed a carton of orange juice and nudged the door shut with her hip.

He tried to phrase something congenial as he watched her walk over to the cupboard, something simple that would allow him to leave the house with a feeling of security, an assurance that all was reasonably well. He opened his mouth. Nothing happened. It was like turning a spigot with the pipes empty.

She filled a glass full of juice and then paused before she raised it to her lips. "I'll see you this afternoon."

By the time he reached the door it occurred to him that he had been dismissed. He turned. "Thank you for cooking tonight," he said. "I appreciate it."

She smiled. "I know."

He drove the six-lane streets. He gassed, he braked, he signaled for every turn. He was halfway to campus before he realized he was listening to some thrash number on the radio at nearly full volume, and now a DJ telling him to avoid outdoor activity. Pollution advisory. How now brown cloud. It happened every winter, when thermal inversions transformed the valley into a Rhode Island–sized garage with a million engines running. He passed through the gate and wheeled into a parking space. His car didn't like the smog either. It had a coughing fit for a few seconds after he cut the ignition, then let out a final gasp before it died. Remarkable. He locked it up and walked to the Econ building with the straps of the two bags crossed over his shoulders, collarbones aching. You were supposed to trust your spouse. He knew that. But knowing and doing were two different things. He wanted to ask Dallas what was going on, but couldn't think of a way to do it without causing more damage than her answer would repair. Even if it turned out to be a misunderstanding, she would take it as an insult. And it would be held against him later. She seemed to keep her grievances on file, waiting for the proper moment to retrieve them. She was a person who forgave, but didn't forget.

He stopped at his office and dropped off most of his materials before heading over to the library. He walked past palms, Mediterranean pines, olive trees, eucalyptus—all marked with the kind of engraved nameplates you saw on most office doors. He crossed an expanse of matted grass where an abstract metal sculpture stood, made out of what looked like leftover machine parts. He descended a long set of steps to the library, the entrance and lower floors located underground. A carpeted bomb-shelter. But Logan didn't mind. It freed him from that tendency to gaze out the window.

He passed through the turnstile and into the hush of the lobby. Here were the computer terminals, the broad reference table, the waffles of fluorescent light. He nodded to the librarian, a lanky woman with a battleship rudder of a nose, and found his usual corner, his usual desk. He unpacked and leaned back in his chair. OK. He could start now. Or he could go over to one of the payphones by the entrance and call home with some excuse just to see if she was there. And what would she say later if he asked her why nobody answered? Gone to the supermarket. The movies. The mall. He let out a breath and opened one of his folders.

His parents hadn't approved of the marriage. They hadn't said a word, of course, as they never spoke about such things, but he had felt the full force of their displeasure across the phone lines. A casino dealer. From Las Vegas. Without a college education. One of the reasons Logan had suggested the off-the-cuff ceremony with the justice of the peace was to save his parents from the obligation of attending it. When they finally met Dallas last Christmas they had overexerted themselves in trying to make conversation, as if she were a refugee from a third-world country with little English and even less understanding of life. It wasn't that they disliked her. They simply didn't want her married to their son. And Dallas's attitude didn't help. She spoke to them with a sugary condescension in her voice, like they were a couple of senile grandparents in a nursing home. A deliberate sign of what she thought of them. So they had settled into a separate peace. Logan's parents called when they knew Dallas was at work and asked about her as a prelude to the real conversation, which tended to be his job—an increasing source of comfort these days among the multi-tiered failures of career and family that surrounded them.

If only they knew what he was doing now. A criticism of mainstream economics via Smith's initial theory and its developments by other thinkers over the course of the next two centuries. Logan spent several hours trying to get a foothold on the material. He finally sat back and stared at his crumpled notes. The false starts, the fierce crossouts. He stood up and decided to look at the introductory chapters of a few old textbooks to see if they would help him pinpoint some of the theoretical changes in the last couple of decades or so. Signs of continental drift. On his way to the stacks, though, he found himself trying to remember that Galbraith quote. How did it go? The problem with economics isn't an initial mistake, but a . . . The mistake of economics is . . . He couldn't quite recall the words, the slightly awkward but incisive sentence from *The Affluent Society*, which was sitting on his shelf at home. It would make a good epigraph, maybe a starting point for his introduction.

He headed toward the *G*s and located the book on one of the lower shelves. He pulled it out, thumbed through it until he found the quote, and then knelt on the floor and copied the words onto an index card. The short-comings of economics are not original error but uncorrected obsolescence. Yes. Exactly. That was the problem. And maybe that was the problem with Dallas. She wasn't a single woman in Vegas anymore, so she really shouldn't behave . . . He shook his head. He eased himself into a sitting position on the floor and folded his hands over his face. In the past, his private agonies had sent him pacing the streets of Philadelphia. It seemed strange to him now, in a city occupying so much land, to have no refuge in its neighbor-hoods, no fire escapes or scabbed brickfaces with old advertisements like faded tattoos, no tangy Chinatown scents or steam rising from subterranean grates, no Independence Mall, no South Street, no long and narrow restau-rants with wainscoting and withered tables, no cinemas walking distance from 24-hour diners, no urban wrack to map his thoughts against. In gradu-ate school, even while he was sequestered with his dissertation during that last year or so, he had met Silas on a fairly regular basis to do those sorts of things. They had even visited the child-friendly Ben Franklin Museum, lin-gering in the large entry where telephones were set up on podiums with a di-rectory on the wall listing the names and numbers of famous figures you could "call" to hear what they thought of the Old Boy. He and Silas had stag-gered with laughter at John Keats's lack of phone etiquette, at Mark Twain's nasal voice, at the listing for Byron, Lord. By the time they stumbled out of there Logan could hardly remember what had been bothering him that day, his stomach punched-out with laughter. But there was no one to call now. He had met a few interesting people in Phoenix, but they seemed indiffer-ent, coated with non-stick surfaces. And try as he might, whenever he and Dallas tried a new restaurant he simply couldn't recover from the process of getting there — the drive to a set of anonymous coordinates near a Sprawl-Mart or a Discount Depot. It didn't feel natural.

He took his hands away from his face. Dusty and battered spines gazed back at him. Tomb silence. The buzzing of fluorescent lights. He hauled himself up off the floor, replaced the Galbraith book, and started to walk away when his mind caught up with what his eyes had just seen. That name. He backtracked and found the book. Nicholas Georgescu. The author Keris had told him about. He pulled it from the shelf and read the first few lines of the introduction, then snapped it shut. He strode back to his desk. This, he thought, would serve him better than a bunch of old economics textbooks that didn't even . . . He came to a halt. He glanced at his watch and realized there was a textbook committee meeting in twenty minutes. And by the time he got out of there he'd have to drive home to meet Deck. The day was essentially finished. He weighed the book in his hand for a moment, then headed over to the circulation desk to check it out. He could carry the extra weight. In fact, he could carry it all the way home. On days like this, it qualified as bedtime reading.

It was like armed robbery. Dallas cashed out and stuffed the money into her purse and walked to her car humming, because basically you don't do that sort of damage to a casino and live to tell the tale. Most people would have kept playing. Not her. She shook another cigarette out of her pack and stopped for a moment to light it. The house edge on video poker was less than a tenth of 1 percent, so if you did the math you'd see she was bound to have a day like this: Four aces, then a royal flush twenty minutes later. The attendant had looked at her like how many rabbits' feet are in this woman's pocket. She got the cigarette going and continued walking. This was the outer limit of luck. She knew it. She had felt it from the very moment she had risen from bed that morning—the steel-edged purity of her thoughts, the deep heat of the shower suffusing her so fully that it radiated through her skin afterward, making every object agreeable to the touch. Juice carton, banana peel, refrigerator door. They liked her. The world liked her today. There was no other way to explain it.

She passed a gigantic motorhome with a couple of dirt bikes harnessed to the back. She passed square-shouldered luxury cars, a gleaming four-wheel drive, a low-rider, a no-rider with bald tires and a cracked canvas roof. Her car was beyond the last lightpole. She had deliberately parked in no man's land so she could get some air, some walking, a decompression period between the video screen and the steering wheel with real life coming at you through the windshield. And there it was—her hag, her wicked witch of the west. She slid behind the wheel and rolled down the window and sat there for a while smoking, her head tipped back, her eyes half-closed. Every magazine seemed to have another piece of advice aimed directly at her, another technique to shatter his complacency or keep him intrigued—the small things that added up to a whole new life, really. But she had made a mistake by mentioning the magazines to Logan. She didn't want him to guess where her behavior came from, otherwise he'd dismiss it. He'd dismiss her from his mind. He'd lose interest.

She flicked the cigarette to the pavement and started the car. The engine ran fine, but the body was falling apart and these days she found herself slowing to read the banners when she passed the dealerships. The shining windshields, the fields of chrome. She had made the mistake last month of telling Logan what was on her mind and he had practically chained her to the kitchen table to prevent her from buying a car. As if the monthly payment would do terrible damage to their budget. As if they even had a budget in the first place. She and Logan said budget-this and budget-that like they had incomes and expenditures written down somewhere, but the spic-and-span truth was that they made it up as they went along, which suited her just fine.

She pulled onto the road and crossed the dusty tracts of the reservation. Beat-up houses here and there. Tufted shrubs. Prickly pear. A few saguaros. Ungroomed desert stretched toward nubbed foothills in the distance, a watertower painted bright red. Near the freeway she crossed the reservation boundary and the transition was instant. It was all strict design and symmetry now. Terra-cotta rooftops. Tile and stucco, trees and grass. This was her first time out here. She had set out for the supermarket this morning but found herself driving farther and farther away, her interest piqued by a billboard that suggested not only loose slots but a whole different universe of luck — and she had followed her hunch. Who could explain this instinct she had for such things?

When she came off the freeway in Tempe she headed for the usual supermarket, not the cheapest place but the most accessible, with the wide aisles and, of course, the best selection of magazines. She parked, locked, walked. The automatic doors parted for her. She selected blemish-free vegetables, a pound of plump scallops, some pasta, some spices, some oils. And what do we have here but nine ways to make him beg for more. She picked up the magazine and thumbed past the ads, the feline bodies and perfume packets spuming up their exotica. She skimmed the article for a moment and then tossed it into the cart. At the checkout she ran her card, their card, through the machine and tried to ignore the woman behind her with the screaming baby on her hip.

There was a time, not long ago, when she had paid attention to prices. She had timed her hunger to her breaks at the casino, forced herself to eat a little hardier because the food was free in the employee dining room, and at the supermarket she had gone generic on everything except toilet paper. That was before she got a grip on the video poker. Those were the days when she and Lucinda would create venture capital by writing checks to each other and gambling with the funds before their banks caught up with the overdrafts. Not anymore. She hadn't gambled at all while dealing blackjack. And now she had it on a leash like a real pet. A hobby. And let's not forget that she was married to Logan, who wasn't exactly on the Fortune 500 list but made enough for them to live like civilized people. That's not even counting today's jackpot, which she was going to stash into her savings account tomorrow. There were clothes she wanted to buy. Shoes, perfume, stockings.

She climbed into her car again. Red light, green light. Sun, sky, smog. She felt a craving for another cigarette but reined it in. Logan might be home. Since last week she had been careful about it, keeping the pack at the bottom of her purse and brushing her teeth whenever breath-quality was in doubt — which, she reminded herself, she should do basically as soon as she walked through that door. Like head for the bathroom before unloading the groceries. She didn't want Logan to have the leverage of knowing. This, she had to admit, was the sort of thing her mother would do vis-à-vis her latest boyfriend, justifying it endlessly to Dallas during that conversational wasteland known as their monthly phone call. Mom gave you the impression she was just full of savoir faire, but she had worked a miserable job most of her life and let a husband slip through her fingers. Forget it. There was more wisdom in horoscopes.

As she approached the house she noticed another car in the driveway, a man with blond hair and sunglasses sitting on the hood. Impeccably dressed. She knew who it was. What she saw now lined up perfectly with that momentary impression of him at the casino eighteen months ago. She pulled past him and into the garage. By the time she climbed out of the car he was approaching her with a duffel bag slung over his shoulder.

"Now this," Deck said, pointing a finger skyward, "is a nice day."

She stood in the open bay holding the grocery bags. "Logan should be home any minute."

"Great."

"He usually parks on that side." She nodded toward his car.

Deck looked at it as if someone else had put it there. Then he nodded. He set down his duffel bag, climbed inside the car, and backed it onto the street, maneuvering it swiftly over to the curb in front of their yard. He came back up the driveway and grabbed his duffel bag again, then raised his sunglasses onto his forehead. "I don't suppose you remember me."

"We've met?"

"The casino. You were busy taking Logan's money, as I recall."

"As I recall," Dallas said, "he won it all back later, plus some." She hit the button to close the garage door and turned to go inside.

Deck stood at the edge of the kitchen while she unpacked. There was the usual small talk about his flight, his interview, the long-time-no-see for him and Logan, and what a shame they hadn't kept in touch since Penn. He had a lean build with some extra bulk worked into the shoulders, a few cords of muscle visible on the forearms below his rolled-up sleeves. High cheekbones, sculpted jaw. The blond hair was fairly short and spiked just a little, showing a hairline that, she guessed, he cherished as a sign that he wasn't aging like everyone else.

"I'm impressed," he said. "This is a real home. Logan is a lucky man."

"We had a good realtor." She had pulled out the cutting board and was rinsing vegetables in the sink.

"I wasn't talking about the house."

It took her a moment to catch the compliment. Then she smiled non-committally and kept her eyes on her work — the same reaction, she realized immediately afterward, that she had used to placate the stag-party types who had occasionally stumbled over to her table at the casino, expecting her to be awed by their charm. That was it. Deck was the kind of guy who thought he was much more attractive than he actually was, who thought he was fooling women with his gentleman routine. Yeah, she knew the type. She knew it too well.

Deck, it should be noted, didn't like the way these things just spilled out of him sometimes when the woman in question had a certain body and a certain way of moving with it. Certain motions indicative of pleasure. He felt like he had just confessed something shameful. He went over to the cupboard. "Mind if I grab a glass of water?"

"Go ahead. I suggest . . ."

He heard a noise and looked back just in time to see her fling open the back door. She stood at the threshold, hissing, making throwing motions with her arm. A sandy-colored cat jumped up to the top of the cinder-block wall that enclosed the backyard and then hopped down the other side. Deck let out a low whistle and went to the sink to fill his glass.

"A stray," she said, as she closed the door. "Logan's allergic."

Deck nodded and gave a wry little smile as he filled the glass, amused at the way some passions erupted, coming up the wrong vent. He wondered if Logan knew what he had on his hands here. Deck, by contrast, was no stranger to this type of woman. He didn't like to talk about it, but once upon a time he had been involved with a waitress and would-be poet in Philadelphia who milked the first I-love-you out of him and then started turning the screws. He understood now. He saw the swerve of Dallas's hips as she moved around the kitchen and knew what she was all about.

He tipped back the glass and drank. Then he made a terrible face. "Oh my God."

"Sorry," Dallas said. "I was going to warn you about that. There's a jug of springwater in the fridge."

He held up the glass. "Does this come from your pool?"

She brushed past him and began drying off the vegetables. "I thought you were from Irvine."

"It was never this bad."

"You've been living in New Hampshire how long?"

"I remember what the tapwater tastes like in my hometown."

"Another finicky East Coaster complaining about the lack of civilization, is what I'm thinking."

He shook his head as he headed over to the refrigerator. "Never mind. Let's just say tapwater goes on the 'con' list. One of the opportunity costs of living here."

"Opportunity costs?"

He pulled the water jug from the fridge and watched her for a moment, working at the counter. The breasts were probably C-cup. The waist was thin, the ass full and nicely rounded. If there were any structural flaws in that body, he couldn't find them. He brought the jug over and set it down next to her. "You're familiar with opportunity cost. You just don't realize it."

She was slicing a tomato with a serrated knife. She glanced at him but didn't say anything.

"It's the true cost of every commodity you buy. When you choose one product over another, you have to include not only the money you're paying for it, but what you gave up as an alternative. The pleasure you would have received from that other thing."

She continued slicing.

"But the most important factor in a consumer's purchasing decisions," he said, reaching past her to dump the tapwater into the sink, "is the law of diminishing marginal utility." He lingered there for a moment, in the subtle field of her body, her smoke residue, her perfume. "It states that each additional unit of a commodity is worth less than its predecessor. You know, the more you have of the same thing, the less interesting it is. The less satisfying."

She cursed, dropped the knife. Deck saw a red slash on her index finger. Welling blood. He didn't move. Right about now, he thought, was the part where he was supposed to take hold of her hand and wrap his handkerchief around the wound or something so they could have a moment together. But he didn't have a handkerchief. And when you were alone with a woman like this one, a woman who slung sex all over the room just to see how a man like Deck would react, it wasn't necessarily a bad idea to let her bleed a little.

She stalked off to the bathroom. He picked up the jug and refilled his glass with civilized water. He called after her, asking if she needed help. She said no. He grabbed his duffel bag, wandered a bit until he found what looked like the spare bedroom, and changed into shorts, T-shirt, running shoes. He needed some circulation after the plane. And that drive. He had picked up his rental at the airport and explored the freeways to see how they measured up. Not that he was expecting Californian sophistication here, but there was something primitive about the whole experience. It had started right away, coming up the ramp behind an open-ended trash truck doling out cartons and wrappers and flapping frisbees of cardboard, sending an extra plastic bag at Deck's windshield just as he was changing lanes. He had slipped past some eighteen-wheelers clogging the lanes. He had maneuvered around a pre-fab house and its chase-car helpfully identifying it as an over-sized load. There had been fast-lane-hugging minivans, fat-hipped utility trucks, self-employed sawed-offs. There had been flatbeds and tankers and truckers, junksters and guzzlers, vintage models with their fins and black exhaust. He had finally come off the freeway disheartened by the whole thing, cruising around until he found a place that made extra-thick smoothies. And it was only then, sitting in the parking lot, sucking pulverized fruit through a straw, that he had thought, all right, every place has its share of wackos. The concentration was simply higher here. You should expect it from a state that didn't have vehicle inspections. You should expect that from a bunch of Zonies.

He came out of the bedroom and found Dallas back at the cutting board with her finger taped up. He eyed the tomatoes, the green peppers, the mushrooms, the onions. He eyed the taper of her thighs and the line of her underwear through her thin cotton pants.

"I'm going jogging."

"Good idea," she said, without looking up.

"You should run those onions under water when you cut them," he said, "or you'll cry."

She lifted her head and looked back at him. "I know what I'm doing."

He left through the front door and began to stretch, standing on crushed gravel where grass belonged. Desert landscaping never did much for him. He was surrounded by blades, spikes, thorns — a yucca, a palo verde, maybe a barrel cactus over there. As he loosened up his quads he leaned closer to the stubbled ribs of a saguaro next to him. And he felt a pang of regret. He hadn't been very nice to Dallas. But he'd fix it. He'd supersize the charm, make her believe, in retrospect, that he was completely unaware of any harm he had done. He knew how to repair damage. He knew how to make people feel better. And with Dallas, he thought, as he began running toward the canal he had seen while driving through their neighborhood earlier that afternoon, he could probably do more than that if he wanted. It was tempting. But she was Logan's wife. And sometimes, knowing that you could do something was better than actually doing it. He began to hit his stride. His lungs expanded, his heart filled. His legs pumped and sent the Earth spinning away from him.

They sat, all three of them, at the table with the usual array of dirty plates and bowls and utensils, wadded napkins. Jazz playing on the stereo. Various permutations of whiskey sat before them — scotch and bourbon, mixed and straight. It had been a real dinner, Deck said. He was impressed. Logan didn't know how to respond to the extra compliments, so he simply nodded and glanced over at Dallas. Ever since he had come home that afternoon he had sensed something between the two of them, a 50/50 mix of hostility and something else he couldn't quite put his finger on.

"If you follow that canal far enough," Deck was saying, "eventually it runs near a dry river bed."

"The Salt," Dallas said.

Deck picked up the shaker and held it out to her.

She did a slow smile. "The Salt River. So named for its high saline content."

He put down the shaker. "How about the Salt Ditch, so named for its low water content."

The music surged suddenly. A trumpet blared. Drums crashed.

"People from the East Coast basically make fun of rivers out here for not having water in them," Dallas said, "because they don't understand what it's like, what sort of place this is, even though they think they have it all figured out the minute they step off the plane." She looked at Logan. "Isn't that right?"

This was meant to cut several different ways and Logan didn't know what to do with it. He took a sip of bourbon. "The river is dry because of Roosevelt Dam, which was built back in 1912, I think, to guarantee a water supply. And, of course, it generates power. Phoenix wouldn't be here without it."

Deck was nodding. "So those canals come from—"

"The Colorado River," Dallas said. "The same water people drink in southern California."

Deck looked at her. "The Colorado runs through the northern part of the state. The Arizona-Utah border. That must be one hell of a pipeline."

"Oh, it is. Enormous. Reliable. It keeps the whole city satisfied."

"Actually," Logan said, "it's a mix of Colorado, Salt, and Verde river waters."

"How do you know all this?" Dallas asked, turning her attention toward him, it seemed, for the first time.

"You remember that faculty function last week. The really boring one I told you about. I met a geologist who mentioned it to me." He glanced at Deck again. "Anyway, I've never walked all the way to the riverbed."

Deck sat back and stretched. "It was a long one. Not that it was a marathon or anything. You should try it sometime."

Dallas rose from her seat and began clearing the dishes.

"I'll help," Deck said.

"I don't need help."

Deck stood and picked up the wooden salad bowl. "You shouldn't have to do all this yourself."

"Logan will help me," she said, pausing for a moment with the plates stacked in her hands, off-centered and slightly splayed, like slipped disks. "Besides, you don't know where anything goes."

"So give me the angle on this place. I look at the menu and see econometrics already listed as the main course with maybe three or four micro appetizers."

This was Deck, much later, on the back patio with a final drink and contemplations. Here were the ruined yard and the high wall, the citrus trees, the unkempt grass. Here was the night sky overhead, swabbed with city-glow and a little bit of cosmos—a half-moon, a hardy star or two. The freeway's steady susurration in the distance. The dull rumble of a jet. It was cold now and they were both reclined on webbed chairs, both facing the mucky pool, both wearing Penn sweatshirts. A coincidence neither of them mentioned. Dallas had gone to bed.

Logan yawned. "Growth. As far as I can tell, Novak wants to expand the curriculum over the next couple of years to give undergraduates training in econometrics. Apparently grad school is too late. Some people are saying we should keep the lower-level curriculum in line with the upper-level. As above, so below."

Deck shifted in his chair and nodded. "The national trend. Although you wouldn't know it at Eastfield."

"Really?"

"I glance at other syllabi and think, What year is this? These guys are still teaching Keynes? Let's add Santa Claus to the reading list and leave some milk and cookies in the classroom."

"I have to admit I still have a hard time picturing you in New England."

"So do I. Forget that gulag of a school for a minute. Forget the bad weather and narrow little roads. I'm sick of that maple-syrup accent. I'm sick of those stony faces. And when they say it's a good place to raise kids, my friend, it's time to pull the ripcord."

Logan smiled. "You're a California boy. Why fight it?"

"The only redeeming feature is the tax system."

"Or lack thereof."

Deck turned toward him. "Exactly. Zero sales, zero income."

"Zero social programs. Zero funding for education."

"The money gets where it needs to go through private means. The market. You know that."

"What I know," Logan said, "is that it's like a car without seat belts or airbags, which is fine unless you're the one having a head-on collision."

Deck laughed. "So you're saying let's dismantle the engine to avoid traffic accidents."

"I don't know what I'm saying." Logan blinked and yawned again. He was reclined with his arms folded, staring into the orange aura overhead. "I'm saying I'm tired."

Deck looked around the yard. "I'm ready for the pillow myself, although I can't say I'm lucky enough to have someone warming up the sheets for me. You've done well for yourself, Dr. Smith."

There was a silence.

"What happened between you and Dallas?"

Deck shrugged.

"You can tell me," Logan added. "I won't get mad."

Deck climbed to his feet and slung the remains of his drink onto the lawn. "There's nothing to tell. Maybe she doesn't like me. Maybe she thinks

I'm trying to take your job or something. Maybe you should tell her I have a different specialty than yours and that we're like an electrician and a plumber working together on the same house."

"Maybe I should."

Deck clapped a hand on Logan's shoulder as he walked past. "See you in the morning."

Logan heard the sliding glass door open and close behind him. A few moments later a square of light appeared on the lawn. When it finally vanished he swung his legs to the ground and sat at the edge of the chair with his hands on his knees. It was late. He stood. He heard a meow. He turned. Puffy jumped down from the wall and came over to him.

"Hey, pal," he said, scratching the soft head. Puffy slanted his eyes and gently butted his skull against Logan's fingers, slinking his backbone up into Logan's palm as he stroked him.

"All right," Logan said. "Wait here." He entered the house through the kitchen, went to the garage, and returned with the food packet. Puffy was sitting in the same spot, faithful and true. They understood each other.

Logan glanced at his bedroom window, at the curtains and the darkness they framed, before he tore open the packet. He could already feel a mild burning in his eyes — the allergy kicking in. "Here we are," he said, dumping the food onto the grass. He found himself repeating it over and over again as Puffy crunched the pellets between his delicate little teeth. "Here we are. Here we are."

Inside, he wrapped the crumpled packet in a paper towel before throwing it away. Then he paused with his hand on the light switch, surveying the kitchen, the clean counters, the pots in the drying rack. The towel was draped squarely over the bar. What's wrong with this picture. Most of the time Dallas could hardly be bothered to put her own coffee cup in the sink, but tonight she had cooked and cleaned like hired help. He turned off the light. On his way through the living room he saw his bookbag on the couch and went over to it. He sat down. He realized he was avoiding the bedroom. Dallas's sleeping shape. He'd have to undress in the dark and slip into bed without disturbing her precious sleep cycle.

He rooted around in his bag until he found Nicholas Georgescu's book. *The Entropy Law and the Economic Process.* The cover was loose, the corners blunted as if it had been dropped down the stairs a few thousand times. The tangy smell of old pages. He never seemed to notice the condition of books until he examined them at home, among the trappings of real life. He turned on the lamp and began to read.

Half an hour later he went to the kitchen and made a pot of coffee. Three hours after that he toasted a bagel and ate it without jam, standing at the counter with his whole body twitching. At some point he looked up and saw the world brightening beyond the windowpanes, materializing into its usual shapes. He closed his eyes for a moment and heard a couple of cars pass on the street outside. Then Dallas's sharp voice. He jolted upright, into sunlight and air, the book that had been splayed across his chest flapping to the floor.

"What is wrong," she said. "What is wrong with you." Her voice was still husky with sleep and she was standing there like someone rudely awakened, her robe cinched, her arms folded tightly across her chest.

He looked at her, touched with a momentary wonder at how beautiful she was, even now, with her tangled hair and sleep-wrinkled face, after eight hours of heavy-duty slumber. "Let's find out," he said.

"What?"

He stood slowly, working the kinks out of his joints. He stooped and picked up the book and brushed off the cover with his palm as if it were dusty. Nicholas Georgescu. Saint Nick. He started laughing—silently at first, but then heartily, surrendering to the storm in his chest. Why? Because he was scheduled to teach today. He was supposed to deliver a flat-Earth sermon. It was either laugh or cry.

chapter 4

Logan read the book twice, filled a legal pad with notes. He tried to contact Nicholas Georgescu but discovered he was dead. No surprise. The book had been written thirty years ago by someone who understood physics, philosophy, calculus, econometrics, history, and at least three languages. A lifetime's worth of knowledge. And in the following weeks Logan tried not to let the contrast between Georgescu's accomplishments and lack of recognition depress him. So what if a great mind had arisen, produced insights worthy of a Nobel Prize, and died in obscurity. So what if Logan had spent ten years in college and graduate school and never heard the man's name. So what if the book was out of print. He paced the stacks at the library and told himself that the new paper he was writing—provoked by Georgescu's book—would be reasonably well received at the convention. He began wearing ties to faculty meetings. He showered every morning with the nozzle at its most brutal setting, ironed his shirts to crisp perfection, shaved until his face burned. He lectured with a grim rigor that made his students suspect a divorce or some other wound in progress. And he surrendered his weekends to Dallas. Like someone loading up on canned goods before the hurricane hits, he was stockpiling credibility to survive the deprivations ahead of him. Not that he realized it. He interpreted his behavior as optimism and renewed commitment. He really did.

Take the following Saturday, for example. There he was, sipping coffee after breakfast, viewing a fine blue vintage of sky through the kitchen window while Dallas read the newspaper. He stretched out his legs. A slice of pulpy sunlight warmed his feet. They had spent the previous night listening to a new CD in the living room and having sex on the couch. They would probably spend tonight in a similar manner. And tomorrow? Tomorrow would consist, at the very least, of Sunday brunch at an overpriced diner, a midday movie, and maybe a stop at the mall on the way home. In other words, he was not only making his quota for the weekend, but exceeding it. And so, believing he was free for the day, he sat back and allowed his thoughts to gravitate toward the work waiting for him in his study, already testing the edges of Georgescu's Flow-Fund Model to see how it might accommodate measurements of—

"The fountain," she said.

"The what?"

She bent back the newspaper and flapped it down on the table. "There. Fountain Hills."

He glanced at the upside-down page but didn't reach for it, dimly sensing trouble. He looked at her. She was wearing her silken bathrobe, but her hair was tied back, her face plain and business-like.

"You mean that cheesy subdivision out on the Beeline Highway?"

"There's a gigantic park with a fountain in the middle of it, and every hour the thing shoots up a geyser three times as high as Old Fateful."

"Old Faithful."

"Whatever. It's a great spot for a picnic, is what I'm thinking."

His chest fell with relief. "A picnic. Sure. Maybe we can go there instead of Binky's." This was the diner where they usually ate Sunday brunch.

She shot him a surprised look. "But that's tomorrow."

"Yeah."

"I was thinking today. Instead of sitting here and doing nothing."

Ah. There it was. He set down the empty mug. Earlier that week he and Dallas had butted heads inconclusively—or at least it had seemed that way to Logan—about whether or not he would work on Saturdays. Now he realized that a decisive victory would involve starting up a second argument about the results of their first argument, winning both of them at the same time, and then trying to work while she brooded all day, radiating resentment through the walls of his study. He'd accomplish little, if anything. And then, to top it off, he would have to make further apologies and reparations afterward. He'd have to be twice as nice tomorrow and it still wouldn't be enough. It was better to be half as nice now and receive full credit for it. This was a simple cost-benefit analysis. It took about two seconds. After all, he loved her.

"Today," he said. "All right." And then, realizing he needed to pump more enthusiasm into his voice: "Let's do it."

So these were the tactics he used, more or less, over the next few weeks as he worked on his paper and monitored the investments he had recently made. This requires some explanation. Although Logan's family had been robbed by a corrupt accountant, this accountant hadn't been able to breach the walls of a trust fund — or, more accurately, a *dis*trust fund — that Logan's grandparents had established in his name. And last October, as soon as Logan had reached the golden age of thirty and come into full possession of the funds, he had tried to give it all to his parents, arguing that it was family wealth and therefore due to them since they preceded him by a generation. Besides, he had a lifetime of work ahead of him in which to generate retirement funds. But they wouldn't hear of it. It had to do with dignity. It had to do with fairness and propriety and the spirit of the law. All that old-world stuff. He had even tried the guerilla tactic of slipping a check into their Christmas card, but his father had torn it up in front of his face. So Logan had finally concocted a plan to invest the money in risky but worthwhile ventures — a chemical-free fertilizer, an environmentally safe dry-cleaning process, to cite a couple of examples — through an old high school friend in Philadelphia, the goal being to double the assets and give half to his parents with the rationale that he wouldn't be any worse off. Sure, the plan was risky. But that first night in Vegas had taught him the value of splitting face cards.

It's worth skipping ahead, now, to a day in early March. A Monday, according to all available records. The conditions were as follows: Dallas at work and Logan in his study, windows open to the bright air, reviewing the Ricardo/Malthus debate about the Corn Laws in preparation for tomorrow's lecture. A pleasant silence. Or what would be a pleasant silence if not for the periodic ringing of the phone followed by a dial tone on the answering machine. Telemarketers, of course. He finally went out to the kitchen and answered one of the calls, under the false impression that by answering one he would be answering them all.

"Is this Logan?" a man's voice asked.

He said it was.

"I understand you're a homeowner here in Tempe."

He said he was.

"Are those single-pane windows you got on your house there?"

He drew back from the receiver. "Who is this?"

"This is Jimmy over at Home Evolution. I'm just wondering if you have single- or double-pane windows."

Logan hit the disconnect button and switched off the ringer and muted the answering machine. Then he glanced down at the catalogs and fliers and credit card offers sprawled across the counter and scooped them up and shoved them into the trash can. He headed back to his study. The window presented itself to him. Single pane. Inadequate. Or so his pal Jimmy would have it. Most economists claimed that consumers' wants were self-generated and insatiable, yet here were these strangers calling him by his first name and trying to create the very wants they claimed to satisfy. The Dependence Effect. Galbraith. He pulled *The Affluent Society* from his shelf and found the page with the folded corner: "The individual who urges the importance of production to satisfy wants is precisely in the position of the onlooker who applauds the efforts of the squirrel to keep abreast of the wheel that is propelled by his own efforts." He smiled. He had tried running that quote past a few people in grad school, only to be treated like a parishioner suggesting they paint a few pentagrams on the walls of the church. Eventually he had let it go. He had let a lot of things go in his life.

He closed the book and put it away. He went back to his desk. He sat down. But then the scent of citrus blossoms came wafting through the window and nearly lifted him out of his chair again with an urge to taste the entire world, to put everything in his mouth. He closed his eyes. When he opened them again he saw all his obligations spread across his desk—the creased notes, the open textbook, the photocopied pages. No. Not obligations. Distractions. He could recite the material by heart. He had been sucking on it like a pacifier instead of writing the final draft of a paper that—let's face it—would do his career no good. He knew that now.

He grabbed Georgescu's book off the top of the filing cabinet and then rummaged through one of the drawers until he found the most recent draft of his essay. He reread the introduction. And he frowned at it. The timid, wincing prose. You could see him apologizing between the lines. He flung it across the room, pages flapping like a wounded bird. Start over. He gathered up some blank paper, along with a few articles he had unearthed at the library, and walked through the kitchen to the backyard. The conference was in two weeks and he had to present a paper and for once it was going to be something he truly believed.

Georgescu's book, by the way, covered a wide range of issues involving science and epistemology, but the central argument went something like this: Since economics has modeled itself on the Newtonian universe, which contains motion but not energy, it depicts every action as reversible and repeatable over and over again, ad infinitum, without alteration or depletion. As a result, the standard textbook representation of the economy is a completely closed system that neither induces qualitative change nor is affected by the qualitative change of the environment in which it is anchored. It is an isolated, self-contained, and ahistorical process, a circular flow between production and consumption with no outlets and no inlets. A perpetual motion machine. And although physics has since developed the branch of thermodynamics to study the fundamental role of energy in all processes—most notably, the Entropy Law, which states that the amount of available energy irrevocably decreases in an isolated system—economics continues on its merry way, refusing to account for the fact that you can't burn the same piece of coal twice. Economics, in short, ignores the Entropy Law, the most economic of all natural laws.

So what did this mean? To Logan, it meant that instead of likening self-interest to "gravity" or some other force, economists should acknowledge the linear nature of economic production—its one-way throughput, just like any other process. Energy in, energy out. Waste by-products. Economic growth was the measure of a supposedly healthy economy, but since the surface of the Earth wasn't expanding at the current interest rate, it was only a short-term solution. Logan continued thinking about it as he shuffled through the yard, flushing butterflies from the tall grass ahead of him. A lizard scampered along the cinder-block wall. The air trembled with hummingbirds. He stopped next to one of the trees and inhaled the scent, then reached out and weighed a plump orange in his palm. Oranges and lemons. The Bells of St. Clements. A song he had learned as a child but hadn't understood until decades later, when he had mentioned it to Judy, his girlfriend at the time. "You know," he had said. "That song you sing in primary school. 'The Bells of St. Clements.'" At which point she had nearly crumpled to the floor with laughter. "Oh yeah," she had finally replied. "Sure. That British song everybody learns at private school." And so another harmless element of his childhood had been exposed, taking its place among the classical pillars and broad mahogany desks and composition books in which he had conjugated Latin verbs.

Enough. He sat down. He pried off his shoes. He started writing and started sweating. The sun heavy on his back. He spent several hours sifting through text, talking to himself, writing and rewriting until his hand cramped. Occasionally he paused and stared into the murky pool to find his thoughts. His only break came when Puffy showed up and reminded him it was lunchtime.

Several hours later, he heard a pair of feet come swishing through the grass. A shadow fell over him.

"Hey, Professor," Dallas said, placing a cool hand on his neck. "Miss me today?"

He smiled and, without looking up from the sentence he was writing, wrapped his free arm around her hips and drew her closer, pressing his cheek to her stiff blouse. Her casino uniform. The ground-in odor of cigarettes, sweat, perfume. "What time is it?" he asked.

"Late. I had to stay an extra forty-five minutes until my replacement showed."

He put down the pen and flexed his hand as he gazed up at her. Her hair was loose but still crimped into an hourglass shape from the way she had worn it at work. She had a depleted look, as if spending the day among other people's cravings had taken something out of her.

"The summer semester begins in June," he said. "You could take a course or two."

"I know."

"You could quit that job," he said.

"I know." She craned her head sideways to look at his notes. "What on earth is that?"

He followed her gaze down to handwriting that had slowly degenerated over the course of the afternoon to a series of wild swirls and spasms, hunchbacked scrawls that only its author could love. "It's the paper I'm going to present at the conference in a couple of weeks. Get a load of this. Between 1950 and 1986, the world population doubled from 2.5 to 5 billion. During the same time period, gross world product and fossil fuel consumption each quadrupled."

"Really," she said.

"And it's still happening. In the last twenty years, fossil fuel consumption has been doubling twice as quickly as population. Meanwhile, conventional Keynesian and neoclassical models continue to assume an economy of infinite expansion, but if you look at the evidence . . . or maybe I should say, if you simply look at what's happening around us, it's obvious that the scale of human activity relative to the biosphere has already grown too large."

He flipped the page and explained the limitations of the free market, the failure of prices to capture the true social and environmental costs of production, the necessity of restructuring the economy to achieve sustainability. He explained what sustainability was. But when he glanced up at her he realized that her eyes were deserted. Or maybe occupied by something he couldn't see.

"So," he concluded, "I'm planning to douse myself in gasoline and become a human torch at the conference as a way of getting their attention."

A moment passed before she blinked and smiled at him. "Great. Now, sorry for switching gears, but I'm starved. Let's scrounge up some dinner."

He lowered his gaze to his notebook.

"I'm in the mood for that leftover pizza, to be perfectly honest."

He nodded mildly. He ran his finger along the edge of the page. "What happened between you and Deck?"

"What?"

"I would understand if you said something," he added. "A lot of women find him attractive."

Her hand was still resting on the back of his neck, but she drew it away. "Where does this come from? This idea. Me and Deck. You think I had sex with him while you were brushing your teeth?"

"I'm just asking why there was a weird vibe between you."

She eyed him carefully, as if deciding how much of it was an insult, how much a gentle investigation. "I don't like his type," she finally said. "And I don't think he likes mine."

"What do you mean by 'type'?"

"You know what I mean."

"So you met him for ten minutes and figured out his phylum, class, genus, species. The whole thing."

"You don't like him either."

"I wasn't the one acting strangely that night."

"Oh, really. Who slept on the couch? Was that me?"

He hesitated, groping for her line of thought. "What . . . what does that have to do with it?"

"Nothing," she said, waving her hand in airy dismissal. "There's no connection."

"I fell asleep reading. I didn't officially 'sleep on the couch' like I meant to spend the whole night there. It just happened."

"While Deck was here."

"Yeah."

"Yeah," she said.

There was a long pause. He almost shrugged. What did she expect him to say?

"All right," she said, turning and heading toward the house. "Let's reheat that pizza."

He sat there for another minute before he rose from his chair, wondering what he had missed. A signal. An opening. A test of some kind. Maybe he was supposed to apologize. Sorry for not stumbling into the bedroom and waking you up that night. Sorry for doing research. Sorry for caring enough about our marriage to ask if anything happened between you and Deck.

It wasn't until they were sitting in the kitchen with a burnt pizza and lukewarm beer, the stereo just loud enough to thwart easy conversation, that he realized she hadn't actually answered his question.

Keris finished her last sun salutation and stood with her arms at her sides, feet together, legs active, spine lengthened, engaging the appropriate band-has for enhanced prana flow. Here she was, sheathed in sweat, wearing a spandex bodysuit with her hair coiled and clipped at the back of her head. This was yoga class. This was one thousand square feet of retail space in the southern end of Tempe, where its oddities slowly dissolved into Chandler's plainsong. A strip mall, of course. But the instructor had compensated with a profusion of mirrors and plants, a poster of the seven chakras, a tiny shrine with its thread of incense smoke rising in the corner of the room. Sitar music played on the speakers. Opaque blinds were lowered against the maya of the parking lot. It was Tuesday afternoon and Keris was supposed to be holding office hours right now but a teacher should be allowed to play hooky every once in a while, correct? Besides, none of her students had asked to see her today and she had posted a note apologizing to anyone who might stop by. Even the most rigid schedule should be able to accommodate some quantum movement here and there.

The standing sequence. Triangle pose. Keris made a wide stance with her right foot turned outward and her heels aligned, her body bent side-ways at the waist, two fingers hooked around her big toe. Not much room for thought here, maintaining the mulabandha or root lock at the base of the spinal column, as well as the uddiyana bandha in which the stomach mus-cles gave varying degrees of support to the diaphragm as she breathed. And she was breathing with awareness. Mouth closed, air flowing through nos-trils and swirling at the back of the throat before entering the lungs and then exiting the same way. The ujjayi technique. It sounded like wind. It sounded like an ocean within her. It was easier to sustain if she found her drishti, her viewing point, and softened her gaze to external things — the room, the play of shadows, the other women positioned on their mats. Of course, without her glasses it was easier to let go of such distractions. She was farsighted. Her glasses allowed her to discover truth, her bare eyes allowed her to under-stand it.

She moved, she heaved, she breathed. Half an hour earlier she had en-tered the studio with her thoughts tangled inside her like ten thousand snakes, but she was calm now. She was systole and diastole. Cleansed of in-tellect. Occasionally there was a class like this, when the instructor's voice lost distinction and the poses seemed to hold her instead of the other way around and she simply became herself, dwelling in the hum of her own heat. Pleasantly undone. There was no other way to explain it. It was a state of being so pure that she didn't recognize it until it had already passed.

Suddenly it was time for deep relaxation and she was lying on the floor in savasana pose, stretched out with her bones loose, her muscles eased, consciousness diffused into a mist somewhere beyond her body. Then bells were bringing her back to awareness. Apparently more time had passed. She sat up. Lotus. Namaste.

Keris drank from her water bottle, ran a towel over her face. She made her way over to the corner, slipped into her sandals and, as she put on her glasses, felt the sudden disorientation of having the world in her face again. Open door, bright sky. She drifted out to her car and sat there for a few minutes, until she fully regained her body. It was dangerous to drive right away. Last month one of her classmates had caused a fender-bender because she hadn't respected the demands of the physical world. Keris took that as a lesson. She waited until the steering wheel seemed important enough for her attention.

Keris had been raised in Tucson by multi-ethnic, multi-lingual, multi-degreed parents, spending most of her adolescence grazing through her father's library. Like her three older sisters, she had dutifully attended St. Mary's Catholic School and recited her prayers. But unlike her sisters, she had viewed the Bible as "a good yarn" with a lot more characters than, say, *Great Expectations* or *To Kill a Mockingbird*. Her parents couldn't purge the heresy from her. Not that they had tried very hard. There's never much discipline left over for the fourth child. But anyway, she grew up largely free of religious stigmata, neither popular nor unpopular among her classmates, eventually sailing into adulthood as a semi-sexy bookworm with an overdeveloped vocabulary. She turned out to be the sort of woman that other women found attractive. That is, her looks were understated and unthreatening: no slim thighs showcased in mini-skirts, no pay-and-display breasts, and, above all, no long blonde hair. "Keris is pretty, don't you think?" a friend would ask her boyfriend or husband on the way home from a party, when the usual debriefing of the evening's events took place. The husband or boyfriend would usually nod in mild agreement — or, once in a while, not-so-mild agreement, which the girlfriend or wife, if she was sharp, would note. OK. So Keris didn't turn any heads when she walked into a room, but if a man looked twice, he kept looking. That was it. In any given crowd, she generated a coefficient of interest whose mean value was about .1, which meant that roughly one out of every ten men would notice her and congratulate himself for having discovered, he believed, the jewel everyone else had over-looked.

Keris started the engine and pulled into traffic. She drove past a complex of offices with dark windows that reflected her own car floating among the palm trees and heavy traffic. Then she turned off the main road. After yoga class she liked to follow this slender residential street—a slower method, but preferable to the drag race out there. She sighed. She felt lighter, leaner, cleaner. Her period was over and so was that bloated sensation. No more low atmospheric pressures within her. No more cramps prodding her into the fetal position. It was, after all, difficult to conduct your daily affairs when you were a human water-balloon sloshing down the halls of the Physical Sciences building. Last Thursday she had taken off her shoes while sitting in her office and, an hour later, unable to fit into them again, had found it necessary to lean back at a ridiculous angle with the soles of her feet against the wall until the fluid drained away. But even that was preferable to the pill—the regulated estrogen levels, the cancer risk, the ten thousand other by-products of simulated pregnancy that science hadn't bothered to identify. A few years ago, after a nasty divorce, she had gone into extensive therapy and made some renovations to her life: yoga, health food, an "I love you" to her daughter every day. And she had gone off the pill and rediscovered that Ferris wheel known as her cycle. The highs were higher, the lows were lower. She was a diaphragm woman now. She was a woman who looked at the moon to gauge what was happening within her. And occasionally—well, she limited this information to a couple of very close friends—when she didn't have a steady male companion, and when the circumstances were safe and favorable, and the energy was right with the man of the moment, she would indulge in a one-night stand. She followed such instincts because life was too short to do otherwise.

Keris turned the corner to her street. The first house had a large ponderosa in the front yard with a tire-swing dangling from its lowest branch, announcing a neighborhood of children. Most of them were roughly her daughter's age. This meant more than any real estate appraisal. And there she was—Sophie, her daughter, brownish and slender, her long braid dangling as she stooped over Chow to unclip his leash. Keris touched the horn as she pulled into the driveway. Sophie looked up and waved. By the time Keris came inside Chow was slurping water from his bowl like a farm animal and Sophie was on the phone.

"Yeah, she's right here," Sophie said, and then held the receiver toward Keris. "It's a man."

And for some reason Keris knew exactly who it was.

"As you all know from the reading," Logan said, "Ricardo's theory of growth concludes that the economy will eventually stop expanding and reach a stationary state. And although he viewed this idea as his greatest contribution to economics — or, as it was called in his day, 'moral philosophy' — modern economists have largely ignored it, instead focusing on his theory of comparative advantage." He was in the classroom, the lecture hall, with its usual space and dead air, its dozing students. His sportcoat was off, his tie loosened like someone deep into happy hour at the end of a rough day. "And the law of comparative advantage is the basis of all modern gospel relating to free trade."

He could already feel himself slipping off the tracks of his lesson plan. But how could he write what he believed in the morning and not teach it in the afternoon? How could he avoid asking the difficult questions?

"What does the law of comparative advantage have to do with free trade?"

He didn't realize how much he wanted an answer until he heard the usual silence spooling out across the lecture hall. It was always worse this time of year, when students overdosed on spring weather and stumbled into class drowsy and sluggish. He could see a lot of bare shoulders and beach-bum stubble out there. A faint coconut scent. The ochre of suntan oil. He understood what they were going through, but he was running out of patience with them. He was running out of patience with a lot of things, now that he thought about it.

He jerked at his tie until it came unknotted, then bunched it up and tossed it onto the podium. "Hey," he said. "Let's do something here. Let's not waste each other's time."

Heads perked up. A few students stopped their automatic note-taking, doodling, love-letter writing — whatever it was — and fixed their eyes on him.

"Forget history for a minute. This is happening right now. Free trade. Open markets. The abolition of all tariffs and quotas. Ricardo's notion of comparative advantage is the foundation for all of it. How many of you took International Econ?"

Most of them raised their hands.

"The production possibilities frontier. Remember it?" He saw some nodding heads, but also a lot of blank expressions, so he went over to the chalkboard and drew the usual half-box—a vertical line and a horizontal line at ninety degrees to each other. "To show the mutual benefits of trade, we simplify an entire country's production abilities to two goods. Let's say . . . oh, I don't know . . . Books and Lingerie." He heard some laughter as he labeled the vertical line B and the horizontal one L. Then he drew a convex curve connecting the two axes.

"The production possibilities frontier. All possible combinations of Books and Lingerie that our country can produce, given our skills and natural resources. If all production is concentrated in the Book sector of the economy," he said, circling the place where the curve met the vertical axis, "then we could produce, say, 200 Books, but zero Lingerie. Conversely, if we concentrate on Lingerie," he moved over and circled the place where the curve met the horizontal axis, "then we could produce 100 units of Lingerie, but zero Books. Those are the two extremes, showing our production ratio of 2 to 1, even though we could produce any combination of Books and Lingerie along this curve, such as 100 Books and 50 Lingerie."

He paused for a minute. He asked them if it made sense. He asked them if they wanted to keep going. Yes, yes, they said, sounding interested, sounding downright eager. Someone made a joke about economic intercourse. Good, he thought. He drew another graph, nearly identical to the first, representing a second country whose resources and skills resulted in a production ratio that was the reverse of the first country's—a maximum of either 100 Books or 200 Lingerie if production were concentrated exclusively in one sector.

"At this point we have a choice. If we want to produce both commodities, we can make, as I mentioned, 100 Books and 50 Lingerie. If the other country wants to do the same thing, they can make 50 Books and 100 Lingerie. But look what happens when each country specializes in the production of only one commodity. If we concentrate on the Books and they concentrate on the Lingerie, we'll produce a total of 200 Books while she produces 200 Lingerie. We can trade 100 of our Books for 100 of her Lingerie."

"Hold on," a female voice said. "What about the exchange rate?"

He wasn't sure where the voice had come from, so he directed his answer toward the mid-zone. "For the sake of simplicity, let's say it's a straightforward barter system. One Book equals one Lingerie." He paused. "Now, if we trade 100 of our Books for 100 of her Lingerie, where does this put us on the graph?"

He paused and let the question dangle for a moment, just in case anyone would bite.

A hand went up. Erin. This was the Dallas lookalike—who, incidentally, no longer qualified for that title because she had spent a few hours at the hair salon over the weekend and emerged as a spiky bleach-blonde.

"Each country," she said, "would be at a point beyond its own production possibilities."

His knees nearly buckled under the weight of his gratitude. "Tell me what to draw," he said.

She told him. He followed her instructions and extended the output coordinates outside each country's production possibilities frontier. The first country would exchange half of its 200 Books for half of the other country's 200 Lingerie. As a result, each would have 100 Books and 100 Lingerie—more than either country could produce on its own. It was beautiful. It was perfect. It was ideal.

"It's beautiful," Logan said. "It's perfect. It's ideal. Could anything be wrong with it?"

"Yes," Erin said.

"What?"

Her lips came together in a straight line. "I don't know. This gasses me out. The assumptions, maybe?"

"How about this for an assumption: Capital Immobility. The belief that capital doesn't cross national boundaries."

Erin's eyes slowly widened as she absorbed Logan's full explanation of how the distinction between domestic and international trade depended, for Ricardo, on the existence of national boundaries that limited the movement of capital from one country to another. Without this limitation, trade between two countries wouldn't be much different than trade between two regions within the same country, in which comparative advantage doesn't exist. And without comparative advantage, the type of trade just described in these models on the board—at this point he gestured back at the graphs he had drawn—is nothing more than a fantasy. Why? Because if capital flows freely to other countries while labor remains immobile, investment is simply determined by absolute advantage in terms of labor costs—or, in other words, whichever country has the cheapest labor. Yet most economists recommend the reduction of trade barriers even though it undermines the key assumption of the very model they're using to make the recommendation in the first place.

He went on for a while, quoting Adam Smith—or, rather, quoting himself quoting Smith, because he was plagiarizing material from his own dissertation now. The purpose of that famous passage about the "invisible hand," for example, isn't to praise self-interest or even to claim that it promotes the best interests of society, but instead to explain why British merchants would continue to buy products made in their own country even if tariffs were removed. Like Ricardo, Smith held certain assumptions about a person's national identity and social relations that have been forgotten. Although Smith believed human actions are largely governed by self-interest, he also believed that the "self" in that interest is first constituted by our relationships with other members of society—a self that naturally favors the well-being of his or her own community as opposed to others'. So if Smith's "self" isn't the same detached and isolated individual presupposed by modern economists, why are we behaving as if it is?

All right, all right. This is somewhat off the topic. The point is that Logan discussed Adam Smith and then responded to questions until he ran ten minutes over schedule. He promised to continue next time. And was it just him, or was there an intense murmur running through the class as it dispersed? Yes. He liked this. He gathered up his papers and climbed the stairs all the way up to his office, which, it should be noted, was on the fifth floor, the final floor, wedged between a supply room and a janitor's closet in an obscure wing of the building. Hard not to take it as a reflection of his status in the department. There was a gunmetal-colored door at the end of the hallway that opened onto an outdoor landing, where he lingered sometimes and gazed at the concrete edifice of the neighboring building. Ten flights jagged down to the pavement. His office was quiet. That much was true. But it was the sort of quiet you experience in solitary confinement. It was why he preferred to work at home or in the library.

He was sitting at his desk, hands clasped, elbows propped on the armrests of his chair, trying to calculate what he had done and what it might mean, when he heard a rap on the doorframe. He swiveled. Erin stood there in ragged shorts and sandals and a paint-spattered tank top that didn't quite cover her navel. He offered her a seat.

She let her canvas bookbag drop to the floor. She wore a frayed leather bracelet on one of her wrists, a silver stud in one of her nostrils. She looked around the office as if it fascinated her.

"This room," she said, "is so pale."

He followed her gaze. "I think it's light green."

"I mean it's untrue. You don't even have like a window or anything."

Ah. Yes. Logan nodded. It always took him a minute to tune in to the slang. He had hung a few art prints on the wall, placed a floor lamp in the corner, and set up a tiny coffeemaker on the university-issue filing cabinet, but it was like trying to decorate a battleship. She was right about that. He couldn't overcome the basic condition of the place.

Erin sat for a moment with her knuckles pressed to her lips as if in serious contemplation, blonde hair jaundiced under the fluorescent light. "I want to do my next assignment," she said, bursting out so suddenly that it startled him, "about what you said today. Free trade."

Logan reminded her that the next assignment wasn't the usual weekly vignette but the mid-term paper. Ten pages. In-depth. She would need to choose her topic carefully.

"Oh, I know that," she said. "And I know it has to be historical in nature, so I can talk about Ricardo or Smith or something. Like when you make a mistake and nobody fixes it, look what happens."

Logan wanted to show how pleased he was, but restrained himself. He didn't want to scare her off. "That's an ambitious topic."

"You know, I signed up for this class because I don't have a major yet and I'm poking around, looking for alternatives to five days of suicide every week and for a while I was this close," she said, holding up her thumb and index finger with no apparent space between them, "to dropping your class. But once in a while you haul off and suddenly it's no longer like, here's this box full of plastic peanuts, but something that really makes sense to me. I mean I was over on Mill Avenue the other day looking at these—I don't know, these mannequins and this cardboard display in the window and I was thinking, you know, they're just going to throw this stuff into the dumpster a few days from now. It's like this thing I saw on the Internet"—she seemed to be shifting to another topic, but at this point Logan knew nothing could stop her momentum—"this newsletter saying did you know that if mannequins were real women, they'd be too thin to menstruate? And if Barbie were a real woman, she'd have to walk on *all fours* because of her proportions? So we're cutting down trees for a display that's going straight into the trash and running these factories that make alien-shaped dummies just so I'll feel anorexic and buy another dress when what's wrong with the one I'm already wearing? So what is all this?" She swirled her hand in the air. "What are we doing?"

She sat back in her chair and gave Logan a look as if she expected a simple, concise answer.

Logan crossed his legs. He took a breath. "OK," he finally said. "You're wondering why the goal of all activity seems to be increased consumption. Consumption for its own sake."

"Yes!"

"A good starting point, then, would be *The Wealth of Nations*. Remember that section we covered a couple of weeks ago about the pin factory? The one where Smith says the division of labor is the key to increasing productivity? Read that section again, then read Chapter 3, where Smith identifies the factor that *limits* the division of labor. Then take a look at his introduction to Book 2. I think you'll see a connection to what you were just talking about."

She pulled out a pen and wrote the chapter numbers onto the back of her hand. She looked at him again. "So you're saying my topic is real?"

"As long as you keep it relevant to the course."

She nodded slowly, as if appreciating a profound remark. "I know what you mean. This is still History of Economic Thought." She gathered herself up and was halfway out the door when she turned toward him again. "You know what's *so* cool?" She leveled a finger at him. "You." And then she was gone.

Logan blushed. He couldn't help it. He listened to the slap of her sandals down the hallway and smiled because her gratitude, her enthusiasm — forget the language barrier for a minute — compensated for a lot of the desolation out there. Even in that cattle drive known as ASU, he could find a few motivated students like Erin who made the job worthwhile. He remembered what it was like to be that age. A questing undergraduate, earnestly seeking truths beyond the three or four standard flavors the world seemed to offer. He remembered how adults had seemed to him then: compromised, resigned, slightly jealous of his freedom as they heaved away at the oars like galley slaves with the whip cracking over their heads, certain that he would join them when he got older and wised up. Well, he was older now. And he had wised up. He understood it was hard to make things up as you went along, hard to embrace uncertainty, hard to look at everyone else and not believe their goals should be your own.

And so maybe Erin was primed for what she would find in those sections of *The Wealth of Nations* — namely, Smith's argument that although "the progress of opulence" occurs when improvements in the division of labor allow workers to become more productive, such improvements require manufacturers to specialize or, in other words, define narrower portions of the market as their own. But such specialization won't happen unless the market expands to support the sale of these increasingly specific commodities. And how does the market expand? Through an accumulation of capital. Simple enough, but the part Smith doesn't spell out — and this was what Logan hoped Erin would realize — is that an accumulation of capital is a fancy way of saying increased consumption. In other words, we need to buy more stuff in order to stimulate the production of more stuff so that we can then, in turn, buy more stuff. This, perhaps, was the point in history when the Great Chain of Being was replaced by the Great Chain of Having.

Logan shook his head and reached for the phone. He keyed into his voice-mail and listened to the usual catalog of excuses from students who had missed the deadline last week. There was a request for the title of Logan's paper for the conference next month. And there was an apology from Keris Aguilar. Logan sat forward. He had called her office and left a message — what, four or five weeks ago? — thanking her for the reference to Nicholas Georgescu and letting her know that it had changed the course of his research. He had also asked a couple questions about physics because Georgescu's book had raised certain issues that he couldn't resolve on his own.

"I'm a lazy dog with this voicemail," Keris's voice said, "and so I should apologize for calling you back this late. You asked about the sun. I think I can answer your questions, but this gizmo is going to beep before I can give the proper answers, so please feel free to call me at home." She recited the number.

Logan put down the phone, picked it up again. He punched the keys. And he was surprised when a young girl answered. He couldn't say why, exactly, but he hadn't pictured Keris as a mother.

"I knew it was you," Keris said. "Your timing is appropriate."

"Why do you say that?"

The lights went out before she could answer. Logan heard a couple of exclamations in the hallway and swiveled toward his open door, surprised to learn other people were up there with him.

"Because the sun gave off a coronal mass ejection yesterday and it's expected to cause a G5 disturbance."

"Does that mean we could lose power?"

"Correct. You're familiar with the phenomenon?"

"I'm familiar with the total darkness here in my office."

"Oh." There was a pause. "It looks like we've lost power here too. Sophie, please don't open the refrigerator because the . . . yes, thank you. Now, Logan, I believe I can answer your question about — let me see if I recall this correctly — the amount of solar energy that reaches Earth."

Logan said she recalled it correctly. Then he sat back and listened to her answer, which included not only numbers, but comparisons to make the numbers vivid. The kind of explanation a teacher would give. He put his feet up on the desk and closed his eyes, listening to the resonant undertone of her voice, the elegant pauses as she searched for the right word or shifted from one thought to another. A voice he appreciated in the dark.

"Well," he said, after she was done, because he didn't know what else to say. "I had no idea it was that much energy."

"Just out of curiosity, why does an economics professor want this sort of data?"

"I'm going to present a paper at a conference next week and my argument . . ." He trailed off.

"Yes?"

"It's difficult to explain. And it's boring."

"Perhaps you can talk it into shape right now," Keris said.

"You want to hear this?"

"I've just returned from yoga class. I'm lying on the couch with a breeze coming through the window. I can smell orange blossoms. My daughter has just gone into the backyard, so if we end this conversation now I will have to stand up and walk across the room to hang up the phone because it's an old-fashioned retro-model with a spiral cord. Don't make me do that, Logan. Please."

Logan smiled. "OK," he said. "Georgescu bases a lot of his work on the Second Law of Thermodynamics. The Entropy Law. The fact that, in a closed system, the amount of available energy decreases."

"It's usually stated, 'The entropy of an isolated system always increases.'"

"Exactly. Georgescu argues that the Entropy Law is the most economic of all laws because the Earth is, for all intents and purposes, an isolated system. We have a finite stock of resources. Or maybe I should say a finite amount of energy that we can tap. And yet we ignore the only source of energy flowing into the system."

"The sun."

"Which, you said, delivers about 175,000 terawatts."

"Correct."

"I want to use Georgescu's analysis as a starting point for a new methodology. A methodology that recognizes limits to growth and true economic value as the amount of energy embodied in goods and services. Think of it this way. In the eighteenth century, a group of thinkers called the Physiocrats believed agriculture was the most important sector of the economy, arguing that economic value came from the productive powers of the land. The Land Theory of Value. Then Adam Smith came along and observed the beginnings of the Industrial Revolution and proposed his Labor Theory of Value. I want to propose an Energy Theory of Value." He pulled his feet off the desk and set them on the floor. "That's it. That's my introduction."

"Write it down."

"In the dark?"

"I'll remember it for you," Keris said.

Logan was fumbling for a pen, anticipating a blind stumble toward daylight at the end of the hall with his notebook. "I need the exact phrasing."

"Call me back later and I'll dictate the sentences verbatim."

He switched the receiver to his other ear. "Are you serious?"

"My memory sets like cement, Logan. I can recall passages from paperbacks I read as a teenager, as well as entire conversations that took place years ago. It's a talent my ex-husband found quite disconcerting during the court proceedings."

Someone came down the hallway with an honest-to-goodness candle and opened the door to the outside world. A sudden gale of daylight, elongated shadows on the walls. Logan heard a chair scrape on the concrete landing, followed by a thud. The door was propped open.

"Your ex-husband," Logan said. "Was he also an astrophysicist?"

"Was and is. A solar physicist, to be more precise. At Berkeley since the divorce. He's working with data from the Heliospheric Observatory to develop a method to predict solar flares and prevent the very situation we're experiencing at the moment. Without, apparently," she giggled, "much success. But the sun is currently at the peak of its eleven-year cycle, so I shouldn't fault him."

"So this is a . . . what did you call it? A coronal something."

"Coronal mass ejection. A blast of ionized hydrogen and helium atoms—in this case, I believe, about 15 billion tons—hitting the sunward side of the Earth's magnetosphere and compressing it, thus causing a geomagnetic storm. Normally the magnetosphere is about 38,000 miles above the Earth's surface. But today it has been squashed to probably half that distance."

"And that causes a blackout?"

"When the magnetic field is closer, it has a much stronger influence on metal objects. Think of all the conductors out there, Logan. Pipelines, power lines. The longer the conductor, the higher the potential voltage and thus the greater vulnerability to disruption."

Logan remembered a section of highway north of town where power lines sagged majestically between broad-shouldered towers. One time, when he had pulled over to get something out of the trunk, he had heard them sizzling overhead like rattlesnakes.

There was a silence. It wasn't awkward.

"I'd like to read this paper when you're done," Keris said.

He laughed. "You might be the only one."

"Is it an unwelcome topic?"

"A blasphemous topic. This could torpedo my career. Or it could put me on national television."

"Don't forget me when you're famous."

"I won't be famous."

"Mention me on your acknowledgments page. And I'll want a signed copy, of course."

Logan laughed again. He thanked her again. He gave fair warning that he was going to call her back later and ask her to recite the exact words he had used to explain his project. And after he hung up, he sat in his dim office for a while, smiling, swiveling back and forth in his chair, which was surprising because there was no reason for it, no reason at all.

The world disappeared. Voices went up. Dallas looked around and saw cigarette embers glowing everywhere like fireflies. Her shoulders dropped. Perfect. An appropriate ending to a day that belonged in the dumpster, if you wanted her opinion. She blew smoke and waited for her eyes to adjust to the emergency lights, slowly making out the silhouettes of other players waiting by their machines like stranded motorists. She could hear jokes, laughter. But without the chiming of the slots it sounded all wrong, like amateur a cappella.

A man's voice came from the corner somewhere, telling people not to move if they wanted to receive credit for outstanding bets.

Dallas stubbed out her cigarette and headed for the exit. The hassle wasn't worth the two dollars or whatever she had left in there. Besides, it would only emphasize the scale of her loss, which at this point loomed overhead like her own personal billboard. Only five hours ago she had hit the freeway with a thick bankroll in her purse, envisioning an afternoon of coins crashing into the hopper like Niagara Falls because this was her lucky casino and it would compensate for the damage she had been suffering after work these last few weeks. She had fallen into the habit of hanging around after her shift was over and basically dropping her paycheck back into the slots. Make that two paychecks. And whenever she came home late and found

Logan already there, she would say she had stayed to cover for someone. It was a stupid excuse, she realized now, because eventually he would look at their checking account with the expectation of overtime pay when the exact opposite was happening.

She climbed a few stairs and passed the ATM, otherwise known as the Great Enabler because it had spit out all those crisp Ben Franklins after her bankroll was gone and she had fed them into the slots right away. Straight out of one machine and into the other. The shortest distance between two cash points was a straight line, and that straight line was her. It was called being a sucker.

She reached the door and shoved it away from her and strode into hot daylight. Blue sky loomed and veered all around her. She squinted, foraged through her purse for sunglasses. And then she halted. She stood there for a minute scanning the lanes. Where the hell had she parked? She closed her eyes and tried to remember, but it was like a videotape spliced in the wrong place — the freeway, then the slot machine with nothing in between because she had been so damned excited to give the casino her money, hadn't she? She cursed. She started walking straight out there. Like it would do any good. Like her car would jump out and say, Here I am, Sucker, and oh, by the way, here are the five paychecks you dropped into the slots this afternoon.

By the time she reached the end of the row her face was trembling. Then her lips curled up and she started to cry. She kept walking, but soon the tears took over and she had to sit down on somebody's front bumper with her hand cupped over her mouth. This was exactly what she had promised herself she wouldn't do. During that last trip to the ATM she had vowed not to become one of those people you heard sobbing in the bathroom stalls at 2 a.m. She found a tissue in her purse, blew her nose. She thought of the payphones near the entrance and imagined calling Logan. She imagined him coming out there and taking her in his arms and telling her the money didn't matter and then driving her home, to hell with her car, let's forget the whole thing had ever happened. But that was impossible. Sure, he'd take her in his arms and tell her the money didn't matter. But he wouldn't let her buy a new car. And he wouldn't respect her. He'd never look at her the same way again.

She went through a few more tissues before the tears finally tapered off and left her in a dead calm. That numb exhaustion following a heavy-duty cry. People began to emerge from the casino. She took a deep breath, hauled herself up, and put on her sunglasses. She started walking again. A few seconds later she spotted her car, tucked behind a brontosaurus-sized RV that had basically altered the landscape with its presence, so no wonder. She almost smiled at it. Thanks for being there. And yet her car seemed especially ugly as she approached it—dented, scarred, damaged down to its very bones like an old prizefighter. The thing was full of warped angles and broken trim. And the interior? She slid behind the wheel. It was a third-world country.

She took off her sunglasses and leaned toward the rearview and of course here was this fat-nosed, puffy-eyed creature staring back at her. She sighed and flopped back against the seat. She needed to start over. She needed to get rid of this car. Like push it over a cliff somewhere and find a dealership that would set her up with reasonable monthly payments. That article she had read yesterday explained how self-esteem was basically inseparable from the clothing you wore because it was one of the ways you expressed yourself, or something like that, and so it was probably even more true about your car, is what she was thinking. She needed an inner-boost. She needed to fix her mistakes. In fact, there were times when she thought of telling Logan about those indiscretions with Felix back in Vegas so she could fix that mistake too, but whenever she actually opened her mouth to say it she felt as if the mistake would only be transferred from one person to another. She'd feel better, but he'd feel worse. Much worse. Maybe incapable of forgiving her. Maybe she was too flawed for Logan, after all. Maybe she didn't deserve him.

She exhaled through her nostrils. He was pulling away from her. Admit it. He was going to bed earlier. He was drinking less. He was slowly cutting down on the hours they spent together like someone shedding a bad habit. And let's not even talk about that night he spent on the couch. She had lain awake for a couple of hours waiting for him to come to bed, hoping there would be some gesture of appreciation for all the cooking and cleaning she had done, but instead he had opted for the couch like it was the most natural thing in the world. Never mind the spectacle it made of her—the proof it offered to Deck that his insulting little comment about their marriage was correct. She couldn't afford to give Logan another excuse for that kind of behavior. The last thing she could do was tell him about Felix. And the second-to-last thing she could do was tell him about the video poker.

She dug the ATM receipts out of her purse and examined them again. The numbers brutal and precise, like the measurements of hell. She put her key into the ignition and twisted it just far enough to engage the battery, then punched in the lighter and, as soon as it popped out, plucked it from the holder and touched the hot coils to the receipts and watched them smoke for a few moments before they finally ignited. She dropped them out the window. This was dangerous, of course, but safety wasn't really the goal anymore. She watched them burn for a few moments, curling and shriveling into black satin until they finally lost their incandescent edges and wafted away in the breeze. Gone forever. It didn't improve her mood as much as she had thought it would. But it helped. She started the engine and put the jalopy into drive. For the last time. It's time for a trade-in, she thought, and to hell with Logan's opinion on the subject. It's my name on the dotted line. It's my money. I can do what I want with it.

And Deck? He was enduring the gray hell of March in New Hampshire. You know the deal. Bare trees, slick air, bleary streetlights. He hadn't seen the sun in weeks. Let's just say snow was almost preferable to this. At night he drove his car, a mag-wheeled, slim-hipped model with enough horsepower to flatten his back against the seat whenever he was in the mood for the gas pedal. What else was he going to do? Call him frivolous, but he needed some surplus once in a while and this place simply didn't have any. He loved his car. He drove it like he hated it. Sometimes he just picked a road and chased it into the woods, finding a little bit of Zen in the double yellow line, in the curves, in the swinging and swaying pavement. He cranked the music loud enough to make the windshield vibrate. He screamed along with the lyrics, slapped the gear shift around. It was his only pleasure. Or so he thought until the night he found a place called the Denominator. He pulled into the parking lot and stared at it for a while. It didn't figure. Here he was, throttling past clapboard houses with ornamental shutters and rustic stone walls and weathervanes that wouldn't swing in a gale — and suddenly *this*. At least, that's what it looked like. Only one way to find out. He found a baseball hat in the backseat and tugged it low over his eyes for a little incognito, paid the cover charge, and slipped inside. An hour later he emerged with a smile.

He returned one week later. Thursday night. A blonde peach of a dancer named Delilah was doing her thing on the runway, strolling up and down with the landing lights flashing, mounting the pole now and then, leaning into the front row and touching herself as if appetized by the exposure, the staring eyes. There was the familiar haze of cigarette and cigar smoke, a male musk that reminded him a little too much of locker rooms. He watched the bounce of Delilah's breasts, the contour of the hip she shot toward him as she unbuttoned her cowgirl vest. The music pumped. Her body glistened. The vest fell open. She pulled it back from the first shoulder, pulled it back from the second shoulder, and then shimmied it down her arms. And although it was strange — he admitted it — he couldn't stop eyeing her high-heeled boots with the five-point spurs, hoping she would keep them on. As for the leather G-string, he hoped she would take it off.

Just then a waitress came over and set a glass of juice in front of him — no surprise, considering most strip clubs didn't serve alcohol, and this was, don't forget, a state where the Puritan attitude was alive and well. He was sitting about halfway between the stage and the back wall. Across the room was a spiral staircase leading up to the Numerator, where you could enjoy the company of the ladies in a more intimate atmosphere. But Deck wouldn't go there. He liked these tables in the corner because they were dark, anonymous, deliberately set away from the glare and the high-traffic areas. The women couldn't see him. Neither could most of the other customers. Which was especially helpful because Delilah just happened to be one of his students. No doubt she was gyrating her way through college with the hope that nobody would recognize her. Big mistake. Deck had felt an initial shock last week when he had recognized her, followed by a more intense pleasure from spying on someone he knew. Especially when that someone was Delilah. She sat near the front of the class with her wire-rimmed glasses and her lopsided smile that he simply couldn't shake out of his mind. She always paid attention. She added funny comments to her homework assignments. And, well, let's just say Deck had a tendency to thumb through all the worksheets until he found hers first. He liked her handwriting. He liked her signature — the high-backed D, the looped ls, the ski-slope finish on the h. She hadn't even bothered to come up with a stage name. Go figure.

Delilah turned her back to the audience and bent over and slowly worked the G-string over her hips, wriggling them a little, like it was stuck, and then slid it down her legs. She kicked the G-string into the air and caught it. There were hoots and howls from the neanderthals in front. Bills littered the stage like confetti until she finally leaned back and opened her legs. The music crescendoed. Deck felt cold liquid on his chest and realized he had been holding his glass halfway to his lips with the rim tilted, slowly dribbling on him. He set it down and brushed at his shirt absentmindedly. A few men were standing now, leaning backward onto the stage with bills sticking from their mouths. Delilah maneuvered herself into position and then plucked the bills away. He could already sense the vague contours of a fantasy that he would enjoy later — Delilah attending his class in her long black skirt and blue sweater, Delilah onstage in her cowgirl pose, and finally Delilah in his apartment at the end of the night, taking a hot shower before slipping under his covers. A woman who exposed herself to everybody, but gave herself to Deck.

A man reached out and touched her leg. Two security guards came cutting down the aisle and chicken-winged his arms behind him and carried him head-first toward the parking lot before he could even react. Thou Shalt Not Touch.

The music wound down. Delilah straightened up and, wearing nothing now except the boots and cowboy hat, made her exit amid great applause. Deck brought his hands together. It would be difficult to avoid smiling at her in class or showing some other sign that he knew her little secret. But that would give away his secret, too, wouldn't it? He looked down at his sticky shirt. It didn't matter. None of this mattered. He had spoken to the head of the hiring committee at ASU and it was simply a matter of signing the contract when he showed up at the conference next week. He was already gone. Say goodbye to the snow, to the cold muddy landscape, to the tight-assed towns. Say goodbye to women you can't touch. Deck was pulling the ripcord. His golden parachute was opening up, billowing in the upper thermals of the atmosphere, in the blue promise of a desert sky. He was already gone.

What is the half-life of a relationship? Keris sat on the patio with her newspaper and her croissant and her cup of green tea. The pool filter hummed. The sun shone. The umbrella spread above her, supplying cool, delicious shade while threads of light came off the pool and wavered over her face. Here it was Saturday morning with Sophie gone to visit her father for the weekend, so Keris should have been enjoying the solitude. Correct? No. Her mood wasn't cooperating with the circumstances. Which made it only worse. Last night she had stayed up late with her laptop and a glass of red wine and Bach's Brandenburg Concertos, updating her notes on stellar pulsation for next week's lecture. "With an incoherent superposition of roughly ten million modes rippling through its surface and interior," she had written, "our star is ringing like a bell." Great stuff. So why, then, had she woken this morning to a vague melancholy, a feeling of autumnal loss in the air? As if the world had altered its valence overnight.

The half-life of radon-219, also known as actinon, is 3.96 seconds — the amount of time occupied by a lingering glance at a party, or maybe a shared ride in an elevator.

Chow was at her feet. Soft, blondish, lion-maned, a refugee from the pound with brown eyes and bat-shaped ears and the disposition of Gandhi, he lay on the ground with his head on his paws, sad-dog aura in full bloom. The birds and lizards had lost their appeal. His favorite chew-stick sat inches away from his nose, meaningless without someone to throw it. And that someone, of course, was Sophie. Once a month Sophie hauled her suitcase out of the closet, and once a month Chow whined and moaned, following her to the door in utter desolation. The departure was always the same: Sophie crouching down and taking hold of his furry head and kissing him, promising to return in two days. And Keris's anxiety was always the same as she said goodbye to Sophie at the airport. Would she emerge in San Francisco to find nobody waiting for her? Would she wander the concourses tearfully in search of Will, exposed to unlimited menace? Of course not. He valued Sophie's visits — if not inherently, as time spent with his daughter, then strategically, as a meeting with his informant. Occasionally Keris suspected him of exercising his visitation rights simply for the monthly reports that Sophie unwittingly provided about Keris's love life. Which at the moment was nonexistent. In the past three years there had been only two men worthy of bringing home and introducing to her daughter.

Keris took another bite of croissant but didn't feel much enthusiasm for it. For food in general, now that she thought about it. What was wrong?

Some glances last longer than a few seconds. Some elevators move slowly. And some isotopes of radon, such as radon-222, occur as a natural by-product of uranium decay in various types of rock. An odorless, colorless gas with a half-life of 3.823 days, radon-222 can seep through the foundations of your house and kill you so gently over a period of years that you don't even realize it's happening.

Keris stood. Chow lifted his head and watched her expectantly, ears perked.

"Stay," she said. "I'll be right back."

But Chow didn't believe her. He followed her across the patio and into the house, waiting for her in the middle of the living room while she searched for the remote. She turned on the television, flipped channels until she found a cartoon that seemed familiar. *The Wallabies*. Yes. Sophie's favorite. Keris set down the remote and went back out to the patio, Chow in tow.

"See?" she said, sitting in her chair again. "Here I am. You must learn to trust me."

Chow flopped down and let out a grand sigh through his nostrils. Keris had left the volume too low, but she could still hear strains of bouncy music coming from the house, animals talking in babyish voices. It made her feel like Sophie was still around.

Keris finished eating her croissant. She sipped her tea. She could hear the drone of a lawnmower somewhere down the street, the sudden blare of a commercial inside the house. The feeling was still with her. She looked at Chow, who met her glance without lifting his head from his paws, eyebrows working as if great calculations were taking place in that mind of his. A melancholy tone to the air.

"I don't know what it is," she said. "But I feel it too."

Dates, encounters, one-night stands. Fermium, produced by the intense neutron irradiation of uranium-238, was discovered by a group of scientists at Berkeley while examining debris from the first hydrogen bomb test explosion in the South Pacific. All fermium isotopes are radioactive, with half-lives ranging from thirty minutes to one hundred days. Dates, encounters, one-night stands.

Berkeley. Keris sat forward so abruptly that she nearly dropped her empty teacup. Chow bolted up and fixed his gaze on her, eagerly awaiting her next move.

"That's it," she told him. She let out a breath and sat back. The light shifted. The sky brightened. The world resumed its normal course. Today was March 15. The Ides of March. The third anniversary of her husband's departure — or, to be more accurate, of the day Keris had thrown him out. It hadn't been until perhaps the tenth or twelfth time that one of his graduate students, a Chinese girl named Yin-Li, had called the house and hung up that Keris had begun to suspect something. Why not sooner? Because Yin-Li was the sweetest, kindest, and — honestly, now — the most sexless young thing Keris had met in her life. She wore boys' shirts and thick-framed glasses and plastic barrettes in her hair. She rode a third-hand bicycle to school. She had joined Keris and Will for lunch a couple of times with a demeanor of such damp-eyed gratitude that Keris wanted to pat her hand and assure her that she was worthy of the meal. Moreover, she had a tenuous grasp of English. This was the hardest part for Keris to comprehend — even more difficult than the physical attraction. What could they possibly talk about besides solar flare classifications and doppler shift measurements? Was he learning Mandarin? Or was he simply teaching her the English he wanted her to know, the sentimental phrases of worship that he had secretly wanted Keris to speak?

So. Eventually there had been a confrontation. A week of haggling and disbelief and crying fits, followed by an almost surreal discussion of legal matters. The factual state of mind that comes from exhaustion. After retrieving Sophie from Keris's parents' house in Tucson, where she had been staying during the upheaval, the situation was explained to her before Will finally moved out. He spent a transitional month or two in a rented apartment before he finally realized his lifelong dream of squeezing a job offer out of Berkeley. He took Yin-Li with him. But apparently they weren't living together these days — this, at least, was according to Sophie, who had yet to meet Yin-Li despite all those weekend visits.

Meanwhile, Keris avoided a complete meltdown by seeing a therapist five days a week — sometimes with Sophie, sometimes without — and immersing herself in yoga, which she discovered not only as a physical exercise but as a process of release through movement and breath. And eventually she began to wake up in the middle of the bed instead of her usual side. Her wardrobe expanded until it occupied Will's section of the closet. She parked in the center of the two-car garage and discovered the glory of extra storage space. She walked into the living room one day and realized that his absence was marked only by a couple of blank spaces on the walls, shelves gap-toothed here and there with the books he had taken. So she did some rear-ranging. It was astonishing how much the household reflected the logistics of the heart.

Cobalt-60, commonly used for radiotherapy, has a half-life of 5.27 years. What does this mean? It means, obviously, that a given sample will emit only half the original amount of radiation after 5.27 years, and then one-fourth after 10.54 years, and so on until the level of radioactivity approaches but never actually reaches zero. In other words, it means that the emissions continue forever, until death do you part.

Keris stood and stretched. She crouched down and scratched Chow's head, his tail brushing back and forth over the concrete. "It's necessary to feel this way," she said. "This needs to happen."

She found herself mulling over the phrase as she headed back to the kitchen for another cup of tea. Where had she heard it before? Oh. Yes. Him. Last Thursday. The day after the blackout. In her office. Sitting at her desk, ransacking her tote bag to find some money for lunch. And then Logan's voice.

"Turn it upside down," he had said.

She had looked up. There he was, standing in the doorway with a legal pad in his hand. White shirt, patterned tie, khakis. She almost hadn't recognized him. His face longer and more angular than she remembered. And maybe it was the contrast with his shirt, but his skin seemed darker, almost Middle Eastern.

"You're saying I should dump the entire debris of my life onto this desk." He nodded.

"You're always proposing extreme measures."

"And you're always rejecting them."

"Not so," she said. "A few weeks ago I pulled the nail out of that shoe and it's still intact. I should have followed your original suggestion."

He nodded at the tote bag. "And now?"

"The junk would come tumbling onto the desk and everything would be revealed and it would be a little sad, I think. No more mystery. No more hope of finding something wonderful whenever I reach inside."

"Like a magician's hat."

"Exactly."

He smiled. She smiled. A moment or two passed before she realized they were looking at each other without saying anything.

"Please," she said, gesturing at a chair.

He sat down and let his eyes roam around her office, taking in the movie posters, the Mexican blanket, Sophie's crayon artwork held to the filing cabinet with refrigerator magnets. "You don't have any . . ." He hesitated.

"Physics decorations? You were expecting a poster of a hydrogen atom. A bust of Stephen Hawking."

"Actually, I was hoping for a nuclear-powered coffeemaker."

"That's down the hall."

He laughed. And as he opened the legal pad she noticed his hands — broad and heavy-looking, but with oddly thin wrists. His fingers were thick. Weathered at the knuckles. A plain quality offset by his wedding band.

"Ready," he said, with his pen poised over the page.

She leaned back in her chair and took a breath and recited the words. He scribbled. He scribbled some more. When it was over he held up the pad and studied it with a frown.

"Whatever I told you on the phone yesterday," he said, eyeing her suspiciously, "wasn't as good as what you just told me."

"I'm not allowed to make improvements?"

"As long as you don't mislead me into thinking the brilliance is mine instead of yours."

"It's the nature of thought." She was about to add something about the necessity of collaboration when her stomach let out a growl.

He raised his eyebrows. "I'm keeping you from lunch."

"I'm keeping myself from lunch," she said, "with my failure to find the cash I stuffed into that bag this morning."

"Do you like Miguel's?" he asked.

This was the Mexican restaurant just off campus with burritos that made her swoon. She nodded.

"Then let's go," he said, standing up. "My treat."

She locked up her office and followed him down the stairwell and into the full blaze of March. Campus at high noon. A great crossweave of heat and potential in the air. Students gliding by on rollerblades and bicycles. Ocotillo tipped with flame-colored blossoms. High-necked palms swaying in the heights. There were booths selling credit cards and religion, a grove of pungent citrus trees, and a makeshift meadow that the irrigation system had turned into a pond, birds of all makes and models drinking and dipping in the water, fluttering themselves clean. There were the buildings of philosophy and visual arts. There was truth, there was beauty. And there were the open doors of the student union, its arteries clogged with fast food and television screens. A fountain gurgled ahead of them. Music. A voice on a loudspeaker. A banner stirring in the breeze, offering cheap long-distance phone calls. Someone tried to hand Keris a plastic bag full of something that, whatever it was, she didn't want.

They never really stopped talking. Keris told him about the courses she was teaching, the latest developments in funding for her research project. Logan told her about the new Economics Institute. By the time they reached the edge of campus they were knee-deep in the personal issues. Keris's daughter. The mysterious disappearance of Logan's family's fortune. And then, finally, he made a passing reference to his wife. OK, she thought. Forget it.

They crossed University Avenue and made their way into a neighborhood where the palm trees were shaggier, the residential yards unkempt. It had been a few years since the retail cleansing of Mill Avenue—a process in which the chains had moved in, jacked up the rents, and sent all the independent stores and restaurants on a trail of tears to this neglected section of town. Here it was: Ruined mini-malls. Dirt lots. By the time they reached Miguel's, which was tucked between a thrift shop and a second-hand bookstore, Keris could feel the sun bearing down on her, heating up her hair. A bead of sweat rolled down her ribs. Logan wiped his hand across his forehead and said simply, It's coming, and she nodded because she knew exactly what he meant. The Heat. The temperature ratcheting upward every week until it reached that five-month inferno called summer. Miguel's door was propped open. They stepped into its hot kitchen breath, the mashed smell of beans and baked tortillas and chili spice. Ranchero music. Fanblades turning overhead. They sat at a vinyl booth and drank tapwater with lemon slices in it to kill the taste.

"And so I still don't know where it comes from," Logan said, after they had finished eating. He was talking about the color of his skin because Keris had asked, matter-of-factly, about his ethnic background. "The last time I interrogated my father was a few years ago."

"And what did he say?"

"He blamed it on my mother's grandmother. It was like this." Logan sat back and crossed his legs with the glass of icewater held at chest level, his face set bleakly. "'That,'" he said slowly, "'is the Ward side of the family.'"

"You're impersonating my father."

"*Your* father?"

"With his cocktail before dinner, making pronouncements. But anyway, I understand what you're saying."

"It's a problem."

"A puzzle."

"I'd go to a genealogical society or something if I thought I could find the answer, but I doubt the records exist."

"You could try to solve it . . ." Keris said, trailing off.

"Or I could accept the mystery."

"Not accept. Embrace."

The waitress came over and cleared away their plates and set the check between them. Logan picked it up. "This is funny," he said, reaching for his wallet.

"What, the check?"

"The tip. Economists really can't explain it. Consumers acting rationally shouldn't pay more than is necessary for a given service. And besides, why do we tip waitresses, but not the people working behind the counter at a fast-food joint?"

She thought about it for a moment. "A tip," she said, "is a reward for quality service, correct? But the person at the fast-food joint simply operates the cash register and retrieves items from that awful rack where all the microwaved food sits, still cooking inside the wrapper—"

Logan laughed.

"—and places it on a tray. After that, you do everything else yourself. You carry the tray to whatever table you like, throw away the wrappers afterward. Et cetera. It's a purely mechanical thing. There's no variation in the level of service. It would be like, I don't know, tipping the cashier at a supermarket."

Logan seemed to mull it over, then nodded suddenly and pulled out his wallet as if her answer was acceptable and allowed him to proceed. "But from an economic standpoint," he said, "tipping simply doesn't work. The marginal benefit of each additional dollar the tipper spends is virtually zero. And most people tip the same amount no matter how good or bad the service happens to be, so it doesn't really create incentives for the waitress or waiter."

She looked at the cash on the table. "Your actions contradict your speech. I see a healthy tip there."

"That's just it," he said. "I don't have to do it, but everybody else does it, so I do it, too. The Tragedy of the Commons."

"Excuse me?"

"It's a term used to describe a kind of trap. A social trap." He made a gesture like he was referring to an object that stood plainly next to them. "It's what causes overfishing in restricted areas. If each fisherman is assigned a limit on the amount of fish he can catch, his incentive is to cheat."

"It is?"

"The quota system creates a perfectly inelastic supply curve. The price —"

"Wait," Keris said, holding up her hand. "I'm trying to remember basic economics."

He described the graph: Price on the vertical axis, quantity on the horizontal, the demand curve sloping downward in order to illustrate that consumers buy more of a commodity when the price decreases.

"So you're saying," Keris said, "the supply curve intersects with this demand curve . . . where?"

"Wherever," he said. "The point is that the supply curve is a vertical line because the same quantity is provided no matter what the price. It's fixed — inelastic, as we say, because there's a limit on the number of fish caught each season. And since the price tends to rise very quickly under these circumstances, you get a lot of money for each additional fish you bring in. There's a strong incentive to catch more than you're supposed to. There's a strong incentive to cheat."

The waitress reappeared and scooped up the cash and thanked them before moving on. Keris closed her eyes for just a moment because she could feel something working underneath what he said, but she didn't know what. Two men in the adjacent booth were discussing politics in Spanish. Music was coming from the speakers. High-pitched horns, maracas, an upbeat baritone.

"All I'm saying," Logan continued, "is that it's a situation in which individual self-interest becomes detrimental to the well-being of others. You're tempted to cheat. Especially when you suspect that others are already cheating. So you think, why not? Why shouldn't I cheat too? Does this make sense?"

"It makes perfect sense," she said. "But what does this have to do with tipping?"

He sat back for a moment, his face flickering a little, losing its edges. Then he exhaled and seemed to recover. "I guess," he finally said, "it's like a fire in a movie theater. If people stood up and walked calmly to the exit, they would be fine. But they see everyone else running, so they run too. They trample each other."

"You're saying economic theory fails to account for such aspects of human nature."

"Or maybe I'm saying something terrible about human nature itself."

She rested her chin in the palm of her hand. "This is making me depressed."

"Me, too."

"We should talk about something else."

"I agree."

They looked at each other. The table was cleared, the check paid. There was no reason to linger. But there was a troubled look in his eyes and she didn't want to let him continue through the rest of the day like that.

"What's wrong?" she asked.

"I don't know. But maybe it's necessary."

She frowned. "What's necessary?"

"Mistakes. Cheating. Overfishing. Resource depletion. Pollution, decay, decline. Maybe you need to know what's wrong in order to know what's right. Maybe this needs to happen."

And that was how it went. Now she was standing in her kitchen with the television whining in the next room and Logan's phrase in her mind. She poured herself another cup of tea. She stepped outside again and returned to the patio. And there was poor Chow. She set her cup on the table and watched him for a moment. Then she reached for his chew-stick. He rose slowly to his feet, transfixed by the miracle taking place before his very eyes. She flung it across the lawn. He exploded into motion and reached it almost as soon as it hit the ground, then trotted back with it, head held high. He dropped it at her feet. She picked it up, threw it again. This was the way it went. It would have been unfair of either of them to expect otherwise.

What is the half-life of a relationship? For plutonium-239, the most dangerous substance on Earth, it's 24,110 years. Like radon, fermium, and cobalt, it's derived from uranium, a natural element found in the planetary crust. But unlike those other substances, it happens to be a source of nuclear fuel with a yield of three million times more energy than an equal amount of coal. In fact, over 99 percent of raw uranium ore consists of the isotope uranium-238, which has a half-life of 4.5 billion years. Give or take ten million. And it's in the air. It's in the water. It's in the ground beneath your feet. So maybe, then, the most important issue isn't the half-life. Maybe it's the amount needed to start a chain reaction. Maybe it's the critical mass.

Dallas pulled into the garage with her new car—a black, sleek, cat-curvy model with tinted windows and automatic everything. She climbed out and stood back, admiring it like a work of art. Even now, with the ignition off and the engine ticking quietly and the feverish smell of coolant coming through the grille, she could feel the pleasure. She had spent the better part of the afternoon on the freeways, enjoying the give-and-take of the thing, because the machine basically took care of you. There were settings, sensors, seesaw switches. The seat assumed her favorite position at the touch of a button, and the CD player paused when she cut the ignition and then, when she started it again, picked up exactly where it had left off. And get this: she wouldn't lose it in the parking lot ever again because she could press a button on this new keychain and the car would chirp to let her know where it was. Why had she put up with that old barge for so long?

She fetched the mail before heading inside. She sorted through it at the kitchen counter. Catalogs. Credit card offers. Loan guarantees. Bills. She shoved it all aside and looked around. The house was quiet. The fridge hummed, empty, aching. The answering machine had nothing to say.

She took the catalogs into the living room and sprawled out on the couch with them. The pages clinging together with static. She had to work her nail along the edge of each one and peel it deliberately, which she soon gave up because what's the point of looking at clothing if you've just bought a car and have to shut down the spending pipeline for a while, is what she was thinking. She stretched, groaned, glanced at the clock. It was the middle of the afternoon. Logan would be at the library for a few more hours. At least. She had allowed him to work this weekend because that meeting or conference or whatever he called it was coming up soon and he needed to be ready. Fine. She had to work tomorrow anyway, so let him destroy the weekend as long as he didn't make a habit of it.

She reached for the remote and started grazing through Saturday-afternoon leftovers—World War II movies, infomercials, bargain-basement sitcoms. Then she remembered something. Her favorite soap opera. She turned on the VCR and rewound the tape. It was programmed to record every episode, although she rarely watched it more than a couple of times per week, which was really all you needed to keep up with it, to be perfectly honest. Lately, though, she had been savoring every moment because Bobby had drugged Darlene and was keeping her captive in his spare bedroom. Don't ask. She propped her head with a cushion, made herself comfortable, and pressed play. A basketball game came on. She fast-forwarded. More basketball. She sat up and whipped her cushion at the screen. The images continued scrolling at quadruple-speed, back and forth across the court, the players scurrying and jumping. Then it spliced right into a daytime talk show that she had taped maybe a couple of months ago but hadn't watched. She hit the play button and slowed it down. The audience was catcalling. People onstage were shouting at each other, leaping up from their chairs periodically while security guards pretended to intervene. Half the words were bleeped out. From what she could gather, a woman was cheating on her husband with her brother-in-law, whose wife was cheating on him with the first woman's husband. Dallas couldn't help smiling. At least it was economical. Four people, four infidelities. Everybody hated everybody.

She turned down the volume. It was better that way. The emotions took on a grand, operatic quality. Besides, after all the cats were out of their respective bags and the chairs had been knocked over a couple of times, it was basically the same thing for the next twenty minutes. A brawl with the occasional shouting match as intermission. She knew this show because Felix had introduced her to it during an afternoon rendezvous in her apartment. They had talked and laughed a lot that day. He had told her about his goals, about investments he had made for himself and his wife, the savings account for his five-year-old son. He wanted a future, he had said. Eventually she understood what it meant. It meant she was a temporary diversion in his life. And that, in her opinion, was the beginning of the end.

Dallas got up and began meandering around the house — not pacing exactly, but sort of casually looking for something to do. Like what? The yard was a mess because Logan had started some sort of excavation project, but that wasn't her department. She had asked him about it and he had replied that they were following the traditional division of labor in which she was responsible for the internal and Logan the external. Fine, she had replied. Fine, fine, fine. She sat down now with a couple of old magazines, scouring them for articles she might have missed. Then she roamed through the bedroom, through the living room one more time, through the kitchen again. She reached Logan's study and stood in the doorway, surveying the open notebooks, the thick editions resting on the bed. The guest bed. Where Deck had slept last month. What had happened between her and Deck? She should have asked Logan the same question — or almost the same question, like what did Deck say about her? What hints did he drop? Maybe that was why Logan had slept on the couch afterward. And maybe that was why she felt like she had been accused of something even though there was nothing to accuse her of.

She came back to the living room and threw herself onto the couch. The couch where Logan had slept with that damn book splayed across his chest. She shut her eyes. She exhaled. All right. Maybe it wasn't a big deal after all. Let it go. When she opened her eyes again the battle was still in progress on the TV screen. The two women were trying to get at each other now, wind-milling their arms while security guards hauled them to opposite ends of the stage.

She groaned. Boring, boring, boring. She grabbed a boring cushion and placed it over her eyes so she wouldn't have to look at the boring walls and the boring sky through the boring window. Say what you want about Vegas, but it had an energy, a high-voltage vitality in the air. You could see good music any night of the week. You could go to epic-scale shows and perform-ances, you could eat in restaurants worthy of Caesar himself. And the gam-bling, of course. It trickled down into her daily life, infusing every outing with a sense of possibility while, at the same time, making each trip to the movies or laundromat or whatever more costly because there was a greater . . . what was it called? Opportunity cost. Like every hour spent at the laundromat was one less hour in which her life could change. And so every option faced stiff competition, which raised the general quality of existence and gave it an edge of desperation. She could be jogging through the most docile apartment complex, surrounded by palms and fountains and groomed landscape, be-having like a downright wholesome girl, and feel it clawing at her. It made the sun rise. It made the traffic flow. It gave the desert meaning.

And now here she was, in feeble Phoenix, with its bland offices and minor-league nightlife, its garage-band music scene. The place needed some black-jack, some craps, some slot machines. It had taken her a while to adjust to the weird silence when she went out in public. A void that Muzak simply couldn't fill. She wanted chimes. She wanted the sounds of luck.

She stood. She sat. No. She needed to rethink her strategy about video poker before going out there again, especially after the damage she had suf-fered last time. Besides, her savings account was empty. And she had just bought a new car, right? Logan wouldn't be happy about the expense, but her old one was dying and what was she supposed to do, walk twenty miles to work? She had burned more than enough money today, is what she was thinking. She would have to occupy herself until Logan came home. A cou-ple more hours.

She heard a meow. She turned and saw that damn cat sitting on the win-dowsill outside, his little nose pressed against the glass. His fur thinning with the warmer weather, bleached a lighter shade of gold. Not that the heat would stop his begging. Dallas hauled herself up from the couch and went to the front door and jerked it open, but the cat was off and running before she could stick her head outside. He knew who she was. She shut the door again. The last thing she wanted was a litter box in the hallway and Logan paying attention to some animal that made him sneeze all the time. Like his work didn't already consume enough of his attention.

She looked at the clock. She looked at the seething television screen. She raised the volume and watched the argument for a while. Not that she was prejudiced or whatever it was called, but why, why, why did those people always have Southern accents? She turned off the TV and fingered the remote's dead buttons. She stood and—well, she could have sworn she was heading to the fridge for a cold drink when she found herself walking out to the garage instead with her purse and her car keys and the automatic door rising majestically, like a stage curtain, to sun and blue sky. No harm in taking a drive out to the casino and testing the waters, seeing which way the tide was flowing this afternoon. She could always get a cash advance—a tiny one, is what she was thinking—on her credit card and then come home if luck wasn't cooperating. And besides, she had a hunch about that machine at the end of the third row. There was a royal flush out there waiting to happen.

One of the few places that reminded Logan of home was the library. But only when he was inside the building. And only when he closed his eyes. The smell of aging paper and fiberboard and dust. The staid air. The silence of accumulated knowledge. All those gothic winter days he had spent in the Penn library during the last two years of graduate school. And now? There was an abundance of heat and light outside and he found himself enjoying the ride in the elevator, bumping and grinding down to the main floor with its wide promenade and banks of computers and, most importantly, the reference desk. He needed to talk to the librarian. He needed help.

"That's a good question," the reference librarian said, which was what she always said when Logan asked for the impossible. She clucked her tongue for a moment. She was a lanky woman with a toucan nose and a flinty voice that intrigued male professors on the phone, then disappointed them when they met her face to face. They expected a pale young thing full of corked sexuality, but instead found the wrinkled old aunt they had been forced to kiss as children.

She directed Logan to a couple of databases. She also directed him to a row of foreboding, red-backed books on one of the low shelves. And in the event of total failure she suggested surfing the Internet, which, of course, was the solution to everything. But actually, she said, pointing at one of the backs hunched over a nearby table, that man was a paleontologist. Logan could consult him, although—she lowered her voice to an even softer whisper — he taught field courses and went on digs in the Middle East for long periods of time, so he was a little . . . she tapped her temple.

Logan said he understood. He walked over and introduced himself.

The guy reared up like some animal at a feeding trough. "You want what?" he asked.

Logan repeated the question.

He huffed and coughed, stroked his grizzly beard for a moment, then finally gestured at the stacks at the other end of the room. "Take a walk down Skid Row."

Something about his tone made Logan suspicious. "You think I'm wasting my time."

The guy smiled cynically. "My advice? Head for ecology. Try Global Ecoscience or Ecosystems Analysis or whatever the hell they're calling it these days."

"Not your specialty."

"You got it, pal. I'm trying to figure out what was, not what is."

"Dinosaurs," Logan said. "Extinctions. Comets."

"Something like that."

"What are the odds of another comet hitting the planet and wiping us out?"

The guy threw his head back and brayed with laughter so loudly that Logan almost took a step backward. There were a few raised heads, evil eyes from people at the other tables.

"First of all," he said, "it was an asteroid. All right? An asteroid. Second of all, the current rate of species extinction is a highly contested issue, but I fall in line with those who say 25,000 to 30,000 species per year. That's three species every hour. So forget the dinosaurs. What's happening now makes the Cretaceous Extinction look like a case of the sniffles. You want to see the asteroid, pal? Look in the mirror. Pick up the yellow pages and read all the names. There's your goddamn asteroid."

Logan thanked him for his help and walked away, past the reference desk, through the rows of computers, and into the inscrutable stacks. Skid Row. He paced for a while, scanning the spines and reciting the titles to himself without really reading them. Eventually he stopped and stood there with his hands on his hips. He rubbed his eyes. He turned and headed back to the elevator and waited, listening to the car thudding and slamming around up there, a few faint voices coming down the empty shaft. The voices faded. The elevator, he realized, was moving away from him. He went over to the stairwell and started climbing — slowly at first, but then taking the stairs two at a time with his wedding ring clinking against the railing, his breath echoing around him.

He felt better by the time he reached his desk. Don't ask why, but lately he had been working in the backyard and it was making a difference in his body—tougher muscles, stronger lungs. His skin had darkened in the sun. He had stopped at the hardware store on the way home from campus last week, and the next morning, shirtless, hatless, he had dug up a section of dead grass beyond the swimming pool, laid down some plastic sheeting to prevent regrowth, and spread xeriscape rocks over it. When he was finished he stood back to survey the results—a six-by-six plot of desert, a reverse-oasis—and saw that it was good. The next day he bought some native shrubs at a nursery and planted them in the same corner. It took most of the day. At one point Dallas had stared uncomprehendingly at the proceedings and asked him what on earth he was doing. He said he didn't know. He seemed to be restoring the backyard to its pre-human condition. Although his motivation was unclear, it can be said with a reasonable amount of confidence that it had something to do with his research. Indirectly. Very indirectly.

He sat forward and opened another book, but the technical terms thwarted him. This wasn't his field. He should just go home. Or maybe call home. Find out if Dallas was there. He shook his head. This was the same feeling, the same seismic unease, that had come over him during a faculty meeting last week. At the time he had considered slipping out the back door and calling her. But what for? What would it have accomplished? Even if she had answered the phone, the conversation would have gone nowhere. And besides, Dr. No had taken the podium at that point and announced a workshop or retreat or conference—the terms kept changing—in Palm Springs to address various issues concerning the public-private partnership. Logan had forgotten about Dallas then, or at least lost sight of her in light of this other suspicion, and by the time the meeting ended he couldn't address all the worries that had accumulated in his mind. So he addressed none of them. Instead he had picked up his legal pad and headed over to Keris's office to write down the sentences she had memorized from their phone conversation. Then lunch at the Mexican restaurant. He could have talked to her all afternoon, but he didn't want to take up any more of her time and . . . all right, maybe there was a connection after all, because that was the day he had stopped at the hardware store on the way home and started landscaping the yard. True. Let's take note of that.

Logan closed the book and reached for a different one. He needed to work. He needed to write the conclusion to his paper, and there were also a few potholes in the main argument he needed to fill. His ecology question had been one of them. Still unsolved. Of course, Keris might know the answer. He'd call her on Monday. Or stop by during her office hours. If she didn't mind. He didn't want to bother her. She probably had a lot of other things going on in her life.

Deck was up there again, above it all, flying the friendly skies into Denver this time because it was a different hub, a different airline, a different institution of higher learning footing the bill. Denver? The place was overrated. Sure, you could see the Rockies in the distance, snowcapped peaks gleaming in the sun like shark's teeth, showing off their rugged good looks. But the city itself was flat-chested and plain. There was the usual sprawl of houses and, directly below him, an expanse of graham cracker fields with hangars all alone out there. A little bit of Kansas right in your backyard. If ever there was a place Deck understood without actually visiting, it was the Midwest. All you had to do was look at the people to know that the mind, confronted with nothing besides space and empty sky, turned inward on itself and eventually consumed its own thoughts to stay alive. A cannibalism of sorts. It produced a certain vacancy in the personality, a blankness reflected in the eyes. That stiff Midwestern face.

Speaking of which, here was this fat old lady sitting next to him — or, let's be more specific, stuffed into the aisle seat with a vacant middle serving as a buffer zone, thank God, between her and Deck's slot by the window. She suffered from some sort of respiratory ailment, which she medicated with a steady supply of soft drinks and potato chips from the carry-on at her feet.

"Chicken or beef?" the flight attendant had asked the woman a couple of hours earlier.

"Beef," Deck had wanted to reply on her behalf, just as a joke, but of course held his tongue.

"Beef," the woman had said.

She was asleep now, head lolling around as the plane banked. And she was snoring — not a gentle rasping, mind you, but a series of gargling, lip-flapping convulsions that was probably setting off instruments in the cockpit. It sounded like she was drowning facedown in a bowl of oatmeal.

When the plane hit the runway she jolted up, looking around wildly. She asked Deck where they were. Deck told her.

"I kinda forgot myself," she said. Her voice a heavy Midwestern nasal, untroubled by nuance or irony. "That ever happen to you?"

Deck said it didn't.

"I got a long drive ahead. Should of flown into Kansas City, but this was cheaper. What can you do, huh."

Deck nodded, wondering how long it would take them to maneuver the jetway into place and pop the hatch so he could get out of this thing. The woman was probably lonely — and, hey, he sympathized, but this was about as much fun as doing laundry. He wanted to get out onto the concourse and take a stroll, have a drink, refine his strategy for the upcoming week. He was arriving at the conference a few days early because it was the beginning of Eastfield's spring break and he was taking advantage of the schedule to do a little reconnaissance at ASU. Last week he had called the department chair — a bumbling caretaker-type who was probably crossing off the days until retirement — as well as the future chair, a man named Novak who seemed a lot more simpatico. He had separate meetings scheduled with them on Tuesday. It was the first step in mapping out the department's political land-scape, figuring out what coalitions existed and where the battlelines were drawn. Assuming there were battlelines. And he needed to know Logan's status. During that last visit he had sensed some resistance, possible trouble on the horizon. Furthermore, he and Logan might be competing for resources. Deck wanted to know what he was up against.

He was walking up the jetway now, into a terminal with skylights and a peaked ceiling high above him, suggesting the grand vaults of a cathedral, its divine space and light. He looked at his watch. Almost two hours to kill. He stepped onto a moving sidewalk and began gliding toward the main con-course, past the gates, the newsstands, the restaurants crammed into honey-comb nooks. One of the slogans on the wall caught his eye: Aesthetics of the Gut. He craned his neck and looked back at it as he continued moving. That couldn't be right. He got off at the next juncture and took the conveyor in the opposite direction. There it was again. An advertisement for some slapdash new restaurant in a place called LoDo. But Veronica wouldn't be living around here, and even if she was, no way would she . . . He nearly stumbled as the sidewalk dumped him onto solid turf again. He came around and stepped onto the original conveyor, feeling slightly shaken, slightly stirred. Aesthetics of the Gut.

He had learned about Aesthetics of the Gut a few months after arriving in Philadelphia, at a place called the Starlight Café. He had been reviewing some Advanced Econometrics, utterly self-contained and unapproachable, when a waitress wearing a red Lycra top had stretched across his table to clear away the plates, exposing a slice of bare waist and breasts with nipples outlined in the fabric. A woman with nothing to hide. He had paid with a credit card and written his phone number on the line reserved for gratuity. She had called a couple of days later. Veronica. Cat-green eyes, black hair, pale skin. Her arms curved and writhed around him like snakes. She wrote poetry full of glaring, terrible rhymes, which she read to him one night in her apartment.

"What do you think?" she asked afterward.

"Uh, I like that rhyme of 'love' and 'dove.'"

Her eyes brightened, watching him intensely. "You got that, right?"

"Of course."

"It was ironic."

"Absolutely. Ironic as all hell. That's why I liked it. No one else could get away with that."

She sat back with a smile, satisfied that he had perceived the depths, and then straddled him right there on her couch. He was in. At least for a while. The truth was that he was sweating through his first semester of Ph.D. work and he needed someone to reinforce his ego. He could admit it now. After all, she took care of him one night when he was sick. She came over to his apartment a few times and cooked gourmet dinners, rearranging the pots and pans in his cupboards without asking, which he loved for reasons he couldn't explain. She slipped him free espresso at the Starlight Café, and he looked up from his work sometimes just to follow the play of her hips between the tables, other men watching with covetous eyes.

One night in December they climbed into a taxi and went to a coffee bar in a deserted industrial area by the waterfront full of warehouses and barren lots, an all-night diner with a broken neon sign. The expressway screamed nearby. This was the site of the monthly poetry reading, whose graces, Veronica had decided, he was finally ready to receive. And it was packed tight, the windows iced with human moisture, a deep-ground smell of sweat and cloves that made him queasy. He sat on a chair with an obscenely tiny seat that forced him to alternate between left and right buttocks. The crooked handle of his coffee cup wouldn't even accommodate his pinky. But he endured it — the rank atmosphere, the discomfort, the poetry hurled at him like off-key jazz, full of gestures and panache signifying nothing except the high opinion the performers had of their own creativity. He couldn't follow the constant shifts, the images that failed to cohere, so he simply nodded when others nodded, laughed when others laughed.

For nearly an hour afterward Veronica talked to some guy with a ponytail who obviously wanted to have sex with her. Deck tried to derail the conversation a couple of times, but it kept coming back to her poetry. Her damn poetry. Or, to be more specific, her two-hundred-page opus. A copy had been sitting on his desk for nearly a month, and he had tried to read it, but by the time he reached the end of each poem he didn't know what he was supposed to think. It was simply there, like a lightpost or mailbox. How do you comment about something like that? Her rallying cry, she said, was Aesthetics of the Gut. Visceral and pure. But he didn't understand that, either.

"Is the manuscript done?" the Ponytail asked.

"Finished," she said.

"I hope you'll please, please let me read it. What's the title?"

"'Laughing at Fashion.'"

"Nice assonance."

"Thanks. Are you going to Greta's next weekend?"

"Are you asking?" he asked.

"I'm asking," she said.

"Then I'm there."

It sounded like sign/countersign. It sounded like a code for some kind of rendezvous. Deck pried her away from the guy and maneuvered her into a corner by the cigarette machine, and before he knew what he was doing told her he loved her. She smiled. You're a special person, she said, and took him back to her place and fucked him until he was raw and exhausted. There was a sense of pity in it that sickened Deck's sleep. When he woke the next morning she was in the shower. He didn't even hesitate. He leaned over, carefully opened the drawer of her nightstand, and pulled out the journal she conspicuously stowed there. His name was all over the pages, scrawled in black ink. Unflattering descriptions, ungenerous speculations, distorted accounts of conversations that he wanted to argue with right then and there. Then he reached a passage that made his stomach go hot with adrenaline. She didn't love him. He was too flat-line, too straight-ahead, too numbered and measured. She wanted to dump him but didn't want to hurt his feelings. If William — was this the Ponytail? — asked her out, then she'd have to gently get rid of Deck.

He replaced the journal, dressed in record time, and went home. She called him an hour later. They needed to talk, she said. He agreed and told her to meet him at an anonymous bar off Rittenhouse Square, where he launched a preemptive strike before she could say a word. He was bored, he said. He was moving on.

"But you said . . ." The words seemed to catch in her throat. "But you said you loved me." She seemed to be glowing now—tragically, it seemed, with an urge to feel deeply, to demonstrate, to have a poetic moment.

"You got that, right?"

She blinked. "Got what?"

"I was being ironic."

Before she could reply he stood and went outside and headed straight into the low winter sun, ice shining on the pavements like white fire, the buildings on Walnut Street festooned with multicolored strings for the holidays, and he crossed the Schuylkill and watched a single rower sculling upstream. Gulls laughed above him. The sky burned, wild and bright. The wind sliced through his coat. As soon as he reached his apartment he went to the bathroom and vomited. Suddenly he understood it. Aesthetics of the Gut. Then he lay down on his bed and started crying.

But that was a long time ago. Now Deck was making a career for himself while Veronica was, no doubt, still waiting tables and filling notebooks with nonsense. Never mind that her supposedly brilliant idea had appeared on an advertisement halfway across the country. He smiled. There was—let's admit it—a momentary temptation to give her a call and say, Guess what I just saw in the Denver airport. Maybe you aren't so original after all. But he wouldn't stoop to that kind of behavior. His ultimate vindication would come when she saw his name in a newspaper or magazine someday and realized what she had missed. She could write all the poems she wanted, she could dress differently, she could fuck like a wild horse, but for every price there is a quantity, for every quantity a price. It was that simple. Happiness equals consumption divided by desire.

He reached the main concourse of the airport. There were terraced shops, full-fledged restaurants, a roof with numerous peaks above him like the largest circus tent in the world. He was going places, he was doing things. He found a brass-and-hardwood bar with a view of the main walkway and sipped his beer slowly, enjoying the variety of life in the crowd—in other words, the variety of women. He had acquired a taste for those no-nonsense heels and stockings, those sharp skirts. At one point he pulled out his cell phone and punched in Logan's number, but then hesitated with his thumb poised over the send button. He turned it off. It wouldn't be smart to tell Logan he was coming early. Not yet. Besides, he wanted some distance between himself and that wife. Dallas. Despite her claims of conjugal bliss, he had noticed Logan sleeping on the couch that night, which was an emergency flare for the search-and-rescue teams if ever he saw one. She was ripe, all right. But if Deck stayed at that house again they'd make a mess of it. There'd be sex on the kitchen floor, then six months of emotional blackmail afterward. No, he thought. Forget it. He couldn't afford to lose his leverage.

chapter 6

Clubs, spades, diamonds, hearts. Dallas stiffened when she heard the hum of the garage door, the guttering of Logan's engine as it entered the garage. Then it all ceased and an airless silence filled the house. She didn't need X-ray vision to basically see his expression as he took in the new car. OK, she thought. She composed herself on the couch with an absolutely transparent face, her emotions on full display. Believe it or not, this was perfectly rational behavior. After a disastrous reunion with the slot machines this afternoon she had realized the only way to meet Logan's anger was show how upset she was—not about the car, which she didn't regret in the slightest, to be perfectly honest—but about her most recent losses. An actress expresses exactly what she feels but calls it something else. Remorse, sadness, weariness. It was all on tap. In fact, her eyes still retained the lurid afterglow of the slots. Assessed from a strictly objective point of view, it looked perfect.

The door opened. She gazed out the front window, at the cacti's needles and pins etched in fading daylight. Good luck, she thought. This machine accepts $1, $5, $10, $20, $50, and $100 bills. Insert bills into slot. Good luck.

"What's that in the garage?"

She faced him. He was standing with his bookbag slung across his shoulder, his hands on his hips. Like he was her father or something. To her surprise, she felt a sheepish smile burning through the fog. "My imaginary friend. Do you like him?"

"You think bankruptcy is funny?"

"I'm trying to make light of an impulse-buy, which I basically regretted by the time I pulled into the garage. It was sort of like . . ." She made a vague gesture, but didn't add anything to it. What could she say? Multi-poker? Bonus poker? Bonus poker deluxe? How could she confess to the juice of it, the electric comfort of the light? Good luck.

He threw his bookbag onto the armchair.

"I admit it wasn't a wise purchase," she continued. "But now that I've done it I've realized that it's basically manageable."

"You've realized."

"We can work it out."

"Oh, really. You have an extra bank account in your back pocket?"

"We can skim a little bit off the top of those investments, is what I'm thinking, and nobody will know the difference."

The words seemed to reach him with a time lag, through the delay of a satellite link. A widened expression came over his face — let's call it shock — followed almost immediately by an odd look of relief, as if he had just heard the answer to a riddle that had been perplexing him for months. "So that's it," he said. "The investments."

She could feel her attitude curdling even before she followed the comment back to where it pointed. "What do you mean, 'That's it'?"

He smiled faintly, with that patronizing air she couldn't stand. "Why didn't you just ask for the money in the first place?"

"Because," she said, the words stiff as cardboard in her mouth, "I didn't want the money. I wanted the car, which you always argued against. And I was just thinking that maybe we don't have to keep every cent of that money locked up when it would help with the monthly payments. That's all."

He sank into the armchair across the room. "Oh, come on." He laughed. "You sound like a mobster's wife. How long have you been planning this?" He seemed genuinely amused.

She let out a rough breath. She had been prepared to minimize the ego. She had been prepared to play it meek and mild under a general attitude of penance for the next few weeks. And she had been prepared, quite frankly, to give him an extravagant blowjob tonight to show him how much she appreciated his understanding — because his understanding, she felt, was ultimately what would emerge from this conversation. But it must be said that these preparations were based on an assumption of *ceteris paribus* — i.e., "all other things unchanged" — in which the effect of her purchase would remain isolated from all other factors influencing their marriage, thus provoking a simple mixture of anger and exasperation at the damage she had done to their finances. Big mistake. She knew that now. She could already feel the prices and quantities shifting beneath her feet. Or maybe it would be more accurate to say that, once again, the cards weren't behaving the way they were supposed to. Jacks or better, two pairs, three of a kind. Straight, flush, full house. Four of a kind, straight flush, royal flush. Good luck.

"What kind of person do you think I am?"

He sighed. "I wasn't saying—"

"If I was a gold-digger, you think I'd go after *you?* You think I'd leave my job, my home, my friends," she said, rising from the couch, "and all the opportunities I had in Vegas, for *this?*"

"Don't take it the wrong way. All I meant—"

"I know what you meant. I know it better than you do."

She expected him to reply to that, but he just rubbed his face wearily, like they had been arguing for hours. Like she was a burden of some kind. She stared at him with every nerve in her body. How could she tell him the truth? How could she tell him that the car was supposed to compensate for all the losses she had suffered? That she wanted it to boost her self-esteem? To make her a better person? To be more worthy of him?

She sat down again. The light was fading. Even now, with the consequences basically right in front of her, she yearned for the comfort of the slot machines, the magic of the silly names: Top Banana, Movers and Shakers, Wild Cherry, Wild Wheels, Lion Fish, Black Rhino, Black Cherry, Black Widow, Diamond Mine, Triple Jackpot, Triple Sapphires, Triple Cash, Triple Bonanza, Hot Peppers, Pure Pleasure, Red White and Blue, Wheel of Fortune, Fortune Hunter, Game King, Lucky 7's, Sizzling 7's, Moolah, Haywire, Mystery Jackpot, Double Diamonds, Double Hearts, Double Desire. Good luck.

Logan entered the white light of the lecture hall the next morning and found exactly what he expected. The padded walls. The chalkboard. The podium. The hollow thud of his own footsteps as he crossed the stage. These were the demands of the classroom. He heard the murmur coming from the tiered seats and tried to gauge the mood because it usually snapped him into focus, told him what kind of lecture he needed to supply for the proper equilibrium. Except he was five minutes late this morning. And these, he realized, looking down at the wrinkled pages in his hands, were the *wrong notes*. He froze. Marx, surplus value, labor power. They weren't scheduled to cover that stuff until the week after spring break. Today was supposed to be Bentham. He looked up at the class—at the spreading silence, the gazes slowly adjusting toward him. He set his notes on the podium. What the hell.

"The greatest pleasure for the greatest number," he said. "The slogan of Utilitarianism as stated by Jeremy Bentham—who, by the way, stipulated in his will that his body be dissected in the presence of his friends."

A ripple went through the lecture hall. Logan took a few steps away from the podium. Admittedly, it was a tabloid-style opening, but he needed to tap a vein if he was going to survive this lecture.

"After the dissection was over," he continued, "the skeleton was reconstructed, dressed in Bentham's favorite outfit, and topped with a wax head to replace the original, which had been mummified according to Bentham's instructions. The body was then put on display in a glass-fronted case at the University of London, an institution he had established a few years earlier with a large endowment. And now, once per year, his head is placed at the . . ." he started laughing, "well, at the head of the table, excuse me, when the university's trustees meet, to serve as a reminder of the principles upon which the school was founded. The greatest pleasure for the greatest number."

Let's be fair about this: He was coming off a rough night. After the argument with Dallas, there had been some halfhearted apologies and an atmosphere of ceasefire rather than reconciliation in the ensuing attempts at sleep. Dallas had churned up the sheets while Logan had stared into the darkness, his thoughts tilting and whirling through his life and the world's problems until they hadn't seemed separate anymore. He had finally closed his eyes around daybreak, only to have the alarm yank him up from the depths again. It had given him a case of the bends. Or something close to it. At any rate, he had staggered through the morning necessities, dumb, dry-mouthed, whitened at the nerves. He had forgotten to shave. And, evidently, he had grabbed the wrong notes off his desk.

Logan continued with the lecture, mentioning the essential facts about Bentham as they occurred to him. Human actions and moral judgments based upon the poles of pleasure and pain. The Pleasure Principle. Hedonistic calculus. A small increase in happiness for many versus a large increase for a few. The question of whether happiness, or utility, can be quantified. The neoclassical notion of marginal utility. He walked around in circles, picked up the chalk, put it down, repeated himself occasionally and jumped ahead to marginal analysis as a response to Marx before he remembered that they hadn't covered Marx yet, at which point he smiled and shook his head and apologized.

"Although Bentham agreed with Smith's theory of the invisible hand, he was also a proponent of social reform. In other words, Bentham didn't see a problem with people seeking pleasure as long as the legal system ensured that individual action coincided with the public interest. He believed that laws based on democratic principles should reward people for doing things that benefit society and punish them for doing things that damage it. The actions of one person shouldn't reduce the well-being of others."

A hand went up. "Are you saying the guy was, like, an interventionist?"

Logan followed the arm down to Erin's earnest gaze. She was sitting with her legs folded up sideways, sandals kicked off. The silver stud still gleamed in her nostril, but the blonde spikes of her hair were less extreme now, softened and tousled like the fingers of a sea anemone.

"Bentham wanted to reconcile individual freedom with the greater public welfare. He believed that social institutions have a major effect on people's actions and, as a result, should be modified to ensure that everyone's pursuit of his or her 'rational self-interest,' as most economists phrase it, was compatible with the long-term goals of society. So, yes, he was an interventionist."

Erin was about to say something else when a male voice erupted a few rows behind her. "But that's politics, not economics."

Logan located the student — a brooding skateboarder, he guessed, judging by the frizzled dark hair, the hooded eyes, the flames tattooed down the underside of his arm. "What do you mean?"

"You're talking about legal stuff," he said. "Laws. But economics is like . . . I mean, all right, so I'm not an expert, but econ is a social science. *Science,* OK? It's supposed to analyze how the economy works so we can increase wealth. Forget social agendas or whatever. Let each consumer decide what's best for themselves."

"All tastes and preferences are neutral," Logan said, to clarify the point. "Why should I tell you — I'm sorry, what's your name?"

"Ozzy."

"Why should I tell you, Ozzy, how to lead your life?"

"Yeah," he said, with a firm nod. "Laissez-faire."

The origin of the term "laissez-faire," by the way, is a matter of some debate. Some historians believe it was Vincent de Gournay, an eighteenth-century inspector of trademarks, who coined the phrase to express his dissatisfaction with the French government's excessive regulations. Others subscribe to the account put forth by the *International Encyclopedia of Social Sciences,* in which Jean-Baptiste Colbert, implementing a program of economic reconstruction in the 1670s, met with numerous businessmen and asked them what the government could do to improve the economy. One of the men, a shopkeeper named Legendre, reputedly shouted, *"Laissez-nous faire!"* Leave us alone.

Logan was about to respond to Ozzy when Erin twisted in her seat and looked back at him. "So you're saying we should delete the value judgments. Let the market decide."

"Right," Ozzy said.

"But that's a value judgment, too."

He hesitated, not quite sure how to respond to that one.

"Like if you scope someone getting robbed," Erin continued, "but you don't try to help him, that's laissez-faire. *Not* doing something is a value judgment, sweet boy. Get off Fantasy Island."

Logan detected a sudden shift out there, like the scattering of birds before an earthquake. He began to smile — not because of the argument itself, but because they cared enough to argue. Maybe he was too easy to please. Or maybe he was simply enjoying a discussion where some essential part of himself wasn't at stake. Yes, that was it. Escape. Despite the errors and fallacies that cropped up in these arguments among his students, they led toward some sort of answer, some sort of illumination. Dallas's comments, by contrast, always seemed to give off more heat than light.

"Hey, don't hang those tags on my toes," Ozzy said. "I'm talking about the free market, OK? Not robbery or murder or whatever."

"And I'm saying if you take the concept of laissez-faire and apply it to *anything else,* it's untrue. How about a laissez-faire doctor? A laissez-faire police officer? A laissez-faire mechanic?"

Ozzy opened his mouth. "But that's not —"

"You want to know why," she went on, "laissez-faire exists? Because it's easier than caring. It's easier than trying to help. It's this belief that, like, people are poor because they don't work hard enough. People are poor because they're stupid. People are poor because they *deserve it*. And that justifies all the neglect, all the callousness, all the denial of actual three-dimensional problems in the world."

She continued for another minute or so, reaching a state of eloquence that Logan felt would have been wrong to disrupt. Call it a laissez-faire attitude. Ozzy, on the other hand, seemed to be stunned, his thoughts floating dead and upside down in his mind.

When Erin was finished she turned toward the front of the class again. A silence settled over the lecture hall.

"You put a long tail on that kite," Ozzy finally said.

Logan considered the best way to mediate. "It seems," he said to Erin, "you're questioning the belief that individual self-interest automatically adds up to the well-being of society as a whole."

"Dead on," she said.

He took that as a yes. "And you," he said to Ozzy, "believe in the free market principle that people acting in their own self-interest will promote the good of society, so we shouldn't interfere with too many rules and regulations."

Ozzy nodded.

"Perhaps, then, the real question is this: Can an individual's self-interested, rational behavior be incompatible with the long-term goals of a larger group or society? In other words, can an individual's rational behavior produce an outcome that's irrational for the group as a whole?"

The class didn't know what to make of that. The question was too big, too vague. Logan scanned the perplexed faces for another moment and then reached for his wallet. He pulled out a single dollar bill and held it up to the class. "This dollar is for sale to the highest bidder. Do I hear five cents?"

There was some hesitation, fidgeting in the seats. Logan looked at Erin until she understood this was some kind of demonstration. She raised her hand obligingly.

"Five cents," Logan said. "Do I hear ten? Ten cents?"

Ozzy's hand went up.

"Ten cents." He lowered the bill for a moment. "By the way, I should mention one rule about this auction. Both the highest and the second-highest bidder have to pay me at the end. OK?"

Nobody objected, so the auction continued, the bids increasing by five-cent increments until it reached a dollar.

"A dollar for a dollar," Logan said, nodding at Ozzy, who had placed the bid. "Do I hear $1.05?"

Silence.

"I guess it wouldn't be rational to bid any higher, would it?"

Erin spoke up. "$1.05," she said.

"Are you sure about that?"

"I just bid ninety-five cents a minute ago. If *that* guy," she said, jerking her thumb back at Ozzy, "wins the auction, then I still have to pay because I made the second-highest bid, right? So I lose ninety-five cents. But if I bid $1.05 and win, then I lose only five cents because the dollar offsets most of the loss."

"How very rational of you, Erin," Logan said. A titter passed through the lecture hall. He looked at Ozzy. "Looks like you're about to lose a dollar, pal."

"$1.10," Ozzy said.

Erin raised her bid to $1.15. Ozzy raised his to $1.20. Logan let it continue for a while, seesawing back and forth between them, the numbers escalating beyond profit and into damage control, each player seeking to lose less than the other. The bidding hit two dollars. Then it hit three.

Erin finally gave up when Ozzy placed a bid of $4.10. Logan slapped the podium. "Sold to the man with the flaming arm!"

A round of applause. One of Ozzy's neighbors patted him on the shoulder. Erin smirked.

"Each of these two consumers," Logan said, "has acted rationally, according to his and her self-interest. Yet the outcome is irrational. How could we change the system to bring individual and general well-being in line?"

Silence again. This was the hard part of the game. The part nobody wanted to play.

Half a mile away, Deck walked among the palms, the pines, the pointed fingers of cacti. The buildings of the central mall surrounded him with their dinosaur muscle. The physique of mass construction. He recognized this system. Obviously the stadium back there—blasted into the side of a mountain, for Christ's sake—wasn't going to win any awards. But that wasn't the point. The purpose was to generate enough team spirit to separate alumni from their cash. Deck smiled. His tie flapped in the breeze. This was an institution dedicated to expanding its market share via high-profile achievements from its faculty. He smelled opportunity here, resources available to those who knew how to access them. Course releases. Sabbaticals. Professional development funds. A PR machine to broadcast faculty accomplishments. Of course, he knew there would be different problems at this place—but overall, he thought, as he passed an arts building with some abstract sculptures riveted to the walls, it was going to be a mutually beneficial relationship.

The walkways were sparsely populated at the moment, which meant classes were still in session. He slowed his pace. He had plenty of time before his first meeting. Everything favored his desires. Yesterday, for example, he had gone jogging across the Mill Avenue Bridge, over some kind of artificial lake in the Salt River bed that hadn't been there during his last visit, and discovered a network of trails winding through Papago Park, the hills thick with creosote shrubs and saguaro and ocotillo, buttes glowing in volcanic hues above the flat stretches where sandstone had been pulverized by a million running shoes. It looked like dehydrated fire. Like the surface of Mars. Little brown rabbits had fled at his approach. Fellow joggers and bicyclists had nodded to him. A few had even said hello, although there seemed to be a disproportionate number of those middle-aged women with their hefty asses and sleeves rolled to the shoulders and tight little baseball hats with the brims adjusted low over their eyes. A local quirk. He'd have to get used to it. Afterward he had explored Mill Avenue and found all the bright signs of retail health. Shops. Restaurants and bars. A movie theater. A bookstore. The chains he knew and loved. He had passed a few cafes and noticed students sitting with their textbooks and calculators and sprawled notes, would-be poets writing purposefully in their journals, having deep thoughts. Deck had pulled out his cell phone a couple of times but then put it away again, resisting the urge to call Logan. It would have been nice to hang around with him. But unwise. Instead he had eaten lunch alone at one of the outdoor tables, the misters hissing over him, mitigating the hot and heavy sun of noon.

He glanced at his watch as he entered the Economics building and realized he was early for his meeting with Silverson. He took off his sunglasses. He ran a hand through his hair. His shirt was spotted with sweat in a few places, his tie askew. And then, as he was heading toward the restroom, he heard a familiar voice.

"Sold to the man with the flaming arm!"

Deck came to a halt before an open doorway. Applause, laughter. Logan's words magnified in the lecture hall. He was saying something about consumers acting rationally but producing an irrational result. It was difficult to catch all the words. Self-interest. How can we change the system.

Deck did a casual glance up and down the corridor to make sure he was alone, then inched a little closer to the doorway.

"It's rigged, OK?" A student's voice. "You're forcing the second-highest bidder to pay, but that's not the way the free market works."

"You're absolutely right. The free market doesn't make the second-highest bidder pay, it makes . . . Yes, go ahead, Erin."

"It makes, like, everyone pay."

There was a murmur in the audience. Logan asked for an example, but after a blank minute or two he had to supply his own. No surprise there.

"How about," Logan said, "open-access resources, such as fishing grounds? Using microeconomic models, we could determine an optimal scale for each individual fisherman — or fisherwoman, yes, Erin — by finding the point at which marginal cost equals marginal revenue." There was the sound of Logan drawing on the board. "You've seen this graph before, right? Here's the number of fish that Erin should catch in order to maximize her profit. If she exceeds that amount, she'll actually begin to lose money. But there are two issues that this model doesn't address."

Deck rolled his eyes. Here we go. In graduate school Logan had enjoyed focusing on the supposed failures of neoclassical models — the various assumptions that, he claimed, stacked the deck in favor of a totally unregulated economy. As if you could redesign the free market according to your specifications. As if you could modify the law of gravity simply because you didn't like it.

"The first thing is cost. Erin's personal expenses don't reflect the impact of her activity on the natural resource as a whole, such as the depletion of the fish population."

There was the sound of his footsteps as he paced around the stage. "And what about scale? Although there is an optimal number of fish that Erin should catch, the issue mysteriously disappears when we shift from micro to macro. According to most economists, it doesn't matter how many fishermen are out there or how many fish they catch. There's an optimum scale for each individual fisherman, but not for the economy as a whole. It can continue growing forever."

What was this, Crackpot 101? Deck had a difficult time believing it was a legitimate lecture, especially since Logan had told him that History of Economic Thought was his only course this semester. Wait a minute . . . A smile rose to Deck's face. Then he smothered it. Hang on. Logan was a friend. Sort of. And anyway there wasn't anything to be gained with this information. It had no bearing on Deck's status in the department.

"How about," Logan's voice continued, "if we do the auction again, but this time with a bidding tax, which would make each person's short-run incentives consistent with our larger goals? For example, if Erin bids ninety-five cents, but now faces a bidding tax of an additional ninety-five cents on top of that, then the situation would change. If she drops out, she loses ninety-five cents, just like before. But if she raises her bid to $1.05, the tax forces her to pay a total of two dollars, and therefore she loses a dollar even if she wins the prize. Maybe, then, her personal cost and benefit would be more consistent with the public cost and benefit."

Deck backed away from the door. He had heard enough. He took an elevator to the second floor and found an empty restroom where he adjusted his tie in front of the mirror and splashed a little water on his face. And for a moment he found himself studying his reflection — the depths of his personality obscured rather than revealed by those eyes, that nose, those curves of the cheekbones and lips. An unpleasant surprise. He wasn't that person on the other side of the glass. He was this person. Why didn't it show? Why didn't it express itself more freely, more sympathetically for the whole world to see?

"I couldn't help noticing," Deck said, "something unusual about the course schedule for next semester."

Novak smiled. He leaned back in his swivel chair and raised his chin slightly. This was a couple of hours later, in Novak's office, with its oak desk and Turkish rug, its overstuffed chair positioned in the corner. A fan sat atop the file cabinet, gently oscillating. Tropical fish swam across Novak's computer screen. The place was bigger than all the other offices Deck had seen so far. It had a window that actually opened.

"You're listed as the teacher for five different courses," Deck went on. "That's quite a load."

"So it seems," Novak said. "So it seems."

Deck chuckled. "You know where I'm going with this."

"But I want to see you arrive." He propped his elbows on the armrests of his chair and brought his hands together with his chin touching his fingertips. "Continue."

Deck sized him up once again. Open-collared shirt, sportcoat, faded jeans. Thick white hair. The brownish and slightly liver-spotted complexion of a veteran outdoorsman. A vigor just below the surface. Deck figured the guy in his mid-fifties, a former womanizer who had finally settled down and decided to seek his pleasures from the neck up. As chair of the hiring committee, he had talked to Deck above and beyond the call of duty during the interview last month. He was planning to take the Economics Institute into places where old-fashioned Econ departments feared to tread, and Deck wanted to know where those places were.

"Silverson told me . . ." Deck caught himself, realizing he had used the name without any sort of prefix, but quickly swallowed it. "He told me that I'm scheduled to teach two sections of Micro 101, with one or two other courses to be determined before the official schedule is printed next month. I could push for Advanced Macro."

"Or?"

Deck smiled. "The new Econometrics course for undergraduates," he said. "That's your baby, isn't it?"

"I prefer to think of it as a prototype that several members of the department helped me to build."

"Yes. A prototype. Which requires a lot of attention. A lot of effort. You'll have to make adjustments as you go along, leave a little wiggle-room in the syllabus for trial and error. Nobody ever said it was going to be easy to explain linear regression to undergraduates." Deck paused thoughtfully. "You'd probably appreciate a lighter load next semester."

"I'm required to teach a certain number of courses every year."

"But you've earned some release time."

Novak had been rocking slightly in his chair, but now he stopped suddenly, his expression stiff. "Who told you that?"

"Nobody. I figured that since you chaired the hiring and textbook committees last semester, you probably have some quid pro quo coming."

He started rocking again. The fan continued oscillating. The fish resumed their merry way across his computer screen.

"I could take those two sections of Macro 101 off your hands."

"That would be very generous of you. But what could I possibly offer in exchange?"

Deck left a silence before he replied. "It seems odd," he finally said, "to offer an Introduction to Econometrics without also offering an intermediate-level course to embellish and deepen our undergraduates' understanding of the material. Especially since econometrics is becoming more important in the discipline these days. And if you really intend to expand the curriculum—"

"Excuse me," Novak said, raising his chin from his steepled fingertips, "but the Institute makes that sort of decision. You understand what I mean."

Deck read the expression in Novak's gray eyes. "Of course. Your role is simply to explain the value of econometrics to the other members of the faculty."

"I couldn't have phrased it better myself."

Deck waited for a couple of heartbeats before he continued. "As a result, the curriculum will probably continue to grow in this area. It's only natural, then, for us to work together on future developments."

Novak shifted in his chair, crossed one leg over the other. Deck noticed the cowboy boots—the brown leather, the scuffed soles. Nice touch.

"Speaking hypothetically," Novak said, "how would you teach a course in Intermediate Econometrics?"

Deck inhaled slowly, as if contemplating the question for a moment, and then recited his answer: matrix algebra, probability and distribution theory, statistical inference, linear regression, non-linear regression, maybe even some autocorrelation and simultaneous equations models. The truth was that he had figured it out by the pool yesterday—an apparently off-the-cuff speech that he had crafted and then stored, spring-loaded in the back of his mind. Because he knew what Novak wanted. He knew the composition of the hiring committee was no accident. And he had decided he could put up with a semester full of introductory courses if it meant bigger and better things immediately afterward. Teaching the introductory stuff was a chore, but an easy one. He could go into the classroom, do his hat-and-cane routine, and then get out. It was like reciting the alphabet.

"That's how I would do it," Deck said, wrapping it up. "Hypothetically speaking."

There was a faint smile on Novak's face. "I'll put in a request for those course releases next semester."

"Are you fairly certain it will be approved?"

Novak's expression broke into a smile. "The course release," he said, "will be approved."

He was referring to Silverson. The lame duck. Deck had showed up at Silverson's office a couple of hours earlier and had his suspicions confirmed so quickly that the meeting was practically a waste of time. The English accent, the vest-and-pocket-watch gimmick, the piles of paperwork that seemed to say, Look how bumbling and incompetent I am, when in fact Deck knew it was a ruse to conceal his weakness. He recognized the type. Silverson was the sort of figurehead who wanted everyone to think he took naps in his office and signed documents without reading them so he could be excused for taking the path of least resistance. The real power was here.

They stood up and shook hands. "Incidentally," Novak added, as if it were an afterthought, "I suppose you've heard about the meeting in Palm Springs."

Deck nodded. "Second week of May. Dr. Silverson mentioned it."

"Are you planning to attend?"

"Well, I just learned about it, so I'm not sure."

Novak fixed him with his gaze. "There will be representatives from various companies and organizations in the audience. People interested in sponsoring future projects with the Economics Institute."

Deck waited for more. Another hint, another clue in Novak's eyes. "Future projects," he repeated.

"If you want them to know you, to be familiar with your research, I recommend an appearance. A good appearance."

"I understand," Deck said, although he didn't. Not completely. It was the tone he followed. The suggestion of the meeting's importance.

They agreed to meet for a drink on Friday, and Deck strode down the hall and stepped into the elevator feeling nearly weightless with joy. Mission accomplished. He could head back to the hotel now, peel off his clothes, and relax by the pool with a sure knowledge of who he was and where he stood. And he could finally call Logan. In fact, it was the perfect time to get together and see how he was doing. Call it a minor detail. The last variable in the equation. Intermediate Econometrics.

*   *   *

Logan turned the key. Nothing. The usual light glowed on the dashboard, but the engine remained silent, refusing to kick or sputter or make a good-faith effort of any kind. He rested his forehead against the steering wheel. Then he popped the hood and climbed out. He opened the lid. The familiar anatomy confronted him. Cracks, corrosion, leaky gaskets, old-fashioned Pennsylvania rust. He wiggled a few wires, checked the hoses and battery connections. In college he had taken an auto shop course, hoping to gain some of the expertise he admired in people who built their own houses and assembled entire vehicles from spare parts, but instead he had discovered that an oil change was well worth the price he paid at the local garage, and he had learned how to translate his mechanic's description of why the such-and-such needed to be replaced. That was all.

He looked around the parking garage, at the other vehicles sporadically coming to life. Everyone seemed to be heading home for the day. He closed the hood. Beautiful. Perfect. Dallas was going to savor every moment of this, taking it as compensation for what he had said last night. But how else could he have reacted? When she had mentioned the investments he had felt a great crashing relief, a joy at discovering that his suspicions had been misplaced. She wasn't involved with anyone. She hadn't done anything illicit with Deck. She was just angling for the money the way a child looks for the best way into the cookie jar. Innocent, playful scheming. OK. But maybe he shouldn't have been so straightforward in showing what he felt. Although he took it for granted that a marriage would always involve secret tactics, he realized now that one of those tactics was to pretend that there were no tactics, that everything was simple and pure.

He retrieved his bookbag and started walking back to his office. He already knew how it would go. She'd sound perfectly neutral on the phone, but then she'd cut through rush-hour traffic and show up with a smirk on her face, music at a soothing volume, the interior flushed with cool air and triumph. She'd enjoy comforting him with the very thing he had cursed twenty-four hours earlier.

He was approaching the Economics building when he recognized Keris coming in the opposite direction. He raised a hand to her, but she didn't notice. She was looking down at her feet and moving her mouth silently, lip-synching her thoughts. Logan stopped and waited. She had a casual flair today — dark blouse, long floral skirt, her hair pulled back with all her earrings exposed. The gigantic tote bag hung from her shoulder.

She nearly ran into him. "Oh! Sorry!"

"You look worried."

"I'm anxious to the bone."

"Sounds painful."

"Very." She reached up and unknotted the band at the back of her head and freed her hair.

"Trouble with the shape of the universe?"

"Actually, it's the shape of Interstate 95 that concerns me at the moment. The clearance of all those bridges. The potholes. The accident potential. But I won't inflict such problems on you. If you don't mind me saying so, Logan, you look a little down in the face, like somebody stole your sunshine."

"My car died."

"Entropy sucks," she said. "You need a ride home?"

"Unless you have a spare car in there," he said, nodding at her tote bag.

"Maybe I do. Who knows? One time I pulled out a friend's credit card and used it to buy a computer. By accident, of course. The salesman had already run it through the machine and I was too embarrassed to admit my mistake, so I forged her signature."

"What happened?"

"I paid her back. She thanked me for the miles on her frequent flier account." She adjusted the tote bag on her shoulder. "Where do you live?"

He told her.

"No problem."

"I don't want to delay you."

"From what? I'm not rushing home to watch game shows. I can spare the time. Besides, Logan, my head is full of mud. If I drive home alone I'll simply mumble to myself and endanger other motorists by running a red light or some such thing. You'll be performing a public service."

"Where are you parked?"

She gestured. They started walking. She asked about his class and he told her about the lost notes, the dispute between Erin and Ozzy, the dollar auction. He told her he had finished his paper and was nervous about presenting it at the conference this weekend.

"May I read it?" she asked. They were walking through the parking garage now, their voices echoing among the concrete pillars.

"You mean, before the conference?"

She pulled out her keys and stopped at a mid-sized sedan with a prematurely fading paint-job. Logan walked over to the passenger side.

"Unless you think last-minute criticism would be too confusing."

"Actually, I'd welcome the input. But I'm giving my presentation on Saturday. That's probably not enough time."

"It is if you give it to me now," she said.

They were looking at each other across the roof of her car. Logan pulled the paper out of his bookbag and flourished it. She smiled, opened her door, and climbed inside. Logan sat down next to her and handed it over.

She glanced at the title before sticking it into her tote bag.

"You're putting it in there?" He couldn't help the note of alarm in his voice.

"This is not the Bermuda Triangle, Logan. Not everything vanishes without a trace. I'll read it this evening and we can talk tomorrow."

She started up her car and drove into hot daylight, into traffic full of passion, pulse, and power. The air-conditioning tried to cool them down. Bach tried to soften them up. Logan glanced in the backseat and saw a frisbee and a couple of baseball hats, a pink backpack, a blanket that looked like it had been dragged through a hayfield. Like her office, it was neither messy nor neat, but gave the impression of subsistence-level organization, a talent for effective triage. These pockets of chaos and neglect existed, he guessed, because she was too busy getting the important things right.

"This isn't going to work," she said. She switched off the air-conditioning and lowered her window. "We're going to overheat."

Logan lowered his window and rested his forearm on the frame. They were stalled somewhere between intersections, next to a motorcycle with a trembling tailpipe, vehicles growling and gargling and exhaling jungle heat. Keris turned up the music, but Bach's harpsichord couldn't compete. She sighed, removed her glasses, and began cleaning them on the hem of her skirt. Traffic inched forward. She took her foot off the brake.

"Um," Logan said.

"Don't worry." She was keeping the steering wheel steady with a raised knee. "I'm farsighted."

"Then why do you wear them all the time?"

She braked and turned toward him, her entire face altered, it seemed, without the glasses. Her hair was slightly tangled. Her blouse shifted sideways, exposing a lavender bra strap. "Because I forget I'm wearing them. Or sometimes I can't find the case and the safest place for them is right here," she said, slipping the glasses onto her face again.

Logan nodded. Another minute passed with everything stalled around them. A horn sounded. A stereo thumped nearby.

"Tell me about Interstate 95," he finally said.

"It's boring."

"Tell me."

She was about to reply when traffic started moving again and she had to merge into another lane. At the intersection they passed a cordon of pink flares, a police officer waving them around some industrial pipes scattered across the road. A flatbed truck stood jackknifed in the middle of it all, hazards flashing.

"That," Keris said, "is what worries me."

"Plumbing?"

"The satellite. I found out today, Logan, that it has to travel on the back of an eighteen-wheeler all the way from the Goddard Space Flight Center to Cape Canaveral. Half the eastern seaboard. What are the hazards of space compared to those of the highway? Tell me, please, that all the clearances will be high enough and that some cockeyed motorist won't slam into it as he's swallowing a cheeseburger at eighty miles an hour and that the truck driver won't become drowsy and have a rollover or continue on his merry way even though the chains have come loose and the satellite is about to go crashing . . ." She placed a hand on her chest. "I'm trying not to rant. I'm not succeeding."

"How much money is this satellite worth?"

She told him.

"It'll be fine."

"You have a strange way of reassuring me."

"The most powerful force on Earth isn't gravity or magnetism or whatever. It's the American bank account. I'm sure the financial stakeholders — whoever they are — have chosen the safest way to ship it there."

"It should be flown on *Air Force One*. It should be lifted by the hand of God and placed on a giant pillow at the launch facility."

They were moving now, speeding up and slowing down with the accordion-heave of traffic until they finally hit an open stretch and the wind began to beat rhythmically through the car. Logan's tie flapped around. Keris's hair whipped, her blouse skewed further to reveal more bra strap, the contour of her milk-chocolate shoulder. Logan forced himself to look forward.

They crossed an overpass with a freeway completely motionless below them, the vehicles caught in a diorama of gleaming windshields and chrome. This was humanity on the aggregate scale. Keris was talking about launch windows, trajectories, vectors. Logan's eyes kept wandering over to her bare shoulder. A couple of years ago he would have enjoyed the wild promise, the possibilities of the situation. But he was living a different life now. A married one. And let's face it: How often had he taken advantage of those opportunities when he was single? The one-night stand with Dallas had been an exception. He didn't have the heart for pickup lines and phony conversation. And when assaults and rapes infiltrated daily life, when AIDS brought the sex-and-death equation into the physical world, seduction no longer took place over a few drinks. It moved in increments of safety and knowledge and therefore required a chess player's patience. Forget video and channel surfing. Forget faxes and fiber optics and world wide webs. Here was the paradox: Sex, like traffic, was slowing down. And there was nothing anyone could do about it.

He directed Keris toward his neighborhood. Now the strap itself was beginning to slip down her shoulder. Look at the dashboard, he told himself. Look at the street. Anything else.

When they pulled into his driveway he immediately climbed out and closed the door and then stretched his arm through the open window for his bookbag. He thanked her for the ride.

"I'll call you tomorrow with my feedback," she said, reaching up and casually tugging the strap and the blouse into place.

He noticed a faint curve, like a sculptor's imperfection, in the shape of her nose, a delicate lift in her cheekbones that centuries of Greek art had tried, and failed, to render. "Call me at the office," he said. "I'll be working there. All day. Or I'll be at the library, so leave a message on my voicemail if I don't answer."

She put the car into gear, backed out of the driveway, and waved to him as she drove off.

He went up the sidewalk and didn't even stop to take a breath, didn't stop at all, as he put his key in the lock and twisted it hard and shoved the door open. He was feeling something deep in his nerves. An equation trying to solve itself.

Dallas stood barefoot at the open refrigerator in her olive shorts and black tank top, embroiled in the usual juice-or-soda debate. They were out of beer. What she really wanted was a stiff drink, but if Logan came home and saw her with a rum and Coke he'd suspect something, like what's wrong with this picture. And don't even think about the pack of cigarettes in her purse. She closed her eyes and inhaled the refrigerator's cool air. The motor kicked into gear and started humming. She didn't move. Her mother had lectured her mercilessly for doing this as a child, pinching Dallas's upper arm with those claws of hers—which, you'd think her mother would have figured out by then, only infuriated Dallas and therefore reinforced the habit. Besides, a clean, bright refrigerator offered a certain kind of comfort.

She heard a car pull into the driveway. The thud of a door, a fading engine. She opened her eyes. A key scraped and scrabbled at the lock before the front door finally swung open and banged against the wall. It slammed shut. She didn't turn around. The argument last night had been messy and she wouldn't be surprised if there were leftovers.

She reached for the orange juice—slowly, like she was picking a flower from a bouquet—and was about to close the refrigerator door when she felt Logan's hands come up around her, his breath suddenly hot in her ear. She reached back and grabbed him. He was kissing her neck and running his hands down the front of her body, between her thighs, and she tried to put the orange juice back on the shelf but she simply couldn't focus on anything and finally let it fall to the floor. She turned. He lit her up. He wanted her. He wanted her through everything and she wanted him too. She was pressed against the open door with her legs spread. She unknotted his tie, she unbuttoned his shirt. He lifted her tank top. The refrigerator hummed. Her foot slipped in something cold and slick on the floor and she realized it was juice leaking from the container. They heaved against the door. Jars rattled. Her teeth found his neck, the salty taste and musk of him. They slid down and now her shorts were off and they were completely naked, the tile smooth against her back, Logan's lips kissing her inner thighs, his tongue finding its way into the pulp of her and her entire body responding now, polarized and keen, humming like a tuning fork. He was inside her and she was wrapping her legs around his waist and squeezing and swearing at him and forcing him to roll over so she could be on top. She had an orgasm. Then he came, his body clenching and tightening before it finally released and went limp.

She sat on top of him for another minute, breathing, her palms on his chest. His eyes staring almost vacantly at the ceiling. A slick of orange juice was slowly spreading across the floor. The fridge hummed uselessly. She stood. He sat up. He seemed dazed.

"Wait here," she said. She went into the bedroom and put on her robe, then grabbed Logan's off the hook.

When she returned to the kitchen the refrigerator door was closed and he was spreading paper towels over the orange juice. Their clothes were piled in the corner. The busted container was in the sink.

"Leave it," she said, holding up his robe for him.

He straightened up, tossed the paper towels toward the trash can, and threaded his arms into the sleeves.

She took his hand and led him into the living room, where they reclined on the couch. This was the way she loved him. She laid her head on his chest and listened to the thud of his heart, the knit of muscles and blood inside him. She could feel him stroking her hair. A breeze stirred the curtains. She wondered if any of the neighbors had heard them.

"How do you feel," she said, surprising herself with the question, "about children?"

His hand paused in mid-stroke, then continued. "They should be banned from nice restaurants and hotels."

"I'm serious."

"So am I. Children are like monopolies. You hate them unless they're yours."

"That's what I'm talking about. Ours."

There was a long silence.

"Are you pregnant?"

"Please."

"You're still on the pill."

She lifted her head and looked at him. "I wouldn't go off it without consulting." Although, to be perfectly honest, the thought had crossed her mind. How would he react to a pregnancy? It would be a test. It would be the next step for her and Logan. Besides, the tick-tock of her biological clock was growing louder by the month and she didn't want to hear it anymore. And a child would keep her away from the slots, is what she was thinking.

"You're not pregnant," he said.

"I'm not pregnant."

He tried to conceal how relieved he was, but she could feel his body relax underneath her.

"So that's what you think."

"Well," he said, "the timing isn't . . . Our finances aren't exactly in the tycoon category."

"That's what you think," she repeated.

"I'm not saying never. I'm just saying not now."

She didn't reply. She felt a hard knot in her stomach, a burning behind her eyes. He was breathing easily now, his chest rising and falling underneath her, lifting her up and letting her down again. Which was what he always did to her.

"Are you all right?" he asked.

"I feel fine," she said. "There's nothing wrong with me. I feel fine."

chapter 7

For Keris the best hikes always turned out to be those last-minute decisions to lace up her boots and drive out to the Superstitions when no one else was around. It returned the world to her. Or returned her to the world. Anyway, take a look at this: Sunlight flaring on bare cliffs. Hills stubbled with saguaro, jumbled cacti, and thickets of brittle brush. A red-tailed hawk gliding overhead. Gravel crunching underfoot. The water main had ruptured at the elementary school that morning and so here they were — Keris, Sophie, Sophie's friend Katie, and Katie's mother, Charlotte. Oh, and Chow, too.

"He wouldn't stop," Charlotte said. "We went out to dinner and then the next day he called and asked me out to lunch. Then drinks the night after that. Then a movie. Perfectly nice about it, but aggressive."

"Stockbrokers will be stockbrokers."

"That's the problem. Suddenly I'm some sort of deal that needs to be done." Charlotte drank from her water bottle and returned it to the sheath strapped to her waist. She had tawny hair, a Scandinavian complexion under her wide-brimmed hat, and always, it seemed to Keris, the scent of high-performance sunblock wafting in her wake. She worked for a law firm in downtown Phoenix and had a tendency to buy more gear than she could actually use. Witness, for example, her pressure-treated walking stick, which was over a year old but still had the manufacturer's gleam upon it.

"He kept saying 'win-win situation' all the time."

"I have to confess," Keris said, "I don't know what that phrase means."

"That's because it doesn't really mean anything."

"We're in a win-win situation."

"That hawk is in a win-win situation."

"My feet are experiencing a win-win situation inside these boots."

This was the nature of their interplay because they were both divorced, both single mothers, and both periodically bewildered by the behavior of their daughters, who at the moment were some distance ahead, Sophie's blue cap appearing from time to time among breaks in the vegetation. Occasionally the view opened up completely and Keris could see Chow trotting behind them, pausing here and there with his ears perked at the movement of something promising, although he rarely gave chase anymore. He knew the pain of leaving the trail. Too many thorns had been pulled from his aching paws.

Keris was breathing through her nose, ujjayi-style, for the extra oxygen. There was a pleasant silence. The steady thud of Charlotte's walking stick. Sophie's or Katie's voice rearing up now and then. Children shouted to each other whether they were two feet or two miles apart.

The trail began at the mouth of a shallow canyon and crisscrossed a sandy creekbed as it worked its way up to a saddle. Keris guessed they were about halfway there. There were switchbacks ahead of them, a few steep ridges before a final hump that eventually dropped away to reveal a spire known as Seaver's Needle jutting up from the floor of the next canyon. On weekends and holidays the trail was occupied by a conga line of amateurs — out-of-towners, for the most part, who confronted the desert in jeans and tennis sneakers, bikini tops and nightclub-caliber makeup that began to streak before the first stream-crossing. They dropped food wrappers and shouted as they barreled down the trail and usually failed to yield right of way. They weren't cruel, but they were careless and thoughtless and it had the same effect.

"So what ever happened to Ned?" Charlotte asked.

"Who?"

"I mean Ed."

"You mean Jed."

"The guy with his own airplane."

"Or so he claimed."

Charlotte threw her a glance. "You didn't believe him?"

"I didn't care. He was in town for the weekend with no strings attached and it was a full moon."

Charlotte blew out a breath. "Can you teach me how to do that?"

"Do what?"

"Not feel guilty about having a one-night stand?"

Keris thought for a moment. "It's like chocolate mousse. You should eat it rarely, but enjoy it when you do."

As the trail narrowed, Keris allowed Charlotte to walk ahead of her. They crossed the creekbed again and passed single file through the relative shade of a mesquite bosque, the limbs gnarled and black and arthritic, quilled with needle-shaped leaves. The path was becoming choppier, cutting up through a field of boulders with sunlight reflecting off pale surfaces, a brilliance almost too sharp to behold. Charlotte's strides had lost some of their nervy bounce. There was a comfortable rhythm now. A steady breathing, a steady sweat. That marvelous part of the hike where you feel like you could climb Everest without serious fatigue.

"So," Charlotte said. "Any prospects?"

Keris stubbed her toe, but recovered without losing her stride. "You mean, potential boyfriends?"

"I mean, it's a full moon this weekend."

"I'm not a werewolf, Charlotte. I don't suddenly grow claws and pounce on the nearest man."

Charlotte looked over her shoulder at Keris. "That was a joke. All I meant was—"

A shriek came from somewhere up the trail. They halted, freeze-framed for a moment, in a state of full alert. Had the scream come from pain or pleasure? Keris called Sophie's name. They waited. Chow's bark echoed down the canyon. Then silence. Keris and Charlotte exchanged a look, measuring their worry against each other, and then started sprinting up the trail at the same time, scrambling over loose gravel and exposed rocks and logs pegged into the ground to control erosion. Panic jabbing through Keris's chest. She was trying to picture something specific because it was better than vague terror. A twisted ankle, a snake bite, a close encounter of the third kind. Anything.

They caught up to the girls at the bottom of the first switchback, strolling along as if nothing had happened.

"Katie?" Charlotte said.

Katie whirled around. "She put a lizard on me!"

Chow barked at the sudden excitement. Keris crouched and laid her hand against the dog's flank to calm him. The usual sighs of relief were heaved, the usual reprimands issued: Sophie for manhandling the wildlife, Katie for overreacting. It took about twenty seconds. Another twenty seconds later the girls were murmuring and giggling about something they clearly didn't want their mothers to hear as they continued onward, stumbling like circus clowns. Keris and Charlotte both shook their heads. There they went—the yin-yang twins. Katie with her dainty deer-limbs, her cropped hair, her alabaster skin coated with the same brand of sunscreen her mother used. Sophie shorter, darker, squatter, baseball cap firmly in place, ponytail swinging.

It was impossible to predict how her daughter would grow up, of course, but these days Keris suspected an outdoor athlete in the making. A seeker of cliffs and whitewater rapids. And thus Keris's worries would never end. When Sophie was a baby the danger had been plain — electrical outlets, unguarded swimming pools, household objects magically transformed into choking hazards — but it had been spreading outward ever since, becoming darker and deeper until it included, now, the car with the unseen driver, the picture with the "missing" caption. Keris occasionally had nightmares about it. There were times when the very workings of the world seemed to threaten her child.

The switchbacks took them over a low ridge. The trail straightened, followed the broad notch of a drainage for a while, and then hugged the flank of a mountain as it continued climbing. The sky was heating up, the air swelling and expanding. Saguaros stood over them with arms arranged in semaphore. Signs and symbols. If only you could read what they were saying. Keris coughed. She felt the beginnings of a parched throat and realized she had been breathing with her mouth wide open ever since she had heard Katie's scream. She pulled out her bottle and drank some lukewarm water.

The girls were pulling ahead again. Where did they get the energy? She imagined Logan making some remark about metabolic efficiency. Or incentives. Or something else. She never knew what he was going to say until he said it and then it seemed inevitable. His paper, which she had read last night, was a case in point. It criticized the standard model of the economy for depicting a closed system lacking any sort of connection to its physical environment. The introductory chapter of most economics textbooks, he said — and she could hear his voice saying it — simply showed a circular flow of goods and services divorced from the realities of resource consumption and waste. It failed to account for energy. For entropy. For depletion, degradation, exhaust. For the fact that all activity involves input and output. It was a fundamental mistake that led to many others — the failure, for example, to study the size of the economy relative to the environment, because although the free market is the best mechanism for allocating a given set of commodities among a given set of consumers, it is incapable of determining how many commodities or consumers there should be. If left alone, the market grows beyond its ecological carrying capacity and becomes too large for the Earth to sustain, no matter how efficiently its resources are allocated.

Keris wiped her brow and inhaled the scent of cactus and dry rock. Logan would love this place. But he would also see the pressures against it. He'd notice the litter, the human impact, the trail ravaged by the crowds. He'd turn and glance downhill, just as she was doing now, and see the haze drifting in from Phoenix, and he wouldn't say anything but she'd feel it haunting the sentences of his next paper. Assuming she read his next paper. He was a person whose work was a window to not only his mind but his—

"Careful," Charlotte said, stopping and looking back at Keris. She prodded a large rock with her walking stick. "That one's loose."

Keris stepped over it and came up next to her. A wall of slick rock loomed above them, butter-colored in the sun. The trail skirted the lower edge of it and then climbed through some sparse vegetation toward the saddle. The girls were a short distance ahead, walking silently, Chow in tow. Almost there. Keris took a swig of water. Charlotte lifted up her T-shirt and used it to wipe her face.

"I'm going to have sex with him," she said.

Keris lowered her bottle. "The stockbroker?"

"He's good-looking. He's sexy. He treats me well. So what if it's not a long-term relationship?" She laughed. "It's a win-win situation."

"But he's married, Charlotte. I wouldn't recommend—"

"Whoa," she said. "Married? I don't know where you got that piece of information, but this guy is a card-carrying bachelor."

Keris could feel her expression faltering. "Of course. Sorry. I must have been thinking about someone else."

In the long silence that followed, Keris could almost hear the speculations gathering in Charlotte's mind.

"Well," Charlotte finally said, taking off her hat, "send her my condolences, whoever she is." She leaned her walking stick against a boulder and peeled her T-shirt over her head, exposing white shoulders, tender skin. Her gray athletic bra darkened with sweat. "Oh, this feels good."

"You'll get burned."

"It's just for a few minutes." She smiled. "The Chocolate Mousse technique." She looped her T-shirt through her belt and set her hat back on her head, then picked up her walking stick and continued climbing.

Keris didn't move. She stood there with the sweet smell of sunscreen hanging in the air. Sometimes it happened like this. Sometimes she accidentally bit into the kernel of an emotion with some trivial comment and she needed an extra minute to absorb its flavor. To an unenlightened observer, she might have seemed upset, or sun-crazed, or stunned by the realization. But in fact she was simply processing it. She was letting it fully occupy her. She was a person who surrendered the moment to understanding. A few minutes later she started climbing again.

*   *   *

"I'm surprised," she said to Logan, "at how well you responded to those suggestions."

It was noon the following day, at a Japanese restaurant with high-grade sushi and an in-your-face view of Rural Road. There were glossy tables, high-backed chairs, framed photographs of pagodas and Shinto temples hanging on the walls. Keris had chosen it despite the strip-mall atmosphere. She was craving protein.

"Everything you said made sense. If I'm going to sell them on the importance of Net Primary Product, then I'd better get the figures right."

"You're nervous."

"I am?"

"You've been rubbing your chopsticks together for ten minutes."

Logan looked down at what he was doing. "I'm scraping off the splinters."

"You're going to start a campfire according to procedures outlined in the Boy Scout manual."

"Don't exaggerate."

"Is that a wisp of smoke I see?"

In a slow gesture of surrender, he laid down the chopsticks and sat back in his chair.

"Your paper will be a success," she said.

He nodded doubtfully. He was wearing a dark sportcoat, a pale shirt, a patterned tie. The outfit seemed to bring out richer overtones in his complexion, nuances to his cheekbones and nose. A sturdy look without the rugged excess you saw in most men. As his eyes roved around the restaurant she could read his underlying distress. She wanted to reach across the table and feel the weight, the density, the charge of his mind conducted through his skin. She wanted to take his hand. The hand without the wedding ring. Stop it, she thought. She looked away and watched the traffic do its usual dance at the intersection. She had called Logan after the hike yesterday and offered her suggestions over the phone because she had lacked the sort of clarity necessary for a face-to-face meeting. The conversation had lasted for nearly an hour. They had talked about Net Primary Product as the amount of photosynthesis absorbed by human beings. They had talked about Keris's corrections to his figures. They had talked about the hike. At one point Logan had made a comment about wanting to go there with her sometime and she had almost replied that, in a sense, he already had. This morning she had selected her favorite green dress, teased her hair into a more pleasing shape, and applied a hint of lipstick — extra touches she rarely employed in her daily life. She knew what she was doing and it frightened her.

Logan was gazing into space.

She waved a hand in front of his eyes. "I'm over here."

He blinked. "They won't accept the theory unless they believe the details, but they won't believe the details unless they accept the theory."

"God is in the details," she said.

"God is dead."

"Really? I didn't even know he was sick."

He laughed. "All right. We'll discuss something else."

A waiter arrived with a platter of sushi and placed it on the table between them. Bright slips of fish on beds of packed rice. They poured soy sauce into shallow dishes, mixed in dabs of wasabi.

"I'd like to see your presentation," she said, picking up a piece of salmon with her chopsticks.

"We're supposed to be talking about something else."

"When is it?"

"When is what?"

"Cut it out."

He smiled. "Saturday. Late afternoon. In a big room with chandeliers and thick carpets. The funeral is immediately afterward. I'm going to be cremated."

Keris was savoring the raw salmon flavor, the tang and afterburn of the wasabi in her nostrils. "If you want, I could sit near the back of the room and fake a seizure to distract the angry mob."

"You have a strange way of reassuring me."

They ate for a while in silence.

He shook his head slowly. "The chairman of the U.S. Council of Economic Advisers."

"Stop it," she said. "We agreed to discuss another topic. How's your car?"

"Dead. Comatose. I don't know. It's still sitting exactly where I left it."

"Then how did you get to campus today?"

He hesitated for an instant with a piece of tuna raised to his mouth. "My wife dropped me off."

Finally. Keris gave a noncommittal nod and continued eating. A cell phone trilled somewhere behind her. A man answered and immediately started reeling off figures and names. She could hear a light sprinkle of harp and flute music coming from the speakers. Traffic rumbling beyond the window. Let's call this an awkward silence. She took a deep breath and decided it was time.

"You and your wife are having problems, correct?"

He kept chewing, but his eyes widened, like he wanted to answer right away. He swallowed the food and gulped some water. "I love her, but it feels like a bad habit. Like biting my nails. Or smoking." He paused for a moment, looking out the window as if expecting to find an answer there. "I don't like the way I love her."

There was a sudden commotion behind Keris. The man on the phone cursed and began rapping something against the table. She looked over her shoulder and saw him—young, pudgy, acne-scarred—complaining that his phone had dropped the signal. A woman at another table seemed to be having the same problem. Keris turned back to Logan.

"I know what the problem is," she said.

He leaned forward.

"A communications satellite."

A perplexed look came over his face.

"Remember that power failure last week? Sunspots. Solar flares. The sun is currently at the peak of its eleven-year cycle."

"I didn't even know it was sick."

Keris smiled. "The moon isn't the only thing with phases, Logan. Solar activity increases every eleven years. Nobody knows the cause."

He laid down his chopsticks. "Jevons said something about it."

"Who?"

"Stanley Jevons. A British economist. A math-happy statistician. In the 1880s he found a statistical correlation between sunspot cycles and economic fluctuations, postulating that the business cycle was caused by variations in the weather resulting from, I think he called it, 'increased waves of heat from the sun,' which he said happened every ten and some fraction years." He paused. "You know, when you said, 'I know what the problem is,' I thought you were about to psychoanalyze the hell out of me and give me something to think about today."

"Maybe I did, Logan." She had meant it as a mild joke, but felt the truth in the words as soon as they came out of her mouth. "Maybe I did."

At the end of the day Logan locked up his office and descended the stairs without his bookbag. Unburdened. Unarmed. You wouldn't shoot an unarmed man, would you. You wouldn't hit a guy with glasses. Lines from old westerns, old cartoons he had watched as a child while his parents were either sleeping or having sex upstairs—not that he had ever been able to hear the difference, their bedroom always as quiet as a bank vault. Maybe it was the heat of his life these days, but he kept remembering those wintry days of his childhood. The metallic air, the pearly light. The colorless after-noons with the streets full of slush and crusted ice. One day in particular his parents had had some sort of argument in the kitchen and afterward, during a heavy blizzard, his father had driven him and his little sister Sarah all the way out to Valley Forge for sledding — and this, it should be noted, involved a complicated route through the Main Line suburbs because the expressway was closed, forcing them onto former wagon trails that curved and fed into each other abruptly with nothing more than a stop sign to warn of the tran-sition. He remembered houses blurred in the storm, swingsets thickened with snow, trees laced and meshed in the colonial woods and all the stone walls fluffed over. He caught a few glimpses of a whitened Schuylkill through the trees before they reached Valley Forge itself and the sky opened up to re-veal the full force of the weather coming across the hills. Not so much a val-ley as a great plain, it seemed to him, with deer poised in the distance, charcoal-sketched in the chalky light. "Reindeers!" Sarah had cried out, point-ing with her mitten dangling from the string that ran through her snowsuit. Dad had put it back on for her and pulled her pom-pom hat down over her ears and then sat her on his lap as they coasted down one of the gentle slopes together. Dad in his overcoat, his fedora, his leather gloves. Logan, by contrast, felt like a professional with his ski goggles and hood cinched tight around his face. He didn't mess around. Lifting his legs high out of the snow and running with the sled clutched to his chest, he threw himself forward at top speed. He loved the effort — the work involved in having fun. He loved the impact in his bones. He loved the numb face and rubber lips, the fluid leaking from his nose.

They returned home and hung their clothes in the laundry room, drank hot chocolate, watched cartoons. Mom didn't kiss Dad, but she cooked din-ner as if everything were fine. And it was, Logan thought. The argument hadn't been resolved, but it had been nullified by their excursion into the blizzard. It often happened that way. If they didn't resolve a disagreement, they'd cancel it instead.

Logan emerged from the Economics building to find the walkways nearly deserted and the bike racks empty. The conference was waiting for him downtown, occupying an entire hotel off Mill Avenue. All afternoon the par-ticipants had been gathering, shaking hands, claiming nametags and folders at the banquet tables — and if Logan walked quickly, he'd arrive just in time to find a seat in the back row and pretend to listen to whatever platitudes this year's keynote speaker had to offer. Afterward he was supposed to meet Deck at the outdoor bar. The invitation had come a couple of days ago, but

Logan had put him off until this evening so he could finish his paper. And minimize the impact. He had noticed Dallas stiffen when she heard Deck's voice on the answering machine.

Despite her reaction, he still didn't think anything had happened between her and Deck—because, try as he might, he simply couldn't picture them together, even for a ten-minute tryst. In fact, the more he thought about it, the more he believed the opposite had happened. An illicit burst of animosity based on pheromones, animal juices, fire and ice. He'd never get to the bottom of it. And, if the truth be told, he no longer cared enough to try. If Dallas wanted to be cagey about it, he'd concede it to her. He was tired of sensing deception in everything she said. He was tired of tracking all the little twists and turns of her mind.

He crossed University Avenue. It was early evening with the sky faded to a toxic glow, the remains of a sunset on the horizon. Dusk. Streetlights and neon slowly coming into being. What would Keris say about this time of day, this moment between day and night? A scientific fact. Something suggestive and indirect. She had refused, after all, to explain that comment in the restaurant. Later, she had said. They had parted in front of the Physical Sciences building, and she had repeated her promise to attend his presentation despite his protests, and he had watched her legs, exposed by the slit in her dress as she walked away. OK. He was attracted to her. But how much of the attraction was authentic, and how much of it was an urge to escape into simplicity, into a world where he could begin all over again?

The hotel was designed in the style of an old Spanish mission, with archways, domes, a colonnade, a courtyard full of towering palms. A waterfall splashed over arranged rocks. Logan and Deck were sitting next to it now, at a table set apart from the others, drinking fishbowl-sized margaritas. Heat lamps glowed against a chilly night.

"Generic speech," Deck said. "The guy got it off an assembly line."

"I wouldn't know."

Deck looked up from his drink. "Let me guess. You stopped listening."

"Right after the part where he said 'Good evening.'"

Deck laughed quietly. "Either of us could have improvised a better speech. Am I right?" He looked around to make sure no one was within earshot, then shook his head and laughed again. He seemed a little jauntier than usual, flushed and relaxed, his self-assurance closer to the surface. He told Logan about the paper he was scheduled to present tomorrow afternoon. He told him about the contract he had signed earlier in the week that officially made them colleagues.

"And I couldn't help noticing," he said, "that you're a member of the Saturday-afternoon panel. The final act of this whole performance. Why don't you give me a preview."

Logan took a breath. "I'm going to examine the conventional model of the economy and describe how it ignores the laws of thermodynamics, mainly the entropy law, and then I'm going to establish, I hope, a method of . . ."

Deck was making a T, timeout, with his hands. "You cleared this with the conference committee?"

Logan shook his head.

"You ran it by Silverson, then."

Logan shook his head again.

"You know what I'm going to say."

"The words 'crash and burn' leap to mind."

"How about 'career suicide'? How about 'the following presentation contains scenes of a graphic nature'?"

Logan gazed into his empty margarita glass. "I have to do it."

"Have to? Unless terrorists are holding your wife hostage, I recommend something different. Another paper."

"What other paper?"

"You don't have a backup?" Deck let out a low whistle. He was silent for a moment. There was the sound of the waterfall next to them, the clamor of the other tables. "You could change your thesis," he finally said.

Logan leveled his gaze at him. "And maybe you could change yours. Come on, Deck."

"Point taken. Look, I'm just sending a warning shot across your bow before the torpedoes start coming. I owe it to you as a colleague. As a friend."

"Thanks, but I made the decision to write this paper knowing what the consequences might be."

Deck didn't reply. He swirled the remains of the margarita in his glass and nodded reluctantly, like someone agreeing to keep a dirty secret. He pulled a menu out of the holder. "I've been tuning in to the department politics this week."

"You mean, here?"

"Home sweet home. I hear you're pushing for a new course in History of Economic Thought."

"They want it."

"Who does?"

"The students. They're hungry for it."

"Hungry." He smiled to himself, as if Logan had made a reference to some private joke. "Sure. Everybody's hungry."

Two days later Logan sat in his study with note cards scattered across his desk. He was dissecting his paper, slicing and dicing the argument for weak logic or careless rhetoric that might jeopardize his presentation. And he was wondering about that fourth paragraph with the—

"What's this?"

Logan looked up. Dallas was standing in the doorway with a packet of cat food in her hand. Sweatshirt, jeans, hair tied back with a plain elastic cord. Was she actually cleaning out the garage?

"What's what?" Logan said.

"This."

"What?"

"This."

"I don't see anything."

"I'm basically about to have a meltdown, so I expect a full confession."

Logan drew a breath. "About what?"

She threw the packet at him and went down the hall and slammed the garage door behind her. Picture frames shook on the wall.

Logan didn't move. He looked down at his desk. The note cards sat there innocently, displaying the main points of his argument. He wished he could do the same thing for Dallas—write a paper describing their heat-energy equations, their throughput, their waste products. He wished she could understand it. But it would be unfair of him to demand what she couldn't supply. He had known that when he married her. He gathered up everything and loaded it into his bookbag.

He showered and shaved. When he emerged from the bathroom he found Dallas's sweatshirt and jeans heaped on the floor by the closet. He called out her name. Silence. He glanced at the clock. He dressed quickly and was still cinching the knot in his tie as he walked down the hallway and opened the door to an empty garage. No car, no Dallas. He cursed. Last night she had agreed to let him use it for the conference. But instead she had left him this: the boxes shifted and restacked, the lawnmower shoved into the corner with the offending box of cat food crushed deliberately under one of its wheels. And there was the old bicycle leaning against the wall. Not so old. Second-hand. He had bought it at a neighbor's garage sale a few months ago with visions of cardiovascular fitness, but then all the end-of-semester obligations had come pouring in and smothered his resolution. Besides, the thing needed serious work. The brakes failed, the wheels wobbled, the chain seized and snagged.

He went back into the house and called Keris, who was on her way out the door and preparing herself, she said, to hide in the back of the room during his presentation and fake a seizure, as promised, and of course she didn't mind giving him a ride.

Dallas, it should be noted, wasn't the kind of person who took a marker. She liked to keep the debt faceless and detached, strictly corporate. And although she had squeezed all the juice out of her first two credit cards, she was using a bigger and better one now, fresh from the mailbox this morning. She had activated it while Logan was in the shower and then basically evacuated the place before he came out of the bathroom. Let him call a cab, is what she was thinking. Let him worry.

She sat in the glow of video poker, working the keys madly. She had hit a few straights and three of a kinds a while back, but had since taken a serious nosedive and was feeling the familiar slump in her spine, the cramping in her thighs that came from sitting with her legs crossed for too long. Her eyes squinting through the cigarette haze. She had visited the ATM a couple of times. It didn't matter anymore. It was only a bunch of numbers on slips of paper. It didn't translate into reality. What were they going to do, take her out to the parking lot and shoot her? Bring it on, she thought. She ordered a drink from a waitress wearing way too much eyeshadow. Bring it on.

She lit another cigarette and glanced around the casino. This was the high mass of Saturday afternoon, coins crashing into hoppers, bells ringing, chimes singing. She knew how the hoppers were designed. It would have been easy to line them with rubber or foam so the coins wouldn't make that clinking and clattering noise when they fell, but the sound of naked metal was primal, like ocean waves, like a baby crying. She turned back to the screen and anted her usual amount before the cartoon cards popped into place. She didn't really want a baby. She didn't have the instinct for it. And setting aside, for a moment, the complete wreck it would make of her body and therefore their sex life, there was the long-run effect on their relationship. The emotional bypass that a child would create. They'd be expressing everything to the kid instead of each other, which was basically the beginning of the end, in her opinion. After all, it had happened with her parents.

Why, then, did she propose it? Why did she ask for something she didn't want? The answer was obvious, obvious, obvious. To hear Logan's response. That ugly logic of his. OK, she thought. So he didn't want children. Or maybe he didn't want children with her.

The screen froze. The machine demanded more money before it would continue. Dallas reached into her purse and pulled out some bills. The payoffs favored the person with deep pockets. You needed to survive the downturns. The situation would improve, both here and at home. To be perfectly honest, she was waiting until the conference was over before she took any further action. He needed to apologize about feeding that cat, for example. He needed to make it up to her. In the meantime, she was going to live her own life.

As she lit another cigarette she saw the flame trembling in front of her face and realized her hands were shaking. She pocketed the lighter, sat back in her chair, and blew out a gale of smoke. Relax. The money wasn't real. Their problems weren't real. In fact, this life wasn't real. It was what most religions taught and she wanted to believe it. She wanted to believe in the light at the end of the swirling tunnel, the white brilliance of her soul's release, herself but not herself, with everything understood and forgiven. She wanted to believe Logan loved her enough to have a child. What was wrong with that? What was wrong with wanting heaven in this life?

It had the unreality of all important events. Like his wedding, like his grandfather's funeral, Logan wasn't feeling anything with the right depth or precision. He knew Keris was out there but couldn't find her in the crowd. So maybe she wasn't there. And everyone seemed a little cleaner and crisper today, glowing in the presence of Nelson Pitlick, the chairman of the U.S. Council of Economic Advisers, who sat in the middle of the room to demonstrate his lack of pretension. Black-rimmed glasses, graying temples. He bore an absurd resemblance to Logan's father, who could also sit for hours, groomed and three-pieced, seemingly at ease with the small talk his colleagues foisted upon him.

The audience settled. The presentations began.

Logan listened to the other panelists read condensed versions of their papers. The first panelist described a two-dimensional application of the maximum principle to illustrate optimal multi-sector growth; the second one gave a comparison of investment-based and innovation-based strategies as developing economies approached the technology frontier; and the third panelist performed an analysis of the transitional dynamics of utility functions. After each reading there were a few questions from the audience, some answers and clarifications. Then it was Logan's turn. He cleared his throat. He gathered up his pages and read carefully, the room swelling, hot and silent, like a fever beyond the edge of the page. When he was done he raised his eyes to the legion of impersonal faces and waited for a reaction. This is the part, he thought, where they start throwing rotten vegetables.

There was a movement next to Pitlick, someone rising from his seat, and Logan knew who it was even before he could focus on the shock of white hair, the expensive sportcoat, the metallic gray eyes of Dr. No.

"My question is simple," Dr. No said. "I would like to know why, exactly, you believe that prices do not reflect resource scarcity."

Logan took a breath. "As I state in my paper, I believe the problem arises from our conceptualization of the economy as a kind of perpetual motion machine — a simple flow of goods and services — rather than a one-way throughput that consumes energy and generates waste along with commodities. We need to recognize the actual physical process of making —"

"I listened to your argument quite carefully, Dr. Smith, but I didn't hear the answer then, and I'm not hearing it now."

"You might, if you let me finish."

A murmur went through the audience.

Dr. No's face took on the expression of someone bearing an insult with great dignity. "I apologize. Please continue."

Logan reached for the glass of water in front of him and took a sip. He needed to loosen up. He was coming off snappy and contentious, playing right into Dr. No's hands. He set down the glass, clasped his hands on the table in front of him, and spoke calmly. "What I meant to say is that I obviously had to leave out certain details in this condensed version of my paper. In the full version, I state that prices function effectively within the limits of the free market, which does an excellent job of allocating a given set of resources among a given set of consumers. But it functions poorly — or, to be more accurate, doesn't function at all — when the task at hand is to determine the proper size of the economy."

Dr. No cocked a white eyebrow. "The size of the economy is quite irrelevant to the —"

"Please," Logan said, raising his clasped hands from the table, "hear me out. In theory, we can double our total resource consumption and the market will come up with the most efficient allocation. But that doesn't say anything about the optimal size of the market. In fact, the size of the economy is completely irrelevant to the market."

"Are you suggesting," Dr. No said, pivoting subtly toward the audience to include them in what he was saying, "that the free market 'contains the seeds of its own destruction,' as a certain nineteenth-century German philosopher once claimed?"

"No. Like most economists, Marx believed in unlimited growth, so I disagree with much of his theory. My point is simply this: A boat that tries to carry too much weight will sink even if that weight is optimally allocated. Asking the free market to solve the problem is like asking a cruise director to come up with the best arrangement of deck chairs on the *Titanic*."

Dr. No shook his head as if he were slightly embarrassed by Logan's behavior. He slid a hand into his pocket. "A colorful metaphor, but I hardly need to point out that the economy is not a ship. Furthermore, your argument ignores the inconvenient fact that growth is the source of financial prosperity. Periods of low or zero growth have been the worst in history."

"That's because our economy is designed for growth. I mean . . ." He hesitated. "A plane will crash if it doesn't maintain a forward motion, but a helicopter won't. We need a helicopter instead of a plane."

"Are you sure the economy is a plane? Why not a shark? After all, the predatory shark," he intoned, "dies unless it continuously surges forward to bring oxygen into its gills." This provoked some laughter from the audience. "Setting these analogies aside, Dr. Smith, I'm curious to know if you have any figures or data—any empirical support at all—for these claims."

"Between 1950 and 1986, world population doubled. During that same time period, fossil fuel consumption quadrupled. In fact, fossil fuel consumption has continued to double twice as quickly as population. This is not simply growth, but exponential growth."

Dr. No glanced down at his shoes and waited, demonstrating his patience.

"The nature of exponential growth," Logan continued, "is that it happens slowly and then all at once. Let's say you accept a consulting job next February. Would you prefer to be paid a thousand dollars per day, or one cent on the first day, two on the second, four on the third, and so on, with your salary doubling every day until the end of the month?"

Dr. No sighed. "We all appreciate the review of high school math, however this doesn't—"

"The second salary makes you a millionaire by the end of the month."

"Yes, of course. But the point—"

"On what day do you become a millionaire?"

"This digression is not—"

"On what day," Logan repeated, "do you become a millionaire?"

"The last day," a voice near the back of the room said. A female voice.

"Yes," Logan said. "The last day. The twenty-eighth day. Half the entire growth occurs in about 3 percent of the time period."

Dr. No shifted his weight from one foot to another. "Even if that entertaining parable were an accurate depiction of resource consumption, it assumes an elasticity of resource substitution equal to zero. It also disregards the development of alternative resources. This is the sort of doomsday scenario that half-baked environmentalists have been predicting for decades, and yet technology continues to render each so-called limit irrelevant."

"Oh, of course. Technology will save us. Technology will provide new and more efficient methods of creating energy." Logan scrubbed a hand through his hair. "Disregarding, for a moment, the issue of pollution, I can't accept that sort of linear thinking. Just because technology has served us in the past doesn't mean it will always continue to do so in the future."

"Are you saying it won't?" Dr. No asked, with an indulgent smile.

"It would be like claiming I'm not at risk of a heart attack simply because I haven't had one yet. And besides, I would ask you to consider what technology has done to this planet during the past century." Logan pulled out a sheet of paper. "According to UN statistics, 90 percent of all plant and animal varieties have been wiped out in the last one hundred years. Of the ten thousand species once used for food and clothing, one hundred and fifty species remain and only four—wheat, corn, rice, and potatoes—account for more than half of the calories consumed by human beings. We've caused more damage in the last one hundred years than we did in the previous ten thousand."

"We have also saved more lives and raised the standard of living by astonishing degrees."

"In the short term, yes. But at what cost? 'Bigger and better' commodities have meant 'bigger and better' depletion of resources, not to mention 'bigger and better' pollution. Technology has been the instrument of environmental degradation rather than its savior. When is this process going to magically reverse itself? When is this miracle going to happen?"

There was a kind of live-wire feeling in the room, people shifting in their seats, talking among themselves in a tone that Logan felt was clearly hostile. He noticed the panelist sitting next to him—a pale math-slinger from upstate New York—fussing with the corner of his paper, afraid of getting hit with friendly fire.

"Once again," Dr. No said, "forgive me for pointing out the obvious, but the use of clean, affordable, renewable energy will occur on a widespread basis at the very moment the incentive to do so becomes strong enough. In addition, you seem to exclude the possibility that scientists will discover, say," he shrugged and made an expansive gesture, "a catalyst to break down water molecules into oxygen and hydrogen, releasing untold amounts of energy from a single gallon of seawater. You're not a scientist, Dr. Smith, and neither am I."

"But I am," a voice said in the back. Heads turned toward Keris as she rose from the crowd. Logan was hit with a few different feelings at once— relief, gratitude, and, most notably, annoyance that she was getting involved. When she had picked him up earlier that day he had noticed something different about her, but he had been too nervous about his presentation to figure it out. Now it seemed more distinct even though she was across the room. The conservative shading of her makeup, the plain-toned pantsuit. A professional demeanor. That was it. She had come here not as Keris, but as Dr. Aguilar. She had been planning to intervene.

"Forgive the interruption," she said. "But as a physicist I feel compelled to point out that Dr. Smith's figures are sound and that his projections are actually somewhat conservative. If you consider, for example, his discussion of net primary production—that is, the amount of solar energy captured in photosynthesis by primary producers, minus the energy used in their own growth and production—you'll see why his points about the exponential growth rate are so important."

There was a shifting motion in the crowd, chairs creaking as people turned to get a better view of her.

"Net primary production," she continued, "is the basic food resource for everything on Earth not capable of photosynthesis. Since human beings appropriate about 25 percent of NPP, it's clear that two more doublings would give 100 percent, with zero energy remaining for all nonhuman species. But of course, at that point we would all be dead anyway because the entire ecosystem would be gone. In addition, I should mention that your example of the catalyst used to create energy from water is physically impossible. Water is not like a piece of coal whose energy can be released by fire. If anything, it's like the heap of ashes left over afterward. The energy of the oxygen and hydrogen atoms has already been discharged in the formation of the water molecules. There's nothing left to 'tap into' or release."

As she was speaking, Dr. No swiveled and shot Logan a craggy look before turning his attention back to her. He caught her as she was about to sit down.

"I understand your point, Doctor . . . ?"

"Aguilar."

"Dr. Aguilar. You seem to be well acquainted with the data in Dr. Smith's paper."

She hesitated before she replied. "I listened carefully."

"But you seemed to hear something he didn't say. Twenty-five percent of net primary production, for example. I don't recall him quoting an exact figure."

Logan felt a jolt in his stomach. "She assisted me," he said. "With the figures. Dr. Aguilar did some fact-checking."

There was a heavy silence. Dr. No turned and aimed his gaze at him. The lights buzzed overhead. Someone coughed.

"Really?" Dr. No finally said. He seemed faintly amused, as if Logan had just confessed to an embarrassing middle name. "No doubt," he said, turning back toward Keris again, "Dr. Smith appreciates your contributions to his paper. A curious cross-disciplinary approach. In fact . . ." He suddenly glanced at his watch. "Well, I would like to continue, but I see that we've run out of time. Perhaps we could resume this debate under more favorable conditions? The Economics Institute will hold its inaugural conference in Palm Springs a couple of months from now and . . . well," he said, chuckling in apparent modesty, "I guess this is as good a time as any to announce that our 'main event,' so to speak, will be a discussion of our future. Not only the Economics Institute, but economics as a discipline. And we would certainly welcome the opportunity to have an inter-disciplinary component of the discussion. Perhaps you and Dr. Smith could say a few words on that topic? Our audience will consist of non-professionals, so we hope to address some of the broader issues of how economics might develop as a profession in the coming years. Please consider it." He nodded to Keris, and then to Logan and the other panelists before he sat down.

The leading panelist a couple of chairs away from Logan rose from his chair. Thank you for coming, he said. Thank you very much.

As the audience dispersed, Logan searched the back of the room until he caught Keris's eye. She shrugged. He gave her a stern look and then wagged his finger, a mock-reprimand. Then he noticed Dr. No out there, nodding slowly in agreement to something Pitlick was saying. But his gaze was fixed on Logan. OK, Logan thought. So Dr. No just saw what passed between him and Keris. Big deal. He began to gather up his papers, feeling the cold clammy remains of a nervous sweat under his arms. A few people walked past him to congratulate other members of the panel. This was no surprise. But he didn't feel the way he had thought he would feel. He had expected a grim satisfaction, the sort of dark pleasure that comes from throwing a brick through the television screen when your team loses the game in the last ten seconds. Instead he felt uncertain and anxious, as if he had won and lost something at the same time, but he didn't know what it was.

Keris sat at the bar with a margarita, her hand wandering toward the pretzel dish now and then. Something about the salt. And the full moon. She felt the familiar ache in her abdomen, the pop of the released egg. A fiery breeze rushing through her. Earlier in the day she had channeled it into housework, a bike ride with Sophie before dropping her off at Charlotte's house for Katie's slumber party, and then high-volume disco music while she showered and dressed for Logan's presentation. She had gone from trying not to think about Logan to thinking about him nearly non-stop. There was a desire within him, half-phased, incomplete. She recognized it in his paper, in his refusal to have his car fixed, in his relationship with his wife. Keris suspected that he didn't talk about his marriage because he subscribed to the belief that it wasn't affecting other areas of his life and that it would eventually correct itself by the sheer power of its own momentum. Which meant Keris needed to stand clear of the whole thing. Keep hands and face away. She couldn't throw herself into the mix because the reaction would probably be disastrous for everyone. Keris couldn't be a catalyst. She was already too affected by the things she touched.

But she was here, wasn't she? She was sitting at this bar like someone expecting a rendezvous. She turned toward the wall of people near her, the blur of suits and nametags, the men outnumbering women five to one. A waitress was working her way through the crowd. It was evening now and there were a few stars poking through the urban glow overhead, a full moon hidden behind the rim of the courtyard. A nearby waterfall splashed softly among the rocks and drained into a swimming pool with lights wavering below the surface, casting a blue glow on the faces gathered around it.

She prodded the ice in her glass with her pinky. This was foolish. She should leave. And then? The truth was that she hadn't made any plans this evening. An empty house awaited her. No offense to Chow. Sophie wouldn't be home until tomorrow morning and, well, Keris thought, there was only the couch, and the microwave popcorn, and the video store a few miles away.

Just then Logan came up and leaned on the bar next to her. "Don't ever jump into the water to save a drowning man," he said, "unless you want to get dragged down with him."

Keris smirked. "In a room full of economists? Nobody could drown in that. Suffocate, maybe."

He signaled to the bartender for a drink. "I've never seen Dr. No bail out of a debate before. That's quite an achievement."

"Dr. No?"

Logan winced and lowered his voice. "I meant to say Novak."

"You were doing quite admirably before I spoke up. I was afraid, in fact, that I derailed the discussion and that you would be angry with me."

"I was. I am. Can't you tell?" He pointed to his own face. "Look at this expression of wrath."

She laughed. "Does that mean I should decline the invitation to Palm Springs?"

He was about to reply when the bartender came over and glanced at Logan's nametag. "For you," he said, handing him a cordless phone.

Logan looked surprised. "Hi," he said into the receiver. "Yeah. Fine. Is everything all right?" He listened for a moment, then blocked his other ear and walked over to the swimming pool. He stayed there for a while, frowning at the water and saying very little before he finally ended the call. As he came back to the bar Keris saw the look on his face and felt her high spirits falling, a decompression in the center of her body, even though she had just finished telling herself five minutes earlier that she had no right to expect anything from him. It was obvious now. Look at the ring on his finger. This is the way of the human race.

It's worth mentioning that Deck had been sitting in the row behind Keris during the presentation. Although the rational expectation was for him to grab a seat next to Pitlick and get in a few words, he preferred a different strategy. He was the kind of guy who created his own opportunities, who distinguished himself from everyone else. In other words, he had done some research and learned that Pitlick was a jogger, and an early bird at that, and so yesterday morning Deck had suited up for a run and then situated himself in the lobby with his newspaper until Pitlick emerged from the elevator, at which point he just, well, bumped into him, shall we say, and accompanied him for a couple of miles before diverging onto a different route. He had dropped a casual hint about his presentation later that day, suggesting it might have something to do with economic policy on Pitlick's level. Plant the seed. And guess what, Pitlick had sat front and center during Deck's presentation. He had even asked a question afterward. Mission accomplished. Not that Deck expected to be a member of the CEA so early in his career. But he was thinking long term. He was paving the road ahead of him.

Now he was standing in the crowd with Novak and Silverson and a couple of lower-echelon drones, making small talk. According to the implicit rule that discussing crackpot theories automatically gave them more weight than they deserved, they had barely mentioned Logan's presentation. And besides, Deck's focus was shifting from the professional to the personal. He had been tracking that Aguilar woman ever since the presentation, intrigued by that crisp appearance of hers. There was just enough of a shimmer in those straight edges to suggest curves below the surface. Just enough sensuality in that voice. A quiet demand for her glasses to be removed, her hair to be released from that bundle at the back of her head. The sexuality was under wraps, but not as tightly as she thought.

In other words, Deck felt a certain desire taking shape within him, and the probability of fulfilling that desire had been disrupted by Logan's appearance at the bar. But it looked like his prospects were improving again. Yes. Logan was handing the phone back to the bartender and saying a few words to Keris. Parting words. And now he was making his way toward the lobby with everything falling into place, beautiful and perfect, until he stopped for a moment and looked back toward her like he might return. Keep going, Deck thought. Get out of here.

Logan finally resumed his walk through the crowd and disappeared. Deck relaxed. The field was clear.

"And we'll be in touch over the next few weeks," a nearby voice said.

Deck's attention snapped back to the conversation and he realized Novak had directed the comment to him. Apparently he was leaving. "Of course," he said, shaking Novak's hand. "I'll send you a copy of that paper." He met Novak's eye to make sure they understood each other.

Novak departed. Soon afterward Silverson wandered off like a senile grandfather, at which point Deck simply said goodbye to the drones and made his way over to an empty space in the crowd. He studied Keris for another minute or so. Call him crazy, but if he looked at a woman long enough he could see her split-sectioned, like blueprint designs, with all entrances and exits clearly marked. This one, however, was harder to figure out. The odd concentrations of her posture, the easy set of her shoulders. Mixed signals. An invitation, but in code. He understood why Logan was probably interested in her, and he understood why Logan couldn't have her.

And—all right, let's admit it—maybe that made her a little more desirable. Maybe.

Deck's drink was half-full, but he set it down on an empty table and came up next to her and ordered another one. While the bartender was working on it he made his move.

"I liked your comment about net physical production," he said.

"Excuse me?" She looked at him as if startled out of a daydream.

"Your point about photosynthesis. That floored me."

"Oh, you mean net *primary* production. I'm afraid it was wrong for the discussion, but I'm glad you found it useful."

"What do you mean by 'wrong'?"

She waved her hand dismissively and finished off her margarita. "Inappropriate. I shouldn't have jumped into the argument like that. I don't belong here."

"That's the most ridiculous statement I've heard today." He tilted his head toward the crowd. "And don't forget what kind of conversations I've been having."

She smiled. "That's very nice of you to say, but I don't think, for example, that physicists would appreciate an economist showing up in the middle of a conference and pointing out the economic ramifications of a new atom smasher." She began tracing the rim of her empty glass. "I don't think I helped anybody."

Deck caught the bartender's attention. "She'd like another one," he said. "Rocks, no salt."

The bartender looked at Keris for confirmation. When she nodded, Deck knew he was on his way. They continued talking and, little by little, he eased her away from the professional stuff. This was the proper way to do it. This was his procedure: Ask her about herself, about her interests, about the way she saw things. He steered the conversation appropriately and paid attention to almost everything she said. Tucson, yoga, physics. Divorce, daughter, dog.

They shifted to more technical matters and he found himself relying, strangely enough, on the documentaries he had watched during those barren winter nights in New Hampshire. Call him eccentric, but he liked this one show in particular, a wild nature series, all blood and guts and struggle for survival, narrated by a voice that remained calm no matter how violent things got. It was much more entertaining than the one about the planets, which he watched occasionally due to sheer inertia because it immediately followed the nature show—and which, he now realized, was a stroke of luck because this woman was not only a physicist but an astrophysicist.

The crowd swirled, shifted, surged. Deck ordered another round of drinks. He talked about Orange County for a while, then told her about his life in New Hampshire. "The stone-cold state," he said, trying to keep the complaint to a minimum, but soon he found himself on a roll, airing all his grievances about the place because he hadn't been able to talk to anyone else about it. He almost mentioned the new job at ASU, but decided to hold off until he knew if it would be an asset or a liability.

"My ex-husband is from New Hampshire," she finally said.

"Then you know what I mean."

"The things I liked least about him," she said, "were also the things I liked least about that place. The stinginess. The need to control everything. 'Live free or die,' they say."

"But the police seem to be everywhere," Deck said, "arresting a college student for having a beer, or directing traffic around a utility truck that's fixing a street lamp or doing something just as trivial even though the truck is completely off the road. I know exactly what you mean."

They were sitting close now, facing each other at oblique angles with their knees lightly touching. He was almost in. He could feel the shimmer of her personal space, the leading edge of her thigh. They both finished their drinks at the same time. They looked at each other. They smiled.

At this point it's important to consider the following objects in Deck's hotel room: Keris's shoes on the floor, kicked off and capsized. Her stockings like discarded snake skins. Her empty blouse and pants. Then his shirt and underwear. Her bra.

Her glasses are on the nightstand. The blankets have been shuffled off in their orchestrations and she is on top now, palms planted against his chest as she straddles him. He doesn't know what to think about this. He doesn't know if he cares. At the moment there is only the focus of every nerve in his erect penis — quite distinct, he feels, from the hidden chaos of her body. He feels warmth, a silken chamber. A sensation that would be unpleasant, perhaps, if he couldn't see her body curved above him, back arched, breasts rising smoothly from the corrugations of her ribs. The dimness of the room cancels her stretch marks, lending depth and shadow to the disheveled hair, the parted mouth, the eyes fluttering closed whenever her body trembles. Because of him. Because of what he can do to her.

He tried staying on top at first, but she shifted around and urged him onto his back only a minute after he entered her. He holds back his orgasm as long as he can because he senses her endurance, but then finally lets it go, looses it inside her, suddenly thankful for the condom, which releases him of obligations. Is it really sex if their insides never touch?

He tries to make conversation afterward because he knows women and men go opposite ways in the aftermath. But she hardly answers, so he lets himself fall asleep.

And then? He wakes the next morning with cold sunlight on his face and finds himself alone. This shouldn't be a surprise. It shouldn't make him upset. After all, this is humanity on the aggregate scale. This is what you want, this is what you get.

Monday morning. Spring break. An urge to renew and straighten. Logan loaded his old bicycle into the back of Dallas's car and dropped it off at the nearest shop, where a guy with dreadlocks and scraped knees promised to have it ready in a couple of days. By the time he came home Dallas was packing a suitcase. The expectation was for him to stand there and watch, so instead he went out to the backyard and set up a lawn-chair near the patch of desert he had established a couple of weeks earlier —the shovel and rake still leaning against the wall, the roll of plastic sheeting still propped against a tree. He peeled off his T-shirt and knitted his hands behind his head, studying pieces of rotten fruit on the ground as if they were runes. His future written in oranges and lemons. When Dallas started slamming around in the kitchen he knew she had seen him through the window. He waited. Doves were cooing in the branches overhead. Ants swarming over the broken and bleeding fruit.

The door slid open behind him. He didn't turn around.

"There you are," her voice said.

"Here I am."

"I'm going to visit my mother."

"Thanks for letting me know."

He heard her sandals rasping on the patio and waited for the sound of her feet coming through the grass, but it didn't happen. She was standing with her hands on her hips, watching the back of his head. He knew that. He knew a lot of things, he realized, without needing to see them.

"I'll be back in a week."

He didn't say anything. A hummingbird fractured the air above his head.

"Don't you want to know why I'm going?" she asked.

"Why are you going?"

"Midlife crisis."

Logan smiled. "Yours or hers?"

"Funny."

"I'm serious." She didn't seem to remember the night when, after a few glasses of wine, he had refuted the very notion of a midlife crisis—not the crisis, but the midlife part of it, which assumed that death would come at the traditional hour. The crisis, Logan argued, was much more continuous because it was pervasive and inextricable from the very act of living. If you don't know when your life is going to end, then any given moment—this one, for example—could be the middle, couldn't it?

"She's having boyfriend problems," Dallas said.

"I didn't know she had a boyfriend."

"She doesn't. That's the problem."

"All of a sudden? She hasn't had a steady boyfriend for a long time."

Silence. This wasn't part of the script. The excuse had probably seemed sturdy enough in whatever conversation she had rehearsed in her mind, but Logan was leaning on it now with some extra weight and it wasn't holding up.

"It's not . . ." She hesitated. "It's just that she . . ." Her tone shifted. "Look, do I have to spell it out for you?"

"Spell what out?"

"M-e-n-o-p-a-u-s-e."

Logan kept his hands clasped behind his head. There was a missing factor in this equation. He had come home from the conference Saturday evening to find her agitated and inconsolable. About? Nothing. She had summoned him, she said, because she simply wanted to see him. Was that such a bad thing? He couldn't say that it was. So they had stretched out on the couch together and watched TV. They had snuggled and kissed. He had ignored the reek of cigarettes on her breath and prepared himself for an onslaught of sex. Except the sex hadn't happened. Instead they had gone to bed at a reasonable hour, churned their separate ways through the night, and then wandered around the house the next morning with different parts of the Sunday newspaper. In the afternoon they had gone to a movie about a subtle conflict between a suburban couple that degenerated until it ended with a spasm of great violence. They hadn't discussed it afterward.

"It seems odd," Logan said, "that you haven't talked to your mother for a few weeks, but suddenly you're going to visit her."

"She called while you were gone. I know this is basically all of a sudden, and I know maybe you were planning for us to spend some time together this week because it's your spring break, but she needs me. She feels alone. I mean, really alone."

Logan pictured Dallas leaning against the table, casually picking at the shredded plastic along the edge. He could hear it in her tone. Making herself quiet and small, seeking sympathy. But for what. For what?

"What time is your flight?" he asked.

"I'm not flying."

Logan resisted the impulse to turn around. "Excuse me?"

"If I buy a ticket at the last minute," she continued, "it basically costs a fortune."

"So you're taking the car."

"I'm taking my car."

"What about me?"

She sighed. "Rent one. Buy one. Here's someone who already has a car but hasn't bothered to get it fixed, is what I'm thinking, so why is this my problem? Did I say you should abandon your car in the parking garage? Did I tell you to ignore it? One week, dear husband. You'll survive without me."

"What's the real reason for this trip?"

He could feel the impact behind him. Everything seemed to stop for an instant — the hummingbirds, the faint rush of traffic, the pulsing of the sky — before Dallas recovered and the world caught its breath again.

"What do you mean, 'the real reason'?"

"You've been acting strange."

"So that's what you think. That's what you think about me."

"I don't know what to think about you anymore."

"Then you haven't been paying attention." The plastic table scraped against the concrete as she pushed herself away from it. See? He had been right about the table.

He heard the door slide open. This was his last chance to see what she was wearing, to see her expression — to see, in fact, if the person back there corresponded with the image in his mind — but he didn't turn around. She'd catch him in the act and ruin whatever integrity he had left. Not that he hadn't already thought of pointing out whose paycheck was financing the car and consequently who should keep it even if the plane ticket was expensive. The car would have served as a type of ransom. She'd come back for it. But would she come back for him? That was what he wanted to know. And he wanted to know how he would feel about her choice.

A minute later he heard the rumble of the garage door and the car idling in the driveway. It lingered for a few seconds, then shifted and finally faded down the street.

Logan put on his shirt and went into the house.

For the next two days he stayed home and ate frozen food. He worked, he read, he wrote. He graded every scrap of paper his students had handed in to him and sketched out lecture notes from Marx all the way through to the post-Keynesians at the end of the semester, working in utter silence because all the best CDs seemed to be hers. He continued excavating the backyard, digging and cutting and spreading rocks. He cleaned his study and hallucinated the sound of her singing in the shower. He went for a walk along the canal with hot air roiling off the parched dirt, replaying all his mistakes with her, the moments when he should have said or done something different—the absences, the odd reactions, the words that cut in multiple directions the more he thought about them—and at one point he lingered on a footbridge and stared down into the water with his reflection silhouetted against the sky's bright abyss, surprised by how easily he dimpled the surface with his tears. His life was failing on both the personal and professional fronts. The debate with Dr. No, he realized, had been a defeat because the repercussions would come subtly, diffused throughout the Economics department, like an exotic form of torture. Death by a Thousand Budget Cuts. But even success had its hidden razor blades. Even if he worked hard, even if he straightened himself out and attained some measure of respectability, he would have to continue publishing articles and participating in committees so that he'd be in a better position to publish more articles and participate in more committees. It was like competing in a pie-eating contest in which the prize was more pie.

When he returned to the house he tried calling a couple of friends in Philadelphia. Silas and Zack. Both were gone. Both answering machines beeped a thousand times to let him know a thousand messages had been left ahead of his. And so he found himself sitting on the back patio with the cordless phone in his hand, the sun hidden behind his neighbor's rooftop, the yard entirely in shadow. He knew Keris's number simply by the pattern his thumb made as it crossed and recrossed the keypad. All those prime numbers. He needed to see her. Which meant, of course, that he shouldn't see her. Why? Because whatever he would say to her now would be the wrong thing. Because the evidence was irrefutable no matter where he looked. He had a knack for screwing up.

He heard a rustling in the bushes, a movement near one of the citrus trees. Puffy. Make that Fuzzy. His coat was thinning in the heat, refining itself, taking on its minimal and essential qualities. Logan went to the garage and retrieved one of the mangled packets, which, despite her tantrum, Dallas had neglected to throw away. Typical of her. Make a spectacle, leave a mess. To hell with whoever has to suffer because of it.

The whole process took about thirty seconds. Puffy ate the pellets as if they were raw sustenance and a gourmet meal at the same time. It must be nice, Logan thought, to live that way. It must be nice to obey only the pulse and muscle of your own body, your physical demands.

The following morning the bike shop called to tell him his bicycle was ready, and he was on his way out the door when the phone rang again. He waited. The answering machine kicked in. There had been a time, before message and identification devices, when a vague hope had come over him in such moments. The possibilities of a ringing phone. But now it was all premeditated. He would screen to see if he wanted to take the call, even though the most likely sound to come over the speaker would be a dial tone. Telemarketers didn't leave messages.

It was Keris's voice.

He walked into the kitchen. "No," he said to the machine. "I can't see you this week."

But then he picked up the phone.

Leave. Leave *now*.

This was how it went: Ill at ease and wide awake as she listened to Deck's steady breathing. When the man of the moment fell asleep Keris often found herself in this condition—alone, but not alone, and therefore lonely. Dissociated. A zero-valence feeling among the foreign silhouettes, the street noise, the sanitized scent of the hotel room. The mattress sagging beneath her. Every guest sat on this side of the bed to use the phone, so the impacts accumulated over time to form this crater, this dropping-off-the-edge-of-the-world contour. She was certain about it. She felt the cause as surely as she felt the effect.

Leave *now*. It was the demand of the situation. Or her own self-interest. Or both.

She slid from the bed and followed the trail of her clothing along the floor, picking up each item as she went. In moments like this she was always grateful for the condom because it prevented certain men from lingering after the pleasure was gone and she simply wanted to be herself again. She put on her underwear and stockings. As she was buttoning her blouse she looked over the room, at the low furniture caught in rectangles of streetlight, the bulbous lamps and television, the decorations that attempted to please everyone and therefore pleased no one. Deck's body nestled beneath the covers. He had been good — or, rather, skillful in all the right places. In fact, she could still feel his imprint within her, like a hat only recently removed. He was a man who knew his way around the female body. But . . .

She nearly lost her balance stepping into her pants. Something about his efficiency and precision and control, even at the very summit of pleasure when most men made faces and lost all sense of shame. At the bar she had detected something odd and pleasantly disjointed below his composure — someone, perhaps, who had studied philosophy in college and went through young adulthood in thrift-store clothing before finding a wife who had normalized him. Or something to that effect. But there wasn't a wife. No wedding ring on that finger and no tan line to suggest the recent presence of one. Instead she detected a subtle calculation in the way he kissed, in the movement of his eyes, in the planned interruptions of breath. Yes. Calculation. He was a person who thought love was a process of fitting Tab A into Slot B.

Leave now.

She reached for her shoes and felt an eddy of nausea. Her sinuses were beginning to ache. One too many margaritas. She steadied herself, checked her tags and zippers to make sure she wasn't wearing anything inside out, and then opened the door quietly, giving Deck a final glance as she stepped into the hall. She eased the door shut. She slipped into her shoes. She found the elevator, the parking garage, her car waiting in its space. She followed the avenues and streets. That was how it went.

The next morning she had an emergency session with her therapist, a woman named Maria who worked out of her house in Chandler and had helped Keris through her divorce by doing such extraordinary things as seeing her on a Sunday morning. They sat in a room filled with plants. A massage table stood in the center. One wall held shelves stocked with essential oils, another framed certificates from institutes certified in alternative medicine. Yes, she was that kind of therapist.

"So it was sex you wanted," Maria said, cradling a cup of tea in her hands.

"Yes. No. I wanted . . ."

Maria waited. She was a Hispanic woman in her fifties with graying hair and reading glasses that she always wore dangling by a chain around her neck. It gave her an air of great patience.

"I wanted the mode of being that accompanied the sex."

Maria smiled. "The fast track to intimacy."

"Yes. Sometimes it seems like the only way to know a man. To get through all the defenses."

"But he fell asleep immediately afterward and you felt cheated."

"Something like that. At the bar he described his childhood in California and his voice took on a vulnerability. I mentioned that I hardly knew the place despite living so close to it. OK, there was that time I tried rock-climbing at Joshua Tree and there was that weekend in Palm Springs with Will back when things were still good between us. But I have hardly been to the coast. The cities. I made a dismissive comment about smog and gangs and constipated freeways and he laughed so hard that he almost spilled his drink." She looked away, gazing at the leaves of a ficus tree next to her, barred sunlight coming through venetian blinds on the window.

"Keep going," Maria said.

"I expected more. But during sex, it seemed like he was participating in some kind of clinical study, and then he fell asleep afterward as if his mission had been accomplished. And I felt like . . . like here was another lover in a long succession of lovers. He already seemed anonymous to me. I felt like a stupid twenty-one-year-old again, wondering why . . ."

Maria sipped her tea and then set the empty mug down on the floor. "Why," she said, "you keep experiencing these periods of sexual misman-agement?"

Keris nodded.

"But there's nothing inherently wrong with a one-night stand, is there?"

"Of course not."

"What's his name again?"

"Logan. No. Sorry, it's Deck. His name is Deck." She did a slow smile and started laughing. "How obvious was that?"

Maria stood. "Somebody had to say it, and I'm glad it was you." She pat-ted the massage table with the flat of her hand.

Keris knew what this meant. She lay down on the table and closed her eyes. Reiki. Energy realignment. Chakra stimulation and healing. Maria placed her hands over the crown of Keris's head and began to concentrate. Keris felt a warmth, a slight tingling sensation. She tended to fade from the room when this happened — not sleeping, not awake, but with her con-sciousness blurred at the edges, lulled into a quasi–dream state with non-sensical visions flitting across her mind and then dissolving and resisting memory when she sat up afterward. This was necessary because there were certain things embedded in her and sometimes talking wasn't enough to clear them.

In the afternoon she herded Chow into the car and picked up Sophie from Charlotte's house. They stopped at a park on the way home and used the swingset together, riding side by side, perfectly coordinated until Keris slipped a little and scraped her hand on the chain and they drifted out of phase again. Sophie hardly noticed. Chow, running joyous and free beyond the picnic tables, was incapable of caring. Perhaps, Keris thought afterward, such injuries were necessary. Perhaps even the worst mistake was good if it yielded understanding. Perhaps you had to discover what was wrong in order to know what was right.

She spent Monday and Tuesday grading mid-term exams and responding to questions from a colleague about the microwave detectors on the satellite and trying, once again, not to worry about the trip down I-95 before it faced the hazards of the actual launch. She imagined herself describing these problems to Logan, phrasing her thoughts a certain way, linking one topic to another to create a certain shape to events, a certain meaning he might share. This was probably what she missed the most about being married. Someone to save her from the monopoly of her own mind.

So what was wrong, then, with having Logan as a friend? What was wrong with spending some platonic time together, like brother and sister? What was wrong with calling him to see if he wanted to join her for a hike? This was her thought, this was her feeling, as she left a message on his machine, at which point his real voice suddenly came over the line.

"You were screening," she said.

"Does that surprise you?"

"What surprises me is that you do it so blatantly."

"Well, it was a screen test, and you passed."

"I'll take that as a compliment." She walked across the living room, stretching the cord across the coffee table. "Would you believe," she said, "that my daughter's spring vacation is next week? The public schools refuse to coordinate their breaks with the university. This week I'm alone in the house. Next week I'll have to hire a babysitter. But anyway, I'm wondering if you'd like to join me for a hike tomorrow."

There was a pause at the other end of the line. "I'd love to. But I have a truckload of exams to grade. Not to mention revisions to the article."

"I understand," she said immediately — a little too immediately, she realized, glossing over his rejection so quickly that it emphasized her disappointment. "Maybe we'll see each other on campus next week."

"Friday," Logan said.

"I don't teach on Friday."

"I mean the day after tomorrow. If I get all the grading done, then I could go on the hike Friday. If that works for you."

Keris reran the sentence in her mind. Had she understood him correctly? "Of course," she said. "Of course that works for me. But I have to warn you that the drive takes several hours each way. We'll leave early and return late."

"Where are we going?"

"A secret place," she said.

"Low desert?"

"I like to think of it as middle desert. Not quite as hot."

"But still hot."

"Oh, come on, Logan. You're tough. You're simpatico with the sun."

"Is that what you meant last week? About the sunspot cycle, I mean. I still don't understand."

She reclined on the couch. "You probably know that the sun rotates, but since it isn't a solid body, the inner and outer layers rotate at different speeds, creating a shearing effect between them, which in turn generates magnetic fields among the electrically charged gases. As the layers continue moving, the fieldlines are stretched farther and farther until they finally snap like rubber bands, whipping outward and disrupting the flow of heat along the photosphere. Flares breach the surface, ejecting plasma and other types of charged particles toward Earth at about 800 miles per hour. Eventually these particles react with the magnetosphere and disrupt equipment of various kinds. I don't know how to tell you directly, so I am approaching it the only way I can."

"I'm getting a better idea."

"It isn't a big thing. It isn't full of meaning. I was simply making a point and perhaps I made it badly."

"We're always talking on the phone."

"We also talk in restaurants."

"And bars."

"A bar. Singular. And that was only for a few minutes last Saturday."

"What time do you want to leave for the hike?"

She told him.

"Ouch," he said. "That's when most people go to bed."

"There are people going to bed now, Logan. Don't worry about other people. Wake up early for a change. Walk in the sun. Do something you've never done before."

Logan walked in the sun. He followed the canal for a while and then made his way on various side streets, the neighborhoods silent and eerie, bathed in the radiation of high noon. So much for resolutions. It had been the disappointment in Keris's voice — the disappointment she had tried to conceal when he declined the invitation — that had broken him. And anyway this lapse should be put in its proper perspective. It was a hike. No big deal. It meant they were settling comfortably into friendship mode.

He emerged onto Rural Road and confronted its lunch-hour convulsions, its rattle and roll, its rising fumes. Some time later he finally reached the bike shop. He stepped inside, into the relief of cool air, and wiped his face on his T-shirt. The smell of fresh rubber. Bicycles suspended from the ceiling. A row of merchandise stretching all the way to the repair counter, where thrash music was playing on a tiny radio. He couldn't see who was there until he walked past a stack of helmets on display in the center aisle.

"Whoa," Ozzy said, looking up from the workbench. "A mirage!"

Logan shook his head. "I'm real."

"Then so am I." Ozzy smiled and shook hands with Logan across the counter, his arm tattooed with flames all the way up to the shoulder, even higher than Logan had realized. His shirt was stained with grease, frayed at the neckline. "Erin says you're letting her color outside the lines a little bit. She says you're dialed."

Logan wasn't sure what to say. "Erin's a good student."

Ozzy nodded slowly, scraping a blackened thumbnail against the stubble on his cheek. He seemed to be weighing something important in his mind. "I hope this doesn't phase you too much," he finally said, "but we started talking after that class."

"The class where I auctioned off the dollar."

"Thanks for not making me pay up, by the way. She sliced and diced me in front of everyone and I wanted to address the issue. You know? Like what's her problem." He looked away and started smiling.

Logan waited. This seemed to be the end of whatever he was saying.

"So," Ozzy said, snapping back. "What's your pleasure?"

"I dropped off my bike a few days ago."

Ozzy's eyes widened. "The purple passion? That's yours?" He went to a row of bikes behind the counter and pulled out one that Logan hardly recognized. It had fat-treaded tires, a taut chain, tight cables, a purple frame that gleamed. Ozzy leaned it against the counter. "Now *this*," he said, "has an opinion."

Logan leaned over and looked at the bike more carefully. "You know, I never wondered about this before, but where's the kickstand?"

Ozzy laughed as he worked the cash register. "Kickstand. That's good. And let's put some plastic tassels at the end of the handlebars. Your jokes come at me sideways, you know?" But when he saw the look on Logan's face his smile faded. "Oh. Hey. You're new to this whole thing, aren't you?"

Logan nodded.

"It's all about weight."

"But a kickstand weighs what, a pound?"

"A ton, compadre. A fucking ton. You don't want that monkey on your back. You've got Titan components, cro-mo frame. You're lean and mean. I don't even like gooing the tires, but you're going to catch some goatheads around here and spend half your life patching flats, so I took care of it for you."

Logan had about nineteen questions he wanted to ask. "Goo?"

"Liquid gunk. Squirt it inside the tube before you inflate. It coats the rubber, seals small punctures instantly." He tilted his head as if conceding a point. "Adds weight, though."

"How much weight?"

He shrugged. "A few raisins."

"That's nothing."

"Hey. Everything counts. Every snap, crackle, and pop works against you. You want to be as kinetic as possible." He was working the cash register again. The total appeared in green digits. "There's your damage. I have an idea for my paper."

Logan handed over his credit card. "Let's hear it."

"This is vacation, right? You probably don't really want to hear it right now. Besides, Erin said your office hours are prime time and she hasn't been wrong yet."

"You've been talking to Erin a lot."

Ozzy smiled as he filled out the credit slip. "We've got a yin-yang thing going on. She's a little bit country, I'm a little bit rock and roll." He swiveled the credit slip toward Logan. "You know?"

"Yeah," Logan said, signing the slip. "I know."

"All right, then." Ozzy stapled the receipts together and gestured at the refurbished bike. "Go hammer."

Logan rode back the same way he had walked. It felt awkward at first. He hadn't biked much in Philadelphia. Once or twice a year, maybe, his parents had pulled the bicycles out of their basement for a trip over to Fairmount Park—which, in fairness to Logan's parents, was all the way across town. They would ride past the art museum and follow the path along the Schuylkill under a high spread of trees, passing behind the boathouses before eventually crossing one of the bridges and coming back on West River

Drive because it was closed to traffic on the weekends. Those were the days of heavy frames and skinny tires, shockless forks, handlebars curling downward like ram's horns. The bar-ends on Logan's new bike, by contrast, slanted upward and forward at a forty-five-degree angle. The chain eased over the gears like silk. It weighed almost nothing. By the time he reached the canal he was feeling pretty good, so he decided to keep going toward the Salt River. He liked this sensation—the circulation and sweat, the steady pumping of his legs, the susurrations of his lungs. There was a fine layer of dust pasted to his skin. The membranes in his nose and mouth drying out.

Ozzy and Erin. He had to smile at that one. If he lost his job at the university he could advertise himself as an academic matchmaker. Discover love through debate. He could open a place called the Discord Café and have people sit down at different tables and argue until they found someone who really made their blood boil. What's your premise? Dispute here often? It would be suitable only for a Hollywood movie, where relationships founded on adversity were sustainable, where people magically overcame the deep incompatibilities that caused the arguments in the first place. And, well, he didn't want to be uncharitable to Ozzy, but wouldn't Erin get bored with him? He wouldn't be able to keep up with her. She'd have to move on.

He could always call Dallas at her mother's house. He could ask her to come back early. He could offer amnesty for whatever crimes she had committed and then, in turn, beg forgiveness for his own crimes after first begging her to tell him what those crimes were. Yes, this possibility had occurred to him. Let's drop the farce of the mother-daughter visit and discuss the real reason you left, OK? But he felt a resistance, almost a repugnance, toward making the gesture—and this wasn't a high school childishness at work here. He didn't mind being the one who called and pleaded. Was it because he needed time away from her? Did he need to contemplate the empty house, the wide bed, the silent shower? Or was he simply sinking into himself? Was he in deep meditation or deep denial?

He was biking near the river now, through a semi-industrial area with corrugated metal and paint-peeling walls on the buildings, cooling units whirring away. High-tension power lines loomed above him. There was some broken furniture by the banks, a couple of wrecked appliances that even the trash-pickers had passed over. And it was right about here that he began to feel weird. A little queasy and shaky. An odd wobble in the Earth beneath him. How long since his last sip of water?

He came to a halt under a palo verde and gazed out at the gravel riverbed, a giant basin with warped air rising, washing out his view of the freeway screaming on the other side. He took stock of his situation, trying not to count the millions of ways he had screwed up. He had walked to the bike shop without water, then biked all the way out here, and now his house was miles away. There weren't any convenience stores in the area. He thought about pounding on a stranger's door and begging for a drink, but he didn't see any homes either. In fact, he didn't see any signs of life at all. It was like being stranded on the moon.

He continued onward, inhaling a cloud of midge flies. They had hatched in the water. Over there. A bulbous yellow wall spanning the riverbanks. The Rio Salado Project. Untold tax revenues had been mobilized to line the dry riverbed with rubber and construct inflatable dams to hold the 1.7 billion gallons of water collected over a period of weeks. The developers had pitched it to the local citizens as a greenbelt in the making, an oasis within the oasis of Tempe itself—although recently the civic project seemed to be taking a decidedly commercial turn, focusing on development instead of parkland along the shoreline. This, of course, was long after voters had approved the tax bill funding the project. The planning and zoning commission had approved permits for three hotels and one shopping center. And the city, apparently, was planning to charge money to people who wanted to launch their boats on its precious waters. Dallas had mentioned going there on opening day and he had cringed inwardly at the thought of it, even though he knew why she was attracted to it. It reminded her of Vegas. It reminded her of home. One week, she had said. A mother-daughter visit. What else could it be?

Don't think, he thought. Pedal. Push. Move. You are alone in this hot, mad world.

He passed a security camera mounted on a pole, a guard in a plain brown uniform strolling the path. He saw a sign listing the regulations against swimming, fishing, feeding ducks, drinking alcohol. Inflatable boats or motorboats or inner tubes were prohibited. So was traveling against the clockwise traffic pattern of the lake. Only registered paddleboats and canoes were allowed, assuming they had paid the mandatory fee. Meanwhile, the girders of the first hotel were rising. And rising. And rising. Apparently nobody had mentioned that it was going to be sixteen stories high, blocking views of Papago Park. How could Dallas think this was normal, that this was the way things should be?

He finally found a convenience store and stumbled inside, stuck his head in the cooler for a few minutes, then bought a large bottle of water and a high-tech sports drink. He drank it in the shade of the store's overhang, watching life come and go in the parking lot. When he felt better he rode out to the concrete riverbank, following a path lined with saplings and transplanted creosote, irrigation hoses darkening the soil. He held his breath as he passed through more midge flies. A recent newspaper article had explained how the city would take care of the problem: Chemicals would be added to the water. Fish would be imported to eat the midge-fly larvae.

Logan stopped, laid down his bike, and looked over the dead water — fishless, plantless, a great big swimming pool where a river once ran. In times of personal doubt he tended to look outward for something concrete, something true. He lifted his head. He closed his eyes. The sun was seething above him with its grand passions, its continuous hydrogen-to-helium conversion, its fusion and fire. Was this the real thing? Was this the truth of the universe? Because the universe was experiencing runaway inflation and unemployment. It was heading for bankruptcy — or maybe, it could be argued, the Great Depression. A big bang had sent it outward, expanding its public and private sectors despite a plummeting Consumer Heat Index, and now it faced an inevitable downturn in the fourth quarter with sales far below expectations, supply and demand shifted too far apart to intersect, trapped in their own singularities. The universe would eventually succumb to the very spaces, the very absences and voids that allowed it to exist.

The sun converts 5 million tons of matter into energy every second, burning itself away. Why, then, doesn't it adopt a better mode of production? Why doesn't it renegotiate its contract with the orbiting planets? Why is the sun spending itself empty? What does it have to gain?

chapter 9

Love. Dallas could hardly feel it anymore. It was a radiance too weak to measure, like a star whose light reached her long after its source had died. She steered, she signaled, she shifted lanes. The road seemed to be full of East Coast tourists driving up to Sedona in rented convertibles with hair flying, shirts off, sunglasses firmly in place, enjoying the Wide Open Spaces and Laid-Back Western Lifestyle they had heard so much about. She got off the freeway just north of town and followed a caravan of boat-towers past Lake Pleasant, then crawled through downtown Wickenburg before reaching the empty road she knew and loved. Her entire life, it seemed, had been spent behind luxury cars and old pickups coughing along at half the speed limit. Make that her entire love life. Or sex life. Or both. People always seemed to say love when they meant sex and vice versa, which is something she probably should have said to Logan a long time ago. He seemed to have put up a firewall between them. The feeling was unmistakable. She wasn't going to hang around for that. No way. Meanwhile, she needed to secure a loan for all the debt she had run up at the slots, so why not do it on familiar territory? After exhausting her new credit card last Saturday and crying in the parking lot yet again, she had driven home and called him at the conference, ready to confess everything as soon as he came through the door. But the expectant look on his face had stopped her. An eagerness he was trying to pass off as concern. She had understood, then, why she couldn't tell him the truth. He wanted it for all the wrong reasons. He wanted her to reveal something terrible enough to give him an excuse to leave.

She was following the curves and cliffs of a two-lane highway now, white crosses staked into the hillsides and trussed with flowers in memory of dearly departed motorists. After a while the road straightened out and she hit a spread of anonymous desert—dirty gold hills, saguaros, thorny scrub, some battered trailers in the distance. Hard to believe anyone could be happy in those metal shoeboxes. She had gone to high school with kids bussed in from the rural wastelands, and they had tried so hard to look sub-urban and blend in that it was basically excruciating to watch if you had a heart. They went home to scuttled vehicles and propane tanks in the front yard. If you could call that a yard. Say what you want about Dad, at least he had paid the child support every month so she and Mom could keep their tract house in a neighborhood as good as anyone else's.

She turned the music up. She turned it down. She turned it off. Wind-shush and engine-thrum filled the car, the wheels rock-solid on the road. It was time to devise a strategy. There were people she needed to see in Vegas. Friends. Acquaintances. A certain net result, is what she was thinking, to pay off the debt. And to be perfectly honest, she missed those old circles. She hadn't really spoken to anyone since moving in with Logan. She wanted to reconnect.

She hit Interstate 40 and drove through a bland sprawl called Kingman before swinging north again, the pale emptiness of the Mojave taking shape around her. It was familiar, so deeply familiar — the naked soil, the yucca stalks rising from their bladed nests, sprigs of creosote growing like weeds through cracked pavement. Rough-cut mountains in the distance. The high noon of a homecoming. She passed an abandoned gas station with blistered placards banging in the breeze, prices twenty years out of date. A sign for a town with the alluring name of Chloride. Guess what's in the groundwater.

An hour later the road began to snake down toward Hoover Dam, the double lanes collapsing into a conga line of RVs and eighteen-wheelers that had slowed to a walking pace by the time she passed the first pack of tourists gawking at the dam like it was the Eiffel Tower or something. She had come out here on who knew how many field trips during grade school and junior high and to be perfectly honest she just didn't experience the awe or grandeur, never mind her family history, the pride she was supposed to feel about having a grandfather who had worked as a high-scaler during the dam's construction in the early thirties. One Sunday afternoon at the nurs-ing home, in the full ecstasy of dementia, he had raved about the heat radi-ating from the canyon walls, the boulders breaking away, the cables snapping, a co-worker plummeting 600 feet and blowing apart against the cliffs. Block 16 eased the pain, he had said with a smile. And afterward, in the car, ten-year-old Dallas had asked her mother what Block 16 was.

"The red light district," Mom had shot back, as if Dallas had been pester-ing her with stupid questions all day. "What did you think it was, church?"

She finally crossed the top of the dam — ground zero, in other words, of the tourist zone, where pedestrians swarmed with their cameras and silly hats, their strollers and smiles, leaning foolishly over the railings to view the Colorado. Then the road began climbing again, eventually opening up to two lanes, and she nearly stood on the gas pedal until she hit Boulder City. She felt a great magnetism in the distance, attracting the iron in her soul.

She had tried explaining to Logan how it could be home and Vegas at the same time, but he had misunderstood. Separate but equal? he had asked, raising his eyebrows. No, she had replied. Together but different, like us. That had shut him up. It was like trying to explain the sky to a child. She could list all the contradictions. She could point out that prostitution was legal everywhere in Nevada except Clark County. She could tell him about her Mormon bosses at the casino. She could mention the atomic bomb tests treated like a spectator sport in the 1950s. But these were simple facts that didn't capture what it was like to grow up a few miles away from the Strip thinking it was normal, the downtown that came with every city, until you became old enough to work there and suddenly it was like wearing your favorite sweater inside out and backward. But that was the way with a lot of things, wasn't it? Love. Marriage. Everything.

One time Dad had stood with her in the driveway and pointed to a column of smoke on the horizon. This was a random memory. A November morning when she was, what, eleven years old? She hardly ever thought about Dad anymore. Well, anyway, it was back in the pre-affair days, when he had still paid attention to her. And who knew why Dad wasn't at work that morning, but there they were, just the two of them, listening to the layered cries of fire trucks while smoke rose and spread into a stratus cloud above the Strip. For a while they tried to guess which casino was burning. Then he started reminiscing about the atomic bomb tests when he was her age. The nearly identical shape in the sky, he said. The flash of light, the rumble underfoot, the green auroras at night with mushroom clouds rising to 50,000 feet, salting the great plains with cancer. Everyone claimed it was harmless at the time.

The *Las Vegas Sun* joked about man-made "earthquakes" and told its readers how to protect their collectibles from the dust. Hotels organized picnics on the hills outside town so guests could watch the explosions while they enjoyed a special mix of vodka, brandy, champagne, and sherry known as the Atomic Cocktail. The fifties were always described as innocent, but perhaps it was simply a case of playing dumb. Why else would doctors recommend particular brands of cigarettes? Why else would miners use uranium dust as fertilizer, the chunks of spare ore as doorstops? The cosmic dictionary contained an entry for human nature that ran as follows: Act first, consider the consequences later.

Halfway through Henderson the freeway widened and ran alongside some walled-in subdivisions, wood frames visible in the newer sections with pantiles stacked on tarpaper roofs. She passed cement mixers in motion. Palm trees gagged and bound on the back of flatbed trailers, bulldozers chained down like King Kong. And finally—*finally* the road crested and gave her a view of the valley: the smoggy backwash in the distance with the pyramid, the tower, the rebus shapes of the New York and Paris skylines. She tuned in her favorite radio station and turned it up loud. She sang, she beat time against the wheel, she resisted an urge to head for the Strip immediately and let the reunions commence. She needed to visit Mom and get it out of the way. Despite the emotional burden, it was a free place to stay and Dallas needed it right now. She took the usual exit, the usual turn, the usual sequence of traffic lights on the avenue only half-familiar now because so many of the stores had changed in her absence, a world of eternal openings and closings, the same places marked with different signs.

Logan has lost her in Edinburgh. Old Town. The stone turrets and towers. The twisted streets. The rubber-throated roar of traffic over cobblestones. But eventually he finds her again on the Royal Mile, unmistakable in her cocktail dress and high heels. On the arm of another man. He knew it. He fucking knew it. Coming up behind her, he still can't see her face, but he recognizes those freckled shoulders exposed by the cut of her dress, the cherrywood hair upswept and elegantly arranged. It's her all right. He steps into the reversed traffic before he realizes his mistake and turns to find a black cab bearing down on him, and suddenly he is awake and staring at the wall of his bedroom. He lies there for a minute, heart hammering. He rolls over and stretches his arm across the empty bed. Morning stillness. Windows gray with pre-dawn light. Sometimes the force of his own dreams astonishes him. Dallas with another man. That part is obvious. But the rest of it? Edinburgh. The Royal Mile. Memories from his post-college trip more than a decade ago.

It had been the usual backpack affair through Europe, except he had done it alone and destitute—alone because he had wanted to roam without negotiations or compromise, and destitute because his parents had refused to support such a frivolous trip. As a result, what he had imagined as a summer of adventure turned into a purgatory of wandering foreign streets with his backpack, hollowed out with hunger, dragging himself through expensive museums. But it's important to start at the beginning: He landed in London and endured its prices for a few days before hitchhiking to Edinburgh. How did it go? The anonymous roundabouts and road junctions, the occasional salvation of lorry drivers. Finally an old Scottish couple returning from a visit to their daughter in Leeds. During this last ride he fell asleep with his cheek resting against the window and woke several hours later to a climate transformed — black sky, spitting rain, houses clustered beside the road with their slate roofs gleaming like tortoise shells. He was dropped off near the train station on Waverley Bridge, sunk in the middle of the city with the castle's ramparts and the buildings of Old Town ranged high above him, the medieval facades layered, overlapping, reluctant to show where one ended and the next one began. Gray stone full of nuance and deep grime, caramelized by the elements. He walked along the edge of the Princes Street Gardens. Uphill. Into the wind. He heard bagpipes skirling somewhere, and as he approached the hostel he saw the player, foot tapping, back arched, face half-lifted to the sky like a jazz trumpeter. Logan threw twenty pence into the man's basket. And he thought, goddamn. I'm here. And that was when he admitted to himself that he had a mission. It was to find Adam Smith's grave.

He read the guide book's instructions and followed the Royal Mile downhill, past the tartan shops and overexposed pubs until he reached Canongate Kirk. The grounds were walled off, the headstones mossed over and protruding from the soil like the nubs of dinosaur bones. Most of the inscriptions were blurred. He wandered down a slope. He wandered up it again. The sound of traffic, busses, machinery radiating from the city around him. He glanced over his shoulder at Calton Hill with its cylindrical tower and what looked like a scaled-down version of the Parthenon. Wrong direction. Closer to the street. In the corner. It was like searching for a sore muscle in his leg.

He found a wall with a tombstone built into it, an iron fence projecting outward and enclosing a rectangular space. The entire plot had a stone base or pedestal, filled with crushed rock. The gate was open. He stepped up. "Here," the inscription declared, "are deposited the remains of Adam Smith, Author of The Theory of Moral Sentiments and Wealth of Nations. He was born 5th June 1723, and he died 17th July 1790." That was it. Plain and simple. No prayers, no biblical quotations, no last-minute ass-kissing before the gates of heaven. The man had simply ceased to exist. Logan nodded. He had started college as an Episcopalian and ended it as a pseudo-Buddhist. But even that belief had been dissolving lately. A fantasy. He admitted it to himself now. The truth was that he didn't believe in a coherent afterlife. He glanced at the headstones bristling with crosses, the plain steeples of Canongate Kirk. It must be nice, he thought bitterly, to take comfort in that fairy tale. Santa Claus writ large.

He looked up and saw a platform of sunshafted clouds in the distance, black-bellied cumulus heaving overhead.

"If you exist," he said, "give me a sign."

The sun rifted through a seam in the clouds and lit the graveyard for a moment, igniting the grass to a bright lime, the moss on the stones to an emerald sheen.

He smiled. "Sorry. Not good enough. I meant something like curing disease or wiping out hunger. If you were omniscient, you would have known that. And you would have done something about it instead of playing parlor tricks." He shook his head. "Not good enough."

The wind blew his jacket open. He zipped it up and folded his arms across his chest. He shivered. He hadn't eaten since London. He looked over at the tombstone again, where a few pennies had been placed on the sill as offerings. Like it was a wishing well. Logan picked them up — not for the money, but to cancel the false tribute, the tokens of well-fed American tourists who claimed Smith's philosophy as their own. Or maybe it would be more accurate to say, claimed their philosophy as his. That, he supposed, was the advantage of reading columns in the business section instead of Smith's books.

Logan left the churchyard and walked uphill until he found a pub, settling down with a pint of dark ale, which had an astonishing effect on his empty stomach. It felt like a heavy-duty hallucinogenic. He drank a few more, slurred his way through a conversation with an Australian he recognized from the hostel where he was staying, and then sampled all the stouts, pretending the prices didn't matter. Some time later he was threading his way through an alley that was either a wynd or a close or maybe just a cobbled courtyard — here, admittedly, the memory is hazy — when a faint nausea mushroomed into full-blown sickness and he found himself on his hands and knees vomiting. Then he crawled away and lay on his back for a while, staring at an archway, black pipes running up the side of a building. There was someone standing over him now. The Australian. He was lifted up. He was floating. Not good enough, he thought. Not good enough. Then he was draped over a toilet in the hostel, his insides exploding.

He woke the next morning with a headache beyond his ability to measure, a jam of neck muscles, blue pressure in his sinuses. This wasn't a hangover. It was a virus. The manager of the hostel brought him bread and bottled water. On the third day a couple of hard-boiled eggs. And he could feel the slow shift of the days continuing out there, sunlight framed in a burning window, the sound of foreign sirens seesawing in the streets like his own delirium, bagpipes bleating, rising and falling along with the melody of his thoughts. His head and neck packed so brightly with pain. He dreamed of finding a guillotine and using it on himself. He dreamed he could feel the universe expanding, the music of the spheres giving way to cold silence, and he tried to scream for help but nothing came from his lungs. Not good enough.

He wakes again. Arizona. His alarm screaming like a prehistoric bird. He reaches out and hits it. He closes his eyes. He opens them. The hike. Keris. She's going to pick him up in twenty minutes. He hauls himself up to a sitting position at the edge of the bed and tries to shake off the grogginess. Now here's something absurd. In the patchwork of stories he and Dallas shared during their time together, he has never mentioned Edinburgh. A mistake. A terrible mistake. How else could he expect her to know him? How else would she understand who he is?

She passed off the visit as a vacation. Logan was fine. Life in Phoenix was fine. They sat at the kitchen table together, sharing a pack of cigarettes as Mom reeled off the woes of the middle-aged dating scene and the insurance agency where she worked. She brought up Dallas's father again, like she always did, a so-called distant memory that came around with the regularity of an unclaimed suitcase on a baggage carousel. Make that an emotional-baggage carousel. But the worst thing, in Dallas's opinion, was hearing about these men Mom dated — and yes, Dallas had met a couple of them — who drove convertibles with vanity plates and wore sportcoats in July. Men who had emerged from the ruins of previous marriages seeking renewal not in love but in love affairs. Obviously, obviously, obviously. How could Mom possibly think these relationships would lead anywhere? But anyway Dallas listened, she nodded, she smoked. Mom had a date that very evening, as it turned out, so she disappeared into the bathroom and eventually came out painted and plumed, permed to the hilt. Dallas tried not to sigh. During the last few years Mom had gradually crossed that barrier in which sexual attraction gave way to pageantry. Instead of looking seductive, she looked as if she had spent an hour on her face — and that, apparently, was the goal.

The next day Dallas tried to call Lucinda, her old comrade-in-arms, but discovered that the number was disconnected and no new listing was available through directory assistance. She drove to the casino where Lucinda worked. Major expansion was in progress, jackhammers going full throttle by the craps tables, and it was only by shouting a few questions to one of the pit bosses that she learned Lucinda had quit eight months earlier. And that, quite frankly, would have been the end of it if Dallas hadn't run into one of Lucinda's catty friends on her way out the door — a woman Dallas didn't like at all — who said Lucinda was working as a hostess at a high-end restaurant across town.

Dallas drove over to the restaurant that evening, smiling at the memory of their desperate days when they would write checks to each other from their overdrawn accounts, cash them simultaneously, and then hit the slot machines with the hope of generating enough winnings to rise above and beyond the debts they had just created. Partners in crime. They would sit side by side at the machines cheering each other on, drinking and smoking and laughing recklessly. Why hadn't she kept in touch with Lucinda?

Dallas entered the hush of the candlelit restaurant. There were skylights, a grand piano, black-tied servers. Vegas's premier refuge from the din of slot machines. And there was Lucinda, standing at the hostess's podium looking healthy, looking well rested, and looking . . . well, looking about five months' pregnant. When she saw Dallas her expression flickered for a moment and then resolved itself into a smile. There was something about it Dallas didn't like. Halfway through the conversation she realized what it was: The look of someone recovering from an unwelcome sight. A reformed criminal facing a ghost from her past.

Lucinda never stepped away from the podium. Glad to see Dallas. Glad to hear about the marriage and marvelous new life in Phoenix. And actually she was busy these next few days so she couldn't go out, and yes, her due date was in September so she was avoiding smoky places and alcohol anyway. She lived with her new husband in a subdivision outside town. A loan? Well. She wished she could. She really did. But with the baby on the way she simply didn't have any money to lend. Surely Dallas understood. Best of luck. Let's keep in touch.

Dallas was about to say something else when an elderly couple came through the door and drew Lucinda's attention away. Dallas felt herself fading from the room. She turned and went outside. She walked out to her car with her face burning. Let's keep in touch? As she started the engine the air-conditioning hit her full blast in the face. A few tears spilled from her eyes before she managed to get hold of herself. No. Don't crumble. Stay focused. If Lucinda wanted to live in denial, that was her problem. Dallas drove to the nearest bar and made a list of names on a cocktail napkin — a hierarchy of those most likely to lend her money—and the next day started tracking them down through their various career changes, their serial addresses, their marriages and divorces, their burned bridges with landlords and shift managers that would have thwarted most detectives, in her opinion.

She saw six people during the next few days. They all treated her with a cheerful indifference, reacting to her loan requests with claims that their spirits were willing but their wallets were weak. She worked her way down the list. She added names to the bottom. In a moment of weakness she even considered asking Mom, who couldn't afford to buy the dresses she circled in the mail-order catalogs, for crying out loud, so scratch that. The furthest she could go was Lorenzo—blond, suave, big-boned Lorenzo, a Texan with a sing-song voice who knew everything about everybody. She had dated him once or twice, to use the term loosely, when he had worked the taxi stand at the casino, because he had pursued her fervently and she had finally decided that having sex with him was easier than not having sex with him, to be perfectly honest. She had regretted it immediately afterward. They were lying there, still linked, when he had joked about stealing a road sign for her headboard that said "Now Entering Dallas." It was like he had flipped a switch. She remembered chasing him out of her apartment, flinging his shoes at him as he hobbled down the stairs with one leg of his pants trailing. He had apologized afterward with flowers and a serenade on her answering machine, but had finally backed off when she took up with Felix, who informed Lorenzo about the new status quo in the parking lot one night. Lorenzo had smiled at her after that, winked to let her know his feelings hadn't changed, but kept his distance.

Someone had mentioned that Lorenzo worked the second shift at Venice, so the next afternoon she napped, showered, applied the proper shades of makeup, and basically prepared herself for an evening on the front lines—short skirt, tight blouse, high heels and stockings. It was the kind of outfit that kept her spirits up.

It was dusk, the day's heat nearly dissolved by the time she left her mother's house. She could see the Strip's perpetual glare in the distance. The moon rising, almost full, with the slim shadow of a sickle blade along its rim. She took the back route near the railroad tracks and cut through a couple of parking lots to avoid the worst of the traffic, then parked near some floodlit fountains. She knew this place. She had applied for a position a few years back, aspiring to the artwork and pasta restaurants, the indoor canals, the Italian sky projected onto domed ceilings. Not that any of it mattered to Lorenzo. He chose his employment based on the quality of the taxi stand, hardly ever venturing inside. Dallas stood by the entrance and watched him for a few minutes, dressed in a gondolier's uniform of black T-shirt, shorts, wide-brimmed hat with a long red ribbon. He sang along with the arias coming from the speakers as he opened taxi doors and ushered passengers in with a flourish, nonchalantly pocketing his tips. The crowd behind the velvet ropes had the usual feel — thrumming, bustling, thrilled to be participating in Vegas's high-performance nightlife — and for a moment she felt a pang for Logan's presence at her side. His underlying confidence in situations like this. The comfort of his hand as they entered a crowded area.

She walked out to the curb alone.

"My Dallas," Lorenzo said when he saw her, spreading his arms wide, "my el paso, my fort of worth."

She forced a smile. "How have you been?"

"As the Swedish say, *Alska mig alltid, eller jag biter Dig i strupen sa att Du da.* Love me forever, or I'll bite your throat until you're dead." He did a Fred Astaire backstep, opened a door, and palmed a couple of bills before shutting it again.

"I saw Lucinda yesterday," Dallas said.

"May she rest in peace."

"You know about her?"

"I know that place where she works. The head chef quit last month and now it's coasting on its reputation. In fact," he said, opening the next door, "I know a much better restaurant on the other side of Highway 91. Wait, did I say restaurant? I meant paradise. First class. Worthy of an elegant woman such as yourself."

Dallas held up her hand and showed him the wedding ring. "Not that I don't appreciate it, Lorenzo, but —"

He stopped in mid-stride and stared at it. "So he finally did it."

"What?"

"I didn't think Felix had it in him. No offense." Another cab pulled up and he reached for the door.

Dallas fixed her gaze on him. "You think I'm married to *Felix*?"

The cab pulled away. Lorenzo planted his feet, thumbed back his hat like a cowboy, and gave her a wide, sunny smile. She remembered, then, why she had reacted so violently to that joke about the road sign. It wasn't the bad humor so much as the delivery — the con man's smirk floating up to the surface and souring the previous compliments, making you feel like a sucker for believing them.

"I just wanted to see your reaction," he said, then pirouetted toward the next cab. "After all, his wife booted him because of you."

"What? Is that a joke?"

He looked at her as he shut the door, stuffing a bill into his pocket. "You didn't know?"

"Come on, Lorenzo."

"These are true-blue words I'm speaking. Felix has been on his own ever since you left town. That was quite a disappearing act you pulled, by the way."

She felt a slow wave of vindication rising through her, threatening to light up her face. But she stopped it. It was important to look sympathetic, concerned. "Because of me?"

"That's the word on the street. The suspect's wife allegedly noticed a hickey on one of his more exclusive neighborhoods, so to speak, and five minutes later his clothes were scattered on the front lawn."

She looked toward the ribbed columns of the portico, the fountains flaring with silver spray. It made sense. Their last rendezvous had turned nasty at the end. She had bitten him. He had shoved her against the wall. She blinked, shutting down the memory. She looked back at Lorenzo. Stay focused.

He was singing again, smiling at the trio of young women he was helping into a cab.

"I'm looking for a few people," Dallas said.

"Such aaaaaaaaas?" he sang, drawing out the vowels to match the aria playing overhead.

"Brett."

"Reno," he answered.

"Maria?"

"L.A."

"What about Liz?"

"She has a beautiful room," he said, gliding over to the next taxi, "at a rehab center in Prescott, Arizona."

"All right, then, where the hell is Lou? I remember when they promoted him to craps and he was excited about the . . ."

Lorenzo was shaking his head and clucking his tongue.

"What?"

"Fired. Blacklisted. Apparently someone was helicoptering the dice right in front of him and, number one, he totally missed it, number two, he overpaid the guy's bet. I love your eyes. If you didn't have a husband I'd drop to my knees right here and beg you to marry me."

A vacant disbelief was washing over her. "What happened to everybody?"

Lorenzo patted the roof of the next taxi and sent it on its way. "You can't step in the same Vegas twice. I'd lend you the money myself if I didn't have my own assets in the frying pan right now."

She shot him a look. "Who says I need money?"

"It's practically in the newspaper. You came to town a couple of days ago trying to shake everyone down."

A prickly heat rose to her face and she was about to say something in response when Lorenzo's expression shifted.

"I have the same problem," he said.

She searched his face, looking for signs of insincerity. "You mean, slots?"

"Sports."

"How deep?"

He shut the door of the next cab, took a few steps toward her, and murmured the amount.

She almost laughed. "I wish mine were that low."

"There ought to be a law that tells you when to stop. You know?" He smiled—not the con man's smile this time, but the pained grin she had seen at the blackjack table when players stood up with empty pockets, trying to convince themselves that the losses were worth it. "Maybe I should switch to poker. Then all you have to do is follow the golden rule: If you sit down at the table and can't pick out the sucker, it's you."

Keris was right on time. Logan came outside with the sun still concealed behind the rooftops and the scent of damp lawns in the air, sprinklers hissing in the final stages of their automatic cycles. Puffy emerged from the bushes and looked up at Logan like he expected to come along.

"Sorry, pal," Logan said. "You'd fry out there."

Keris was sitting behind the wheel wearing sunglasses, a faded green tank top, and gray athletic shorts. Something was different about her, but he couldn't say what it was. As he set down his daypack on the seat behind him he noticed a pair of hiking boots on the floor with socks stuffed into them.

"Is that your cat?" she asked, backing out of the driveway.

"Puffy. He's a stray."

She turned to Logan with a wide-eyed expression behind her shades. "You haven't adopted him?"

"It's a long story."

"He's a beautiful cat."

"I know."

"It is clear that Puffy loves you, Logan. Adopt Puffy. Share your life with Puffy."

"Tell me where we're going."

Keris took a breath. "We're going to a national forest approximately the size of Rhode Island. Elevation 4,000 to 4,700 feet. High Sonoran Desert. Native flora include agave, lupine, Fairy-duster, cholla, cottonwood, mesquite, saguaro, and prickly pear. Fauna most commonly seen this time of year are warblers, hooded orioles, hummingbirds, several species of hawk, and turkey vultures. I should also mention bobcats and mountain lions."

He poked her with his index finger. "Is there a CD-ROM in there?"

"It's dangerous to tickle the driver while traveling at a high rate of speed," she said, trying not to laugh. "You're also undercutting my highly scientific and objective tone."

"How much coffee did you drink this morning?"

"I'm excited for open air and the crunch of gravel under my boots. I want the smell of cacti. I want the sky. I want the mountains looming peacefully ahead of me."

"You're stir-crazy."

"Correct."

They were driving south on the freeway, near a complex of malls and car dealerships with multicolored banners suspended from lightpoles. As the sun broke over the horizon, Logan could feel the change coming into everything — the glass, the stucco, the plains of concrete and chrome. Subdivisions with terra-cotta rooftops blushing in first light. They seemed to be traveling backward in time, the houses becoming younger and younger until they passed unborn neighborhoods with stacked lumber and dumptrucks full of gravel, bulldozers sleeping in sections of mauled earth. He was trying not to look at Keris too much. What was different about her? Hairstyle, clothing?

As the subdivisions tapered off to empty interstate, his eyes relaxed into the low hills and saguaro. They passed farms with irrigation pipes stretched across the fields, a few towns where entire livelihoods seemed to be staked on the commerce of highway exits. They passed Picacho Peak. And then Tucson. Compared to Phoenix it appeared suddenly, buildings and signs sprouting up next to the highway, and Keris started talking about it, eventually pointing in the direction of her old neighborhood. She told him about her parents. She told him about her sisters. She told him about her ex-husband, about his affair with the graduate student and the sudden termination of their marriage. Logan was silent for a minute after she finished. Tucson had disappeared and the landscape had reverted to simple desert again. "It was a relief," he finally said.

"The divorce?"

"The affair. I mean, what the affair revealed about him."

There was a long pause. "Yes. I guess you could state it that way."

"You sensed something kicking around inside him. Something bad. Something inevitable. But you didn't know what it was until he finally did it, and then it was a relief to have it revealed, even if the marriage ended because of it."

"How do you know this?"

"I'm inferring. Deducing. Tell me if I'm wrong."

"You're correct. But there's one more thing."

"What?"

"That marriage was the best mistake I ever made."

"You mean, you don't regret it?"

"No."

Logan took this in slowly. "Fair enough," he said.

Keris lowered her chin and peered over the frames of her sunglasses. "Something is happening up there."

Logan looked ahead. They had come up behind a truck towing a horse-trailer, a pair of brown rear ends swaying with the rhythm of the road. And yes indeed, something was happening. The anus on the left was opening up and releasing a large hunk of dung that exploded into a cloud of green hay as it hit the pavement.

"Look out!" Logan shouted.

Bits of manure rushed over the car. Keris started laughing. A sharp and murky smell came through the vents.

"Shut off the air!" he yelled, leaning over and fumbling with the switches. "Which one is it?"

Keris was laughing too hard to answer. The horse released another grenade, and then another, bursting into gales of confetti.

"Slow down!" Logan cried. "Back off!"

She shook her head and gestured behind her. He looked back. An eighteen-wheeler was there, and a large van was on their left, preventing them from changing lanes.

"We're trapped in a shit-storm! Oh, what a horrible way to die."

A tear streamed down Keris's cheek. "Stop," she managed to say. "Please, stop."

He clasped his hands together and begged the heavens for a swift and painless death amid the feces suffocation. He prayed for the anus to close. Hi-ho, Silver, away. Keris began to swat him with her free hand—cut it out, she said, or she would crash—her voice pinched, weak with laughter, until the assault finally ended and the air cleared and the smell dissipated. Keris wiped away her tears. Logan sat with the back of his hand pressed to his forehead in mock distress.

"Are we there yet?"

"Don't be so teleological," she said.

They turned off the highway and passed a strip of convenience stores before finally hitting a gravel road—rutted, washboarded, loose rocks thunking against the underside of the car. There was a fringe of barbed wire on either side and, beyond it, cows dispersed among emaciated scrub, heads down, tails swishing. After a few miles they crossed a cattle guard where Logan saw a stable and a corral and stacked bales of hay, a house with a satellite dish on the roof. Then more cows, more barbed wire. Another house and stable. The pattern repeated a couple more times before they ran over a final cattle guard and entered a thicket of cacti and chaparral. They dipped through a wash, then continued on into the foothills. At one point Logan saw some all-terrain vehicles, like oversized tricycles, parked in one of the turn-offs, a couple of coolers on the ground, men dressed in fatigues shooting empty beer bottles with handguns.

"I'm sure they'll clean up the broken glass afterward," Logan said.

"Are you kidding?"

"East Coast irony," he said. "Here's another example. Honey, can you run to the store and pick up some milk?"

"A reference to the long drive on this road."

"Exactly."

"But that's what makes it beautiful."

They came to a gate with a sign that said they were entering a privately owned nature preserve.

"Are we breaking the law?" he asked.

She didn't answer. She parked in a small gravel lot with four or five other cars. There was a shallow creek nearby, a single-level adobe house, and a wide path leading uphill to a line of other adobe buildings that Keris called *casitas*—a fancy Spanish word for cabins connected by a few common walls and arranged, mission style, into a square. Sycamore trees loomed overhead. The slopes were studded with cacti, a few ancient saguaros branched skyward, their stalks arranged like moose antlers.

He followed Keris into the house, which turned out to be a visitor center with books and videos for sale, a large desk where a woman wearing a flannel shirt was typing at a computer. She looked at them over a set of bifocals and smiled, welcomed them, asked them to sign in. She handed them a map. She pointed them toward the trailhead.

Back at the car Keris was lacing up her boots when she glanced over at him. "Where are yours?"

"My what?"

"Your hiking boots."

He looked down at his sneakers. "These aren't good enough?"

"Lucky for you I have a blister kit."

She took off her sunglasses and put them in the glove compartment before closing up the car.

"What about you?" he said, looking at her and realizing, stupidly, what was so different about her appearance. "You're not even wearing your glasses. You're going to lead us straight off a cliff."

She batted her eyelashes and smiled. "Contact lenses."

They put on their baseball caps, shouldered their daypacks, and started walking.

She resisted it for a while. She drove up and down the Strip, sitting numbly at the ten-minute traffic lights and ignoring the tourists who fancied themselves gamblers in the city of light. She smoked. She played the radio. She wandered the avenues through the bland retail districts. She even tried to kill some time at a bar, but left without finishing her drink because a man came over and started hitting on her and she didn't have the energy to fend him off.

The guitar stood as always, multicolored, golden-necked, its Olympian proportions gleaming. She almost parked in the employee section by mistake. She sat there with the engine off and heat slowly creeping into the car, watching the clock on the dashboard. When it reached a certain number she checked her makeup in the rearview mirror. She climbed out, adjusted her skirt, and walked over to the entrance where the music was pumping, cabs inching toward the crowd massed behind the velvet ropes. Dallas passed through the golden doors. She entered the familiar space of the casino — the old weather and light, the slots ringing their eternal song. She deliberately narrowed her focus as she walked, trying not to let nostalgia or the force of the place penetrate her. Basically it was tunnel vision, otherwise she wouldn't be able to keep her cool as she walked by Felix's station. She didn't even glance at him. She wove her way past the craps games, the blackjack tables deprived of her presence, if such a judgment is allowed, and finally sat down at the bar.

Twenty minutes later Felix was sitting on the stool next to her. He faced straight ahead, as if studying the bottles on the glass shelves. It was midnight. His shift was over. The timing of her arrival wasn't a coincidence. They both knew it.

"As a former employee," he said, "you could get in trouble for failing to notify security that you're on the floor."

"And you could get in trouble for failing to report me."

Felix caught the bartender's attention and ordered a drink for himself, a refill for Dallas.

"He's new," she said, watching the bartender walk away.

"Everybody's new. Surveillance is probably watching me right now, but they're third shift. They won't recognize you. Pretend I'm a stranger who just said something interesting."

"The stranger part I can pretend. But interesting?" She swiveled toward him and was so surprised that she nearly forgot what she was going to say next. He was bald. His scalp was marble-smooth. And to be perfectly honest, she felt an urge to touch it right then and there. Not many men could pull it off, but it worked for him. It really worked. He had talked about shaving his head all the time, like a kid saying he wants to be an astronaut someday, and finally here it was. Maybe getting kicked out of his marriage was the kind of liberation he needed.

"What brings you back?" he said.

"This is home," she said, lighting a cigarette. "Do I need an excuse?"

The bartender set down their drinks. She pushed her empty glass aside and took up the new one. "And anyway I like to drop in on friends without warning. It's the only way to get the real story." She exhaled and watched him through the smoke.

He lowered his eyes. "You heard about me and Sharon."

She mustered as much sympathy into her voice as she could. "I'm sorry."

"No, you're not. But that's all right. I deserved it. I just wish I could see my son once in a while."

"Is it that bad?"

"Brutal. Absolutely brutal. She nuked me right away. Claimed I molested him. Can you believe that? The charge won't stick, of course, but it'll take forever for the court to sort it out. Meanwhile, he's getting older. I'm getting older."

This, it seemed, was a new Felix — the naked head, the shifting facial expressions, the glasses with thinner frames. She had always sensed a tenderness below his sarcasm and overconfidence, and now it had been released. She nodded and frowned, demonstrating the proper concern as he related all his difficulties to her. She asked questions. She listened to his answers patiently. And from time to time she glanced around the bar for familiar faces, maybe an old co-worker or waitress who might recognize her, but didn't spot anyone. Felix continued talking. She waited for an opening.

"Then she must have taken all of your money, too," Dallas said, some time later. They had ordered another round of drinks.

Felix shook his head. "She's loaded. It was a big secret, but the only way to prevent her father from disowning her was to sign a pre-nup. I guess he didn't trust me." He laughed. "The old bird was right about that. I couldn't be trusted. I got this job just to show him I wasn't afraid to work for a living. Saving money for Jason's education. That was my excuse." He laughed. "Like nobody else was going to pay for it. Anyway, I guess it's a good thing I did that. Now it's my savings account."

Dallas could hardly restrain herself from jumping in, but she let him continue.

"What a terrible thing I did. I should have told Sharon years ago that I wasn't happy." He looked at Dallas. "Were you going to say something?"

"It's not important."

"No, go ahead."

She took a final drag from her cigarette and stubbed it out. "I'm in trouble," she said. "Financial trouble."

"What kind of financial trouble?"

"The usual kind."

"Slots?"

She nodded.

"How much?"

She told him.

He let out a long breath.

"You know why I'm telling you this, Felix."

He was running his index finger around the rim of his glass.

"I'd make monthly payments. You could count on it like the sunrise. Basically it would be my new religion."

The din of the machines was beginning to subside, the crowds thinning. Soon the music would fade with the downward arc of the night.

"I might be able to swing it," he finally said.

Dallas almost sagged against the bar with relief. She felt as if she had been holding her breath for a month.

He looked around. "Let's get out of here. I feel like I'm still at work."

"The Hard Eight is quiet."

He tilted his head slightly, as if to say it wasn't a bad suggestion but not a great one either. A coy expression on his face. "I was thinking maybe my place."

"I shouldn't."

"You shouldn't, or you don't want to?"

She hesitated for a moment, the sudden glare of his proposal catching her off guard.

His expression fell. "I get it," he said. "I understand. For a while there I thought you actually cared about me." He rose from the stool.

"*No.* Felix. Wait." She reached out and grabbed him by the hand. "That's not what I meant. Of course we can go to your place for a drink. I was just trying to remember . . . I mean, I told someone at work that I'd call her today to let her know if I can cover her shift next Thursday. But what time is it?" She brought his hand closer and turned it over to look at his wristwatch, making sure his forearm touched her breast. "See, it's already too late to call her. It's not today anymore. It's tomorrow."

They hiked through a mesquite bosque and then climbed a hill full of scrub juniper and prickly pear, flowers and tall grass poking up among the chaparral, purples and reds and blues all around them. At the crest they saw pincushion cacti and segments of cane cholla lying on the ground like amputated limbs. The trail continued along a series of hills until it reached a flat stretch with mountains visible in the distance.

"Is that where we're going?" he asked.

She shook her head. "You can't see where we're going."

The sun strengthened behind them, the vegetation rising thick and high enough to offer some shade in a few places. They dipped through sandy washes, crossed open sections with plates of broken sandstone scattered across the ground and sweet dust hanging in the air. A couple of times Logan almost stepped on animal droppings. Not that he studied such things very closely, but it seemed to have a knobby texture, full of corn-kernel-sized berries. At one point Keris stopped and showed him a pile that actually had hair in it.

"Mountain lion," she said.

"Should I be afraid?"

She shrugged noncommittally. "If you see one, which is unlikely, don't run. Never run. Stand tall. Slowly back away."

The trail narrowed and they walked single file with Keris in front. He watched her feet, her thick socks scrunched above the tops of her hiking boots, her brown calves powdered with dust, the faint workings of her muscles leading up to her pert backside. The firm swerve of her hips. He could feel the skin on his own heels and toes heating up with the friction of the long walk, the constant rubbing. He tried to ignore it. He started talking to distract himself and pretty soon he was telling her about Dallas. He told her how they met. He told her how the relationship happened. He told her that Dallas was visiting her mother in Vegas, which he only half-believed, and tried to explain that he was operating on deep instinct, a raw-survival mentality he couldn't shake because he felt like something rough and necessary was happening and it needed to play itself out and he didn't know how he would emerge, in what condition or state of being. Keris nodded. She asked a few simple questions, almost logistical in nature, but didn't force any assessments or advice on him afterward.

They sat on a boulder in the full glare of noon and had a lunch of trail mix and lukewarm water. The sun high and hot. He felt salty-skinned, loose-boned, energetic but slightly sluggish, too. There were scrapes across his legs from all the thorns he had brushed against.

At one point Keris looked at him like she was about to say something, but then stayed silent.

"What?" he asked.

"Nothing."

"Come on. Out with it."

She hesitated for another moment. "The last time we had lunch you said, 'I don't like the way I love her.'"

"Yeah. I remember."

"And I think you should consider the effect of that."

He lowered his eyes to the boulder they were sitting on, the deep heat against his legs. "You mean, the effect on her."

"Her, you, everyone. What happens when you don't like what you want?"

Silence. A bird or animal screamed somewhere far away. He could feel the remark cutting into him slowly. But she was right. "OK," he said.

"I'm sorry if that hurts you."

He reached out and touched her forearm. "I'm glad you said it. Now," he said, shifting to a lighter tone, "tell me where we're going next."

"Straight ahead."

As he followed her line of sight he realized the land dropped down again, sinking into a small canyon that had been concealed in the seemingly flat distance. "Let me guess," he said. "The name of that place is Hidden Canyon."

"Rustlers' Canyon. Many a stolen herd of cattle were stashed away there in the late nineteenth century. See those trees?" She pointed toward some bright green leaf-cover where the canyon opened out into the desert. "Cottonwoods. They always grow near sources of water."

"Smart trees."

"They have shallow roots. The early settlers could spot water simply by looking for them. We'll follow a wash down into the canyon, then hike along the creek."

"Sounds dangerous."

"Even a Pennsylvania boy wearing sneakers can do it."

"Just for that," he said, reaching into her bag of trail mix, "I'm going to eat all your raisins."

She casually brushed a piece of grass off his shoulder. "How are your feet, by the way?"

"Fine."

"Really?"

"Really."

She hopped down and picked up her pack. "I just don't want anyone to get hurt. Understand?"

"I understand," he said, although he didn't absorb the tone of her voice until they were walking again and it was too late for a meaningful reply.

They hiked down into the canyon and along the creek, lingering under the cottonwoods. Leaves shimmered and glittered in a faint breeze coming off the water. They dunked their heads and reclined on a flat boulder for a while, talking, falling silent, listening to birds call from the cliffs and splayed branches above them. They saw a hawk wheeling overhead, a fox hiding in a grove of oak. And not too far from the parking lot they saw a gang of gray, bristly, ugly creatures that looked like wild boars but which Keris claimed were javelinas.

When they reached the car Logan sank into the passenger seat and waited for Keris to change out of her hiking boots. He kept his sneakers on. He didn't want to see the devastation of his feet. He imagined himself at home in a bathtub filled with icewater, cubes clinking merrily around him. He closed the door and buckled his seat belt. Keris did the same. But when she turned the key, something clanked under the hood and there was a detonation of some kind followed by a hissing and gurgling noise. Steam began to rise from the grille.

Logan lifted the hood and immediately spotted the burst hose, its ragged strips hanging. Fluorescent green fluid was gushing and pooling on the gravel.

"Look at all that coolant," Keris said. "We should stop it from washing into the creek."

Logan headed toward the visitor center and met a man coming out the door with an armful of rags. He wore a straw hat, blue jeans, a white shirt as spotless as hospital sheets.

"Heard it all the way up in the office," he said, handing the rags to Logan. "These'll soak up most of the fluid. I'll get a shovel to take care of the dirt."

Twenty minutes later the mess was cleaned up and the man, who turned out to be the caretaker of the property and the husband of the receptionist, tossed a trashbag full of dirty rags and tainted soil into the back of his pickup truck. The sun was setting. A gold slant falling across the hills. The ripening colors of dusk. He invited Logan and Keris into the visitor center and, after they had washed their hands, explained the situation. The only garage in town wouldn't send a truck all the way out to the nature preserve. He'd be happy to give them a lift so they could pick up a new hose, but it would have to be tomorrow because it was, let's see, five-thirty, and the garage was already closed. They had one *casita* available tonight, but they'd have to make do with a futon because the bed broke last month and they hadn't got around to replacing it they were so damn busy lately with the watershed restoration. It wasn't a five-star hotel, but they were welcome to it.

Logan and Keris thanked him. At this point it was dusk and they had difficulty making out each other's features in the dimness of the office. The caretaker turned on a lamp. He said he'd get the room ready for them, but then the receptionist came in and said it was already done — the futon, such as it was, made up for them and fresh towels in the bathroom. The only thing left to do was notify the people waiting for them at home. Keris called her friend Charlotte and made arrangements for Sophie to spend the night there, then called Sophie to explain the situation. When she was done she handed the phone to Logan, but he shook his head. There was nobody for him to call.

His hope for a couch or another alternative disappeared right away. The futon, it turned out, *was* the couch, now folded flat in the living room with a pair of pillows, a bottom sheet, a comforter, and extra blankets stacked on an armchair next to it. He inspected the rest of the place while Keris was taking a shower. Besides the living room and bathroom there was a fully equipped kitchen and a bedroom with a big empty gap where the bed had once stood. Tile floors. Mismatched second-hand furniture. Adobe walls adorned with electrical conduits and framed artwork of cowboys sitting by campfires. The living room looked out onto a courtyard with palo verde trees. He could see lights in the other *casitas*, but no other signs of life.

He lowered himself into the armchair and was about to unlace his sneakers, preparing himself to face the ruins of his bare feet, when he heard a knock on the door. He rose slowly and shuffled across the room, muscles already stiffening.

"Thought you and the wife could use this," the caretaker said, handing over a bottle of wine and a casserole dish. "You ain't vegetarians, are you?"

"Wow. Thanks. Thank you very much. I mean —"

"Joanna made this lasagne last night and the wine is just to say we feel really bad about the situation. Pete just doesn't take to people pestering him after hours." He slid his hands into his pockets. "That's the guy owns the garage. 'I'm not a freakin' doctor on call twenty-four hours a day,' he says. Riles him to no end. Go figure. So anyway, accept this token." He gestured at it, then turned and walked away.

Logan called out a final thanks before shutting the door. He set the wine on the counter and removed the foil from the lasagne, resisting an urge to plunge his face right into it then and there. He turned on the oven and set the dish inside. He limped back into the living room. As he was settling into the chair again he realized what the caretaker had said. Too late. Always catching these things too late. Thought you and the wife could use this. The shower stopped running. He heard a final sluice of rivulets and dribbles, the plastic curtain sliding back. "She's not my wife," he said quietly.

Logan showered, put on his dirty clothes again, and came out of the bathroom to find the lasagne sliced and served, the wine poured, and a clean outfit draped over the armchair. Flannel shirt, jeans. He was holding them up to measure against himself when Keris came out of the kitchen in a pair of sweatpants and an oversized T-shirt that said Hot Stuff.

"Don't laugh," she said.

"I promise you," he said, laughing, "that I won't even smile."

"What's the caretaker's name?"

Logan went back to the bathroom to change. "I keep forgetting to ask," he said through the door.

"He thinks we're married."

"I know."

"You didn't correct him?"

"Didn't have a chance."

Logan waited for a response but didn't hear one. He finished buttoning the shirt, tucked it in, and looked at himself in the mirror before he opened the door again. She was setting the table in the kitchen.

"What about you?" he said, coming through the doorway. "Did you correct him?"

"You look rustic," she said.

"And you look like Hot Stuff."

She swatted him. Her brown hair was damp and loose, her skin blushed in the afterglow of the shower. There was a fresh scent emanating from her. Slightly rooty. A forest after rain. Logan told himself that fatigue and the rustic setting were amplifying his feelings, but nevertheless he looked into her eyes as she was talking and accepted the truth that she was beautiful, utterly and totally beautiful, and he hoped by acknowledging it he would be able to move on.

Halfway through the meal he caught a chill from the open window and got up to close it.

"It's actually cold outside," he said.

"When you spend all your time in Phoenix, it's easy to forget how much the desert cools off at night."

"All that asphalt and concrete."

She nodded. "A heat-island effect."

There was a silence.

"How many planets," he said, "are like this one?"

She took a sip of wine. "Zero."

"Let me rephrase that. I don't mean how many planets have oak trees and freeways and the evening news. I mean, how many planets have somewhat complex creatures capable of thought and language."

She laid her knife and fork across her plate. "Zero."

"No, really. I mean creatures who may be completely different from us, with tentacles and brains made out of chlorophyll, or whatever, but who have technology of some kind. Tools. Shelter. Maybe even simple machines."

"Zero."

Logan threw up his hands. "You're no fun."

"I assume you're talking about evolved forms of life, Logan, rather than the sort of extremophile bacteria found inside geothermal vents and nuclear reactors."

"Exactly. I don't want to hear about single-celled creatures living in pools of sulfur. That bores me." He helped himself to more lasagne, happy to be talking about something outside their lives.

"As it should. You are, in fact, thinking about science fiction movies where people whiz around in spaceships that exceed the speed of light and routinely encounter aliens who speak English."

Logan wanted to respond, but he was still chewing. He held up a finger.

"I know I'm making a parody of what you asked," she continued. "Nevertheless, your question is based on faulty notions about the universe."

Logan swallowed. "But I've read articles about this. The sheer size of the universe, the number of planets that are out there. If you do the math, the odds of life are . . . what's the matter?"

Her head had fallen back in exasperation. "The Drake Equation. An estimate based on grossly inaccurate assumptions about star and planet formation, solar system dynamics, and the ambient conditions of all known galaxies."

"You're saying it's wrong?"

"Sadly, yes."

"Explain."

She did. As Logan finished his lasagne, she told him that, contrary to popular belief, our sun isn't average. In fact, it's completely unique: not only a solitary and stable star with planets orbiting in a relatively orderly fashion, but also neither too close nor too far from the center of the galaxy to suffer ill effects. Regions closer to the center, for example, experience heavy bombardments of comets and asteroids because there are more stars passing each other, while at the same time experiencing more intense X-rays, gamma rays, and ionizing radiation. By contrast, even in this unusually quiet section of the galaxy, we have Jupiter to suck in the most harmful debris. And did Logan know the characteristics of all the planets discovered outside our solar system? Giants. Similar to Jupiter in size, but with wildly eccentric orbits, exacerbating the destruction and instability of smaller planets by constantly slinging cosmic debris at them instead of absorbing the debris and thereby protecting them from it. And although the edges of most galaxies don't have these problems, their stars lack elements such as iron, magnesium, and silicon,

213

which are essential for the formation of planets with sufficient gravity to retain atmospheres. Such elements are also necessary for plate tectonics. Without the slow churning of the Earth's crust into the hot interior, we wouldn't have enough variation in landscape and climate for biodiversity and therefore the evolution of complex life forms. And turning our attention to the moon for a moment, let us note that it was formed when a Mars-sized object struck the Earth during an early stage of its formation—a freak occurrence at exactly the right time, with incalculable odds in and of itself, never mind all these other factors, and so we have the moon stabilizing the Earth's tilt and climate, again allowing the evolution of complex life.

By the time she had finished talking the wine bottle was empty and the remains of the food had congealed on their plates. Plate tectonics, Logan thought. A fuzzy warmth suffused him. The glow of physical fatigue and, yes, the wine. Keris's hair was dry now, strands of it falling forward, which she kept brushing away from her face.

"Everything I have learned, Logan, tells me that this planet is the jewel of the universe."

"And we're treating it like a business in liquidation."

She sat back in her chair. "Maybe our job is to teach students what they need to know in order to prevent that from happening."

A hopeless mood settled over him, like it usually did whenever he thought of the human race as a whole. "But what if we don't deserve it?" he said. "What if we aren't worthy of this planet?"

"This sounds incredibly pessimistic."

"Here's the paradox. I would never think that an individual person doesn't deserve to live. But what about the human race as a whole? What if we're too stupid? I mean, stupid in a spiritual or maybe existential sense. Why are we so much less than the sum of our parts?"

She began to rise from her chair. "It seems that every time we have a meal together, we talk about something like this."

"I'm sorry." His gaze was fixed absently on the space where she had been sitting.

As she was picking up his plate she leaned in close. "I meant that we tend to bare our souls to each other across the dinner table. We're both weird that way."

He stood up, carefully avoiding her face, the lips he easily could have kissed, and helped her wash the dishes. Afterward they went over to the futon and sized it up.

"I can sleep on the floor," Logan said.

"And I can sleep hanging upside down in the closet. Please." She nudged him with her elbow. "I think we can share it like reasonable adults."

She kicked off her sandals and got under the comforter in her T-shirt and sweats. Logan considered his options. Then he took off the jeans and went to bed in his boxers and the caretaker's flannel shirt, using one of the extra blankets as his separate cover. This seemed reasonable. He moved his feet gingerly, careful not to rub his blisters against the bottom sheet. They lay there for some time in silence. The hum of the refrigerator, the window slightly open with the mingled scents of the desert wafting in — a pungent odor of soil and cacti, flowers and trees. He could feel the warm sheen of Keris's body next to him. Her rooty scent, her breath. He felt an erection coming on and knew there was nothing he could do to avoid it. Where was the mind-body split when you really needed it?

"The flaw of your argument," he murmured, "is that you're assuming other life forms have the same basic requirements that we do. What if asteroid impacts don't destroy certain creatures, but feed them instead? What if they eat lava? What if they drink fire? What if they love things without consuming them?"

"It's possible," she whispered. "I hope you're right."

"Remember what you told me about the sunspots?"

"Yes, I remember."

"I understand it now."

There was a silence.

"And?" she asked.

"I'm scared."

He thought he felt a movement next to him, like she was coming closer, settling into the raw spaces between his limbs, but that wasn't quite right, a dream-feeling, a half-asleep sensation before zero gravity took him and the sequence was done.

He woke up warm. Too warm. Sweating, a damp chill between his shoulder blades. Flannel shirt, thick blanket. He writhed awake and lay there blinking, trying to remember where he was. Something was different. Purple shadows on the wall. The room full of moonglow and nightshade, faintly featured, detailed, delicate. He was lying in the middle of the futon. Alone. He sat up. Keris was curled up in the armchair with the comforter wrapped around her, gazing out at the courtyard. A full moon hovering beyond the branches of the palo verdes.

"What's wrong?" he asked.

She didn't look at him. "It was foolish of me."

"What was foolish?"

"I thought I could get away with it, Logan. I really did."

He blinked and rubbed his eyes. He was about to confess he didn't have the slightest idea what she was talking about when she spoke again.

"I thought I could avoid loving you."

Logan didn't move. He wanted to make sure he had heard that correctly. If it was what she had actually said or what he wanted to hear, although — and this was confusing — it felt like what he wanted and didn't want at the same time. Such a condition was, of course, impossible. There can't be two demand curves for the same person.

"I'm split," he said. "I'm cut right down the middle."

She nodded. She wiped a tear from her cheek. "Things are complicated enough between two people without adding a third. I think we both agree on that."

"What if I left Dallas?"

"Would you be leaving her for me, or leaving her because you want to leave her? Even if it meant being alone?" She turned and looked at him, her eyes damp, gleaming. "Be honest."

It would have been easy to say that the marriage was beyond salvation, that he had been planning to ask for a divorce before Keris started this discussion. He could have pulled it off. She would have believed him. And, without question, it was in his best self-interest for his feelings to be clear-cut. But they weren't. They simply weren't.

"I don't know," he finally said. "I think I'd be leaving her for you."

She nodded slowly. "I don't want that."

"But I'm going to be in love with you," he said.

"Going to be?"

"How long have we known each other? I can't say I love you yet. But I will. So what's wrong with taking the time to—"

"Stop."

"But I want—"

"Please," she said. She sniffled again and wiped her nose with the back of her hand. "We have to drive back to Phoenix together. Please, stop."

The sun was high, the car an oven by the time she left Felix's apartment the next morning. She had forgotten to put up the sunshade when she arrived and who could blame her. Sweat immediately bloomed across her forehead as she slid behind the wheel. Hot air caught like smoke inside her lungs. She closed the door and put the key in the ignition, but hesitated before starting the engine. She pulled her stockings out of her purse and rummaged through it until she found Felix's check, made out for the grand total of all the money she owed. It still had his wife's name printed on it. But everything was in order. Everything was right. The debt and its spiraling interest finally put to rest, supply and demand at equilibrium, intersecting at a point of mutual satisfaction.

She stuffed it back into her purse and glanced at herself in the rearview mirror. The remains of her makeup were smeary and moist, her face dissolving. She gripped the steering wheel and let it burn her hands. The parking lot spread abjectly before her—the glass and chrome, the palm trees, the aluminum mailboxes. Basically if she had any sense she would start the car right now with the air-conditioning set to maximum. Sweat was already running from her armpits, dribbling down her ribs, collecting in the hollow between her breasts and moistening the creases behind her knees, wetting every portion of skin that happened to be touching something else. Blots appeared on her blouse as if she were bleeding.

Felix had slowly reverted to his old habits over the course of the night. He had talked about sports. He had complained about his co-workers. And then, while they were sharing a cigarette, he had patted Dallas's bare ass like it was a thoroughbred he had just ridden, making the transformation complete. She managed to hide her hostility. As she was getting dressed she casually reminded him about the loan and he asked her to fetch his checkbook for him. She did it without hesitation. She even smiled and thanked him afterward, as if she hadn't earned every cent of it.

And now, drenched and smelly, she realized that even when she had felt most compelled by Felix, even when she had wanted him deeply and insatiably, she had secretly hoped to expose him as the second-rate fink he really was. The day would come when he'd be caught at something. But wait a minute—he had already been caught at something, hadn't he? That something was Dallas. His wife had thrown him out, and now there he was, marketing himself as a wounded soul who needed love and understanding. Make that sex and understanding. Felix was the kind of person who would always get away with the things that were most important to him. He'd clean out Fort Knox one bar at a time.

Her lips were becoming scorched in the rotisserie heat of the car. The brutal leather seats. The windshield and its one-way allowance with the sun. A greenhouse effect. She could smell Felix all over her skin, his gooey moisture between her legs, gamey and oily with excretions. This was the price she paid for the loan. A trickle of sweat leaked from her hairline and ran straight down her nose, hanging there until she wiped it away.

She started the engine. She needed a week at a luxury spa, but instead would have to settle for a tepid shower at her mother's house. And here was the hard part. Maybe the worst part. She had to walk through that door. Mom would be waiting for her, supposedly watching TV or reading a magazine, but in truth hanging around so she could witness Dallas in this condition. But it didn't matter. To hell with Mom. To hell with Logan and his complacency. Dallas wiped her sleeve across her eyes. It's my body, she thought. I can do what I want with it.

chapter 10

April in New Hampshire. A gust of warm weather came surging through the White Mountains like a train behind schedule, shaking the pines awake. Snowcrusts began to melt. The sky regained color, the grass resumed growth, winter sobriety burned away like morning fog. Let's call it spring and it's about goddamn time. Deck stood onstage with his sleeves rolled up, collar open, gripping the podium as he spoke to his congregation. It was a renovated lecture hall with cinema-style seating and padded walls, but the old coiled radiator still emitted heat, the antique windows still shuddered in their frames. He could never forget where he was. He guessed maybe half his students were absent this afternoon, chasing frisbees across a quad somewhere. That was OK. It was all right. He had built a couple of extra days into the schedule — safety compartments, if you will — for this kind of disruption, and he was taking advantage of the opportunity.

"Every demand function," he said, "contains both a predictable systematic component and an unobserved, unpredictable random error component."

He tugged his tie loose for extra effect, like let's get down to serious business, folks, because he was taking a risk, he was being reckless, he had set aside his lecture notes in order to try a little bit of econometrics on them. Call it a taste test. A focus group. He was leading them through the basic concept of a statistical model with sample information, a likely component of the undergraduate course he had discussed with Novak last month. Not that he could measure their response with complete accuracy. Even if he discounted the weather, he still had to factor in the Thursday-afternoon hysteria — the unofficial end of the week in academia with the tide of parties approaching. Look at all those blazing faces. Whether it was actual interest in what he was saying or simply the season's hormones, he didn't know. This was still long-sleeve weather, in all honesty, but there were bare arms and legs out there, sunglasses raised onto foreheads. California dreaming. It was in their nature to lean hard against the winter's tilt, dressing not for the climate as it was, but for what they wanted it to be. As if dressing would make it so. Hard not to smile at such dreams.

"Let's call this random error component e," he said, heading over to the chalkboard. "In a demand relation, for example, it's possible that the proper controls haven't been established for taste. Or maybe an important variable has been omitted. Or you could even claim, if you wanted to, that human behavior has a random component."

He picked up the chalk and wrote the appropriate formula, full of xs and betas, explaining, quite simply, that the part of the function all the way up to and including the last beta was the systematic part, while the e — at this point he added it on with a flourish — was the nonsystematic, random error component that was present but couldn't be observed. This was exactly the sort of moment when he hoped other people could see as deeply into the work as he did, apprehending the truth of the equations, the beauty of the intersecting curves. This was human nature sectioned and diagrammed like the overlapping transparencies of an anatomy textbook.

As he continued talking he caught sight of Delilah — his blonde, supple-breasted, hearty-hipped stripper-student — in the seventh row with her head down and notebook open, scribbling away. Maybe she was transcribing his every word. Maybe she secretly appreciated him the way he appreciated her. After all, he always kept her on the radar, noting her absence, her presence, her location in the lecture hall. He had gone back to the Denominator a few times to enjoy her performances since returning from Arizona last month. And it would be a lie to say he hadn't driven straight home and masturbated afterward. It would be a lie.

"Now, to make this statistical model complete, you need to identify the source of the error, or errors. Is it the result of unobserved random variables? If so, then you need to be specific about the means and variances of these random variables and maybe even the distributions that they were drawn from." He smiled and shook his head. "But I'm getting ahead of myself. The important thing to remember is that assigning the error, or errors, a random interpretation transforms the equation into a statistical-probability model and establishes a basis for statistical inference. Then you can estimate unknown parameters and test hypotheses about them."

He was going too hard, too fast. He could see his words disappearing on their faces like the patterns in passing clouds. He stopped. He nodded and said, all right, all right, I'll back up, as if several students had raised their hands and begged him to go over it again. He did some cartoonish simplifications of the process until he was satisfied with the level of understanding they showed him. He checked his watch. Then he waved a hand over the crowd, absolving them of the last five minutes.

The lecture hall emptied like a fire alarm had gone off. He collected his notes. He descended from the stage. He walked down a creaking hallway and unlocked the door to his office. Call it quaint if you want—and some people did—but Deck didn't care for life among the ruins. His office suffered from an impotent radiator, a water-stained ceiling, a north-facing window that would have admitted little daylight even if you trimmed the ivy and demolished the clock tower over there, tyrannically gonging the hours. It was yet another reason to say game over, I'm done.

Deck dropped into his chair. He rubbed his forehead. The econometrics primer hadn't been received with the level of understanding he had hoped for. But it's important to identify the real source of his mood: Keris had called a few days ago. The phone had startled him out of a nap and he had answered it without a thought in his head, and maybe a moment or two of elation had passed before he found himself fending off questions about his family's medical history and his HIV status. Whoa, whoa, whoa. This was the woman who had left him in the middle of the night, but now she wanted to know if he was a terminal case with schizoid grandparents. I'm clean, he had said. And so is my family. Not that it would have made any difference to you that night.

And that was it. Like a fool, he had answered her questions and simultaneously given her a reason to hang up. A dial tone filled his ear. He called directory assistance and tried the various caller ID functions on his line, but her number was unlisted, blocked, top secret. He had let her get away. In the following days he tried to dismiss her interrogation as misplaced guilt and anxiety about the one-night stand—although, he had to admit, condoms weren't 100 percent reliable, so maybe . . .

He heard a knock. He swiveled toward the door and found Delilah in her pink T-shirt and denim cutoffs, a handbag slung over her shoulder. And was it Deck's imagination, or was there a slight hint of a smile, a knowing look in her eye?

"Can we talk?" she asked.

An uneasy jangle ran through him. Can we talk. He had never heard those words followed by good news. He nodded. She sat in the chair next to him and crossed her long, cool legs. Deck dutifully fixed his eyes on hers. Back in California he had seen a beloved professor's career derailed by a few careless glances and some words taken out of context. Besides, he had seen more, so much more of Delilah at the strip club these last couple of months. He tried to steady himself with the knowledge that he had taken every precaution to mask his presence — parking at the supermarket down the street, sitting in the club's dark mid-section with his jeans and hooded sweatshirt and baseball cap, studying the spotlights over the stage to confirm that the dancers couldn't see more than two rows into the audience — but the truth was that he didn't like the sound of this. He didn't like it at all.

"I know this might not be the right time to talk about this?" she said. "But I feel it's important?" Her voice rose at the end of every sentence, converting it into a question. The vacancy, the high melody of soap opera. A cartoon mind, he thought. And yet she seemed to be opening subtle negotiations, he suspected, for a better grade.

Deck coughed and told her to go ahead.

"Are you sure?" she said. "Because you should be in the right frame of mind when you hear this. I mean, you'll probably want to think about it? And so maybe I should come back during your office hours?"

He said it was no problem. He had plenty of time.

"Well . . ." She trailed off, a half-smile rising to her lips again. "This is kind of like, I don't know." She wrinkled her nose. "I guess you could call it a proposal?"

He waited. His pulse was clicking hard and heavy in his ears. "Say it," he said.

"Well . . . I have an idea for the paper we're supposed to hand in next month? And I know we're only supposed to write about the topics you listed on that handout, but I had a real inspiration in class today, and I'm afraid you'll shoot it down. But I'd like to explain it first if that's all right?"

It was like a circus tent collapsing — the poles yanked away, the canvas coming down around him — as he realized what she was saying. A wild and pleasant relief in his heart. He recovered his composure and smiled. "I'd be happy to hear it," he said.

"See, I work at this club? And most of my wages comes from tips? So we have incentives to spice up the performance. I mean, we're trying to extract money from the customers as quickly as possible? And so everyone uses different, I don't know, strategies? And, well, I want to see if I can set up those kinds of functions you were talking about. All the different factors? And maybe I could correlate everything? It would be interesting because of that error variable you mentioned. I mean, there are certain things you just can't account for. You have good nights and bad nights. You know? But maybe I could figure out what each factor contributes to the tips and then we could actually improve our . . . service, I guess you could say, based on that — and am I being completely outrageous or am I on to something?"

Deck was nodding, trying to maintain a neutral expression, but his relief was slowly draining away without anything else to replace it. He shifted in his chair. Her proposal, he said, was quite outside the range of topics he had given to the class a couple of weeks ago. They were supposed to take a recent article from a business magazine and discuss the impact of whatever topic it covered on either aggregate supply or demand, using the specific equations they had learned in the course. But he'd think about it.

She smiled. She stood. She slung her handbag over her shoulder and swiveled toward the door like it was part of her stage routine. Deck felt a heat flooding his face. Was this a joke? It seemed to be a mockery of her own performance — the pumping and heaving motions, the final pose where she stretched back and displayed herself with shameless ease. There seemed to be an edge of vulnerability to it at the same time, something that always cut into him like the memory of a traumatic dream.

It wasn't until she glanced back at him from the doorway that he realized he had been watching her legs.

"Have a nice weekend," she said. And then she was gone.

He sat there with the scent of her perfume lingering in the air. A colleague walked by his open door without a glance. Students filed past, complaining about an exam they had just taken. He checked his watch. Not that it mattered. He had nothing else scheduled for the rest of the day.

He picked up his materials, packed up his briefcase, and locked up his office. He followed the hallways, the stairs, the paved paths across campus, walking with his head down as he passed the brick buildings with their faux-Roman entryways, the clock tower with its ding-dong bells, the flagpole and flapping colors, let freedom wave. By the time he reached his car, the weather was turning sour again. Clouds were massed into a low ceiling. There was a sluggish breeze, a smell of dampness in the air. He shook his head and cursed. This whole damned place. There was a reason they called it New England and not New Italy. On the way to campus that morning he had heard a forecast for clear skies and, like a fool, he had believed it. The measure of every science was how accurately it predicted the future, but meteorologists screwed up half the time and still kept their jobs.

Raindrops dotted the windshield as he drove home. Lately it had occurred to him that the cycles of the free market pertained to the love market as well. The stages of a relationship. Boom, Panic, Recession, Depression. There was the Boom of the initial infatuation, followed by the Panic of discovering your lover's flaws, the Recession of desire, and eventually the Depression of familiarity. So why bother? What was the point of loving anyone when it always led to the same thing? Boom, Panic, Recession, Depression.

He stopped at his apartment for a few minutes to pack a bag and then drove to the gym as the rain thickened and began to fall like a biblical punishment. He spent some time in the weight room, pushing the chrome bars away from him, pulling them in close. He ran on the treadmill while the storm beat its fists against the windows. There were televisions hanging from brackets in the ceiling with the usual options — cartoons, music videos, news, drama — but he spent more time watching a hot young thing in black spandex on the stairclimber in front of him. The silky motion of her legs, the shifting of her rump inviting desires he couldn't afford to express. He thought about sex too much. And he thought about it in all the wrong ways. It was an unseen rudder guiding his movements, and if anyone discovered it then his reputation, his career, his life would be over.

He went back to the weight room and lifted a few extra sets. The point of exercise, for most men, was to make themselves bigger, but for women it was to make themselves smaller. Or so Keris had claimed that night at the hotel. She had also claimed that yoga did both for her at the same time, which was impossible because they were mutually exclusive. He shook his head. She'd probably drive him nuts eventually. Forget about her. His feelings that night had been the product of his own excitement after the conference, the spillover of professional success. Any woman could have cracked him open with a kiss. Any woman could have turned his own desire against him. Any woman could have probed him with her fingers until she found the small of his back — the place where the spine caves in for a lover's hands.

Friday was better. Much better, as a matter of fact. After lunch he put the finishing touches on his revised article, spell-checked the thing for crying out loud, and printed it and squared the edges and stapled it and then went to the gym again in the afternoon. Afterward he checked his voicemail at the office and discovered a message from Novak, who would be honored if Deck would agree to team up with him for the debate in Palm Springs next month. It was all coming together.

Saturday evening he went to a sports bar to watch a baseball game and had a couple too many. He needed the release. Sure, the Denominator was still out there, but it didn't hold quite the same attraction anymore. He was tired of Delilah. He had seen all he needed to see. He was done with her. So instead he enjoyed his beer, his pretzels, his team-pride vindicated with a grand slam at the bottom of the eighth inning. He ran into a colleague who invited him to a barbecue the next day and Deck surprised himself by accepting. And that was what sank him. The barbecue was generic in every way — house, kids, cat and dog, a few other colleagues from the Econ department and a lot of collateral friends from the guy's intramural basketball league or something. But it was more than that. They seemed to have a shared history of ski trips and beach excursions, parties and movies and dinners. Throw in some clear afternoon weather that reminded Deck of Irvine and it's easy to see why he imagined a life with plenty of reasons to pick up the phone when it rang.

The decision came that night. Sunday night. Too late to rent a video, too early to go to bed. Not sleepy, but washed out from his visit to the sports bar the previous evening followed by an afternoon of snacks and burgers and pissy golden beer. He turned on the television and ransacked the channels until he found a documentary about Antarctica, figuring he'd see a few seals and penguins, maybe some parka-clad scientists taking wind readings, which would make him feel better about being stationed here in the Granite State. But instead it was a surreal, moody piece, a meditation on barrenness with fast-motion photography of clouds furling over empty white landscapes and serrated mountain ranges, the sun burning weakly, like a heavy star, through blizzards. A lone cello playing. A slow tinkle of piano keys. A slant of diluted winter light. He couldn't recognize the scientists because the camera showed only one piece of them at a time — a gloved hand here, a torso there, a pair of boots squeaking on dry snow. Body parts instead of people.

The katabatic, the narrator said, is the most powerful wind on the planet, reaching sustained gusts of over two hundred miles per hour. Yet it begins as only a slight breeze at this South Pole research station, where air currents, drawn southward by the Earth's rotation, descend from the upper atmosphere into a climate so dry that the moisture condenses into ice crystals — a glittering haze known as diamond dust.

Deck remembered the night with Keris. He remembered waking alone in the hotel the next morning and, after a sullen breakfast at the cafe downstairs, driving to the airport and returning the rental car and then boarding the plane in the grip of what he told himself were post-event blues. The letdown you feel after a wedding or reunion. Of course, returning to New Hampshire hadn't made it any easier. The gray landscape, the stone-cold skies. That night he had sat in his living room with shawls of snow descending in the glare of the streetlight outside, the glass rimmed with cloudy moisture, every lamp burning and the television offering nothing more than a second-rate martial arts movie with way too much talking and not enough fighting. What kind of woman had sex with you after a few hours of sweet talk and then slipped away like that? Not the kind of woman he wanted. But when the phone rang he nearly leapt for it and had to hide his disappointment when it turned out to be Prentis calling from an airport somewhere — hungover, lethargic, sated after a long weekend in Vegas. He gave Deck the highlights. And Deck kicked back and laughed along with him, thankful for the distraction. Soon he began to tell Prentis about his encounter with Keris, redeeming himself as he talked, shaping and solidifying the experience so he could put it on the shelf and know that was the way it happened, that was how it went.

Diamond dust adds twelve inches of ice to the South Pole every year, pushing the outer layer thirty feet closer to the coast. Researchers dig below the surface to read patterns in the stationary pack created by drifting snow over the last century, cross-referencing those patterns with meteorological records to establish an index of the general climate. Ice-core samples are then extracted from half a mile down, serving as biopsies, if you will, of the Earth's weather during the last six thousand years. And the results? Millennia of climatic stability have apparently given way at the beginning of the twentieth century to carbon dioxide levels rising one thousand times faster than in any previous era.

He crossed his arms and stretched out on the couch. The assumption, among women who knew Deck but hadn't slept with him, was that he was incurably selfish in bed. But the opposite was true. He serviced them. He devoted himself to their climaxes. In fact, he was usually so focused on his partner's pleasure that he sacrificed his own, or at least postponed it until the next morning when he was safely alone in the bathroom. And believe it or not, this behavior made sense. It was a rational choice. A satisfied woman was a woman who would come back for more — and he always wanted the woman of the moment to come back for more, even if he didn't particularly care for her. He wanted her to need him. He wanted her to rank him higher than he ranked her. The values of the equation fluctuated, but the results were accurate and true. Happiness equals consumption divided by desire.

He watched ice floes travel over one thousand miles to the coast, splitting and cracking, squeezing through narrow mountain passes until they eventually flaked off into gigantic bergs and crashed into the sea. He surveyed the McMurdo Dry Valleys, where the ice was actually in recession, retreating from the ocean instead of moving toward it. Although the cause of the movement was unclear, it appeared that the katabatic became warmer as it descended from the Pole's higher elevations, preventing ice from forming on the black rock of the Valleys. But the mummified remains of a few penguins and seals, the narrator said, attest to the brutality of this climate no matter what the trend may be, the corpses scoured down to skeletons by the kata-batic's unforgiving power.

He kept expecting a commercial until he finally realized he was watching public television. He looked away from the screen. The empty symmetry of the furniture, the stiff poses of the lamps and chairs. He could use another phone call from Prentis. Or Keris. Sure, he'd answer the phone if she called again. He might even apologize.

On the television screen, wind was whipping sheets of snow across vast distances with an orange sunset burning like a pyre on the horizon, eerie organ music filling the room. The misery of Sunday nights. It had always been a problem for him. He'd trade one of these evenings for ten Monday mornings without a moment's hesitation.

The temperature plummets to minus 40 degrees in the summer. Water snap-freezes. Breath stings the lungs. Penguins visit the coast only to breed. When the Weddell seal gives birth, the newborn pup emerges tail first into an environment 140 degrees colder than the one inside the womb.

Why would she call him about his family's medical history and HIV status? He sat upright. Hang on. What about *her* HIV status? OK, it was probably negative if she was worried enough to call him about his, but it still gave him a right to seek her out. It gave him a right to certain dividends after that night together—or, to be more accurate, a couple of hours together. Which was exactly the problem. She owed him more than that. But how was he going to contact her? He had already thought about e-mailing and calling her number at the university, but knew she'd ignore any message he left there.

Seven million square miles of ocean are frozen every winter, equal in size to South America, the ice pack advancing two and a half miles per day. The Antarctic dome contains 95 percent of the world's fresh water. It resembles the moon more than anyplace else, explored only with elaborate life-support systems.

Logan. Deck brought his fist to his forehead. Of course. Why hadn't he thought of it sooner? Logan had her number—and, along with it, he had to admit, a certain claim, a certain degree of intimacy that he had earned over time. But Deck would override it. He would prevail. He would treat Logan as an aid rather than an obstacle, drawing on the guy's own resources to surpass him. Step one, quite simply, was to call him with some plausible excuse for getting her phone number.

The documentary ended. The credits began to roll. Deck picked up the remote and turned it off. Normally he'd have to suffer through these last ten minutes of tooth-brushing and alarm-setting before bed. But now he reached for the phone. He was halfway into Logan's number when he glanced at the clock. He hung up. Even though Logan was three hours behind him, it was still too late to call. He didn't want to come off as desperate. And besides, it would be more convincing if he did it during business hours and mentioned Keris as a tangent to some conversation about the conference in Palm Springs. He stood and made his way toward the bedroom, feeling calm but elated. Maybe it was because he had settled on a course of action. Or, to be more precise, maybe it was because the course of action was a single phone call. He favored subtlety. He favored elegance. A room full of gasoline requires only one match.

OK, so there's something about Keris you haven't been told. There was a missed period, a pregnancy test purchased at the local pharmacy, and then a visit to her gynecologist. Results positive. She cried for three days — which was inevitable, of course, given all the warning signs she had ignored. Why hadn't she acknowledged, for example, the sudden two-hour naps? Why hadn't she paid attention to her tender breasts, her queasiness at the smell of alcohol, her fatigue after climbing the stairs to her office? After all, isn't that what had happened during her first trimester with Sophie? Let's chalk this one up to the simple power of denial, which had her believing, for a week or so, that these things were just symptoms of depression after the hike with Logan. But the evidence finally defeated her.

So. After seeing the gynecologist she went back to Maria, her therapist, and spent an hour talking to her and then three hours lying on a massage table receiving Reiki in order to have her chakras cleared and realigned. She had been back several times since then. The possibility of an abortion had entered her mind like an icy draft before she shut the door on it. No. Deck had used a condom, and she had used her diaphragm. This child wanted to be born despite all probabilities and precautions. She couldn't deny that.

Keris was working in the lab now, sifting yet again through a computer program that had been revised more times than she cared to estimate. Sophie sat across the table from her, backpack on the floor, math book open, wrangling with her own empirical demons. Fluorescent lights hummed overhead. A few friends had visited this place expecting white coats and armored doors accessed via exotic security measures such as fingerprint scans. But it had a plain door with an old-fashioned key. It was in the basement of the building. And it was ugly. There were mismatched computers and assorted electronic equipment, cables and cords and wires stretched across portions of the floor like dead snakes. Pieces of one of the microwave detectors sat on a workbench, color-coded entrails spread across the surface.

Sophie stopped jotting. She put down her pencil and flexed her hand, her fingers protruding from the bunched sleeve of Keris's sweater—which, it should be noted, she wore because Sophie had forgotten her own and the room was air-conditioned to an almost polar temperature for the sake of the equipment. "What happened to that man?" she asked.

Keris glanced at her. "What man?"

"Oh, you know. The one you liked. The professor."

Keris hesitated before responding the only way she could. "You mean Logan? He has been busy lately. We've both been busy. He's just a friend."

Sophie looked down at her worksheet, averting her eyes the way she did whenever she received a disappointing answer.

"Is something wrong?" Keris asked.

She shook her head.

Keris was readjusting her gaze to the computer screen when Sophie spoke up again. "You were happy when you talked to him."

Keris looked at her daughter in bewilderment. "What do you mean?"

Sophie shrugged. "You were happy, that's all." She shifted her buttocks on the chair and returned to her math problems with the air of an adult resuming important business. These moments of sudden maturity had been coming over her recently, fading immediately into some typical childlike expression, which took place now with her tongue peeking out between her teeth. It reminded Keris of Will. His irritation with data that refused to coalesce, as if the physical world were trying to thwart him. She hoped the attitude would ripen differently in Sophie. Especially since she was going to be somebody's big sister pretty soon. Keris's eyes watered up suddenly. She blinked. She released her shoulders. She breathed. She couldn't tell Sophie—or anyone else, for that matter—until she cleared the first trimester.

According to her calculations, the baby would arrive around Christmas. There would be maternity leave. There would be a vast depressurization of her finances, which would be difficult but not impossible to handle. The most frightening aspect of the whole process, however, would be her solitude in it. Despite the problems between her and Will, he had remained at her side throughout the morning sickness, the shooting pains in her sides, the flatulence, the hormone circus, and of course the astonishing weight gain. He had picked up the phone and wrangled an immediate visit to the doctor when she spotted blood one day, the specter of a miscarriage haunting them for sixteen hours before it was revealed as a false alarm. He had taken on all the extra duties of the household when she was hollow-eyed with exhaustion during the first trimester and then, during the rest of the pregnancy, when bending and lifting became Olympic events. And he had loved her, in some small way, every night. She had never felt alone.

Sophie closed her textbook and slid the worksheet across the table toward Keris. "You're supposed to sign this," she said.

Keris examined the page. The text at the bottom read, "My son/daughter has completed this assignment without the use of a calculator," followed by a line for parent or guardian signature.

"Long division?" Keris said. "When did you start learning this?"

"I dunno. Last week, I guess. Only a dummy would need a calculator, but Mrs. Brolin is such a tight-ass."

Keris opened her mouth, but Sophie beat her to the reprimand.

"I know, I know. Watch your language." She flopped her hands on the table and looked away.

This sullen mood had been hanging over Sophie for the past few weeks — which, now that she thought about it, was about how long it had been hanging over Keris. True, she had been doing most of her crying in the shower and generally putting on her best face for Sophie, but it was foolish to think she could shield her daughter from such heavy radiation.

Keris signed the page and slid it back toward Sophie. "Hey, I love you," she said.

"I love you, too. Can I get a chocolate bar?"

"Are you sure you don't want some more grouch pills?"

Sophie began to smile.

Keris reached into her purse and pulled out some money. Sophie took it with a flourish and left, the door snapping shut behind her.

Keris returned to the computer screen. A moment later she leaned back in her chair and took off her glasses. She *was* happy when she talked to Logan. Correct. True. She couldn't deny it. She hadn't spoken to him since returning from the hike because it had seemed like the only way to avoid a disastrous affair. Nothing physical had happened between them, but it didn't matter. When they were together, they were lovers. It had been hard enough before the pregnancy. And now? She wanted his love even more, but deserved it even less.

At least that was what she had thought until yesterday. Yoga class. Late afternoon. She had unrolled her mat and recited the opening chant with an odd tightness, a stiffness of the muscles. Her breath shallow, her thoughts scattered among the minor errands she hadn't accomplished. But then the instructor had started speaking softly during the sun salutations. No pose is worth restricted breath. No pose is worth tensed muscles. No pose is worth the loss of your smile. And she had gone down into child's pose and sobbed softly, unable to resist the naked feelings welling up in her. The urge she felt for everything. For the life humming inside her. It was silly. It was true. She couldn't close herself off to the possibility of loving Logan simply because it was inconvenient. The real problem was that she didn't know if she could face him. What would he think of her when he discovered the truth?

She picked up the phone and called his office, the numbers illegible without her glasses, but she knew the pattern of the keys. He probably wouldn't be there. She'd leave a message saying she wanted to continue working with him.

His actual voice came over the line.

"OK," she said. "I'm willing to read the next draft if you're willing to send it."

"Send?"

She surprised herself with this condition. Now that she was talking to him, she knew she couldn't take the plunge right away. "Campus mail. We can discuss revisions over the phone."

"What about Palm Springs?"

"I'll drive separately and meet you an hour before the presentation to review any last-minute details. I have to be strict about this, Logan."

"I miss you," he said.

She closed her eyes for a moment. "And if we could keep the talk on a professional level, I would appreciate it."

"All right," he said. "Historical materialism. Base, superstructure. Capital accumulation. Labor power. Surplus value."

"What are you saying?"

"I'm keeping the talk on a professional level. Today's class was about Marx." She heard the squeak of his chair, the soft thunk of what she guessed was a book landing on his desk. "Last summer I read his biography to learn some personal details about him. Just to add some color to the lecture. But the more I read, the more I understood how his theories were natural outgrowths of his life — and I don't mean simply that his analysis was subjective. Everyone knows that. What I mean is, even the driest parts of the analysis were deeply personal for him in ways that no one will ever understand."

"The personal and professional are inseparable."

"You said it, I didn't."

She wanted to ask him when his wife had returned from her trip and if the relationship had improved. But, following her own rule, she held off. "Continue," she said.

"Expelled from Prussia and France for his political writings, he fled to London. No job. No prospects. He lived with his wife and children in a two-room slum."

"How many children?"

"Three. Plus a maid."

"A maid? How could he afford—"

"She bore him an illegitimate child at one point."

Keris paused. "I don't like the term 'illegitimate.'"

"You know what I mean."

"What do you mean?"

"Born out of wedlock."

"OK. Continue."

"He went to the British Museum every day and read whatever he could get his hands on, from obscure government documents to the works of classical economists such as Smith and Ricardo. Did I mention he suffered from boils and piles?"

"You can skip that part."

"I hope zat ze bourgeoisie," Logan grumbled in a deep German accent, "vill have cause to remember my carbuncles. And you know, he was right about some crucial things."

"Such as?"

"The whole process of capital accumulation. Employers investing their profit in equipment to raise the productivity of labor, which causes unemployment and, ironically, decreased demand for the very goods they're producing. It eventually leads to a downturn. A depression. The economy recovers only when excess goods have finally been sold and prices begin to rise and the whole process happens all over again. But each cycle involves more labor-saving equipment and more overall production with a dwindling amount of labor involved. Each glut becomes longer and more severe. And furthermore, the downturns allow bigger companies to gobble up smaller ones. Businesses with greater financial resources gain increasing shares of the market until a few large ones control everything. There's a preponderance of mergers and conglomerates, mega-corporations. Sound familiar?"

Keris remained silent. You would be happier with me, she thought. You would recognize your own potential.

"I haven't mentioned all the problems with Marx's theories," Logan said, "but that part of it seems accurate to me. It seems correct."

"It feels right," Keris said.

"Exactly." He paused. "I've talked too much. What are you working on?"

"The program for the microwave detector. Drudge-work." She glanced at the computer screen, at the printouts and handwritten notes spread across her desk. It was all an underwater blur without her glasses. "I'd like to see the latest draft of your paper. Tomorrow, if possible."

"Why the rush?"

She hesitated. She could feel him listening. "Because I miss you, too," she said, and softly hung up the phone.

She exhaled. She gripped her nose with her fingers. Stupid, stupid, stupid. She was sending him mixed signals. If she didn't know what she wanted from him, how could she expect him to supply it?

The door opened suddenly and she reached for her glasses like a naked woman going for a towel. Sophie came into the room. The chocolate bar was nearly gone, the gold wrapper smeared and creased. Wait a minute. Keris glanced at the clock. A trip to the vending machine shouldn't take that long.

"Were you listening at the door?"

Sophie's eyes widened. "Me?" She popped the last of the chocolate bar into her mouth and shook her head. "Uh-uh."

But Keris knew the expression, the buried smile, the diversionary food-in-the-mouth tactic to camouflage her reaction. Keris turned away. She looked at her computer screen and tried to concentrate on it, but saw only Logan and herself in all the figures, star-crossed, canceled out. This, of course, didn't even include the other factor in the equation, the other phone conversation she had screwed up: Deck. She had tried to get through it quickly—too quickly, like a chore that could no longer be avoided. She had misspoken. He had reacted badly. She had hung up on him. But enough of that. It was over. She was moving forward. She would take all the appropriate measures to ensure the baby's health, and she would continue to interact with Logan. After all, she was an alchemist at heart. She believed in the process of making happiness from her daily struggles. What else is life for?

chapter 11

Let's look at it another way. Since happiness equals consumption divided by desire, the best way to solve the equation is to begin with a value for consumption, which itself consists of two basic components. The first, called Autonomous Consumption, is simply the proportion of consumption independent of income, while the second, known as the Marginal Propensity to Consume, is the proportion of each additional unit of income that is spent rather than saved, which is usually assumed to be greater than zero but less than one. So far, so good. The problem with such a simple equation, however, is that it assumes an exact or deterministic relationship between income and consumption, when in fact the relationship between these variables is inexact. It is necessary, then, to modify the consumption function by adding what is known as a disturbance or error term—i.e., a random variable that has well-defined probabilistic properties. This variable may be said to denote all those incalculable factors that affect consumption but cannot be taken directly into account, such as a gambling addiction or an unexpected pregnancy.

The only thing missing now is a value for desire, and this, it might be said, was the issue for Logan as he biked along the Rio Salado, gliding past the freshly painted lightpoles and benches, the rippling water, the shoreline garnished with desert plants. He followed the curve where some palo verdes stood, wired and braced, irrigation hoses coiled at their trunks. His eyes burned. His mouth was parched all the way back to his throat. It was the first 100-degree day of the year, officially speaking, and he was sweating, he was breathing, he was cycling with a steady motion and his hands were holding the handlebars loosely, forefingers resting on the brake levers. He was wearing a helmet that felt much better than it looked—and it only looked bad when he caught a glimpse of himself in the reflective glass of an office complex. His backpack held his books and papers, along with his tie and shirt and pants folded badly, but he shouldn't be judged too harshly for that. He learned these things by trial and error.

Keris's phone call had invigorated him, but he didn't want to admit it. So he didn't. Instead he clicked into high gear and accelerated down a hill too subtle for motorists to notice. He told himself that the real source of his happiness these days was Dallas rather than Keris. The only problem now was how to tell the former about the latter. Dallas deserved the truth. In fact, he had been planning to confess everything to her as soon as she returned from Vegas, steeling himself for a summit meeting in which everything would be revealed and the future of their marriage decided. But she had preempted him with a meek and agreeable attitude, a tearful apology for her behavior during the last couple of months, because, she had said, her boss had implemented some tedious on-the-job procedures and reneged on his promise to promote her to poker dealer and she had been taking it out on him. Could he forgive her? He had faltered before her trembling voice, her pleading eyes. And so instead of a great reckoning there had been a great lovemaking. Instead of resolution there had been renewal. Instead of lawyers and paperwork, there had been openness and honesty.

OK, here was the issue: For the past few weeks he had respected Keris's wishes and kept his distance even though it depressed him. And now suddenly she called and said she missed him while at the same time imposing strict regulations on their interaction. What new procedures would she demand tomorrow? Neither of them would benefit from that kind of relationship. He had to be fully present in his marriage. And that meant, of course, telling Dallas everything. But he still couldn't seem to overcome a deep reluctance to bring it up. He had avoided telling her before because things were bad. Now he avoided telling her because things were good.

He passed a pair of security guards on bicycles of their own, sporting sleek helmets and wraparound sunglasses, radio microphones clipped to their chests with spiral cords dangling. These days swimmers were being warded off on a regular basis. Patrols had been stepped up. Surveillance cameras had been fitted with infrared lenses. The fish were scheduled to arrive next week, at which point the launch ramps would be available to those who paid the fee and obtained the proper permits. Logan followed this route because it was relatively sheltered from traffic, leading to the canal that went through his neighborhood. Today, though, in a bold mood, he took a shortcut across Rural Road, waited for a stoplight that miraculously parted rush-hour traffic, and then followed some sidestreets through the residential neighborhoods, past empty sidewalks, houses pressurized with air-conditioning, a playground where kids risked sunstroke on the monkey bars.

He coasted into his driveway. He dismounted, grabbed the mail, and went into the garage, where he leaned his bike against the wall. Dallas's car was huddled there, still radiating heat from the afternoon commute. He hung his helmet on the handlebars and went inside.

"Hey you," Dallas said. She was standing at the stove in a frayed tank top and shorts, a casserole bubbling in front of her. Her hair loose and sexy and beautiful. The television was blaring in the living room. The central air was humming. She came over and kissed him.

"Tastes like you went swimming in the ocean," she said, smacking her lips.

"An ocean of sweat. I should take a shower."

"Can I show you something first?"

He nodded. She stepped away and lifted up her hair to expose a nicotine patch below her ear.

"Surprised?" she said.

Logan hesitated. Surprised that she had quit smoking? Surprised that she had taken it up again without telling him? Surprised that she was acknowledging it at all? He eased his arms out of his backpack and let it drop to the floor. He tossed the mail on the kitchen counter. "Yeah," he said. "I'm surprised."

Her expression faltered. "You probably hate me now."

"No. Of course not." He took her hand. "I'm glad you told me. It's just that I'm . . ."

"You're hurt. You're mad because I deceived you."

"I just wish," he finally said, "that you didn't feel the need to hide it from me."

An audience began clapping in the living room, a saxophone bleating out a theme song.

"To be perfectly honest, it didn't start like 'Hey, I'm gonna take up smoking again.' It was because of that stuff at work. The hassle. The stress. Basically it's one cigarette to take the edge off and then maybe another one, and pretty soon I'm having six or seven a day. But it never felt like I was a smoker, like the habit was official. So I wanted to make sure I was off it again before I told you about it. That was my thinking on the issue."

He considered mentioning the fact that only a life-threatening case of pneumonia would have prevented him from smelling and tasting it all over her, but she seemed to feel terrible enough already, so he let it go. He wasn't about to pour gas on that fire.

"Is that where you're supposed to wear it?" he asked, looking at the patch.

"This is where it works for me."

Sirens trilled on the television. A car crashed. A woman screamed.

"How about a trade? I'll take a shower if you turn down the volume."

"In five minutes," she said, heading over to the stove. "After the lottery drawing."

"You're kidding."

"I'm feeling lucky, OK?"

He picked up his backpack. "In that case, I'll take care of my books first. I don't want to get caught with shampoo in my hair when we win."

He went into his study and closed the door behind him and set his backpack on the desk. Glancing out the window, he saw a large patch of barren soil where the pool had been and it actually surprised him—or surprised his eye—before he remembered the restoration in progress. Last week he had drained the pool and then hired a crew to demolish the concrete basin and fill in the hole. He had even called someone with a chainsaw to cut down the citrus trees, but at the last minute ordered a stay of execution. He didn't have the heart. Sure, they sucked up ten times more water than native plants. They didn't belong there. But it felt wrong to kill them.

He unpacked his folders, his books, his papers. He shook out his clothing and laid it on the guest bed. And when he unzipped the outer compartment of his backpack, Marx's *Capital* fell out and hit the floor with an angry thud. He grabbed it by one of its dog-ears and set it on the desk. The students had responded well to the material—that is, to the cleaner and more eloquent passages he had selected from the text. There had been a few arguments of the Ozzy-and-Erin variety about the Labor Theory of Value underlying Marx's critique. Some tirades against Communism. Ditto capitalism. He had reined them in whenever their speeches wandered too far from the topic. And was it just his imagination or did there seem to be more students in the room than were actually enrolled for the course?

He shook his head. Forget it. He had to think about Palm Springs. The conference was happening in three weeks and if history repeated itself—scheduled, this time, as farce—then he was going to face not only Dr. No, but an unsympathetic audience as well. The fallout from their last confrontation had settled over him so heavily that he seemed to glow during faculty meetings, pulsing in the coded silences and occasional traces of innuendo suggesting that, among other things, the new Economics Institute would have very little room for historical analysis or examinations of the epistemology behind neoclassical theory. Perhaps Logan could emigrate to the Philosophy department? He suspected that the debate was a set-up of some kind: Target practice on a naysayer, or maybe an opportunity to provoke him into a sin terrible enough to warrant excommunication. After all, the audience would consist of private sponsors whose funding would largely determine the direction of the Economics Institute — including, perhaps, the very existence of certain faculty positions. And if Logan's position didn't receive any funding . . . He shook his head again. Forget it.

He began sorting through his materials, putting each item in its assigned place. Research articles on one shelf, lecture outlines on another, printed spreadsheets on his desk along with some notes he had jotted down in between classes that day. He couldn't help it. Where there had been chaos, there was now order. He had organized his study a few weeks ago — OK, the day after he had returned from the hike — and discovered that he couldn't stop organizing. He had developed a habit of sifting through the debris of each day's experience, as if a day could never be finished, never truly assimilated or understood, until he unpacked his bag and found a place for everything. He thought through the physical world.

As a final gesture, he turned his backpack upside down with all the zippers open and shook it. Something flapped out and hit the floor. A booklet from the registration office. This was his latest prop to encourage Dallas to sign up for classes at the university — or at least, he hoped, to quit the casino for a job that would give her some measure of satisfaction. He was trying to facilitate the process.

He came out of his study and, finding the kitchen empty, stuck the booklet into the pile of mail so Dallas would think it had arrived along with everything else. He glanced into the living room and saw her standing with her arms folded in front of the television, cages full of numbered ping-pong balls whirling on the screen. He went into the bathroom. He turned on the shower and stripped. And then he caught a glimpse of himself in the mirror. Usually this would be an unpleasant moment — the unflattering proportions, that extra dough around the waist — but this time he realized all the biking and yardwork was beginning to show. Muscles were emerging from plain surfaces. Flab was disappearing. His mid-section was more sharply defined. And his skin was darker from all that time in the sun. Dallas had commented on it last night in bed. She had smiled, she had kissed him, she had moaned into his ear and wrapped her legs around his hips like he might float away. Again that neediness, that guilt. It made him uneasy. It was possible, of course, that she simply appreciated the physical change in him. Or maybe she understood it as a manifestation of deeper things. Keris. His research. Conclusions that weren't restricted to the page. After all, it isn't always necessary to understand the parameters in order to understand the equation. This, at least, was Logan's thought, this was his feeling, as he stepped under the nozzle and tasted his own salt as it rinsed away.

Dallas turned off the television. Not even close. She had played the digits of her birthday, Logan's birthday, and their wedding date, seeking some kind of confirmation in the drawing—the right numbers in the wrong order, perhaps, or maybe even a few key numbers spread too thinly between the tickets to win anything. That would have been enough. But the cosmos seemed to be laughing at her. She dropped the remote on the coffee table and went into the kitchen, stirred the casserole for a minute, and then began sorting through the mail. Catalogs, advertisements, credit card offers. A booklet from the university, courtesy of a certain husband who will remain nameless. And a letter from the bank. Dallas held the thin envelope between her fingers for a moment. Then she tore it open and unfolded the page. The words flamed out at her. No. That couldn't be right. There was no way that could be right. She leaned against the counter and read it again, hands trembling, juddery all over, and finally folded it up again and stuffed it in the junk drawer, below dead batteries and masking tape and tools they never used.

The casserole was bubbling like a witch's brew. She went over and stirred it again. Peppers and tomatoes and onions. Chicken, rice, and spice. Breathe, she thought. Relax. It was a mistake. Either her bank or Felix's bank had crossed their numbers or debited something that should have been credited or made some other error along the way. She glanced at the clock. Long past closing time. She'd have to go over to the bank tomorrow morning in person because it took you forever to work your way through the touch-tone menu and she wanted to see the evidence before she called Felix. Which she doubted she'd have to do. It was a mistake. And besides, Felix could always write out another check.

But she had already mailed her own checks to her credit card companies and now those checks would come back with penalty charges and—stop it, stop it, stop it. She cupped her hands over her nose and mouth. Trembling. She needed a cigarette. But she was basically already having a cigarette, wasn't she? She touched the patch on her neck and considered adding another one, but Logan would probably notice. She had waited a couple of days for Felix's check to clear and, since she hadn't heard anything from her bank, had assumed no news was good news, to be perfectly honest. And now, a week later, here was this letter saying—

She heard the shower shut off. OK. He would be out of the bedroom in ten minutes and she'd have to get through dinner and the rest of the evening without showing panic. She could do it. She knew how to maintain Logan's illusions. She hadn't had an orgasm, for example, since returning from Vegas. Something seemed to be locked up inside her. She couldn't relax. She couldn't achieve the proper release. But she thrashed around like a shark-attack victim just the same, giving the impression of ecstasy.

By the time Logan came to the table the wine had been poured and the casserole was steaming on their plates.

"What did I do," he said as he sat down, "to deserve such a feast?"

She smiled at him. It was a funny thing, showing the opposite of what she felt. Like developing a new set of muscles. She detached her face from the usual circuits and let it function independently, shifting into the proper expressions at the proper times. It was automatic. And it was effective. Nobody knew the difference.

She leaned across the table and kissed him lightly. Then she wrapped a hand around the back of his head and did it again, more fully this time, savoring the taste of him. This was the closest she could come to telling him the truth.

He gave her a perplexed smile. "What was that all about?"

"Affection," she said, as she sat back in her seat. "Is that allowed?"

"Not only allowed but encouraged. It was just a surprise, that's all. A happy surprise."

"After some unhappy surprises."

He paused with a forkful of casserole raised to his mouth. "Come on. Don't be so hard on yourself."

She shrugged apologetically. They ate without speaking for a while. The quiet clinking of utensils, the crunch of food between teeth. She had forgotten to put on some background music and was really beginning to regret it. A silence like vinegar in the air. When he complimented her on the casserole, which she hardly tasted, to be perfectly honest, she looked across the table at him and realized he had no idea anything was wrong. Which was exactly what she wanted. So why did it make her feel worse?

"You know," she said, as if the thought had just occurred to her, "I should stop playing the slots after work."

He raised his eyebrows. "What's this?"

"Oh, you know. After work sometimes. I take a little bit of money and blow it on the slots."

"When did this start?" He had stopped eating.

She shrugged. "A few weeks ago. Maybe more. I mentioned it to you."

"You didn't mention it to me."

"I mentioned it to somebody named Logan who was also my husband. Tell me if that description fits you."

"I don't remember this."

She sighed and finished off her wine before replying, like he was quibbling over something foolishly minor. "Anyway, it's a waste, is what I'm thinking these days. Whenever I win something, I just lose it later."

"That's because it's a social trap."

She laughed. "You mean an anti-social trap."

"Economists call it a social trap because the long-term costs and benefits are inconsistent with the short-term ones. For example, if you play a slot machine for an hour, you might hit a jackpot, right?"

"A royal."

"A royal jackpot."

"A royal flush. That's the highest payoff."

"All right. So you hit a royal flush. But the machines are programmed to pay out, say, eighty cents for every dollar you play over the long term. You might win a lot of money now and then, but those winnings won't compensate for heavier overall losses. You end up losing a total of twenty cents out of every dollar you play. But what if the short-term and long-term effects were the same? What if someone reprogrammed the machine so that every time you played a dollar, only eighty cents came out? You wouldn't play very long, would you?"

"Did I say I played for a long time? When did I say that?"

"It's just an example. I don't mean you, Dallas. I mean the rhetorical 'you.' It sounds less formal than 'one.' My point is simply that we can address a lot of problems by modifying an individual's short-term incentives to make them consistent with the long-term goals of society. Global warming, pollution, resource depletion — all of it could be addressed more effectively with this kind of system." He was pinching the stem of his wineglass, but hadn't lifted it from the table.

"So you'd have to be a fool to play slots, is what you're saying."

"No, no. Of course not. For someone who plays a little bit now and then, like you, it's just recreation. But when the losses start to accumulate? When you see the general effect of it? You have to wonder what's going on in someone's mind." He lifted his glass and drank.

She looked away for a moment. There was a greasy heat all over her. She picked up the bottle and refilled her glass. Nothing like a cool white wine to keep the spirits afloat. Although it increased her ache for a cigarette. The patch lacked that crucial element of cigarette-ness that she needed right now. She exhaled through her nose.

"What's wrong?" he asked.

"I'm wondering how we can reconcile the short-term benefits of leaving your car in the parking garage with the long-term problem of having only one vehicle."

He laughed. He stretched his legs under the table, his feet bumping hers. "Guilty as charged. First-degree car-slaughter and gross negligence. What's the penalty?"

"You have to clear the table and put everything in the dishwasher."

"Ouch."

"And then you have to make love to me."

"Cruel and unusual punishment." He rose from the table and began picking up the dinnerware. "But I guess it's what I deserve."

She sat there with her wine, smiling, feeling wrecked inside, watching him carry the dishes over to the sink and then rinse them carefully before loading them into the dishwasher.

"By the way," he called back to her. "I forgot to ask if we won the lottery. Are we millionaires?"

"Of course we won." She reached up and touched the patch on her neck to see if it was still there. The after-dinner urge for a cigarette was absolutely ferocious. "We hit the jackpot. What else did you expect?"

It's worth noting that, on the same day Dallas received the letter from the bank, Deck went for an HIV test at a clinic in Portsmouth. It was the logical thing to do. The test was free and anonymous, and if the condom had been faulty, he reasoned, then it had been faulty in both directions. So he called the clinic and made an appointment with a woman who said she needed to write down his name, even if it wasn't his real one, to hold his time-slot. He didn't hesitate. Logan, he said. Then he hung up and laughed. At least he had a sense of humor about it.

He drove under black skies, a cold misty rain. Headlights at noon. He blared music and tried not to think about what might be happening in his cells at that very moment. Because of her. The conventional wisdom was that women didn't have as many sexual partners as men, which meant that either a few sluts were making up for the virtuous majority or most women were covering their tracks. Deck went with option number two. He knew women pretended to be discriminating in their choices and more interested in love than sex, but in fact they didn't care who they fucked. They simply cared who found out about it.

He parked in a public lot five blocks away from the clinic. He wore his raincoat with the hood up, grim reaper–style, in case he happened to pass anyone from campus who might recognize him. He gave his fake name at a desk. Two minutes later someone called him — or, to be more accurate, called Logan — and he followed a middle-aged woman down a hallway to an office that clearly didn't belong to anyone. Generic chairs. An empty bookcase in the corner. A second-hand desk with nothing on it except a box of tissues, like he might burst into tears or something. The walls were adorned with propaganda posters warning against venereal disease, which struck him as a case of too little, too late in the worst possible way. Put them up in night-clubs, he thought. Put them up in bars. In this room it was nothing more than a sermon for the eternally damned.

The woman had a cemented perm and an expression that belonged on a totem pole in the middle of the African jungle. She sat straight in her chair with her hands folded in her lap and stared at him as if he had been caught breaking a window during recess. He crossed his legs. The inquisition began. Why did he want to be tested? Had he thought about what he would do if the results were positive? Did he have sexual relations with men, women, or both? How long since his last unprotected sex?

"Just give me the test," he finally said.

"We'll do that in a minute. Do you know that if you've been exposed to HIV, it takes between six weeks and three months for it to appear in the test results?"

His thoughts halted in their tracks. He began to click backward, calculating the weeks since his encounter with Keris. "No," he said, feeling his blood rise. "The woman didn't tell me that on the phone."

"Well, then it's —"

"Why didn't she tell me that on the phone?"

The inquisitor paused. "If you'd like to come back in a few weeks . . ."

"No," he said. "This is it. Let's do it."

They moved to another room stocked with minor-league medical equipment, a few instruments and first-aid supplies in glass cabinets. He sat down, rolled up his sleeve, rested his arm on a pillow. The woman tightened a strap around his biceps, applied the alcohol swab, and then punctured him with the needle, the vial filling with his ripe blood. When it was finished he drove home in a fury and went to the gym seeking catharsis with the free weights, but suffered through a lackluster workout instead — a sign, perhaps. He went back to the clinic the next day. Results negative. Of course. It was too soon. He'd have to do the damn test again in a couple of weeks. In the meantime, he'd get Keris's phone number from Logan and call her, using the HIV issue as an excuse. He needed every ounce of leverage he could get.

Dallas waited until Logan biked off to campus the next day before she retrieved the letter from the kitchen drawer. She read it over one more time and tucked it neatly into her purse. She knew how to approach this. She had figured it out last night in bed, in the numb aftermath of sex. She went into the bathroom now and applied some low-key shades of makeup. She dressed herself in medium heels, slacks, a prim blouse — not because it would make a difference to the people at the bank but because it would help her to maintain the proper composure. Emotional displays would only weaken her credibility, is what she was thinking. Not that it would even reach that point, she told herself as she drove to the bank. The teller would probably punch a few keys and tell her it was a mistake. She peeled the nicotine patch off her neck and checked her face in the rearview before she went inside. The letter, she told herself, was obviously wrong.

It was right. She came out of the bank twenty minutes later, striding through the hot glare of the parking lot, the plains of white fire. She stopped at a convenience store on the way home and bought a long-distance phonecard because she didn't want any evidence on the bill next month. By the time she reached the house it was an oven. She turned down the thermostat and heard a soft thud somewhere in the recesses of the central vents, followed by a weak whisper of air. She picked up the phone and dialed the special number on the card and then punched in her code and then finally Felix's number, standing there at the kitchen counter, sweating in her stupid outfit.

"I've been meaning to call you about that," he said, after she had calmly and reasonably explained the situation.

"You knew this would happen?"

"A couple of days after you left," he said, sighing, "I got into this thing with Sharon. She called me. We're not supposed to talk to each other, but she called and started threatening me over the phone. The bottom line is that she wants me to pay for Jason's education after all. She's really taking me to the wall. It's terrible. Absolutely terrible. Don't ever get divorced."

"What about," Dallas said, steadying herself, "the check you wrote out to me?"

"I'm really sorry about that. I had to follow my lawyer's advice and stop the payment on it. I'm going to need that money. I hope you understand."

She stood there in a choked silence, staring out the kitchen window at the dead grass, the shallow ditches, the piles of dirt in their backyard. Her legs were shaking. She asked him to repeat what he had just said.

He repeated it.

"Listen to me," she said. She tottered over to a chair and lowered herself onto it. "Felix, listen. You can't do this. You can't take it back. I already wrote out the checks to my credit card companies."

"I feel terrible."

"Don't listen to your lawyer. Listen to your heart."

"I shouldn't have promised the loan without thinking it over more carefully. It was thoughtless of me. I can't believe I did that. You probably hate me now."

"We spent the night together," she said, hearing the plea, the helplessness in her voice. There were times when she hated her own behavior even as it was happening.

"And it was wonderful. We never laughed like that before. Why didn't we —"

"I mean," she said. "I spent the night. I spent the night with you, Felix."

"Wait, wait, wait. Are you saying what I think you're saying?"

She bridged her hand over her eyes. Her face was on fire. Her forehead slick and feverish. "What I'm saying is that we have a connection, you and me, and you're spoiling it by basically taking back the loan after you already gave it to me."

"You hate me," he said. "I knew it. That's why I couldn't bring myself to call."

She looked down at herself — her plain brown shoes, her ordinary slacks. This wasn't going to work. Like an iceberg, 90 percent of his refusal was below the surface and no amount of charm or persuasion would ever melt it. She knew that now. And she knew that he had planned it from the very beginning.

She rose from the chair, tightening her grip on the phone. "Take some time to reconsider your decision. All right? Do you understand what I'm saying now? You lend me the money, like you promised, otherwise I tell the casino how you met me at the bar that night without reporting it to security. I call your wife and offer to testify that I heard you say you molested your son when you talked in your sleep one night. Think about it. Think about the long-term costs and benefits."

"You'd lie?"

"Yes," she said, almost believing it herself.

"You'd make up a story about me and tell it to the judge?"

"You got it."

"In that case, there's something else you should know."

"What?"

"I've been recording my phone calls ever since that last conversation with Sharon. My lawyer recommended it. You're on tape right now."

The air left her. Her mouth fell open. "Nice try," she finally said. "But I don't believe it. Reconsider the loan, is what I'm saying. Two days. Forty-eight hours. That's when I start making phone calls."

She pressed the disconnect button, slid the phone across the counter, and started pacing the kitchen. She cursed. She kicked off her shoes and flung them into the living room and then pursued them with some vague intention of throwing them around some more, but when she bent over to grab them she kept going all the way down to the floor and collapsed there, sobbing, her forehead pressed against the cool tile. She turned onto her back and wept. She shook. She cried hoarsely through her throat. When it was over she felt so exhausted that she almost fell asleep, but she couldn't breathe through her nose. Eventually she picked herself up and found a box of tissues in the guest bathroom, carefully avoiding the sight of her swollen eyes in the mirror.

The phone rang. It was like an electric current in her chest. Felix was capable of changing his mind. He really was. And just enough time had passed for her empty threat to sink in. Had he actually believed her? But she didn't run to answer it. She walked into the kitchen like a civilized human being and cleared the hair from her face before she picked up the receiver.

It was Deck. She almost hung up the phone.

"I thought Logan would be there," he said. "Isn't this his day off?"

Dallas said it wasn't.

"I'd like to leave a message, if it's all right with you."

Dallas said it was. She was speaking softly, frugally, to hide the congestion in her voice.

"Do you have a cold?" he asked.

"Allergies," she said.

"Really. What are you allergic to?"

"Name it. People moved here from different parts of the world and basically brought those parts of the world with them. You want to leave a message for Logan?"

He cleared his throat. "It's more like a question. I just need some information about the woman he works with. For the purposes of the debate next month. He'll know what I mean."

Dallas had picked up a pen to write it down, but she stopped with the point resting on the page. "The woman he works with."

"The astrophysicist. His co-author and collaborator. You should hear the buzz ever since that last conference. My prediction is that Palm Springs is going to be standing room only."

"They're writing a paper together," she said.

"Come to think of it, that's probably why he's on campus today. I'll call him there."

"No," she said suddenly. "You won't reach him."

"Why not?"

She could feel the gears beginning to turn somewhere, lights coming on inside her. "He's at the library. All day. I'll give him the message when he comes home."

There was a silence on the other end of the line.

"Are you still there?" she asked.

"You know," he said. "I don't need this information directly from Logan. If you could do me the favor of finding out her phone number—I'm sure he has it written down somewhere—then I wouldn't have to bother him with it. In fact, I probably wouldn't even mention it at all."

She asked Deck to spell the woman's last name. She was already walking toward Logan's study. His address book was in the top drawer of his desk with the evidence written in pencil on the very first page, like something temporary and harmless. She read the number to him.

"I appreciate it," he said.

"So there's no message for Logan," she said.

"Consider this whole conversation null and void."

She looked at Logan's desktop, at the papers and books stacked neatly on the shelves, the corners of each object obsessively squared with its neighbor. How could she have missed it? How could she have believed the changes coming over him didn't involve another woman?

"Take care of those allergies," Deck said.

"I'm already taking care of them," she said, reaching up and, before she realized what she was doing, peeling the nicotine patch off her neck. "I'm trying a new medicine now."

chapter 12

Half a month later. Midweek, midafternoon. Keris was walking on Mill Avenue, through the window glare and dragon's breath, the fast-food pheromones. The sun burned. The pavement baked. The misters hissed over vacant tables. Most of the restaurants had settled into their siestas by now, but everyone else seemed to be muscling their way through this sluggish part of the day. She warded off a marketeer handing out deodorant samples and then, almost immediately afterward, spare-change requests from a couple of teenage panhandlers who weren't homeless, but homefree, having rejected the bourgeois lifestyles of their parents, and so she donated not her coins but the banana she happened to be carrying in her bag. She couldn't eat it anyway. Morning sickness was upon her.

Make that all-day sickness. It had started a few days ago with a general nausea that never quite coalesced into vomiting. Unlike her first pregnancy, in which the mere sight of cheese had sent her running to the bathroom, this time around it simply had the effect of deadening her appetite. Yesterday she had struggled through her usual breakfast — a cup of yogurt with some wheatgerm and dried cherries mixed in — before switching to a raisin bagel with peanut butter. Carbohydrates didn't banish the queasiness, but they seemed to make it bearable. And, anyway, weren't carbs supposed to give her more energy? Weren't they supposed to alleviate her deep fatigue, her bone-heaviness, her clug-and-slug through the days when, despite her naps, she followed Sophie immediately to bed? She had cut back on yoga, on her hours at the lab. And thank God Sophie had enrolled in a swimming class after school, otherwise Keris simply wouldn't be able to keep up.

She reached the cafe where she had agreed to meet Logan and stepped into cool air. Rainforest murals. Flute music. Why was the sound of nature always a flute? Potted trees stood among the tables, their branches spread so profusely into the configurations of the room that moving them would have meant amputating limbs. She waited in line behind the usual assortment of students and office workers, running her fingers through her hair to free a few damp strands pasted to her temples. She shook out her skirt. It was long and loose and earth-toned, but still managed to generate a greenhouse effect down there. Right about now she felt the urge to lie down and catch a two-hour snooze. Delicious sleep. After all, she had walked, full tilt, through the heat so she could arrive early and choose a table in a conspicuous location before Logan got there. Her goal was to discourage intimacy. Why, then, had she agreed to the face-to-face meeting? Because there was too much to do in too little time. They were at a final stage of the collaboration requiring quick, numerous exchanges of figures and graphs that no means of telecommunication could satisfy. And so Keris had suggested this cafe, and she had deliberately assigned herself the duty of picking up Sophie and Katie from swimming class in a couple of hours even though it was Charlotte's turn. It was an external boundary based on internal law.

Logan showed up five minutes later. "You're early," he said, sitting down at the table.

She shook her head mildly. "You're late."

He was wearing a T-shirt and shorts and funny sneakers that clicked on the floor like tap-dancing shoes as he walked. She didn't have to ask. She had seen enough students clipping into their bike pedals outside the Physical Sciences building to recognize the device. It kept the feet aligned and equalized the effort between them, thereby increasing the efficiency, the energy-to-output ratio. It meant he was becoming serious about his biking. It also meant that his leaner and browner appearance wasn't the product of her imagination.

She didn't comment. Instead she adopted a strictly business tone, scribbling some corrections and clarifications and refinements on the pages he showed her, and then handed over the report she had drawn up the previous week. She sipped her peppermint tea and watched him as he read it. The knowledge seemed to take hold of him like an illness. His expression darkening, the lines deepening in his face. She looked away and tried to ground herself in the activity of the cafe — the fan blades spinning overhead, the cool vents blowing, the smell of burnt-earth coffee and flavored syrups — but it was too late. The inner glow of everything was shifting, taking on an altered mood, like the pivot between late night and early morning.

Logan folded over the final page of the report and remained silent for a moment. "Two and a half more Earths," he said at last.

"It must be wrong," she said, sipping her tea. "This isn't my specialty. You should be working with an ecologist or someone else in the environmental sciences."

He tossed the report onto the table and scrubbed a hand through his hair. "Two and a half additional Earths would be required to support the world's population at the standard of living currently enjoyed in the United States."

"I'm jeopardizing the entire project by drafting up such a figure. I myself don't believe it."

He tapped the pages with his index finger. "This is solid. This is a conservative estimate that, if anything, grossly understates the case. I'm willing to bet the total is closer to three, maybe three and a half more Earths. Where are we going to find these extra planets?"

"As I mention in the report, we have to account for advances in technology. Fusion. Solar energy. Improved productivity of farmland through —"

He tilted his head back in exasperation. "If I hear somebody say 'technology is going to save us' one more time, I'm going to do a backflip through that plate glass window and drown myself in the Rio Salado."

"Technology is going to save us."

"You don't believe that."

"I want to see you do a backflip."

He sighed. "Are you going to deny the implications of your own research?"

"It would be irresponsible to announce these figures."

"You mean it would be irresponsible to withhold them." He picked up the report. "Six million hectares of productive land lost every year due to encroaching deserts. Eleven million hectares of tropical forests due to deforestation. Thirty-one million hectares of forest dieback as the result of acid rain in Europe alone. Soil oxidation and erosion, 26 billion tons in excess of formation. Soil salinization from failed irrigation projects, 1.5 million hectares per year." He flipped a page. "This is the part where you don't give numbers because the amounts are impossible to quantify. Draw-down and pollution of groundwater. Fisheries exhaustion. Declining per capita grain production. Ozone depletion. Increasing levels of atmospheric carbon dioxide."

"Lower your voice, please."

"Even if somebody invents a super-duper solar panel this afternoon and allows us to use the — wait a minute," he said, flipping a few more pages, "the 175,000 terawatts of energy from the sun . . . Even if somebody does that, we still have to acknowledge the damage we've done by using only 10 terawatts of commercial energy." He set the report on the table. "And what about waste absorption and processing? Let's assume for a moment that we can defy the laws of physics and grow wheat in the Sahara and catch fish in empty oceans. We're still producing waste faster than the Earth can break it down. The limiting factor isn't only energy. It's waste. Why can't we announce this?"

She cradled the cup of tea in her hands — feeling a chill, believe it or not, from the air-conditioning. Why couldn't they announce it? Because she didn't have the strength to defend it. Because she had already spent too much time and energy on this extracurricular activity. Because she secretly hoped he could defend his position without her. Because she even more secretly hoped he couldn't. Because every particle of matter has a corresponding particle of antimatter somewhere in the universe, the measurement of one affecting the measurement of the other, no matter how many billions of light years they're apart. Because the principle is called entanglement. Because she was pregnant with somebody else's child.

She reached across the table and took his hand, preparing him for what she needed to say. Logan returned her gaze. But then he raised his line of sight above her and withdrew his hand. She turned.

"I see signs," Dr. No said, standing there with a faint smile on his face, "of rigorous preparation."

"Fact-finding," Logan said.

"My uncle used to say that fact-finding and soul-searching are the same thing. But he was a statistician." He met Keris's eye. "Dr. Aguilar, I presume?"

Keris endured the formal introduction. The polite handshake, the courteous smile. She almost called him Dr. No by mistake. His dark sportcoat seemed identical to the one he had worn at the conference, but the faded jeans and cowboy boots gave him a down-home effect that, she suspected, had been cultivated to set other people at ease and compensate for certain deficiencies in his personality. Not that he wasn't attractive. There was a vibrancy in those shocks of white hair, a vigor in the etched lines of his face. Gray eyes gleaming with top-percentile looks. It was the inner hydraulics she sensed and disliked. And, wait a minute, here was something interesting: He was holding a to-go cup in his hand, which meant he had been in the cafe for a while and had, perhaps, heard part of their conversation before approaching their table.

"What a coincidence I should see you now. I just finished typing up the announcement."

Logan raised his eyebrows. "Announcement?"

"It seems that the Assistant Secretary of Commerce is planning to attend the debate."

Keris gazed into the tepid remains of her tea and felt the window of opportunity closing firmly, the lock cinching tight. What she had been about to say a few minutes ago had been necessary then, but impossible now.

"Why is the Assistant Secretary of Commerce interested in what a couple of economics professors have to say?"

"Because they're saying it in Palm Springs," Dr. No said. "I spoke to Assistant Secretary Groscost himself on the phone this morning, and he told me that the chairman of the CEA was impressed enough by our disagreement to bring it up at a recent meeting." He chuckled. "Normally you couldn't pry someone like him out of Washington with a crowbar, but he hinted that coming out to the conference is just the kind of 'official' duty that might lead to a working vacation."

"So this," Keris said, looking at him carefully, "might not be attendance in the true sense, but only face time."

He turned the full force of his gaze on her. "I wouldn't presume to judge," he said, "what the Assistant Secretary considers important and what he doesn't. Nor would I presume to judge how his opinion about a subject might change in the wake of a lively debate." He glanced at his watch. "Well, the classroom awaits, and I still have to share the good news with Dr. Moore."

"Who?" Logan asked.

Dr. No stopped as he was about to leave. "Dr. Moore. Your friend? I assume you've spoken to him recently."

"What does Deck have to do with this?"

Dr. No glanced at each of them to make sure this wasn't a ruse. "Dr. Moore is going to be my partner in the debate. I thought you knew."

She missed Logan's reaction, whatever it was, in the terrible heat flooding through her. Dr. Moore. Deck. Logan's *friend?* She didn't want to believe it right away. She wanted to indulge in a few minutes of denial before slowly acknowledging the possibility, then the probability, and finally the undeniability of it. But it was one of those stark and instant truths, like a fatal traffic accident, that didn't give her time to think. After all, Deck had left two messages on her answering machine last week and now it all made sense.

"That's news to me," Logan said. His expression had tightened as if he had a headache.

"Certainly you don't expect an old man like me to face two energetic opponents without some assistance?"

"Of course not. I'm looking forward to it."

"Good," Dr. No said. "I'll see you soon."

Logan waited until Dr. No had passed beyond the window outside before he slumped in his chair, arms dangling at his sides as if he had been shot. Keris remained absolutely still. Her first instinct was to seek refuge in the ladies' room, but certain facts, she realized, needed to be confirmed.

"This other person. Deck. Is he really your friend?"

Logan seemed to consider his answer seriously before he replied. "I don't know if that has ever been an accurate description. We went through graduate school together. When you're in a foxhole, everybody's your friend."

"What does he look like?"

He narrowed his eyes. "Look like?"

"Help me put a face to the name."

Logan gave her some basic details: tall, athletic, corn-colored hair. It was more than enough. She started giggling. She pressed a hand to her mouth, but couldn't stop. She snorted. She laughed. She keeled over sideways in her chair and surrendered to the feeling, the weakness, the softening of the muscles in her torso, and she wondered why there wasn't a Laughing Hyena pose, or something to that effect, in yoga. The purge, the release. The understanding it yielded. What you did in private had consequences that spread outward and became increasingly public until the resemblance between the two was completely lost.

Logan handed her a napkin to wipe her eyes. "Are you going to share?"

"It's nothing," she said.

"It's something."

"The universe, Logan, is mostly nothing. But that makes it something to us because we're incapable of handling empty space."

He gave her a skeptical look, refusing to be put off.

"I laughed because," she said, finally rescuing herself, "I was thinking of you doing a backflip through that window."

He watched her for a moment, deciding whether or not to believe her. Then he picked up his iced coffee.

She looked over at the murals on the wall, where happy monkeys lurked, camouflaged in the leaves. Maybe Deck had called simply to discuss the awkward situation. Why, then, had he called her home number? Her unlisted number? How had he gotten it? It felt like pursuit. And something else she couldn't identify. That night in the hotel room she had caught a steely glint in his eye as he was looking down at her, redefining the angle of his body against hers. She had shifted him into a different position after that. She had placed her hand over his heart and felt a dead chill instead of heat.

"We need a name for it," Logan said suddenly.

She blinked. "What?"

"We need a term," he said, "to describe the amount of land required to sustain the consumption of a given population."

She took a breath. "Call it a Footprint," she said. "A Biophysical Footprint."

He straightened in his chair. "You're a genius. Did you think of that just now?"

"Yesterday. I knew that you would want to call it something."

"You're a double-genius."

"But you have to note the period of time," she said.

"Excuse me?"

"The definition of Biophysical Footprint is, I believe you said, 'the amount of land required to sustain the consumption of a given population.' But for how long? Over what period of time?"

"Forever. That's what sustainability means. It goes without saying."

She shook her head. "It needs to be said."

He swirled the ice in his glass. "How about this. If your only source of income is a bank account, then you want to live off the interest, not the principal. And right now we're living off the principal."

"Nothing that a few extra planets wouldn't solve," she said.

"But even that solution is temporary unless we change our behavior."

"Yes," she said, as a fresh strain of nausea rose through her. "Unless we change our behavior."

The Assistant Secretary of Commerce. Dr. No. Keris. Dallas. Deck. Logan tried, for a while, to believe in the balance of disparate forces, in equilibriums that emerged from the apparent chaos of individuals pursuing their own self-interests. So why, then, did he stand at the podium reading off the entire roster? Why did it matter if the faces didn't match the names? Call it misplaced anxiety. Suspecting that the population of the lecture hall had increased unnaturally over the last few weeks, he wanted to find truth in official numbers, but discovered instead that it was simply a case of perfect attendance. Which was inconceivable. In a class this size there was a certain proportion of students missing even in the best of times — somewhere, it may be said, around 3 to 4 percent, like the unemployment rate in a booming economy. Yet here it was.

He put the roster away and did a quick recap of what he had covered in the previous class. John Maynard Keynes. National income. Fiscal policy. Output and unemployment. Savings, investment, and the interest rate. He had explained the propensity to consume, the inducement to invest, the marginal efficiency of capital. He had fielded questions about liquidity preference and the multiplier effect. He had brought everything together and distilled it into Keynes's basic belief that open economies were inherently unstable and that the source of the instability was financial markets. That's right. Financial markets. Irrational, knee-jerk wheeler-dealers who would sell their grandmothers into slavery for a higher return. And although Keynes favored the removal of trade barriers, he also favored the use of fixed exchange rates and restrictions on the flow of investment capital over national boundaries. These were the kind of regulations necessary to ensure that investors remained investors rather than speculators. Because speculators, Keynes believed, were the ones who caused most of the trouble, artificially swelling and deflating entire economies at the merest flicker of a percentage point.

So that was how it had gone and, aside from that crack about the wheeler-dealers, it was a pretty fair summary. Logan had covered the material efficiently — so efficiently, as a matter of fact, that he found himself with some leftover time today, an opportunity to deal with questions such as this:

"What's wrong with him?" This was Ozzy, mender of bicycles, vendor of shoes. His hair was still long, but it was tied back. The eternal five o'clock shadow was gone. And the reason for the changes, it's safe to say, was the young woman named Erin sitting next to him. She knew what was good for him.

Logan said he didn't understand the question.

"We're waiting for the slam," Ozzy said. "The piledriver. Come on, man. Take him out at the knees. What did Keynes screw up?"

Logan assimilated this slowly — not so much the question, but what the question meant. He looked over the class. Then he looked back at Ozzy. "I hope you don't think that's what I've been doing this whole time — describing each economist in detail just so I can tear him down afterward. These were all brilliant and, for the most part, well-intentioned people. Many of their theories were valid at the time they conceived them, so if they seem wrong now, it's only because our collective knowledge has grown or because the economy itself has changed. Or both."

"Whoa," Ozzy said. "Easy on the vermouth. I'm just asking for some realness. I mean the . . . you know . . ." He hesitated.

"What he means," Erin said, "is you gotta bite hard to get to the blood."

Logan looked at her, perplexed.

"It's like this," she continued. "I took an Econ course last year, and the whole time it was just la-di-da, here are some graphs straight from God, absolute truth on the chalkboard. But guess what? A couple of weeks ago you drew the same graph and said it was neoclassical analysis and you explained where it came from. Nobody ever told me that. Why didn't anyone tell me?" She glanced around the class. "It's like these other teachers are only telling us what they want us to know. You get trapped in these theories and equations because you accept the assumptions without realizing it. It's like . . . it's like trying to tell someone you love him when you don't know the word 'love.' So maybe you use another word instead, even though it doesn't feel right, but you can't say why. And that leads you to this cardboard feeling that keeps getting worse and worse because one thing always leads to another." She sat back in her seat.

Ozzy nodded firmly. "That's me. What she said."

"OK," Logan said. "If you really want to know Keynes's biggest mistake, it's the growth paradigm. The belief that a growing economy is a healthy economy, as measured by the size of its GNP."

"Size doesn't matter," Erin replied.

"Oh yes, size matters. And what you do with your economy matters even more. But we'll talk about that later," he said. "The question I want to ask now is, what is GNP?"

"What *is* it?" someone repeated.

Logan nodded. "What is it? Plain and simple."

A few students threw out phrases. Gross National Product. National income. The total market value of the goods and services produced in the economy during a given period of time.

"Yes," Logan said when they were done. "In essence, we can say that GNP is the amount of money being spent. So let's look at something that causes GNP to increase. How about if you leave class today and head over to your favorite bar for a drink? It's a positive contribution to GNP, right? And if that drink leads to a few more? Even better. In fact, the best thing you can do for the economy is drink yourself into a stupor, get behind the wheel of a brand-new car, and cause an accident involving as many other people as possible, because the alcohol, the car repairs, the medical bills — everything — is a positive contribution to GNP." He was wandering around on the stage now. "This is how we define economic prosperity. In other words, our ideal citizen is a chain-smoking, alcoholic wife-beater with a large collection of guns living next to a nuclear power plant."

Ozzy clutched his head. "You're blowing my mind."

"Measuring economic welfare with GNP is like having a doctor assess your health by taking your pulse and blood pressure and then sending you home."

There was some murmuring, some confusion.

"Because," he added, to clarify the point, "it's all about circulation. Flow. This is how Adam Smith understood the economy a couple of centuries ago, and for all intents and purposes, he was correct at that particular time in history. The scale of human activity relative to the environment was too small to make a significant impact. But the basic design of that model has never been modified. And so what do we have now?"

He paused and felt a vibrant sensation, a magnetic silence in the lecture hall. This was it. This was what he wanted. Most of them would forget these ideas, lose them in the breezes of general opinion almost as soon as they left the room. But a few of them wouldn't. And maybe that meant something.

"We have," he continued, "the standard model of the economy depicted in almost every introductory textbook. Open it up and take a look. You'll see a picture of goods and services endlessly 'flowing' from one sector to another over and over again. Completely self-contained. No input or output. No energy, no pollution, no wear and tear."

They were stirring, making comments to each other. One of them actually pulled out a textbook and began flipping pages.

"Tell me something." He was pacing the stage, unable to stand still now. "How are we supposed to follow a model of development in which every single nation on this planet becomes a net importer of raw materials? How are we supposed to believe every single nation can export its waste? How are we going to get through the day if everyone consumes more than he or she gives? What kind of life is that?"

"Speak it," Ozzy said, nodding vigorously. "Speak it, brother."

Logan's chest was opening up, a weight lifting from him. Why had he waited so long? Why had he been so afraid to do it? "That model of the economy is a *cartoon*," he said. "It's a pipe dream. It's a car without a gas tank or an exhaust system, with parts that never wear out, with a body that never rusts, with endless legroom and higher RPMs all the time even though the engine never grows." He leaned forward and pronounced the next words with dramatic emphasis. "And it's making us sick."

Erin said something, but it was lost in the choruses that began to rise from the other students, the sudden clapping and cheers, like the hearty assent of a gospel church.

"We want a new paradigm!" Erin shouted.

"What?" Logan cupped his hand to his ear.

"A new paradigm!"

"I can't hear you," he sang.

Several students chimed in. "A new paradigm!" they yelled in unison.

The clapping increased until it finally coalesced into a full round of applause. Someone tossed bits of paper in the air like confetti. Logan clapped along with them, as if rallying them to face an opponent or adversary, as if there would be a distinct opponent or adversary to face.

Two additional factors should be noted. Externalities, if you will. The first was Dr. Novak, who happened to be standing just outside the classroom with his arms folded and his gaze lowered in solemn concentration. He turned now and walked back to the elevator as the applause died down. He had heard quite enough. And although he had considered eavesdropping on Logan's class before, it may be said with a reasonable degree of confidence that the incentives had never been strong enough until he had spoken with Dr. Moore on the telephone the previous day, during which time Dr. Moore had made several subtle but unmistakable suggestions that Logan's conduct in the classroom was inappropriate. Most people wouldn't have picked up on it. But Dr. Novak's antennae were sensitive — achingly so, at times — and therefore receptive to codes and frequencies of all sorts. Again, this is what the evidence suggests.

The other factor was Dallas, who left the classroom with the students and followed the general movement down the hallway until she found herself outside under a colonnade of palms. She almost hadn't done it. A last-minute gush of sympathy had threatened to undo her. Chalk it up to her period. Her hormonal seesaw. Her bloated legs, her oily pores, her tender eyes wincing from the merciless assault of the sun. Useless, ugly, fat — that was how she felt. And obviously past her expiration date. Everybody was ten years younger. But she had managed to hide at the back of the lecture hall with her head pitched low, ducking behind some broad-shouldered kid whenever Logan looked in her direction, and by the end of the class she had realized where her husband had gone. The man she had fallen in love with — the real Logan — was right there onstage, splitting face cards without her. He wasn't at home anymore. She had watched, in miserable wonder, as he had left the room with a bunch of groupies in tow. Not the sort of confirmation she had wanted. Terrible as it seemed, she had wanted the other kind — and yes, let's get it over with — provided by the private investigator who had followed Logan to the cafe, among other places, and taken photographs of him with Keris. Yesterday he had handed over the photos with a shrug. He seemed to think she'd be relieved. Two weeks of surveillance had produced no hotel rendezvous, no stop-and-pop at some house identified as the other woman's. Not even a kiss in a public doorway. Hand-holding in a cafe. A gooey look between them. That was it.

And that was the worst thing, to be perfectly honest, because it gave her all the cost and none of the benefit of catching Logan in an affair. In all the melodrama she had anticipated, in all the amateur porn that could have been lurking inside that envelope, she hadn't expected to find that expression on his face. Had Dallas ever seen it? That glow, that life in his eyes? Sort of. It was the same light, but from a different angle, like the difference between the tropical and polar sun. She had wanted something heavy enough to balance the scales against what she had done with Felix. But this didn't balance the scales. It only added more weight to her side.

She stopped at a junction of two grand walkways, trying to remember which direction was the right one. She cursed under her breath. Then she spotted a campus map housed behind a pane of glass and went over to it. The four points of the compass. You are here. The problem, though, was that she always got lost between here and there, between the bet and the payoff, between the short-term twist and the long-term turn, so sometimes she wondered why she bothered at all.

She traced out the path on the map and tried to hold it in her mind as she continued walking. Part of the problem was this campus basically resembled the one at UNLV in all the wrong ways. The concrete buildings seemed to blur together until they canceled each other out and she was left with nothing. She kept walking, kept sweating, kept cursing the cramps in her abdomen. She wound her way past thorny landscaping. A grove of citrus, a procession of palms. Bicycle racks in multicolored glare. Students bopping along with their backpacks, their happy-go-lucky swing and swagger. She didn't belong here. Logan was deluded for thinking she could go splashing into college without drowning. It would be embarrassing. There. Let's just acknowledge it. She'd flunk her courses, or at the very least receive low grades after months of head-pounding effort, and the truth would be revealed. This was the sort of person she was.

She found the visitor lot. Finally. She zigzagged her way through burning chrome and unlocked her car and then plopped down behind the driver's seat. An oven. The tinted glass didn't do a thing. She fired up the engine, the music, the air-conditioning. She drove away. She obeyed the traffic laws like an honest person. Ten minutes later she was home, crying softly, almost casually, as she sorted through the mail at the kitchen table with a box of tissues by her side.

She filled out paperwork, she signed forms. These weren't papers of separation or divorce. They were withdrawal forms she had culled from Logan's files. Authorizations to liquidate stock. A few days ago she had quit her job and so it was easy to intercept the mail every afternoon before Logan came home. The last of the checks were arriving. She simply forged his signature now and then. It was ridiculous what you could get away with just because you were married to someone. The procedure went like this: She deposited the checks into their joint account and then, a few days later, transferred a corresponding amount to a personal account she had opened at another bank. Money in, money out. She had already gathered enough to pay off her debt, but her attitude toward it had changed in the meantime. She had come up with a plan. Cash was required. Liquidity preference, as Logan had phrased it onstage today. One of the few things she understood. She raised her head for a moment and looked out the window at their ruined backyard. Make that Logan's backyard. She just lived here. She was his roommate, his cook, his whore. She dabbed her eyes with a tissue but realized she had stopped crying, so she tossed it aside. He wanted a new paradigm? Well so did she.

chapter 13

Deck paused with the ball of shaving cream raised to his face. It was the sight of his flexed arm, the beef-jerky biceps, that caught him. Look at that. A sinewy knot. A glob of muscle clinging there, contingent and temporary, like a lump in somebody's throat. Strength on a minor scale. How many sets did he do at the gym every week? How much lift and howl? It didn't matter. His body didn't want to grow that way. It wanted the scrawny days of youth, the violin days, the days of exclusion from Irvine's sunny streets. He blinked and shook off the feeling. It would kill him if he let it. So he didn't. Instead he smeared foam over his cheeks and jaw, he lifted the razor, he drew it down, he dipped it in the water, he lifted it again and he drew it down again and then he wiped steam from the mirror, determined to resist this seizure of melancholy.

The room was both foreign and familiar, like your home rearranged in a dream. Where was he? The hotel in Tempe — the very same one where he had stayed during the conference a couple of months earlier — because the prices and quantities of his life dictated it. He needed reliable logistics. After sprinting through his final exams at Eastfield, he had caught a flight to Phoenix and ignored the frowns over his early departure. His tests were marked and filed, his grades posted, his academic duties fulfilled. What more did they want? He laughed quietly now, remembering the looks on their faces when he had told them about the new job. They had underestimated him. And let's not even mention that little trick of waiting until the last possible minute to give notice so he could buy his plane ticket with the last of his professional development funds. The rental car, however, was coming out of his own wallet. No way to avoid that. True, he could have flown straight to Palm Springs, but he had some business here in Tempe first. He had requested a meeting with Novak this morning to coordinate their presentations, although it wasn't totally necessary. His real purpose, it should be acknowledged, was to have an "accidental" run-in with Keris. He had done his research. The university's website listed the information for every final exam — the time, the location, the instructor — and he had simply figured out where Keris would be and when she would be there. He would just happen to be walking by her classroom when she finished. Hey. Wow. Funny seeing you here.

He dragged the blade up his neck. He cleared the underside of his chin. He dipped and scraped, dipped and scraped. Delilah's special project, by the way, had been a complete mess. Not to mention her final exam. Now that his disgusting little infatuation with her was over, and now that she had ended up with the C-minus she deserved, he could admit the truth: She was a candy-brained idiot.

The water in the sink was pasty now, littered with the floating ash of his whiskers. He wiped the mirror again. He opened the door to let out the moisture and did a double-take when he saw the room. The gaping suitcase, the mangled sheets. The curtains open to palm fronds and a slice of blue sky. Exactly as he had left it before taking his shower. Now, though, he recognized it for what it really was: the culprit of this low morning mood. Call him sensitive, but it reminded him of that morning after Keris disappeared.

He finished shaving. He sluiced his face with cool water and toweled off. He lifted each arm like a chicken wing and slaked on the deodorant, then spent a few rough minutes with the tweezers plucking nostril hairs. His eyes watered up when he yanked them, his nose running afterward almost as if he were crying. Almost.

He drove. He wasn't stupid about the heat. He wasn't the kind of guy who showed up at a meeting looking like he had been doused with a firehose. And besides, there was Keris to consider. Using a map left over from his last visit, he found a visitor lot at the east end of campus and walked directly to the Physical Sciences building. He admired the thing. It had a smooth edifice with a creamy look to the edges, shimmering and melting and reforming as you approached it. He went in through the main entrance. The air thrummed softly. There were a couple of nerds by the vending machines, but otherwise the place was vacant and silent. He strode down the clean hallways, the floors glossy as gray ice, following the numbers toward Keris's coordinates. He knew he was getting close when he heard some shuffling ahead of him and passed a few students coming the other way. A minute later he was fighting the tide of an entire class.

He nearly bumped into her when he rounded the next corner. She looked different. She looked better. Her hair was slightly shorter and, although he usually didn't go for that sort of thing, it was appealingly swept back. So his reaction couldn't have been more natural, he thought, as he came to a halt and brightened his face in surprise.

Her expression, on the other hand, closed like a Venus flytrap. He didn't waver. He went through the prelude exactly as he had planned it. The wow. The hello. The you-teach-in-this-building? And then the pause as he gave her just enough time to think, but not ask, what he was doing here, before preempting her with the information so she would think he was volunteering it.

"If you're wondering what a guy like me is doing in a place like this," he smiled, "the answer is, I'm lost. I'm whipped. Maybe it's heatstroke, but everything looks the same around here. I was on my way to a meeting when I stepped into this building just to cool off and look at the map. North, south, east, west. Who knows? I figure there's a door at the end of this wing that'll put me closer to the Econ building." He didn't like the sound of his own voice, the choice of his own words. Too bright and buoyant. Don't overcompensate, he thought.

Keris didn't move. She had a stack of exams in her arms, a tote bag slung over her shoulder. "I believe," she said, "you're heading in the wrong direction."

He nodded. He shook his head. Silly him. What a screwball. He paused, testing the silence in the hallway. The last of the students had trickled away. They were alone. He lowered his eyes to the exams and saw his opportunity.

"I'll help you with those."

"Oh no, I'm fine. Really."

But he was already reaching, already taking hold, already lifting them away from her. It was the only way to overcome her reluctance. He managed to hang on to his briefcase underneath it all with a couple of fingers hooked through the handle. A few moments later he was walking her toward the stairwell. He even managed to hold the door open before following her up the stairs, watching the firm curves of her ass, the suggestion of dark underwear through her thin cotton skirt. She wasn't fooling anyone. The enticement was deliberate, yet subtle enough to pass off as a mirage, a figment of your own loin-ache. She made it seem like the attraction was your own problem, something you projected onto her. And that was what made it powerful.

They climbed. Their footsteps rasped on bare concrete. Their voices echoed as they talked about the upcoming debate. Yes, she knew Deck was working with Dr. Novak. Yes, she understood it was important to keep their personal feelings out of it. As she reached the next landing Deck touched her arm so she would stop. She turned and confronted him. And despite her expression, he couldn't help admiring the delicate slopes of her face — the slightly crooked nose, the fine taper of cheekbone and chin. Her skin seemed to be touched with the stairwell's pale fluorescence as if it were candlelight. This was what Deck wanted. An authentic woman. No daily application of artificial turf in the bathroom every morning. He knew that now. And as she adjusted her tote bag over her shoulder, he could see the edge of a black bra strap peeking from the neckline of her blouse, and he felt, once again, the missing factors inside him, the equation only her quantities could solve. He wanted her right there. He wanted to drop the exams and ride that skirt up over her hips and take her against the wall. But instead he asked if she had received his phone messages.

She nodded slowly. "I felt uncomfortable calling you back."

"Why?" he said. But he said it too quickly, too emphatically, as if it weren't a question. Just the sort of thing to scare her off. Relax. Downsize the anger.

"How did you get my number?" she asked.

"Your number?"

She nodded again.

It occurred to him that he hadn't covered this gap in the story. Stupid, stupid. "Directory assistance, I think."

"They don't provide unlisted numbers."

He worked a look of surprise into his face. He shifted the exams in his arms. "Maybe it was when I talked to Novak — Dr. Novak — a couple of weeks ago, and I mentioned that I wanted to call you." He realized he was talking his way into the lie, not sure what it was going to be until he got there. "And he gave it to me, I guess." He shrugged. "Hard to remember, to tell you the truth, with all the preparation for the debate, because I just wanted to clear the air before we see each other in Palm Springs." He allowed himself a pause. "But if you're too busy before the debate, we can see each other after it's over. Maybe go out for a drink."

"I'll be leaving immediately afterward."

"I meant here, in Tempe."

"How long are you in town?"

"Permanently," he said. "I'm moving here."

Her expression seemed to crack. "I don't understand."

"My new job. Logan must have mentioned it."

"He never mentioned it. And neither did you that night at the conference."

He shifted his weight and braced the small of his back against the railing. The exams were getting heavier. "The job offer wasn't official at that point, and I didn't want to ruin it with a positive forecast, if you know what I mean. Let's go to your office so we can dump these things."

She put her hands out. "I can take them."

"No," he said, nodding at the stairs ahead of them. "Go on. I'm right behind you."

"At least give me half."

"Let's talk in your office."

"I'd like to carry them."

Neither of them moved. She was still holding out her hands.

"You sneak off in the middle of the night," he said. "I wake up and boom, you're gone. No note, no explanation. Then a month later you remember who I am. You ambush me on the phone with . . ." But he trailed off as the awareness finally took hold of him, now that he was looking at her, that in all the fuss about his HIV status he had overlooked the obvious.

"You're pregnant."

She jolted. "No. That's not true."

"Then why did you call me?"

"At the time, I thought I might be. But it was a false alarm."

"You're sure about that."

She fixed her eyes on his. "I'm sure."

He should have felt a great expansion, the lifting of a terrible weight, when he heard the news, but instead it seemed to sink more deeply into him. This wasn't how he was supposed to feel. "Then what about that night we spent together? I thought that meant something."

"And I thought you understood it was just one night and nothing more. I didn't know you were moving here. I thought we'd never see each other again." She surprised him with the tone in her voice. "Is this making sense, Deck? Tell me this is making sense."

"Of course it is, but —"

"But what?" she said. "Why is it so difficult for you to accept that a woman might want to have a one-night stand? You're intelligent. You're mature. You know what it means when a woman doesn't return your phone calls. You know," she said, shifting her tone slightly, "that I'm not interested in a relationship. I'm sorry to be point-blank with you, but you persist in this manner and now here we are in the Physical Sciences building with our voices echoing in the stairwell."

He surprised himself with what he said next. "I want to know what scared you away."

Her eyes narrowed slightly, as if he were receding in the distance and she couldn't quite make him out.

"I want to know why you changed your mind."

Her expression began to soften, resolving itself into pity and he couldn't tolerate it, absolutely couldn't stand something like that based on a false understanding of who he was.

"If you believe—" he said, but then stopped himself, sensing possible damage unless he refined the thought and switched it to a more diplomatic channel. "If you think you really know me after a few hours at a hotel, you're off the mark. Way off." He could feel his spine collapsing from the weight of the exams, his arms becoming sore.

"I don't believe any such thing. I simply know what's best for myself right now, and I'm sorry, Deck, but it isn't a relationship. Not with you. Not with anyone. Now please," she said quietly, holding out her arms. "Please, please, please, give me the exams."

He looked into her eyes. A steely expression. Now—*now* he knew what it was. He knew the answer. She was under the influence of bad advice or maybe an obligation to some secondary lover whose feelings she didn't want to hurt. Yes. Of course. He could address it. He could correct whatever false belief was misguiding her, say something that would put a line of best fit through the whole messy dispersal of her feelings and make her understand the truth. But he couldn't do it now. He needed to regroup, reassess. And so, with as much dignity as he could muster, he handed over the exams and said goodbye.

Carrying only his briefcase now, he descended the stairs until he heard a door slam above him. He stopped. He looked up. Emptiness. Railings angled upward, layered and overlapping in his line of vision. The symmetry of concrete flights. He uttered a curse and listened to it echo sonorously. It wasn't simply her resistance. Something had gone wrong inside him during the conversation and he was identifying it only now. Here it was: His motive had been to find out if she deserved the place she occupied in his mind. And he had wanted her to come up short. He had wanted to find a fatter ass, wider thighs, sagging breasts, or maybe even a vague colorlessness to her personality— anything that would have devalued her. He wanted to correct the balance sheet. He wanted to stop wanting her. And yes, he knew rejection was a strong possibility, but rejection didn't matter if it came from someone he had already assessed as unworthy. Think of it this way: He had wanted the grapes to go sour, but they had sweetened instead.

He turned and continued descending the stairwell, clutching heavily at the rail. If he had understood his own motives better, he would have designed a different approach. He would have put up some guardrails to keep himself on course. But the problem with self-knowledge is that it usually comes from making mistakes — that is, mistakes too serious to repair.

He was gaining speed now, taking each flight of stairs faster than the previous one and wheeling around the landings in downward-spiral mode until he finally boomed out the bottom door. Sunlight slapped him in the face. He was outside. Hot concrete everywhere. Blinding fire. He fished his sunglasses out of his pocket. All right. Beautiful. Perfect. He had gone past the main floor of the building and come out the wrong exit. A walkway in front of him ran in opposite directions. Which way to the Econ building, genius? He turned around and entered the building again, back into the coolness of the stairwell, and pulled out his map. And he almost laughed at himself. Shelter from the heat. A place to look at the map. His excuse for being in the building had been a lie when he had said it fifteen minutes ago, but true now, after the fact, because the lie had created the circumstances which had then, in turn, made the lie true. But let's not dwell on it. He was orienting himself on the map. More importantly, he was resisting the urge to punch a hole in the wall. Stupid, stupid, stupid. He had screwed up.

The suspicion spiked through him again that something was happening between her and Logan. It was the only explanation. And if that was the case, then what would happen if their relationship became a little more bearish? What would happen if Logan found out the truth about Keris? He folded up the map and fit it neatly into the outside pocket of his briefcase. He began to smile. He reached for the door and for some reason shoved it open with far more power than was necessary, banging it against the outer wall. Because it felt good. The force, the release. The course of action identified.

The bluebooks slanted and spilled across the desk as Logan shifted his feet — because his feet were up there too, in his biking shoes, the right one crossed over the left, shedding grit everywhere. He didn't look up. He was reading Erin's final exam, caught in the jagged peaks of her handwriting. The mad additions squeezed into the margins, the crossouts and corrections. She worked by association, avoiding the chronological lock-step that most students performed as they marched through the answers. This was more like a dance number. Sure, she stumbled occasionally—a step in the wrong direction here, an awkward landing there—but it had the kind of raw muscle and nerve that he appreciated. He spent a lot of time writing out comments at the end, balancing praise with a few cautious words about her tendency to wander too far off the topic. He wrote an *A* and circled it. He closed the bluebook. He lifted his arms and stretched, his chair squeaking as it tipped back. There were only a few exams left and he was pleased with what he had read. A high proportion of them were working through the material confidently, providing their own connections and criticisms rather than churning out blocks of undigested material. They seemed engaged with the subject more closely, and with greater care, as if they were writing about something that had happened to them instead of something they had read about. Maybe that was it.

There was a knock on the doorframe. He brought his feet to the floor and swiveled around. Ozzy and Erin. Tall and dark, short and blonde, they stood side by side, almost touching.

"Those," Ozzy said, pointing at Logan's shoes, "look like they're working."

"I can't take them off," Logan said.

Ozzy's eyes widened.

Erin elbowed him. "He's kidding." She looked at Logan. "I have a mega-favor to ask. I mean, I'm asking for the moon. You know that final essay we turned in last week?"

Logan glanced at the pile—that is, the other pile—of paper on his desk. This was the final research essay, which he had collected during the last class and graded over the previous weekend. He hadn't returned them to the students yet, so Erin didn't know that, unlike her exam, she hadn't done well on this one.

"It's mush," she said. "Don't tell me the grade. But I have a solid excuse." She turned and shot a look at Ozzy. "Don't I?"

Ozzy lowered his head and muttered something.

"What?" Erin asked, hand cupped to her ear. "Didn't quite catch that, boss."

"Somebody, namely me, grabbed her computer disk by mistake and left it on the kitchen table in my apartment. And then," he turned toward Erin, "my roommate, namely not-me, spilled a brew on it. All right?"

Logan sighed like a parent. "Why didn't you tell me this last week?"

"I didn't think it was worth the scrabble, you know? But then I saw this article in a local mag yesterday and, like, the thing possessed me and I started rewriting the essay." She paused. "Re-rewriting it, I mean. And I'm gonna cap it off tonight if you'll just read it tomorrow and burn the old one, please-please-please."

Logan rubbed his forehead. The student-teacher classic. Disk ruined, paper lost, deadline extension requested. Except she had already given him an essay. She wanted a second chance. And let's face it, she deserved one. But the logistics would be difficult.

"I have to turn in my grades the day after tomorrow," he said, thinking aloud, "and I wasn't planning to come on campus until then. But I guess I could bike here and pick up the paper from you."

She put out her hands. "Wipe the thought. I'll drop it at your house."

Logan thought about it for a moment. He agreed. He told her his address. She promised and double-promised to deliver it no later than noon and did he know that he was a specimen of a rare species known as *Superious professorius?*

By the time he deciphered the compliment she had already shifted to another topic. "Love that Georgescu," she was saying. "All that entropy. Thermodynamics."

Georgescu. Yes. Of course. It's worth mentioning that, after some input from the class, Logan had compressed the material about neoclassical synthesis and then, after working in some of Galbraith's dissent, devoted an entire period to excerpts of Nicholas Georgescu's book, which he had photocopied and distributed to the class. Why not? Georgescu was an economist. He was history. And the class was History of Economic Thought.

"You know what I'm putting at the top of my essay?" Erin asked. "As an epitaph?"

"Epi*graph,*" Logan corrected.

"A quote from Georgescu. 'The economic process is a continuation of the biological one,' thank you very much."

Ozzy nudged her and then tapped his wrist with his forefinger. "Ticktock."

She sighed and nodded. "OK. Know anyone with a spare room? We're shacking, Ozzy and me, as of next week, but both our leases are done before the new lease starts and we need a place to spend the limbo."

Logan actually considered his guest bedroom for a moment, but then perished the thought. There was the student-teacher boundary, of course, even though the semester would technically be over by then. But more importantly, there was Dallas. She had been incredibly sweet and tender to him these last few weeks and he didn't want to jeopardize it.

He slowly shook his head. "Sorry. But if I hear of anything I'll let you know tomorrow, when you . . ." He trailed off deliberately.

"When I drop off my essay," she said, picking up the cue, "no later than noon." She smiled and shot him a goodbye with her finger.

Ozzy saluted likewise and they moved off together. Logan sat there for another minute watching the empty frame of the doorway as if it might reveal something—a parallel universe, perhaps, where Keris could be substituted for Dallas painlessly and guiltlessly, and therefore happily. He let out a breath. He turned back to his desk and tried to forget it.

Half an hour later he was outside, under the eternal commerce of sun and sky. Logan swallowed his recommended daily allowance of midge flies as he biked, his legs churning, his feet married to the pedals by his special shoes, his mind a toneless hum. He passed some ripped-up earth where a few tractors and dumpers were gathered, a crane with its neck stretched above the heap—dormant now, but arranged like a medieval catapult or torture device with its chains and shackles and irons. The smell of oil and diesel. He blistered through it all. He was done. He had finished his grading, except for Erin's essay, and now he needed to prepare himself for Palm Springs. The debate. Eager for it and fearing it at the same time.

He arrived home in a lather of sweat and dust. He put his bike in the garage and called out his usual greeting as he entered the house. Dallas's voice called back from the bedroom. A tingle of expectation rose through him as he walked toward it. A couple of weeks ago, on an afternoon a lot like this one, he had come home to find Dallas reclined on the bed in black lingerie and stockings, refusing to let him shower because, she had said, she wanted him exactly as he was. Apparently the dirt had been some kind of turn-on. Afterward they had stripped the bed and stuffed everything into the washing machine, the linens streaked with russety grime and the secretions of sex.

But this time he found an open suitcase on the bed. Dallas was in the bathroom, wearing plain shorts and a T-shirt. He went over and stood in the doorway while she faced away from him, packing her toiletries.

"It's all Lucinda's fault," she said, stooped over the counter. "She's having a baby shower this weekend and there's basically no way to refuse the invitation."

"Who?"

"I told you about her." She raised her head and met Logan's eye in the mirror. "Old friend. Also a blackjack dealer at the casino. I tried to look her up when I visited my mother last month, but no dice. Anyway, she called today because someone finally told her that I was trying to find her and . . . you're disappointed."

"Surprised," he said, although that was only the mechanics of it, the reversal that stunned him — the slap that hurts so much more when you're expecting a kiss. "I mean . . ." He made a gesture toward the suitcase on the bed. "It looks like you're leaving today."

"Tomorrow morning."

"For how long?"

"Five, six days, is what I'm thinking. Mom would kill me if I came to town without spending some quality time with her." She zipped up her case. She turned and faced him. "You remember Lucinda."

"I think so. Vaguely. A story or two."

"Wild oats," she said, coming up to Logan now, wrapping her arms around his sweaty neck. "History, dear husband. She's married now, with a baby on the way. Bulging like a blimp."

"How do you know that? I thought you hadn't seen her."

She smiled. "According to her own description."

"On the phone."

"On the phone." She gave him a light kiss. "Come on. Don't pout. It's only a few days. And besides, you'll be at that conference anyway."

"So I guess you're driving to Vegas."

Her expression fell. She dropped her arms. "So that's it. The car."

"I didn't mean it that way."

"Yes, I'm taking my car to Vegas. I have a car, you have a car. Yours, if I remember correctly, has been sitting in a parking garage for how long?"

Logan received this in silence, enduring the full glare of his mistake. Sometimes he mixed emotions with logistics and expressed one in terms of the other. "Sometimes," he said, "I mix emotions with logistics —"

"Thank you, Dr. Smith." She grabbed the toiletries case from the counter and stepped up to him with her arms at her sides. "Excuse me."

He stood aside and let her pass into the bedroom, a slipstream of mingled perfumes and lotions in her wake. The scent of her hair. "Please listen," he said. "I'm trying to explain."

"I'm sure there's someone else traveling to the conference who will be happy to give you a ride." She tossed the toiletries into the suitcase and turned toward him. "This really isn't a problem."

There was a long silence.

"I'm sorry," he finally said.

She turned back toward her suitcase and closed it. "So am I."

The next morning, in the backyard, Logan worked a shovel into the hard soil. He pushed, shoved, dug. His shirt was off, his body bare except for a pair of old shorts. He levered chunks away from the ground until they resembled plates of broken ice on a river. As difficult as this was, the conversations with Dallas last night had been worse—all effort and no progress, striking bedrock over and over again, exhausted into silence. They were trying to uncover something. Or at least he was. No matter how much debris he cleared away, Dallas seemed to cover it up again with other topics, other issues. It was a strange type of resistance—like a work slowdown or stoppage when the boss wasn't looking. Except he wasn't the boss. And she wasn't a worker. So why did it feel that way? He stabbed the shovel blade into the soil. The polished handle slid against his sweaty palms. He was taking refuge in blisters and minor aches. At least his stomach was finally settling down. After Dallas had left a few hours earlier, all chatty and bright, he had forced down a bagel to convince himself that everything was fine. "Everything's fine," he had said, sitting alone at the kitchen table. "Everything's fine."

He rested the shovel in the crook of his elbow and drew his forearm across his face. Here was his yard in the process of becoming. Piles of turned-up topsoil. Yanked-out shrubs gathered and withering in the corner. What little grass remained was starved at the roots. Yes. The necessary derangement.

"You're wasting your time," a voice said behind him. He knew who it was even before he turned around. Deck was standing at the entrance to the yard, where the wooden door had fallen off the hinges a couple of weeks earlier. He had one hand in his pocket, the other on his waist, sunglasses firmly in place. "The treasure's buried in someone else's backyard. I saw the map."

Logan smiled out of the corner of his mouth. It was the best he could do.

"I rang the doorbell," Deck said, coming forward, stepping carefully around the holes and scattered dirt. "Then I saw you through the house."

"Through?"

He jerked a thumb toward the sliding glass door. "Lines up perfectly with the living room window. You know that, right? You looked pretty funny out here, talking to yourself."

He stopped a few feet away from Logan. Shorts, T-shirt, sneakers—this was Deck in casual mode, but it gave an unnatural impression. The colors seemed overbright, pressed and pleated as if they had been dry-cleaned.

Logan didn't move or change his stance. "I didn't expect to see you until Palm Springs."

"Local business. And local pleasure. Novak wants all the *i*s dotted and *t*s crossed, as you might expect."

An incomplete note hung in the air. He had specified the business but not the pleasure, and Logan knew he was supposed to notice the omission. And he also knew they could circle each other for a while, or get it over with and have Deck out of there in half the time. So Logan asked about the pleasure.

Deck hesitated. "I don't want to speak out of school."

"We're not in school. We're at my house. Speak."

He laughed. "Wow. The new and improved Logan Smith. Tan. Lean. A man who speaks his mind." He glanced away, then looked at him again with a chastened expression. "I should have told you about my role in the debate. I should have sent the signal. Sorry about that. I wanted to call you a thousand times, but I've been going full tilt the last couple of months just to stay in the race, you know?"

He went on about his nose-to-grindstone existence, his lack of satisfaction with Eastfield, the major work he had been doing without revealing any detail about what, specifically, that work was. By the time he was done he was sweating lavishly, his T-shirt darkened at the armpits and collar. Unacclimated. This was the part where Logan was supposed to invite him inside.

Logan drove the shovel into the soil and left it standing up. "Thanks for stopping by," he said. "But I need to shower and get some work done. Preparations, you know, for the conference."

"Don't tell me your paper isn't finished."

"Dotting the *i*s and crossing the *t*s."

"That shouldn't take long."

"It shouldn't, but it will." He wiped his hands on his shorts and began moving toward the house. "Besides, I need to turn in my grades, pack a suitcase, rent a car."

"What do you mean, rent a car?"

Logan hesitated, already sensing the mistake. "Dallas is visiting a friend in Vegas for a few days. And my car is out of commission, so—"

"Say no more. I already have a car."

"You shouldn't feel obligated—"

"Don't be ridiculous. Why should we drive there separately?" He took off his sunglasses and blotted his forehead against his shoulder. Then he squinted at Logan with his bare blue eyes. "Besides, we could use the bonus time, you and me. Am I right? As future colleagues, we need to discuss the schematics of the department."

"I have to turn in my grades tomorrow morning."

"No problem. We'll swing by campus on the way out of town."

Logan was trying to think of some other excuse when Deck put on his sunglasses again and started heading toward the gate. "And hey," he said, stopping as if struck by a sudden thought. "Tell me if it's none of my business, but why aren't you driving there with Keris?"

Logan was silent for a moment. "It's complicated," he finally said.

Deck nodded solemnly. "I understand. Because you know when I said 'business and pleasure' earlier, I misspoke. It's not really pleasure. More like, I don't know, loose ends. We spent a night together."

Logan stood there dumbly.

"I don't know if she told you. It was during the conference here in Tempe." He shrugged and glanced down at his feet. "I saw her at the bar afterward, and one thing led to another. Anyway, there's a lot of mopping up to do. Emotionally."

Logan listened to the words, trying to fit them together like puzzle pieces. He heard the long flute-note of a dove calling somewhere behind him. The shush of traffic beyond the walls. Conditional silence.

"You're talking about Keris," he said.

"She didn't tell you?"

Logan shook his head slowly. "We're colleagues. It's professional. It's not that sort of relationship."

"Right. I shouldn't have mentioned it. I'm overstepping." He glanced at his watch. "Anyway, I'll pick you up at eight."

"The registrar's office doesn't open until nine."

"Eight-forty-five, then. And if we drive in the fast lane, we can squeeze in nine holes before the keynote address. So many golf courses, so little time."

"I don't play golf."

"Lessons," Deck said as he reached the gate. "It's never too late to learn."

Logan stood there afterward with the full weight of the sun on his back. Keris and Deck. No. Impossible. It was like an orange full of razor blades. He pulled the shovel from the ground and continued working, driving the blade harder, deeper, flinging the soil away. At one point he stopped with the handle raised. That day in the cafe, she had asked for a description of Deck and then laughed when she heard it. No, not laughed. Giggled. As if the coincidence . . . He lowered the shovel. No, wait. Hang on a minute. It wasn't his business. He had absolutely no right to judge her sexual behavior. She could screw the entire university football team if she wanted to. She had her life, and he had his. Yet even as he reasoned it out to himself, his mind was spooling back, helplessly, through all the conversations, all the confessions and admissions they had made to each other over the last couple of months—which had accumulated, he felt, into a kind of intimacy. Yes. There it was. They had discussed his problems with Dallas during that hike through the desert. He had said he was afraid as he drifted off to sleep that night. And she had said she loved him.

He started digging again. It wasn't fair of him to demand anything beyond that. They were friends. And, after all, maybe he was expendable. Maybe he didn't matter to her anymore.

He heard a meow. He turned. He dropped the shovel.

Puffy had slash marks on either side of his face and a mangled left ear, favoring one of his back legs as he walked. Logan reached down and carefully picked him up. He cradled him, hot and soft, trembling faintly against his bare chest—his skin reacting immediately with a poison-ivy prickle. But the allergy didn't matter anymore.

"Who did this to you?" he whispered. His shoulders began to shake and suddenly he was crying. He couldn't help it. He cried like a little boy. Puffy purred and nuzzled him, which only made the sobs come harder, louder. He wanted to erase pain everywhere. He wanted to undo all the terrible things that had been done.

He heard footsteps in the dirt behind him. He raised his head. He wiped his eyes with the back of his hand and cleared his throat before he turned, still hugging the cat, not sure if he could withstand another conversation with Deck.

Erin was standing at the entrance flourishing her revised essay, but when she saw Logan's face her own expression deflated. "Oh," she said, "this is a bad time." She lowered her eyes to the ground. "A really bad time."

chapter 14

She stayed at the superlative hotel — the newest, the largest, the grandest place in town — recently constructed over the debris of a mobster relic. She remembered watching the implosion of the old structure on the news, a comic-relief segment in which the lower stories detonated according to plan but then sent a dust-cloud billowing up and swallowing the nearby buildings like a biblical disaster. Not that it delayed the construction. The casino had opened maybe three weeks ago to a fireworks concert and free champagne. The theme? Old-fashioned elegance. It had the look and feel of a ballroom. There were marble floors and grand staircases, crystal chandeliers, vases full of fresh-cut flowers atop the slot machines. The dealers wore tuxedos and evening gowns. Even the cocktail waitresses wore silk. Modeled vaguely on Monte Carlo in the middle of the previous century, it recalled an era before electronics and mass tourism, before all the verbs of the world had been fully conjugated.

Furthermore, the place had energy. Impossible to deny. Kinetic in the casino, potential in the rooms. If you took the elevator up to the seventh floor — which was the one Dallas had requested, for good luck — and followed the hallway to her room, you'd find a new mattress tight and ripe in its bedframe, the carpet bright, the curtains fresh. The furniture had sharp-edged definition. The bathroom's gleam came not from scrubbing — not yet, anyway — but from the quality of the fake porcelain itself. Dallas was there now, nestled among the bubbles, her knees poking above the surface like the humps of a sea serpent, her hair upswept and pinned, her eyes closed as she sang an old saucy ballad to relieve the tension. She had arrived a couple of hours earlier with discretion worthy of a queen. She hadn't advertised the shopping bag full of money. In fact, she hadn't mentioned it at all. No request for a safe-deposit box, no hello-I'm-a-whale. She wouldn't get the comps, of course, so forget about the penthouse suite and the free meals, but she also wouldn't have security checking everything down to her shoe size and adding her picture to their database. She didn't want that kind of attention. And so the money was under the bed, and the room was locked from the inside, and the doorknob was collared with the DO NOT DISTURB sign.

She finished singing. She stirred, she shifted, she wriggled her toes. Cash under the bed. This was what it came down to. But she needed the seed money, and it was borrowed, not stolen, so don't even think in that direction. How else was she going to erase her debt and, fingers crossed, rise above and beyond it if she stuck to the minimum bet like some housewife from Topeka? She needed deep pockets. She needed a bankroll equal to the debt itself. Never mind the paradox, she thought, of already having the amount of money she was hoping to win. Of course, there was the obvious risk factor. She could end up losing everything. This was where her mind usually stopped — or, in this case, fabricated a brand-new reality instead. Logan's blessing for this little venture. Better yet, his presence. He was opening the door now, he was climbing into the bath with her — no, wait, they were in bed now, plain and simple.

She knew what was coming next, but she delayed it an extra moment, lifting her arm from the suds and swabbing herself with the washcloth, gently scrubbing her neck and her shoulders, working her way down below the surface until she reached all that difficult territory. The nooks and crannies unseen. The water was warm and deeply sensuous, the way bathwater was supposed to be, and pretty soon the washcloth was gone and her bare hand was between her legs and she was masturbating, thinking of Logan, his tongue, his hands hot against her inner thighs. She shook. She splashed a little. When it was over she sobbed. But then she straightened herself out, like she usually did, by focusing on the nuts and bolts of the moment, the simplicity of constant errands, the protocols and procedures, the demands of the physical world.

Sitting forward now, she spread shaving cream into her armpits. She reached for the razor. She scraped away the stubble. The legs were more difficult, of course, but the rewards it brought were more worthwhile, if you wanted her true opinion on the subject. She cleared swaths along calf and shin, along haunch and thigh, until smoothness seemed to be the natural condition. She rose from the bath. She toweled off and opened the bathroom door to check the clock on the bedside table. Plenty of time before dinner. Good. This was how she wanted to do it — calmly, slowly, resisting the nerves at play in her stomach.

She aired herself on the bed for a while, head propped, robe open to the cool air with the TV volume low, enduring the day's endzone of news and re-runs. She held the remote against her hip and grazed through it all. The room flickered and danced in the kaleidoscope light. No matter how hard she tried to let her mind wander, anticipation kept her tethered to the big issue and she could travel only a limited radius before helplessly coming around to it again. She turned her head toward the window. Her room faced north, away from the Strip, with a view of residential lights and mountains matted sharply against the blush of a distant sunset. The sky fading to bruise-purple. It was consoling — the heat pressing up against the glass, the city chugging and churning out there. She closed her eyes for a moment and imagined life as a teenager again, napping on a Friday afternoon before Mom came home from work, a simple dinner in the kitchen, then an hour or so in her bedroom with the music on high as she tried different makeup and clothing combinations, the countless experiments, she and her friends competing and criticizing each other during those years when they were so much more comfortable with sexuality than sex itself. How did those nights go? How many boyfriends with cars? How many nights when the gyroscope of her heart responded to everything, the movements of jetstreams and ocean currents, the tensions of the moon and the sun and the stars?

She opened her eyes. The remote had fallen softly from her hand. The clock claimed only a few minutes had passed, but her body knew better. She had been somewhere. A sense of travel lurking in her glands like jet lag. As if she had lived another life in those moments. As if she had returned to Arizona with her winnings, paid off the debt, replenished the accounts, and used the leftovers to surprise Logan with an all-expenses-paid vacation to an island with their own bungalow on a golden beach. As if she had set the tickets on the table, quietly triumphant, and confessed to everything. The gambling. Felix. The borrowed money. As if Logan, in turn, had admitted to having an affair with his colleague but promised Dallas it was over because he loved Dallas and wanted to be with her and nobody else but her. As if the vacation had allowed them to heal. As if it had given them an opportunity to begin again, their relationship renewed, their love wiser.

As if. The truth was that he was probably spending more time with that woman now that Dallas was away. Which wasn't fair. He was supposed to be the one missing her. He was supposed to be the one lying in bed like this, silent and alone, wishing she were lying there next to him.

She stood. She shut off the TV and went into the bathroom and began preparing her face for the evening, bringing it into proper focus with lipstick and eyeliner, base and shade. Afterward she shrugged off her robe and began putting on the outfit she had bought at the mall earlier that week. It started with black silk underwear and a strapless bra. It continued with a pair of lace-top stockings. She sat at the edge of the bed with the first one gathered in her fingers, gently easing it up her leg, readjusting it several times until the seam lined up correctly. She repeated the process with the other one. And finally the dress—deep red, almost maroon, with an oriental pattern and a network of whip-thin straps crossing her back. It was cut slightly higher than mid-thigh, with a slit up the side for good measure. She tested her profile and then pulled out a chair and sat down properly, sideways to the mirror, legs crossed. The slit exposed a hint of lace. Perfect.

She put on her shoes, checked her alignment one last time, and counted out a fat wad of cash. It barely fit into her little purse. Then she stopped with the door open. She stepped back into the room. She took off her wedding ring and added it to the shopping bag under the bed. Not that it changed anything. She was still married. She wasn't going to do anything to contradict that. But the appearance of a wedding ring could only hurt her tonight. She examined her bare finger and was surprised to find no mark there—no tan line, no skin irritation, not even a minor blemish. She took it as a sign of good luck.

She felt the eyes right away. They looked up from cards, from dice, from slots, following her through the smoke and energy, the cinematic glow. This was gravitation. This was magnetism. This was a force—strong on her side, weak on theirs. This was luck, self-generated and erotic. This was how you rearranged the world in your favor. Even an ugly woman could do it if she wanted to. It was all in the presentation.

The casino agreed with this philosophy. Look at it: The chandeliers shimmered. The vases overflowed with foreign flowers. The marble exuded rich creamy tones. She walked slowly, absorbing it, processing it, dowsing for the right vibe until she finally found a craps table where all the dealers and pit bosses happened to be male. She stopped, stood, watched. She didn't say a word. After a moment or two her presence took hold and the bodies parted agreeably. Open sesame. Good. Very good. She could feel the heat coming off the table, chips on nearly every point, the thrower avoiding seven like it was mathematically impossible and everyone shouting and clapping in celebration. She pulled a few bills from her purse. She tossed them on the table and immediately felt the craving for a cigarette. The blood-ache. The sudden rage of appetite. She asked the guy next to her if he could spare one and he practically spilled his drink getting the pack out of his pocket. She didn't have to ask for a light. A flame appeared in front of her. She smiled, she got the cigarette going, she leaned forward to pick up her chips.

It started beautifully. She bet the passline and kept piling her winnings on top of her original stake, watching them grow exponentially. And then it turned. Dealers shifted. The dice became evil and people vacated the premises like a bomb had gone off. Which is when she made her first mistake. Never chase bad money. But she did. She chased it like a hellhound because she wanted to recoup her loss before she quit the table and of course that made it only worse. Two hours later she went up to her room and got more cash out of the shopping bag. Then she did it again some time after that, not sure exactly when because she'd had a few drinks to loosen up the mood. But she kept her composure. She maintained her appearance. She went to the bathroom periodically for inspections and adjustments — a repositioned lace-top, a shift of the bra, a twist of the dress — because it seemed to protect her, to be perfectly honest, from the outward signs of loss. Men talked to her all night, supplying her with endless cigarettes. There was a dinner invitation from one, a weekend in Hawaii offered by another. Such was the price you paid for the accommodation, the vortex of male attention that brought luck along with it.

Too bad, then, that it didn't seem to be working. She ranged, she roved along the rim of the table, changing positions, altering strategies, pushing chips at anything that moved. Finally she took a break and tried roulette. She tried slots. She tried blackjack even though it basically rankled her to be on the other side of the deal, knowing the cut and shuffle, the give and take, sweet memories of her old edgy life lashing away at her. She knew the way the game always ended but she stayed for three hours anyway. When it was over she stood up slowly, uncoiling herself from the table. The clown next to her asked her out to breakfast and she didn't even reply. She walked to the elevator and felt the autumnal tone in the air — the crowd thinning down to the lean and serious, the night-shifting professionals. She went up to her room.

She stepped out of the shoes. She peeled off the stockings. She unzipped, unclipped, unbuttoned. She released herself from the bra and underwear. It felt good to be naked with the imprints of straps and elastic bands, like blank tattoos, across her skin. She coughed for a minute, her lungs raising a mild protest against all those cigarettes.

She washed away the makeup in the shower and then stood under the nozzle for a while, hands braced against the tile. When she was done she wrapped a towel around her head and crouched by the bed and pulled out the shopping bag and counted the money, her expression dead, absolutely stiff. More than half the cash was gone. It was all right. It didn't matter. She'd sleep. She'd eat. She'd take some sun by the pool tomorrow and go for a full treatment at the spa. She'd hit the casino again, renewed, relaxed, recharged.

She checked the DO NOT DISTURB sign, then safety-locked the door from the inside and yanked the curtains shut, overlapping them at the edges to basically bombproof the room against daylight and, at last, numb with fatigue, she crawled into bed with her skin still damp, the towel still wrapped around her head.

Keris sat at the dinner table pushing pasta around her plate. Was she depriving the baby of nutrition by eating so little today? Blame it on her paltry appetite. Blame it on her queasiness. It had taken her an hour to decide what to cook and now she still didn't want to eat it even though she had livened it up with a garlic-and-white-wine concoction, having prepared a separate tomato sauce for Sophie. And Sophie, for once, had cleaned her plate. She had consumed every single vegetable and sucked up the pasta, and now she was swabbing up the last of the tomato sauce with a hunk of bread. Chow had been fed and relegated to the backyard to prevent covert assistance under the table. This was her own handiwork.

Sophie got up and went to the freezer and returned a moment later with a carton of chocolate ice cream and a spoon large enough for a witch's caldron. Keris couldn't let this go.

"Use a bowl, please."

"Aw."

"And a normal spoon."

Sophie trudged over to the cupboard. When she came back she opened the carton and began working her spoon into the cemented surface of the ice cream. She grunted.

"Let me do that, honey." Keris took the spoon and began prying away some slabs. She popped one into her mouth. Not bad. In fact, the sugar was quite—

"Do you have a tumor?"

Keris's mouth stopped in mid-suck. "What?"

"Katie says you might have a tumor."

"Why on earth would she say such a thing?"

"Because I told her you're eating just bread and other crap like that, and Katie said that's what her grandfather ate when he had a tumor in his ass."

"Sophie —"

She slumped her shoulders, preparing herself for the reprimand.

"First of all, don't swear. Second of all, I don't have a tumor. I'm perfectly healthy."

This came out more harshly than she intended, and when she saw the impact on Sophie's expression she felt sick inside. She couldn't hold it back anymore. She set down the spoon. She took both of Sophie's hands in hers.

"The fact is, I'm going to have a baby."

Sophie's eyes widened. "Boy or girl?"

"I don't know yet."

"If it's a girl can I name her?"

Keris hesitated. It was as if she had announced they were buying a big-screen TV. "Um, we can discuss that later. The important thing right now is that we can't tell anyone."

Sophie's face puckered. "Why not?"

Keris calmly explained the concept of trimesters and the possibility of early miscarriage and other complications that could arise. She promised that when the time came, Sophie could tell as many people as she wanted.

"But until then, don't say a word. Especially to Katie this weekend. OK?"

Sophie nodded reluctantly.

"Can you promise me?"

"I promise."

Keris looked carefully into her eyes. She hoped this would stick. Sophie was sleeping over at Katie's house while Keris attended the conference in Palm Springs. And Katie was Charlotte's daughter. It would be embarrassing to have the news leak out this way, especially after that hike a few months ago when she had taken such pride in the way she handled one-night stands.

She dismissed Sophie, who headed straight to the living room for her one-hour ration of TV. Then she let Chow inside and fed him some of the pasta she hadn't eaten. It would have been a shame to waste it all.

Lying in bed a couple of hours later, she was awakened by a jolt in her abdomen. Her joints and ligaments loosening up to accommodate the enlarged uterus. While carrying Sophie she had endured a sleepless night because of it — not from the pain itself, but from a fear that it signified an ectopic pregnancy, the baby growing in her fallopian tubes. Now, though, it simply nagged at her. You're awake, you're pregnant. This sort of thing usually didn't affect the ten-hour coma she experienced every night — or even, for that matter, her afternoon naps — so she kept her eyes closed, trying to visualize a meadow in the mountains somewhere but instead finding herself back in the stairwell again, seesawing between guilt and vindication as she lied to Deck. She hadn't planned it. But she had realized almost immediately that if Deck knew the truth, he'd try to bind her with it. He'd try to claim her like lost property. At some point, of course, he'd find out — especially now that he was moving to Tempe — and she'd have to fend him off again. Perhaps she could tell a darker lie. Perhaps she could say the baby was somebody else's.

She woke in the morning with the hiss of sprinklers outside her window, the bark of a dog, the bleating of a car's false alarm. She hauled herself upright, let Chow outside for his morning business, and trudged into her study to check her e-mail before she had to wake Sophie for school and start packing for Palm Springs. A gallon or two of coffee, she thought, would be nice right about now. The first trimester was when she needed it the most, but also when she could justify it the least. As she waited for her messages to load she looked around the room. She had never got around to replacing the art prints Will had taken with him. She had never filled the shelves convincingly with the extra books from her office, the reams of old research she knew she'd never touch again. As if she had known she'd have to give up this room. As if she had already placed the crib along the far wall, the changing table in the corner by the window. She closed her eyes. She had already spoken to her mother and sisters about tag-team assistance after the baby arrived, but the idea of caring for a newborn as well as Sophie was still too exhausting for her to comprehend. Assistance was exactly that — extra help. It wasn't partnership. It wouldn't change the fact that she'd be alone.

The screen materialized. She clicked on the first message, forwarded by a former colleague at the NOAA's Space Environment Center. A solar flare was expected to cause a geomagnetic storm of strong-to-severe levels sometime this afternoon, possibly affecting satellite operations and power grids. The northern lights would be pushed as far south as Denver and Washington, D.C.

Keris sat back in her chair. The temptation, right about now, would be for her to take this as a sign — or simply as a measurement, like barometric pressure, of the weather in her life. After all, she believed in auras and chakras and reincarnation. But this very belief prevented her from interpreting cosmic events with any kind of determination. She hated horoscopes and astrological charts, for example, not because she thought the movements of the stars and planets were irrelevant to earthly events, but because she knew that everything was connected to everything else with such complexity and endless permutation that it was beyond our ability to decipher.

She sorted through the rest of her messages and made the essential replies. Then she shut down her computer. She stared at the dead screen for a minute. Her suitcase awaited her. Logan awaited her. The conference. What had seemed like a chore now seemed like a plunge into dark waters. The day would end much differently than it began. This was what the solar flare told her. This was the universe's sign.

Logan sat in the passenger seat, his mood suspended in the heat and pressure of the landscape — the distance, the sky, the shadowless veins of shrub and branch. The addictive desolation. He understood, for once, the appeal of isolated towns with their fast-food monopolies and civic pride tattooed on the crests of nearby hills. He understood the need to be surrounded by emptiness. An odd sadness coming over him as they took the bridge across the Colorado, the transition from vibrant Sonoran to malnourished Mojave. They were both called deserts, but it felt like an insult to the first one, a compliment to the second.

Deck didn't seem to notice. He talked about work and baseball and current events. Logan engaged in the conversation now and then simply to keep the momentum going, offering nothing of substance. He was balled up like a porcupine. They both knew it. They ranged over various topics, but avoided Keris the way most people avoided talk of death in a nursing home. An absence that sucked everything toward it.

The mountains. The space. The dead hills and slabbed rocks, angled into positions of worship. The limp-wristed creosote. Scarcity in abundance. Driving this very same route a year earlier, he and Dallas had pulled into a rest stop designed like a bunker with bombproof bathrooms, plates of stainless steel bolted to the wall instead of mirrors, vending machines caged and padlocked into full body-armor. It had sparked a discussion of eastern versus western highway facilities and what they signified about life in general and he had felt that he could easily spend his life with her. He closed his eyes. He wanted her to come home. But he didn't want to see her. Figure that out.

They came off the interstate to a corridor of fast-food and convenience stores like any other. Was this really Palm Springs? The buildings were run-down, the vacant lots gray as moonscape and littered with old tires and shopping carts and wrappers clinging to stunted cacti. But then it started to change. Plants rose up. Yucca and Joshua trees filled the medians. Grass appeared. At one point the buildings suddenly gained height and clustered together with shops and restaurants and cafes — a theme park, Logan guessed, for people who wanted to experience authentic urban life. They kept driving. The road curved lazily, halting at traffic lights to admit the gleaming barges of retirement. The vacant lots were less frequent now. A few brimstone mountains stood ahead of them, raw and sharp and gaunt, like the foothills of hell. As they passed the edge of a bright-green golf course Logan finally realized where the uncanny feeling came from. It was like a Hollywood set. You had to cut your vision down to movie-screen size and look only in certain directions for it to seem real.

They arrived at the resort. They checked in. They parted ways with a final burst of goodwill that, Logan knew, was simply relief in disguise. He unlocked the door to his room, dropped his bag, and threw himself onto the bed. He rolled over and lay there, starfished, motionless, gazing at the blank ceiling. There was a disk mounted to the surface with a red light inside, blinking every few seconds. A fire detector. He glanced at the phone and almost reached for it. No. Even if Dallas were there, her mother would answer first and he'd have to fight his way through ten minutes of pleasantries before he could even get Dallas on the line. Besides, what would they say to each other over the phone that they hadn't already said face to face? I'm suspicious of you and, oh, by the way, I adopted Puffy?

Twenty-four hours earlier, in the vet's waiting room, he had settled on it regardless of the consequences. What did this mean? For the moment, it meant that he needed a catsitter while he was gone to the conference, and since Erin had so generously given him a ride to the vet's office and then home again, she seemed the natural choice. OK. So she and Ozzy could stay at the house for a few days. Logan charged them with Puffy's care. In the meantime, he forbade them to answer the phone, because if Dallas found out he was running a boarding house as well as an animal shelter, the damage would be irreparable. He had given them the number of the resort along with instructions to call him if the door so much as creaked differently. When in doubt, he had said, call me. A hundred interruptions are better than returning to the charred and smoking remains of my home. Our home.

He rolled off the bed. He opened his bookbag and carefully extracted the books, the rubber-banded folders, the loosely gathered notes. He had hardly thought about the debate today because it was so close, so large, so beyond additional preparation at this point that his mind shied away from it. He unpacked his suitcase. He changed into his swimsuit and then, as he stepped into the bathroom to grab a towel, paused for a few moments in front of the mirror. He couldn't help it. He had been working in the yard and riding his bike for weeks with no visible change, but now it seemed to be happening all at once. It seemed like the only positive development in his life.

Towel, sandals, baseball cap. Room key. It was enough. Lately he seemed to find comfort in the heft and texture of simple objects. A way of grounding himself. He listened to the thud of the door behind him. The click of the latch. The towel was clean and nappy, squeaking between his fingers — a sensation more than a sound, as acute as the creaking of his joints. What was happening to him? He didn't know. He wouldn't know until it was finished. Assuming it ever finished. Whatever it was. He draped the towel around his neck, adjusted the brim of his baseball cap, and went in search of a swimming pool.

Erin didn't think the way most people thought. At least that's how she caught it. The line usually went something like this: Erin, that idea is overcooked, or: Erin, you have a tendency to choke on your own talent. Everyone said it at some point. Teachers, parents, ex-boyfriends. Especially ex-boyfriends. Her latest, before sweet Ozzy, had been a guy named Leo who argued her all over the room whenever she questioned his dogma. Make no mistake. She was liberal. But this guy was a fervent Communist, which meant, in essence, that he thought people would rewire their desires someday and rise up in glorious union. Welcome to Fantasy Island. He described a mistake, for example, as a "Trotsky" — like "I made a Trotsky when I calculated the tip" — and referred to his second-hand dishes as the People's Republic of China. His cat was named Chairman Meow. Meanwhile, Erin wanted to disprove some of his claims but simply didn't have the ammunition. Thus the Econ class — although the truth was that Leo was long gone by the time the semester actually started, but still. She wanted to finish the arguments just for her own personal satisfaction.

Anyway, the point is that Erin had these hunches, these laser-fine insights that could slice the bones from a fish they were so precise and serious. For example, here they were at Logan's house, she and Ozzy, working in the backyard with a couple of shovels, continuing the landscaping work. Their only duty was to care for Puffy and otherwise ensure that his life continued, but they were taking some liberty with this chore. They liked Logan. And they appreciated the shelter. And so they were digging and hefting like members of a chain gang minus the misery — in the zone, it may be said, sweetened with a good-deed feeling — when she happened to step inside for a swig of sports drink from the fridge, at which point the phone rang and a voice came on the answering machine. A man with something-something-something Trust Company. She couldn't remember the name if you dangled her over a volcano, and normally she would have sluffed it off because it was none of her business, but the guy seemed alarmed. Something about I just returned from the Caribbean yesterday and why did you liquidate everything while I was gone. Please give me a call.

She felt sorry for the guy, obviously wondering what had gone wrong. But more importantly, it was the note of high-finance danger that she respected. Although she didn't have much tolerance for the nit-picky fine-print bullshit that took place on Wall Street, she understood the effect it often had. Most natural disasters couldn't compete with it. And so the longer she stood there in the kitchen, the more important it seemed. She picked up the phone. She called the number Logan had pinned to the little message board. A receptionist put her through to his room. Voicemail. She talked. She summarized the stockbroker's message as best she could and apologized for bothering him with something that was probably nothing, but you said when in doubt, call, so I'm calling.

She hung up. She chugged more sports drink and popped it back in the fridge. She went outside, picked up her shovel, and resumed the toil, stopping now and then to frown at the dirt where the pool had been. What a shame. She and Ozzy agreed on this, the way they agreed about all the important things. Getting rid of that pool was a total shame.

The table. The misters. The umbrella. The shade. Logan and Keris sat across from each other with their folders and glasses of iced tea. Palm trunks and cactus blades surrounded them. Waiters strode through the heat with brimming trays. You had to angle yourself a certain way to catch the moisture and therefore relief from the misters, but it was worth it, Logan felt, to breathe some real air.

"And if we aren't sure," he was saying to Keris, "I think we should simply ask each other who wants to respond to certain questions. Honesty is our best approach. We have nothing to hide, right?"

"Correct," she said, without lifting her eyes from her notebook. She flipped pages, wrinkled her brow, flipped some more.

For a moment he thought his last words might cut a certain way, but she didn't seem to notice. They were in professional mode, professional demeanor. He was wearing a sportcoat and a collared shirt, boycotting the tie for effect. She was wearing a one-piece dress that fell straight and loose, a couple of small pockets on the side, looking less like a professor and more like the kindergarten teacher every boy fell in love with.

The sky. The sun. The postcard glow. The mountains in the distance brassy with afternoon sunlight. Everything in town was lush. Everything outside it was parched and starved, suffering from rain-deprivation.

Keris closed her notebook. She looked up. "I don't like the term 'emergy.' It sounds like a child trying to speak with a mouth full of chocolate."

"No problem. I'll tell my writers to come up with something else."

"What?"

He gave an exaggerated shrug. "I'm feeling very Hollywood today. It's the setting. Relax, baby, my people will get in touch with your people and we'll have the deal signed *mañana*. Isn't that how they talk?"

"I have no experience with Hollywood."

"But you have experience with other things, don't you? Extrapolate, baby. Extrapolate."

"I've heard the word 'baby' twice now and yet there are no infants in sight."

He sat back. He looked away. "Look at this place. It's Phoenix, *reductio ad absurdum* and *ad infinitum*."

"You mean *ad nauseam*."

"I mean *ad infinitum* and, *ipso facto*, *ad nauseam*."

Her expression shifted toward a smile, but then faded.

"Granted," he continued, "it's not the most beautiful landscape in the world to begin with, but there's something terrible and absurd about what they've done to it. The violation. The way they're tearing it up. Ransacking it."

There was a silence between them. Murmurs at other tables. Hissing misters.

"Thank you," she finally said.

"For what?"

"When you said 'violation' I held my breath, waiting for the word 'rape' or 'defile' or some other term equating the landscape with female sexuality."

He considered it for a moment. "You mean, like 'virgin forest'?"

"Correct."

"Mother Nature."

"Exactly. Landscape described in terms of sexual availability. Either a virgin or a whore. Or else a sexless mother figure that nourishes and provides."

"You've given this a lot of thought."

"Most women do."

No, he thought, most women don't. It was one of the things he liked about her. Of course, another thing he liked was her quiet vitality, but today she seemed weary. Shadows under her eyes, a slight droop in her posture. "You look tired," he said.

"I'm fine."

They looked at each other for a moment.

"Speaking of landscaping," he said, shifting his tone, "my backyard is almost complete. A couple of my students are probably working on it right now, even though I said it wasn't necessary."

"What's this?"

He told her about Dallas's sudden trip to Las Vegas and the subsequent arrangement with Ozzy and Erin. He couldn't help it. His personal life always seemed to come spilling into conversations with Keris and he didn't know how to change the habit. Although he didn't mention the incident with Puffy.

"I'm not worried," he said, talking about Erin now. "She's going to call me if anything goes wrong. I made her promise, otherwise she'd try to handle it herself. She has a real problem with authority."

"How do you know this?"

"She said, 'I have a real problem with authority.'"

"And your response was . . . ?"

"What makes you think I said anything to that?"

Keris waited.

Logan sighed. "All right. I put my hand on her shoulder and said, I'm sorry, but these next fifty years are going to be really difficult for you."

Keris laughed. Her face opened up and she threw her head back and when she looked at Logan again her eyes were bright and alive again. He realized, then, just how much he had missed her.

"Wow," he said. "It's you. I remember you."

Her laughter drained away, but her face was still flushed and he understood with terrible clarity that he wanted to be with her. The voice. The eyes. The twists and turns of her thoughts. The indexes of love.

One more thing: A minor detail that, under normal circumstances, wouldn't be worth noting. Logan forgot a folder in his room and went back for it. The plastic keycard. The give of the latch. The folder on the bedside table and the red light flashing on the phone. A message. He picked up the receiver. He pressed the appropriate button and listened to Erin's voice as it came over the line. When it was done he listened to it again and then called the house and started talking into the machine until she finally answered, sounding languid and sweaty, not a care in the world, and he grilled her about the message until he felt pure death entering him, the cold certainty of it, an absolute zero of the heart.

He thanked her. He hung up the receiver. Then his stomach roiled up and he ran to the bathroom and vomited. His whole body seemed to be bursting. Sunstroke. Heat-shock. Wrung-out glands. A heavy pressure inside his skull, like a headache about to go nuclear, his heart pounding in his ears. When it was over he removed his sportcoat and his shirt and then bathed his head in the sink. He brushed his teeth, gargling the thick foam before he spat it out. He toweled off and finally dressed again.

Sitting on the bed with a baby-sized glass of tapwater, he dialed his broker and confirmed what Erin had told him. Everything was gone. The signatures on the paperwork appeared to be his. Was there a mistake? the broker asked. Logan said he'd get back to him and then hung up before the broker could ask another question. Yes, of course, there was a mistake. What else could it be? And for a couple of minutes he actually believed it. A misunderstanding that he would sort out when he called Dallas at her mother's house. Or, if she wasn't staying there and if her mother didn't know where she was, he'd start calling hotels on the Strip until he tracked her down. He'd find her. They'd talk. In the meantime he would avoid jumping to any conclusions. He gulped the awful tapwater. He gripped his forehead with his fingers. But didn't the fact that he had to track her down in the first place mean that his worst conclusions were true, no jumping necessary?

He grabbed the phone again and was about to dial Nevada information when the clock gave him the evil eye. He was supposed to be at the conference right now. In fact, he was late. He hung up. He stood up. He lowered his head and shut his eyes. Sustainability, he told himself. Emergy. Biophysical factors. The only way to survive the debate was to crowd out personal thoughts with economic ones. Empty his mind by filling it. He had done it before. He had taught classes through his parents' bankruptcy and all his turbulence with Dallas by saturating himself with work until nothing else could be absorbed.

He gave his ghost a quick look in the mirror before stepping outside. The heat clobbered him as he crossed the main drive toward the lobby. The curb. The contoured pavement. The islands of vegetation, bristling by design. There was a gargling fountain in the middle of the cul-de-sac, marble pillars by the belldesk where uniformed men were discussing something in Spanish. The doors parted with an electric sigh. Cool air washed over him. It seemed appropriate that it should happen like this, walking the vast and desolate hallway by himself, a couple of potted ferns standing guard by the entrance to the conference room. The devil-skin pattern in the carpet. The processed air. The white light and voices of the crowd.

And the folder? Exactly where he had left it. On the table next to the phone.

chapter 15

It should be clear by now that Deck had more than his fair share of days like these, when he wrapped his hands around the rubberized grip, lifted the club behind him, and struck the ball with every bone and nerve devoted to the motion only to see it careen awkwardly toward the trees as if he had whacked it with a polo mallet. This is when all his surplus values melted away, leaving him flatlined and alone by the sandtrap. His true condition. There. The truth. The guy was alone.

He wiped the sweat off his forehead. He climbed into the cart, manhandled it down the course until he sighted the ball, and then climbed out with the appropriate iron. He crouched down for a moment. The ball was ugly and white, pitted with acne scars. It deserved to be hit. It deserved to be buried over there: the pale green lilypad, the limp flag at the end of a pole. Like a cartoon island with a lone palm. The castaway with the beard and ragged clothes. Ha, ha.

He wanted people to give him tacit praise. He wanted them to acknowledge the faint outlines, at least, of who he was. Was this too much to ask? Apparently it was. Keris was simply too obtuse to know what was good for her. Eventually she'd regret her decision. She might even see him at the presentation this afternoon and change her mind. It had happened once before — an ex-lover emerging from the crowd at a conference, obviously seeking to relive history. No, not Veronica. Someone else. But anyway the offer had been clear: Sex with an ex. Deck had turned her down. This was difficult to explain, but the refusal had given him a greater charge than the actual sex would have. He had lived off that juice for weeks afterward.

He straightened up again. He set his stance. He swiveled his upper body, lifted the club, and then swung smoothly, keeping his eyes focused on the ball. There. *There.*

He sheathed the club in the bag and checked his watch. He had enough time to finish this hole — the seventh hole — before heading back to his room and performing his ablutions. The front nine would remain incomplete today, but for once the numbers didn't matter. This was solo time. This was an opportunity to clear his head. After the presentation was over he'd socialize to the hilt, proving once and for all that he had plenty of camaraderie when he wanted it. Not to mention a distinguished career ahead of him. He was moving on to the next thing, and then the thing after that, the steps rising ahead of him like a spiral staircase toward a penthouse full of lifetime achievements. This would be an impressive place. A Nobel on the mantelpiece, perhaps. The walls hung with photographs of him in the company of presidents. Theorems that would survive him into eternity.

Of course, there had been other possibilities for a while. A woman's touch. A nursery. He felt a darkness nibbling away at him as he drove the cart onward and continued with his usual life. He halted the cart and climbed out. He drew his putter like a sword. This feeling was temporary and silly and insignificant — a by-product of the exchange with Keris. An externality he'd remedy with the usual taxes and redistributions of the soul. Right now the important thing was to continue. Don't think about the step beyond the next one. Don't think about the next hole. That's not for you. That man over there at the eighth tee, sharing a laugh with a lanky-legged woman — that isn't you. You're on the green. You're holding the putter. You're making your par. You're sweating and thinking and feeling. This is you. This is the self no one will ever discover. This is humanity on the aggregate scale. This is what you want, this is what you get.

Dallas slept just fine, thank you, even as the world tossed and turned behind the curtains. She sensed it vaguely in the spaces between her dreams, like the sounds of a lover snoring or talking in his sleep. The world seemed to be ill. It had a fever. It hallucinated rainforests into tundra, deserts into marshes. It believed, somehow, that its meridians had switched places with its latitudes and that its tropics had become poles. No wonder the weather was so screwed up. Its stratosphere ached. It had runny rivers and stuffed-up shores, a lethargy around the equator, a nasty cough in the temperate zones that simply wouldn't go away. Take some aspirin, the sun said. Take some antibiotics. And while you're at it, sign up for a detox program and get rid of those people, please, so this doesn't happen again.

It was early afternoon when she woke, instantly aware of her situation. Usually there was a pleasant moment or two of oblivion before her memory booted up and she remembered who she was and what kind of day awaited her. But not this morning. She felt the air vents thrumming. She sensed the money lying under the bed, nursing its wounds. She could still taste those last couple of drinks at the blackjack table, which always showed up double-sized in her inventory the next day, so no surprise there. She sat up and allowed the damage to reveal itself. A mild case of hammer-head. Alcohol-induced windburn. Actually, not too bad given the circumstances, is what she was thinking as she trudged to the bathroom and splashed water on her face. Afterward she dressed in neutral blouse and jeans and headed downstairs for a few gallons of coffee, sitting sideways in a booth with her back against the wall while the caffeine slowly graced her with its presence. And then, as she smoked a cigarette she had bummed from someone at a nearby table, she began to feel the kick-start of a new day. A clearance sale with optimism as the featured item. In fact, she thought, as the waitress came over with her food, why wait until tonight? It was Friday. The raucous weekend crowds would arrive in a few hours and she'd have to fight for space at the tables. Do it now. This afternoon.

She ate syrupy pancakes and a side order of home fries, craving the starch, craving the sugar, craving the salt. Upstairs in her room again, she applied subsistence-level makeup, changed into a black silk blouse to go with the jeans, and tied her hair back casually. This was the way to go. No nonsense. Functional. She would ignore the sirens of the slot machines. She would sail past the rock of the blackjack table, the hard place of roulette, and let the dice decide her fate. It was simple. And it was ferociously liberating. She grabbed a wad of money from the bag and went downstairs.

Forget quantum mechanics for a minute. Forget general relativity. Forget the vibrations of string theory, which nobody understands anyway, and consider the simple truth: Every object continues in a state of rest or uniform motion unless acted upon by an outside force. Take Logan, for example, as he entered the room ten minutes late. Voices subsided. Heads turned. Attention shifted toward him with a Coriolis effect that nearly knocked him sideways as he walked down the aisle, and he took his seat on the platform with a full understanding of what it meant — the judgment about to be passed, the execution that would surely follow. The only thing missing was a guillotine. Fine. He'd smile at the blade. There was nothing left in him to damage, nothing left to steal. He folded his hands on the table and felt the air settle around him. Numb acoustics muffled the last of the murmurs and squeaking chairs. The platform. The sconce lights. The pale blue color of the clinical walls. His change in motion during the last couple of months had been proportional to the force of Dallas's behavior, which had been so utterly sweet and loving and kind that he had ignored all indications of it being artificial. Make that fake. Fool's gold. The shining edges of her guilt. It was occurring to him now—really occurring to him—that the true betrayal wasn't the theft of the money itself but the premeditated nature of the theft. She had methodically liquidated the portfolio, consolidated the cash under her name, and timed her departure during the conference to maximize her getaway. *I*s dotted, *t*s crossed. And he had been gullible and obtuse to the very end. His face burned. A general self-loathing rose up in him as he sat there, his thoughts fashioned into a supreme awareness of everything he had ever done wrong in his life—the mistakes, the failures of perception, the retreats from difficult truth. For every action, there is an equal and opposite reaction.

"Thank you all for coming," Maxwell Silverson said. "First of all, I would like to thank Optimus and the Midnight Corporation for co-sponsoring this event. And I would like to extend an especially warm welcome to Assistant Secretary Groscost from the Commerce Department, as well as Mr. Pang from the Council of Economic Advisers, who have been kind enough to . . ."

"Are you all right?" a voice next to him whispered.

Logan turned. Keris's face detached itself from the general blur like a figure in a child's picture book. Her eyes fixed on his with a look of concern. Professional concern, he thought. No doubt she sensed the trauma in him and was worried that it would affect his performance in the debate. But there was also a tenderness at the edges of her expression, a faint softening of the eyes and mouth because—yes, admit it—most of the things she said or did were compromises for the more intimate gestures she really wanted to make, and she loved him, and he loved her, and he had given it only minor expression over restaurant tables and phone lines because he lacked the courage to love her the way she deserved to be loved.

He shook his head vaguely. He glanced away. Not yet. Two hours until the presentation was over. Then the warmth would pierce his frostbitten nerves and he would start screaming. Was it possible to postpone a total breakdown? He reached for the pitcher of water on the table in front of him. He tipped it. Ice cubes clanged into his empty glass.

Silverson flicked his eyes toward Logan like a headmaster noting something too trivial and juvenile to merit a rebuke. He continued to speak, detailing the format of the debate in a cadence softened by long-term exposure to American slackjaw. The inner accent, though—the very meat of the words—still retained its quality. Listen to those pitch-perfect vowels. And make no mistake about Silverson. He knew his status. He knew his role. His position and velocity in the profession were as follows: Lame-duck chairman of the Economics department. Old school. Old world. A fine old clipper ship ready to be decommissioned. And the truth, of course, was that no one wanted it more than Silverson himself. He wanted to spend more time with his wife and continue working on his wood carvings, perhaps make a few improvements to their cabin in the Bradshaw Mountains. And so here he was, moderator of the debate, chosen for reasons that had less to do with his diplomacy than with his symbolic presence as a member of the old guard, like the senile grandfather placed at the head of the table. So be it.

The stage arrangements were simple. There was a backdrop with the insignia of the new Economics Institute, flanked by the emblems of Optimus and the Midnight Corporation — the private sponsors whose board members were in attendance along with those of a few other companies. There was Silverson at the central podium with an overhead projector next to him and tables extending in either direction, angled slightly toward the audience to make a shallow V. Logan and Keris on one side, Deck and Dr. No on the other. Logan looked across at them for the first time. Dr. No had violated his own private dress code with a deep gray suit and a bright pink power tie, his white hair cropped neatly, his face tanned and chiseled into high aristocratic composure. Deck, on the other hand, looked like something straight out of the corporate mill. A blue suit-and-tie combo. Logan felt contempt boil up in him. So that was Keris's choice for a lover. It called her taste into question, among other things.

Silverson's voice ceased. Everyone seemed to be looking at Logan, which meant, apparently, that he was supposed to lead off the discussion. He pulled the microphone toward him. He took a breath and paused, his free hand grasping dryly at the tabletop. The folder wasn't there. It was still in his room. Perfect, he thought. Beautiful and perfect. He looked out at the audience, which had become globby and grotesque, like cells on a microscope slide. He closed his eyes. He opened them. Then he heard his own voice come over the loudspeaker.

She bet the passline for a while, adding extras to the fours and fives and sixes and eights and nines and tens when the lucky shooters began to hit them, the crowd working itself up into a froth of claps and cheers before the streak ended and the heat dissipated in the usual manner. There were gains and losses, losses and gains. She rode the pendulum for hours, which was better than losing outright, but not by much, is what she was thinking.

She tried to shake the dice out of it. She threw them savagely against the opposite wall when it was her turn. She switched from soft drinks to mixed drinks. She lit cigarettes with her left hand instead of her right. She broke the taboo of betting against the shooter and she even put money down on the hard eight just for the hell of astronomical odds. Nothing. The dice remained noncommittal. Staid. Complacent. At one point she counted up her chips and realized she was ahead by five dollars, which amounted to third-world wages, to be perfectly honest, so she might as well get a job in a clothing factory overseas.

In other words, it was frustration. And it was hunger because the pancakes and home fries had disappeared from her stomach like Chinese food. Null and void. Satisfaction quotient, zero. Her appetite seemed to make the day's lack of progress intolerable, so when the shooter next to her crapped out, she was fully aware of what she was about to do. She scooped up her chips. She stubbed out her cigarette. She looked at the nearest dealer—a guy with a droopy smile and a tux a little too tight around the collar, if you wanted her opinion on the subject—and she piled everything on the passline. Droopy called back to the boss. The boss turned, noted it with a nod, and kept watching.

It was her turn to shoot. She grabbed the dice and flung them with extra whiplash toward the other end of the table, where they landed and bounced and rolled and finally came to a halt with their snake eyes showing. Craps, the dealer said. The other players groaned, more from empathy than the loss of their minimum bets. Dallas shrugged. She said she'd be right back.

It occurred to her, even as she was riding the elevator up to her room to fetch the rest of the cash, that she was doing it for the terrible reason of wanting to feel something different. She was bored. She was tired of trying to renovate her life. She wanted to demolish the old one—implode it, collapse it—and build a new one over the ruins. She simply wanted to get it over with.

As she plopped the rest of the cash on the table she could feel the electronics in the ceiling taking a sudden interest. Not to mention the dealers and other players. The dynamics of the table adjusted accordingly. She felt the extra space they gave her, the gravity of their looks. New chips appeared. Orange and black. Tiger-striped. As she picked them up she recalled a certain time in grade school, maybe when she was seven or eight years old, when the teacher had handed out a series of self-directed reading assignments that were color-coded according to level of difficulty and everyone's folder seemed to be orange while Dallas's was green with envy.

A player at the far end was shooting. She watched the dice fly and hit the wall below her. Seven. A winner.

"The charm of neoclassical economics," Logan said, "is that it provides an internally consistent theory in which the marginal costs of goods and services determine the level of supply, consumer desire determines the level of demand, and the interaction of these forces in competitive markets determines their exchange values. Producers and consumers, trading freely among themselves, allocate resources optimally. Who could argue with that? After all, it's a natural process. Or so the argument usually goes. Individual producers and consumers are the best decision-makers. Intervention by an outside force—the government is the most frequent example—would bring about suboptimal prices, reducing overall welfare." He had been letting his gaze wander, unfocused, around the room, but now he aimed it at more receptive regions of the audience. "Most economists show an almost religious commitment to the free market as the best method of determining value and maximizing wealth. Most of us, trained in the neoclassical school of thought, behave as if all the issues of economics have been essentially resolved within the context of the basic neoclassical paradigm." He paused. "Give or take an externality or two."

The smoke was clearing and, despite the absence of his notes, he was finding his way into what he needed to say. He knew the broad outlines of his speech, but what surprised him were the details coming to the surface. Phrases he had shuffled and retyped on his computer so many times that he remembered them like the verses of his favorite song.

"This is all fine and well as long as we ignore the basic physical conditions—that is, the biophysical framework—necessary for an accurate understanding of the economy. Although wealth seems to be produced through economic policy, it actually occurs through the exploitation of natural resources, usually in an increasingly non-renewable manner, and almost entirely through the escalating use of fossil fuels. Cheap oil and its derivatives continue to be used to alleviate the impact of depletion and environmental degradation and mismanagement, often giving the appearance of solutions when in fact solutions are only being postponed. In short, most economic development 'works' because we extract fossil fuels out of the ground to make it work, and because we encourage people to run through resource stocks by giving them incentives to do so. Economics is about the exploitation of resources. To say otherwise is to deny reality."

The opposition shimmered in his peripheral vision. Deck's navy-blue shape. Dr. No's tie glowing like an emergency light in an airplane cockpit.

He was about to continue when Keris touched his elbow. "Give me your room key," she whispered.

He covered the microphone with his hand. "What?"

"Give me your room key, and I'll get your folder."

He fished the plastic card out of his pocket and handed it over. And then he sat there dumbly for another moment as she rose and walked down the center aisle like it was the most natural thing in the world.

"I'd like to talk about economics as a discipline," he said, "because I believe it suffers from some severe problems. Fundamental problems. Problems which, for the most part, can be traced back to a basic paradigm that ignores the physical characteristics of economic systems. The standard model of the economy, which usually represents it as a perpetual motion machine unlimited and unconstrained by the laws of thermodynamics, is not only unrealistic, but also irresponsible and dangerous. We need to examine the economic process itself and construct a more realistic model. We need to think about the long-term ramifications of what we're teaching our students. We need to think about our goals."

And the goal, in this case, was either a seven or eleven on the first roll. Or, barring that, basically anything except a two, three, or twelve, which is called craps, and which gives the game its appropriate name. After that the seven, which you love dearly, becomes evil incarnate and it's all about setting the point and hitting the point over and over again, payoff after payoff, like a long night of sex. And Dallas was beginning to feel that way now. The repetition. The rhythm. The secretions and glandular discharges polluting her bloodstream. The eternal ring of the slots, cheering her on. Her pile of chips was growing bigger and bigger, good and plenty, and she was letting it ride, and she was taking risks, and it was paying off. But when the inevitable crap-out happened and curtailed her hottest streak, she kept rolling heavy. Why not? This was the way to live, this was the way to die. She wanted to know what she was made of. She wanted to know what kind of person she really was.

The crowd around her intensified, obeying the universal biorhythm of the day that manifested itself as teatime in England, siesta time in hotter places—unless, of course, the hotter place happened to be here. Here it meant more gambling. It also meant turning up the air-conditioning an extra notch. The sun was hammering away at the rooftops out there, at the palms and cacti and pebbled soil. It struck everything into its sharpest color-essence. The asphalt, the cinder block, the stucco, the glass, the rubber, the chrome—it never felt so pure. The sun made everything what it was. The sun was doing an honest day's work.

Unlike her. She was losing now. It was becoming consistent. She was placing the equivalent of yearly salaries on the line with every roll of the dice, and with almost every roll of the dice the dealer was taking it away.

Keris opened the door and went straight for the bedside table without even thinking about it. Of course the folder was there. And of course there were signs of struggle by the phone—the uncapped pen, the notepad gouged with an unidentified number. Ambushed by bad news. That was the only explanation. She turned and, halfway toward the door again, halted as if stung by something. This was no time to linger, but she looked around anyway. What was it? The room held her. There were his sandals on the floor. His sunglasses on the table. His empty duffel bag sitting on the couch. There was nothing special about it, nothing to learn from his baseball cap or his crumpled T-shirt or his swimsuit draped over the shower curtain in the bathroom, but her urge to linger was powerful and she knew right away it was because she could feel close to him here without the risk of actual closeness. That's what it was. The presence without the person. It was safer. And it was why, in the days when she had still loved Will but hadn't been able to tell him her deeper thoughts anymore, she had found excuses to stop by his empty office instead.

The door shut itself behind her. The walkway led her back through the enchanted forest, where hoses hissed and gurgled among the vegetation, turning lawns into lakes. It was almost dusk. The sun had dipped below the horizon, tarnishing the upper flanks of the mountains, leaving them hip-deep in shadow. Jets of ionized gas were probably striking the magnetosphere at that very moment. Maybe nothing would happen. After all, the most dangerous regions were those directly facing the sun. Maybe they were safe.

She walked briskly, her shoes clacking on the pavement. Rooftops around her thrumming with the sounds of manufactured air. The heat was beginning to release its grip and she could smell the cacti among the resort's foliage, tart odors fermenting in the dusk. She inhaled through her nose, ujjayi style, air swirling at the back of her throat, ribcage expanding, intercostals lifting, and then exhaled the same way. It compensated for not only her fatigue, but also the thin atmosphere of the conference room.

She had been prepared for the odd rituals and customs of a different profession. But the audience had taken her by surprise. Maybe she was naive, but she hadn't expected the lowest common denominator to be so evident in their faces. And the presence of corporate sponsors had made her only more suspicious. She wasn't sure if Logan's presentation suited the occasion. In fact, she wasn't sure if it suited anyone in this type of setting. The best strategy, she suspected, was to convince other economists of his ideas and let them gradually trickle down to the general public through the process of teaching and publishing. Trickle down? No, she thought. Cancel the supply-side imagery. Infiltrate. Then she realized she was revising the thought based on Logan's reaction to it, or what his reaction might be if she were speaking to him. This was the problem. They inhabited each other's thoughts.

The path ended. The parking lot stretched ahead of her. She crossed it haphazardly, weaving through the rows of sleeping vehicles, her eyes stinging in the second-hand heat. She was sweating like a marathon runner, but she quickened her pace as she passed the grand fountain near the entrance. Why? Perhaps it was a sudden urgency. Perhaps it was the sunspot activity, the solar flares. Perhaps she secretly wanted Logan to get an unexpected phone call, or whatever it was, and be disturbed to the very core. A conjunction of events. A crossing of the stars. She entered the lobby and headed toward the conference room, feeling it now in the entire length of her spine. Everything was becoming itself. Everything was being revealed.

Logan took a breath. "GNP is only a partial measure of the conditions that contribute to the improvement of our happiness and well-being. It measures the total output of goods and services. That's all. Plain and simple. It ignores the proportion of output devoted to necessities versus luxury goods, bypassing questions about the distribution of wealth. Furthermore, GNP doesn't account for either the proper functioning of ecosystems or their degradation, mainly because such processes don't interact with markets. The hydrologic cycle, to cite just one example, is probably the most important factor in most of the world's economies, but nobody pays rainclouds for their services, and as human activity disrupts the hydrologic cycle, there's no way for the market to account for the loss of its natural processes. Throw in the fact that GNP counts so-called defensive expenditures—that is, expenditures needed to remedy the effects of drought—as positive contributions, and you can see how it compounds the problem.

"But most importantly, GNP measures only the flow, and not the stock, of natural resources. Why do we count the depreciation of a factory in our estimates of GNP, but not the loss of natural capital, such as trees and soil? Why do we continue to use GNP as an indicator of economic well-being even though it clearly encourages high turnover and the construction of inferior products? GNP rises when people buy more goods to replace shoddy or seemingly 'obsolete' ones, creating more pollution and reducing the resource base even further, and yet we interpret this rise in GNP as a good thing. Meanwhile, we support development policies in the third world whose principal goal is to increase GNP, encouraging other nations to liquidate their stocks of forests, to cite just one example, as rapidly as possible to gain monetary flow. But when the rivers flood, or when droughts strike regions where the buffering effects of the forests have been removed, there is no system to account for the losses to GNP. And forgive me for repeating myself, but GNP actually increases as the towns destroyed by floods are rebuilt."

Dallas kept sending the chips out there because the shooter on her left, a man with long sideburns and an Oklahoma drawl, was staying alive. He hit eight twice before Dallas finally made the commitment and tagged it for herself. Too late. Seven reared its ugly head. She cursed. This was not the time to be wishy-washy. This was not the time to be meek. How much had that hesitation cost her? Don't add it up. Learn from the mistake. Move on. She set down another heap of chips. She bummed another cigarette from a gum-snapping college girl next to her and lit it with shaking hands. Smoke jetted from her nose as she waited for the next shooter to throw. Seven, she thought. Just think of it, and nothing else. Think of yourself playing dice. But then she remembered something Logan had said one night. It wasn't so much what he had said but the way he had said it. His tone. Like he was referring to something she couldn't possibly understand. And so she hadn't asked for an explanation. She had let the comment die between them because anyway it was a stupid thing to say. A stupid expression. But she remembered it clearly now: God does not play dice.

Keris came strolling up the center aisle like a game-show contestant with the precious folder. Logan thanked her as she handed it to him. The satisfying thickness, the weight of accumulated thought. He opened it and thumbed through the documents, selecting something he had designed, he realized, probably while Dallas had been forging his signature at the kitchen table. He shoved the thought away. He stood and made his way over to the projector by the central podium and switched it on.

He cleared his throat, and for a moment, just a moment, his mind slipped out of its groove and he felt the stabbing loss inside him. He squeezed his eyes shut. He opened them again. He loaded his disk into the computer and opened the file. A graph filled the screen.

"What GNP measures quite accurately," he managed to say, "is the amount of fuel consumed in an economy. This graph plots two figures — fuel consumption and GNP — in the United States over the last one hundred years. As you can see, they mirror each other, almost point for point."

The image was of two lines staggering upward together from left to right, as if drawn with a twin-pointed pen, from the turn of the previous century to the turn of this one. Logan had suspected that it was going to be the toughest part of his argument to sell, and he was right. Murmurs from the audience. Vibrations of disbelief.

"I've done similar graphs for five other industrial nations and four developing ones, and the relationship is nearly the same. What does this mean? It means, I think, that the driving force, and the primary source of value in an economy, is energy. And yet energy is the one factor consistently overlooked in standard production functions. As I mentioned a few minutes ago, the standard neoclassical model depicts the economy as a closed system in which the flow of output is circular and self-perpetuating. But in reality, of course, the human economy is an open system embedded in a global environment that depends on the continuous input of solar energy and fossil fuels. We use these energy sources to support labor and produce capital. Energy, capital, and labor are combined to refine natural resources into more useful goods and services. Economic production, in other words, is essentially the process of upgrading matter into highly ordered structures." He switched off the projector. "In this sense, the term 'production' is a misnomer. It's consumption. This is the economic process."

He looked over at Keris. She was ready. Her notes were open, her microphone switched on.

"Each time you spend a dollar," she said, "nearly half a liter of oil, or its equivalent as coal or some other fuel source, has been extracted from the ground somewhere and burned to create the good or service represented by that dollar. No energy use, no economic product. We may think of this energy as 'embodied energy' — or, for more convenient reference, a new unit of evaluation called 'emergy.' Emphasis, please, on the second letter. That's *m* as in 'monkey business.'"

This last comment drew some laughter, which she cultivated—intentionally or not—with a sip of water, a faint smile as she set down the glass. As Logan made his way back toward his seat he searched the audience to see if the goodwill went any deeper than joke-appreciation, but the results were inconclusive. He glanced over at the enemy. Dr. No was chuckling politely. Deck had a grin on his face. When the grin disappeared, though—and it disappeared quickly—it exposed, for just an instant, another expression below it, something that made Logan do a double take as he sat down. Too late. It was already gone. But it was like a mugshot of the soul. Maybe it was his imagination. Stress, he told himself. It's stress. Instead of reviewing his notes, though, which is what he should have been doing, he continued watching Deck for another glimpse of it, whatever it was, in the shifting planes of his face. It reminded Logan of something. That sharp light in his eyes. It reminded him of . . . of what?

"Emergy, quite simply, is the energy required to make something. By measuring goods and services this way, we can evaluate all the resources in an economy using the same unit, allowing us to make easy comparisons. Think of it as a common currency in the truest, most physical sense of the word. Of course, you might think this concept runs contrary to the sacred assumption of economics, which is that price determines value. Yes. This is correct. But we should not forget that the price of a product reflects nothing more than our preference for that product, our willingness to pay for it. It can also reflect the amount of human services 'embodied' in it, if you will. But a valuing system based on human preference alone assigns either arbitrary values, or no value at all, to necessary resources and environmental services. Emergy, as a unit of evaluation, avoids these problems because it is a quantitative measure of the ability to cause work, independent of price. The actual value of a resource should be determined by this ability—that is, its ability to stimulate the economy. A gallon of gasoline will power a car the same distance no matter what its price. Its value to the driver is the distance it allows the vehicle to travel or, in other words, the work it produces— again, regardless of price. And here we arrive at the heart of the matter. Price is usually inversely proportional to a resource's contribution to an economy. Plentiful resources often have low prices, despite the crucial roles they play, while scarce resources have high prices even though they hardly matter at all. Two hundred years ago, salmon was abundant in New England

and contributed enormously to the welfare of society even though its price was low. Today the opposite is true."

Logan saw Deck's gaze shifting toward him, but he looked away before they connected. Keris introduced the concept of the biophysical footprint. The amount of land and water required to provide the resource flows, or consumption, for a given population over a given period of time. On average, she said, urban regions of over three hundred people per square kilometer appropriate the bioproduction of ten to twenty times more land than the regions themselves contain. She went into the basic land and sea categories, the assimilation figures, the carbon sinks, the regeneration cycles. Logan picked up his water glass and stopped with it raised to his lips. He knew what Deck's expression reminded him of. Dallas. The look on her face last January when she had goaded him into sex on the living-room floor. She had ripped open his shirt and bit his neck and slapped him until he finally took her down and did what she said. Like he was following instructions. Fuck me hard, she had told him. Fuck me like a whore. He had gripped her hips and pumped away, calling her a whore, a stupid whore. But when he was done he had felt sick. His penis deflating in shame. And she had stood up with a look of amused contempt on her face, as if she had been trying to get that confession out of him for years. Then left him there. Downgraded. Reduced. It wasn't right, he thought. She had made him believe it for a few seconds, but only because she had believed it first.

"Logan?"

The room came back. The tables, the chairs. The audience. The stage. Keris said his name again — matter-of-factly, but with her hand covering the microphone, an urgency in her eyes. He could feel his nerves misfiring, twitching faintly across his face. He needed to say something.

"Dr. Smith," Keris said to the audience, "will speak now about a possible new direction for economics, since it is unlikely we will discover the additional two Earths required to sustain the rest of the world at our current standard of living."

He nodded. OK. Yes. His thoughts returning, snapping back into place. He found the microphone in front of him. He knew what he needed to say.

As the final chips disappeared she felt utterly black inside, like a burned-out building, gutted and exposed for everyone to see. This was the part that surprised her — not the death, but the public spectacle that accompanied it. The humiliation of standing there with all her empty windows and charred timbers on display. She lit another cigarette and watched the table reset it-self. Dealers sorted chips into the rack. A few of the players shifted at the rim and leaned down to place new bets. Someone squeezed in next to her, but she couldn't give him the appropriate space. The paralysis of the final loss was still with her. So she stood there instead, smoking vacantly and wonder-ing, with numb fascination, what she was going to do with her life. Return-ing to Logan would have been difficult enough with a ton of winnings. But now?

"Blow," a voice said.

A hand appeared in front of her with a pair of dice resting on the open palm. The lifelines and lovelines, the cross-hatchings of someone else's fu-ture shoved right in her face. She looked over at him. Was he serious?

"I'm guessing you didn't see how much money I just lost."

"Blow," he repeated.

He had wide eyes. Mildly blunted features. A plain collared shirt and jeans. He could have been anybody. He was probably nobody. She looked at the dice again and felt an urge to slap the hand away and send them flying. He wanted her to blow? Fine. She'd blow. She took a long drag from her cig-arette and then, focusing her lips, blasted them with smoke.

"All right," the guy said, nodding. He brought his arm back and released the dice with a backhand motion.

Seven. Cheers went up. She smiled bleakly. Of course. Good luck for everyone except herself. She was about to step away from the table when he caught her.

"Whoa-whoa-whoa. Stay right there, you goddess. Don't you move."

"I'm basically done," she said.

"Love well, whip well. You know what I mean?"

She gave him a skeptical look. It was time to go upstairs and drown her-self in the bathtub, is what she was thinking. This was extra voltage she sim-ply didn't need.

He held out the dice again. "One more time. Please."

She would have walked away if it hadn't been for the desperation in his eyes. The dog who drops the ball at your feet, so easily pleased. She sighed. She brought the cigarette to her lips and repeated the trick. Then he threw the dice and repeated the result.

"See?" he said, shouting through the cheers that surrounded them. "You're a goddess. I worship you. What's your name?"

She told him. He nodded vigorously, like he loved it, like it was the best name he had ever heard in his entire life. She asked his. Then she asked him to repeat it. Ouch, she thought. Logan had told her about this kind of thing. People from the East Coast so warped by their confinement to the prep-school circuit that they didn't know how their names sounded to people outside it.

He scooped up the dice and presented them for her blessing once again.

She humored him. It was something to do. The spic-and-span truth, actually, was that the more she thought about her room upstairs with its drawn curtains, its empty shopping bag beneath the bed, its discarded high-style clothing and damp towels and bunched-up sheets, the more she realized she didn't want to go back there ever again.

It was much easier to blow smoke. To watch him throw the dice. To participate in a winning streak even if it wasn't hers. There was a certain pleasure, to be perfectly honest, in urging him to raise his bets without bearing the risk—a low-calorie thrill that sustained her for a while. He kept playing. He tripled his take. Even after he crapped out and passed the dice to the next shooter, she came up with the idea of smoking his chips, curing them like salmon, before he placed them on the table and it seemed to have a similar effect. He praised her. He paid homage to her eyes, her voice, her opinions on the game. He swiveled his hips, Elvis-style, and threw a finger in her direction—which, he confessed afterward, he did simply to hear her laugh. And so she was actually sort of enjoying herself, really, savoring this tiny slice of joy while it lasted, when she happened to notice that his chips weren't the fifty-dollar ones, like she had thought, but five-hundred-dollar lookalikes with only those little red slash-marks on the side to distinguish them. The cigarette nearly fell from her mouth. Don't ask why the casino designed them that way. Or maybe her eyes weren't as sharp as she thought. Maybe she needed glasses. But anyway, the guy had been raking in piles of them for quite a while now and they added up to how much?

It was his turn again. He picked up the dice and held them out. She blew smoke accordingly, but she was feeling a little spacey now, almost weightless with the numbers in her head.

Seven. A winner.

He set down an even larger pile to accompany the one already out there and said a couple of words to the dealer, who nodded and gave him back a single chip, a simple black-and-white one, when the next roll came up seven. Again. A stadium roar in her ears.

"Those chips," she shouted, leaning against him.

He raised his arms in victory. "Yeah! These chips!"

"No, I mean *those* chips." She pointed.

"The zebras? What about them?"

"You know how much they're worth, right?"

He held out the dice again. His eyes seemed slightly bulbous, as if amazed at everything they saw, his face half-lit with a smile. Everyone was whooping and clapping, calling for her smoke. "Zebras are endangered species, sweetheart. You could trade one for a sportscar. Blow."

She looked at the dice. Simple things. Like the chips, they were black and white. Modestly dressed. But they doubled your fortune with every roll. She was finally learning how to accept the magic.

"I need another cigarette."

She held out her hand, index and middle fingers parted, until somebody reloaded it. A lighter appeared. And as she leaned toward the flame she felt the relief of zero gravity taking her, the springs of her soul released. Is this how it happens? Is this how your life is made? By blowing smoke? By surrendering to the forces that make you who you are? The slots were chiming all around her, the voices of the players singing her praise. She was the center of the universe, the brightest star of surveillance, the image burning on every screen like the object of an ancient god's lust. This is how it feels to be alive. You are the blackjack dealer, you are the dealing. You are the ringing in the air, the pouring of the drinks, the promise and payoff of every bet. You are the fire and you are the burning. Yes, you are the burning.

"The difference between science and economics," Logan said, "is that science attempts to understand the behavior of nature, while economics attempts to understand the behavior of models. And many of these models have no relation to any state of nature that has ever existed on this planet."

This was the homestretch. He talked about the unrealistic assumptions of neoclassical economics. He talked about the lack of empirical testing to validate even the most widely accepted models. Switching on the projector for an example of what he meant, he displayed a textbook image of the Phillips curve—a downward-sloping graph showing the supposed trade-off between inflation and unemployment—and then superimposed a line of actual data over it, which cut backward and looped over itself and then curled and dropped and rose again like a child's scribble.

"Furthermore, these types of models demonstrate only a specific set of internal relationships. As Dr. Aguilar discussed earlier, price doesn't always reflect scarcity. But even if it did, we would probably fail to notice it because the prices of all goods, including resources, would inflate together as a general trend, staying the same relative to each other and thus masking the underlying scarcity. And further still, consider the fact that we have compensated for resource depletion by using more energy-intensive methods to extract and upgrade lower-quality materials, producing more pollution for each unit of the resource — which, again, is not reflected in prices. Neoclassical models don't indicate air quality. They don't indicate increasing greenhouse gases or ozone holes. They don't indicate losses in soil fertility or fish stocks, and they don't reflect species extinctions or oceanic dead zones or the weakening of the Gulf Stream or even rising sea levels. They don't capture the effects of deforestation. In fact, they might even demonstrate a more efficient outcome.

"So where does that leave us? It leaves us, I think, with a belief held by the French physiocrats in the eighteenth century — namely, that the Earth itself is the origin of wealth. We need to approach macroeconomics from a thermodynamic perspective, emphasizing the production of goods rather than their exchange according to human preferences, which is what neoclassical analysis has always done. We need to acknowledge the very basic fact that the production process is a unidirectional, one-time throughput of low-entropy fuel that is dissipated and, for all intents and purposes, lost as waste heat. This process depends, quite simply, on the availability of free energy."

Logan clicked another image onto the screen: The standard circular-flow model, as copied from a Macroeconomics 101 textbook he had used in his own courses. Then he clicked again, replacing it with a "Biophysical Throughput Model" he had created himself, which consisted of a box within a box, like a framed painting, with the larger box named "the ecosystem" and the smaller dubbed "the economic system." Moving from left to right, it showed a sun radiating a single arrow toward the ecosystem, which contained the words "matter" and "fossil and atomic fuels" within it, fattening the arrow before it crossed the border into the economic system. Logan pointed out that the economic system, as he depicted it, was almost exactly the same as the standard circular-flow model, but that it was embedded in an environment, sending "waste heat" and "degraded matter," represented by arrows continuing toward the right, into the ecosystem and then passing beyond it, presumably into space, as "low-grade thermal energy."

"This would require an extensive rethinking of production functions to include natural capital," he said. "It would require integrated assessments of waste sinks and regeneration capacity. And it would require an entirely different accounting system in which resources are valued according to their contributions to the economic system. In short, it would require a different kind of economics. An economics based on an Energy Theory of Value. A biophysical economics."

He switched off the projector and looked out at the audience. Their faces were reserved, inscrutable. "I haven't drafted any specific equations to quantify such a theory. In fact, I'm not even sure it's possible to quantify it at all. All I know is that we, as economists, are on the wrong track. I'm proposing a move in what I believe is the right direction. And I need your help. This isn't something one person can do alone. Thank you for listening."

Applause. Tepid applause, it seemed to him, as he made his way over to his chair, already feeling the deflation, the wilting of his nerves that came after deep stress. A tired and dirty feeling like smoke in his blood. Keris leaned over and complimented him. He returned the favor. He drank water and pressed the cool glass to his cheek and resisted an overwhelming urge to leave the room. To leave himself. To forget who he was.

Dr. No drew his microphone forward and angled himself toward the audience like someone preparing for an intimate chat.

"Thank you, Dr. Smith," he said, without looking at Logan, "for an earnest criticism of neoclassical theory. It certainly could use some fine-tuning, couldn't it?" His face broke into a gentle smile. "The world seems to be in such a terrible state. Doomsday is here. Our natural resources are almost gone. Population growth is outpacing food supply while at this very moment mass extinctions are taking place in our oceans and forests, which themselves are disappearing at an alarming rate. By the way," he said, dropping his voice slightly, "we're distributing free antidepressants at the end of the discussion."

Laughter rose up. Dr. No waited pleasantly for it to subside. "The problem with these pronouncements, however, is that they happen to be wrong. Despite an overwhelming urge to view natural resources in physical rather than economic terms, the truth is that we're dependent on oil because it happens to be abundant right now, just as we used to be dependent on coal when it was readily available, and wood before that. Although the resources of the Earth are obviously finite, the real question is whether their finite nature has economic relevance. And the answer is no. In fact, the main constraint on resources is not scarcity, as many alarmists would have you believe, but the increasing costs of extraction, since the process of finding and utilizing the vast—and I must emphasize the word 'vast'—reserves now known to exist is an expensive process indeed. This doesn't even include the reserves that have not yet been discovered. And . . . are you ready for a shock? Known reserves of fossil fuels and basic minerals have actually increased during the last few decades. But don't take my word for it. The proof, as they say, is in the prices."

Logan turned and shared a puzzled look with Keris. Had Dr. No been asleep during their presentation?

As if in answer, Dr. No rose from his chair, made his way over to the overhead projector, and loaded his own image onto the screen. "This table lists eleven of the most commonly used minerals in the world today, showing the ratio of price per ton to the hourly wage in the manufacturing sector — in other words, the relative prices of these minerals for each decade during the past century. As you can see, there has been a continuous decline in resource prices for the past one hundred years. If we were 'running out' of these resources, as Dr. Smith seems to believe, I think we'd certainly know it by now. In fact, I would like to make a wager with Dr. Smith."

Logan raised his eyebrows, feeling the sudden heat of attention on him.

"Choose a few minerals — nickel, copper, chrome, or whatever else you like — and calculate the amount, by weight, that you could purchase with a thousand dollars. Ten years from now, we will recalculate the price of that metal in inflation-adjusted dollars. You pay the difference if the price falls, I pay the difference if the price rises. What do you say?"

Logan nearly laughed. "One of the main points of my argument is that price doesn't reflect scarcity. Didn't you hear that? Price is usually inversely proportional to a resource's contribution to an economy." He looked toward the audience, the gallery of expectant faces watching him. "I hope that was clear in our presentation. So, actually, I expect the price of most mineral resources to decline during the next ten years."

"So you reject the wager?"

"I just pointed out that price is a false measure of resource depletion. Your response is to propose a wager about resource depletion in which the winner is determined by price. Do you see the problem here?"

Dr. No nodded. "You reject the wager. Aluminum, cement, copper, gold, iron, nitrogen, and zinc constitute more than 75 percent of global expenditure on raw materials —"

"Expenditure. Not *use*. That's what I mean."

"— and despite an increase," he continued, holding up a finger, "of between two and ten times the amounts being consumed fifty years ago, the available reserves have, again, actually grown."

Logan was about to jump in with another comment when Keris put a hand over his forearm. He sat back. OK, OK. Save it for the rebuttal. He glanced at the audience to see if they understood what Dr. No was trying to get away with, but a haze of pleasant expressions had formed out there. Nods of agreement. They were engrossed. Logan brought a hand to his hot forehead. Then he clenched it and almost slammed it down on the table. This wasn't right. He wanted to scream at everyone. It wasn't right.

They were causing a commotion. Make that a circus. Like the only things missing were the horses and the clowns, is what she was thinking, as the crowd thickened around them, hooting and applauding, parting sluggishly for the waitresses to deliver drinks. You could have sold tickets. Of course, the casino tried to disrupt the proceedings with the usual tricks: Dealers came and went. The dice were replaced several times. The racks were re-stocked, the drop box emptied. Management did everything except pull the fire alarm, to be perfectly honest, but it was impossible to change the energy. Her smoke. His money. Matter and antimatter. Cameras watched from sev-eral angles, trying to spot something suspicious, the barest hint of an irregu-larity. But what could they do, tell her to stop smoking? Tell him to stop throwing the dice? Meanwhile she shut the numbers out of her mind and simply watched the black-and-whites double over and over again. Her thoughts glittering with nicotine. Everything was pure and sharp. Her emo-tions distilled from high-octane adrenaline.

But then the guy violated protocol. He raked it all in and placed the min-imum bet out there. A hunch, he announced. She protested. He rolled any-way. Snake eyes. There was a debate between them about whether or not his reduction in the bet had affected the dice, like don't assume you'd roll the same number with a different stake, was her thesis, which he eventually ac-cepted, but the damage had been done. It was basically an engraved invita-tion to the manager, and sure enough, a few minutes later she sensed rearrangements in the crowd, an opening beside her, and then a dark sport-coat hovering in her peripheral vision.

"How are you this evening?" the manager said.

She glanced over at him. He had squarish glasses, graying hair, a sagging face. One of those anonymous men from the upper end of the demograph-ics who were useless to her and therefore difficult to acknowledge even when they were front and center. She was about to reply when she realized he was actually looking across her, focusing on the guy, as if she were some kind of buffer or safety barrier.

"As you can see," the guy said, picking up the dice again, "we're cleaning house. We're gonna own this place pretty soon."

Dallas brought the cigarette to her lips.

"You know," the manager said, "your craps game is a little too hot for us. How about if you play something else instead. Blackjack. Roulette. Slots."

The guy threw back his head and gave a big horsey laugh. "Are you nuts? This is our game, pops. This is the bonanza."

"It isn't a suggestion," the manager said.

The guy's face cleared. He shot Dallas a look, then eyed the two security personnel providing backup. "You aren't serious," he said. "You can't pull us off the table just because we're winning."

"A casino," Dallas said, "is a private establishment where they can basically do whatever they want. They can say everyone wearing a blue shirt has to leave."

The manager shifted his eyes to her for a moment—grateful for the comment, she guessed, even as he noted it as another suspicious element in the winning streak. "Enjoy yourselves," he said, looking at both of them now. "But not at the craps table."

The guy stammered. He looked at Dallas. Was this for real? She said it was. And then, for proof, she nodded toward the table. The dice were sitting out of reach, neutralized. Their chips had been consolidated and stacked, ready for collection. It was over.

With one swift motion the guy leaned over and gathered up everything, stuffing it all into his pockets. This let the air out of the crowd. Moans. Hisses and boos. She stubbed out her cigarette and turned toward the manager to throw him a final, cutting glance, but he had already disappeared.

They worked their way through other crowds, other action, other tuxedos and evening gowns in the light of the chandeliers. Even now she wondered what was happening elsewhere, what she might be missing. They sat down at the bar and ordered drinks.

"I still don't believe it," he said, shaking his head. "We were behaving like real citizens."

Dallas sipped a gin and tonic. "He probably did us a favor."

"Don't hand me that."

"The wave was about to crest." She unbound her hair and ruffled it out, already turning her mind to the next order of business. "How much did we take in?"

"We?"

"You and me."

"That's one way of looking at it." He gulped at his drink and wiped his mouth with the back of his hand. He nodded and smiled. "That's one way."

She didn't reply. She sat there with a completely detached look on her face, letting him think about it. Now that the flush of the game had faded she saw that his wide-eyed expression, which she had taken for excitement, had already become brutish, as if he ogled everything he looked at. Life with this guy meant dirty underwear on the floor and fantasy football with the guys. It meant a forced march through Valentine's Day. It meant sleeping with someone whose idea of great sex was to thrust away at you for hours thinking you absolutely loved it.

"I guess," he finally said, "I could be persuaded to share the wealth."

"What kind of wealth are we talking about, is what I want to know."

He drained his drink. "Let's go up to my room and count it."

She nodded. She was ready for this. She followed him toward the elevator and rehearsed the magic words in her mind—the spell that would allow her to receive her fair share of the winnings while at the same time avoiding the sexual favors. He pressed the call button. A few moments later the doors opened and they had to stand back as a tide of would-be winners poured out. The car was empty now. They stepped into it. He pressed the number for the top floor. Good. Perfect.

"Hey," he said, as they rose in cushioned silence. "You know what Freud said about elevators?"

"A couple of centuries ago," Dr. No said, "Thomas Malthus predicted widespread famine for Great Britain, basing his claim on the notion that food production grows arithmetically—that is, by increases of equal increments, such as one, two, three, four—while population grows exponentially—or, in other words, by a process of doubling in which one becomes two, two becomes four, four becomes eight, and so on. The math seemed irrefutable. In only a few years, he said, population would outstrip food supply and there would be massive starvation. A crisis was at hand." He paused for a moment and smiled wryly. "But tell me, when is the last time you saw a television commercial asking you to adopt a British child for three cents a day?"

Laughter. He looked toward Silverson in mock apology to show no insult had been intended.

"And so Malthus began a long dynasty of doomsday prophecies that continues to this very day. Just pick up the newspaper—or, better yet, open your junkmail—for another gloomy report on the state of the world, and please send your donation right away to the League of Environmental Justice or NaturePrime or whatever group is profiting from your fear. The funny thing about these reports or so-called studies is that they always contain erroneous predictions of when the world's natural resources will run out. For example, did you know we were supposed to exhaust our oil reserves last week? Oh yes," he said, continuing with mock gravity in his voice. "According to the Club of Toledo's report, issued seventeen years ago, the final drop of crude oil was supposed to be burned last Friday on the Ventura Freeway."

More laughter. Dr. No sat back, flipped some pages, and quoted more old reports, all of which predicted the exhaustion of food, fossil fuels, and mineral resources by dates settled safely, and comically, in the past.

"I have a question," Logan said suddenly.

"Excuse me?" Dr. No looked up from his paper in surprise. "I believe there will be plenty of time for questions during the rebuttal."

"If your doctor diagnoses you with cancer and gives you three months to live, does it mean you don't have cancer if you're still alive four months from now?"

"I would like to finish my —"

"An incorrect prediction doesn't necessarily mean the diagnosis is wrong. And by the way, if all the shipping and transport systems broke down, isolating Britain from the rest of the world, everyone on the island would be dead within six months. Like every other developed nation, the U.K. is a net importer of resources. But anyway, go ahead," he said, flicking his hand at the report Dr. No was reading. "Don't let me interrupt."

OK. So this wasn't the smartest thing to do. It should be stressed, however, that Logan was sick of appeasement strategies and reasonable approaches. After all, look what it had gotten him. Dallas had led an alternate life right under his nose. She had taken everything. There was a man involved. Of course there was a man involved. This was his latest thought. He was the worst kind of fool. He lifted his glass of water and gulped it down, hearing a high, faint, whistling noise in his head. His hands were shaking.

Dr. No gave the audience a half-embarrassed look — see what I have to put up with? — before he continued. "Let's take a moment," he said, "to look at the economics of exhaustible resources. If the market for a given resource is near equilibrium, then the net price of that resource — that is, the market price minus extraction costs — must be rising at the current rate of interest for that type of investment." He paused and raised a finger. "Now, I must emphasize this. A rising net price doesn't necessarily mean that the price to *consumers* is rising. If extraction costs are falling — and, as I demonstrated a few minutes ago, they have fallen consistently for the past century and will probably continue to do so — then the price to consumers can remain constant or fall lower through time. And if we look ahead to the distant future, to a time when the resource becomes so costly to extract that the market price rises and the rate of production falls accordingly, we will indeed reach a point where the price becomes high enough to choke off demand. At that moment, production ceases. The resource will be exhausted at the instant that it has priced itself out of the market. The Age of Oil or Zinc or whatever will come to an end and the Age of the Next Cheapest Resource will begin at the very same moment. We move laterally, in a process of substitution, from one to the other, the cheapest resource being replaced by the next cheapest resource, and so on, guided by the free market."

Keris slid a note over to him. ARE YOU ALL RIGHT? it said, the words glaring at him in capital letters. He shrugged stiffly, without looking at her. It was too late to be all right. He'd never be all right again.

"Let's look ahead to the Final Stage, if I may be so bold. At some point in this process, we reach a technology capable of substituting for a mineral resource at relatively high cost, but with a virtually inexhaustible resource base. Let's call it a 'backstop technology.' This can be nuclear fusion, it can be solar energy, or it can be something we haven't even discovered yet. Since it doesn't have the scarcity rents associated with mineral resources, this technology will function as soon as the market price rises high enough to cover its extraction costs, and it can continue to operate indefinitely, providing a ceiling for the market price of the resource. In other words, successive grades of a resource are mined until the last and highest-cost source is exhausted, at which point the market price has risen to the exact level where the backstop technology becomes competitive."

"Which is fine," Logan announced, "as long as you continue to use energy and matter interchangeably."

"Logan—," Keris said.

"Do you see the problem here?" Logan continued, stabbing the table with his index finger. There were ripples running through the audience, but he didn't care. "Whenever you reach a limit with materials, you switch the analysis to energy without bothering to acknowledge the switch. And then, whenever energy becomes a problem, you refer to resources. Well, which one is it? The solar panels and nuclear reactors have to be made out of something. Matter matters. An 'endless energy' scenario simply won't cut it. You can't just cobble together an abstract model with the advantages of both but the limits of neither. This is what I was talking about earlier."

"I must remind Dr. Smith," Silverson said, who had risen and taken hold of the microphone at the podium, "that we have a strict and orderly format for this debate. You will have a chance to respond accordingly. Until then, please restrain yourself."

"Sure," Logan said, running a hand over his face. "No problem. Sorry."

More murmuring in the audience. Dr. No resumed his speech.

"The key, of course, is not simply technological progress, but the degree to which technological progress allows us to substitute one resource for another. Current evidence, not to mention the general trend of technology, suggests a high degree of substitutability. In fact, the elasticity of substitution between exhaustible resources and other inputs is quickly approaching unity or bigger, suggesting that other factors will soon replace natural resources in the production process, allowing a positive level of per capita consumption forever."

Logan tilted his head back in exasperation. Other factors? What other factors? Was Dr. No expecting deliveries from another planet?

Dr. No continued speaking as if he hadn't noticed. "The world can, in effect, get along without natural resources, so exhaustion is just an event, not a catastrophe. The economy will continue. We will all continue. And as Dr. Moore is about to demonstrate, organizations such as the Economics Institute will continue to guide us in this process."

The audience's attention shifted toward Deck, whose posture seemed to lengthen in the ensuing silence. He flexed his wrists like a TV news anchor preparing himself for the camera. In Logan's fevered vision he looked like a figure composed of straight lines and surfaces, his clothing welded into casements over his body. As if something had been neutered out of him.

"Contrary to what you may have been told," he said, "growth actually has a positive and *equal* effect on the incomes of both rich and poor. I've assembled data from eighty countries over the last four decades showing that the average incomes of the poor rose by the same percentage as incomes of the rich. Growth, as it turns out, helps everyone. If this is the problem with growth, then I say let's have more of it."

He continued by citing standard-of-living increases, development benefits, education and health indexes rising steadily over the past few decades.

"In the last five hundred years," he said, "world economic growth has increased one hundred and twenty times, allowing us to enjoy a quality of life higher than at any other time in human history. So is there a problem, after all? Yes, there is." He paused. "The problem is that we could be doing better. Our only failure, if you want to call it that, is our failure to adequately assess the few environmental problems that exist. Take, for example, the greenhouse effect—an externality caused by the production of carbon dioxide,

317

methane, and nitrous oxide at inefficient levels. We can analyze the costs and benefits of the greenhouse effect in terms of two fundamental functions. The first, capturing the costs to society, can be called the Damage Function, while the second, representing the cost of slowing or eliminating greenhouse warming, may be understood as the Mitigation Function. From these two functions, we can calculate the most efficient strategy to reduce the costs of climate change and maximize Net Economic Welfare."

It took all of Logan's resolve not to lower his head to the table in utter frustration. There were too many things to say. He felt as if he had spent hours proving that the Earth was round, only to have his opponents respond by calculating the size of the sea serpents waiting for ships that sailed too close to the edge. Of all the things he had anticipated from Dr. No and Deck, he hadn't expected such a deliberate refusal to address the substance of his argument.

Deck went to the overhead projector and flicked it on. His two functions were illustrated on a graph whose vertical axis represented the monetary values associated with greenhouse gases—that is, the costs of damages and mitigation—while the horizontal axis measured greenhouse gas emissions as a percentage of uncontrolled quantities. He described the equations he had used for the Mitigation Function, admitting to possible shortcomings, oversimplifications, inaccuracies. Then he delved into the complications of the Damage Function.

"This," he said, "is much more difficult to calculate because the greenhouse effect will surely harm the economy in some ways, yet it will also bring certain benefits. For example, lower agricultural yields will be offset by the fertilization effect of higher carbon dioxide levels. In fact, recent EPA estimates of crop damage are less than the study's margin of error. The forest products industry may also benefit from this fertilization effect. Greenhouse warming will increase the demand on cooling systems but decrease the demand on heating systems, having a small net impact on the energy sector. Construction in temperate climates will benefit from longer periods of warm weather. Recreation and water transportation will be affected both positively and negatively, depending on the region. And to top it all off, the vast majority of the economy—the manufacturing, mining, utilities, finance, trade, and most service industries—will hardly be impacted at all.

"Obviously, several factors have been omitted from this calculation. Human health. Biological diversity. The aesthetics and amenities of daily life. There are no current studies indicating significant costs in these areas, although a recent report by the National Research Council actually suggests major amenity benefits from global warming. Suffice it to say, further study is needed. In the meantime, however, we have to proceed with the information we have and make our 'best guess.' And this best guess leads to a rather surprising conclusion. Global warming will probably have a net benefit to the world economy."

He flicked off the projector for dramatic effect. "Don't get me wrong. This isn't an argument in favor of climate change. As a matter of fact," he said, turning on the projector again and clicking to another graph, "we can see that the optimal reduction of greenhouse gases occurs at the point where the Marginal Cost of Mitigation is equal to the Marginal Damage caused by each additional unit of gas. For the values I've assigned the various components of these equations — which, I should note, are available for review — the efficient outcome is an 11 percent reduction in the level of greenhouse gases."

He went on for some time, adding a joke about the additional jobs provided by the mitigation activities, or "mitigation sector" of the economy, as he phrased it. From there he began to wind his way toward a conclusion, citing general feel-good figures about human progress. In the last fifty years, he said, the world population has doubled, but food production has more than doubled, while at the same time the world food commodity index has fallen by half. Calories per capita are higher. Fewer deaths from famine, starvation, and malnutrition than ever before. And by the way, did anyone realize that cancer rates are decreasing? That the deforestation issue was a myth? Statistics from the United Nations indicate that biomass stocks of European forests have been increasing for the past few decades. American forests are — brace yourselves — in excellent health. And although it's true that tropical forests have been shrinking, the rate of loss has been declining during the last decade and will soon reach zero. In addition, we should take into account the fact that biodiversity loss has been exaggerated — the loss of only one bird during the last two centuries, for example, has been documented in the eastern United States — and understand how this raincloud hanging over our heads is largely a fabrication of sensationalist media and environmental groups seeking to keep their coffers full.

Logan was leaning sideways with his elbow on the armrest, his hand cupped over his mouth to prevent a sudden outburst. Keris reached under the table and took his free hand. But instead of helping, it brought everything closer to the surface. He squeezed his eyes shut. He wanted to scream.

He wanted to throw chairs around the room and collapse into tears, and then he wanted be absolved of it afterward.

There was a silence. Deck was staring at Logan across the stage. He flicked off the projector and smiled flatly.

"Go ahead," he said to Logan. "I'm done."

This caused some confusion. A few seconds passed before Logan realized what it was. From his position on the stage, Deck was the only person who could see Keris holding his hand. Logan released it and brought both arms onto the table. He let out a breath.

"An 11 percent reduction," Logan said. "That's lovely. That sounds so precise and scientific. Just don't forget to send a copy to the Marshall Islands and several other microstates in the Pacific before they sink underwater."

Deck gripped the podium. "Tell me something. What's so special about your theory? People have been predicting Doomsday ever since they could talk. You haven't put together a single coherent model. You don't even know how to make an equation."

"That's not the point."

"What is the point, then? Inventing a new job for yourself? 'Biophysical economist for hire.' You really expect everyone to go back to the horse and buggy just because we might run out of petroleum a couple hundred years from now?"

"Excuse me," Silverson said, rising from his chair.

Deck held up a hand. "I want to hear this."

"I didn't come here to argue about whether or not we're running out of gas this week. It doesn't matter. None of those figures matter." He turned toward the audience. Ordinary faces. Men and women. Maybe they could understand. "Don't you see? At some point we have to start caring — I mean, really caring about the way we live. It's all connected. How are we going to treat each other if we keep treating the Earth like a business in liquidation?"

There was a long silence. His throat was dry. His eyes burning, threatening tears. He didn't know what else to say. He was about to excuse himself when the lights went out and did it for him. Darkness. Startled voices. A slow commotion began to roll through the room. Logan stood. He wished, like he had never wished before, that the electricity would stay off until he could escape. Let it end this way. He made a move toward the door — or where he guessed the door was — and bumped into someone almost immediately. Keris. He didn't back away from her. He didn't say a word. He stood against her, feeling the warm length of her body, her hands on his chest, and he took hold of her and kissed her because he felt as if he would die if he didn't. It was the only thing he knew.

The guy's room was pristine. Dallas noticed it right away. The bed untouched, the closet empty. There was a small suitcase on the floor where he had obviously dropped it before heading straight down to the casino, but otherwise nothing. Which made the process easier. It didn't feel like she was stepping into his lair, is what she was thinking, as she watched him empty his pockets onto the bed. When he was done he went over to one of the chairs by the window and sat down. It was nearly dark now, the signs in full-blown hysteria behind him, multicolored lights shifting and shimmering like the strobes on an empty dance floor. He leaned back in the chair and knitted his hands behind his head. Apparently it was her job to count the money.

It was even more than she had hoped. She divided the chips into two equal piles and gazed down at them as if they were rare jewels. These pieces of plastic solved her problems. They solved her life.

"What's that?" he asked, nodding at the piles.

"What's what?"

"The split you just made."

"You answered your own question, partner."

"That's a funny way to talk about my winnings."

"You mean, your original stake. Multiplied by my smoke."

He smiled. She could see his puggish features more clearly now, his bulbous eyes exaggerated by the harsh light of the lamp beside him. His name suggested privilege. An effete, polo-playing life. But the longer she looked at him, the more he resembled the half-wit who mucked out the stables. She could come out and say it to herself now: She didn't like him. She didn't like him at all.

He stood up. He came over to the bed and stretched out sideways on it, his head propped in his hand. "You'll have to be more persuasive than that," he said. "A lot more persuasive."

Here we go. Finally. She lowered her eyes. She summoned up a look of embarrassment. "That's not really an option for me. You see," she said, tracing a pattern in the bedspread, "it's that time of the month."

She looked up at him after she said these last words. His eyes lost their intensity for an instant. He exhaled slowly, almost a sigh, and rolled onto his back. Victory, she thought. The chips clinked and jumbled as his weight shifted on the mattress and she put a hand between the two piles to prevent

them from mixing. And while she was at it, she decided, why not start picking them up and casually putting them into her pocket like it was a done
deal. Possession is basically nine-tenths of the —

"That limits the options," he said. "But there's something else you can
do." He turned his head toward her.

Her expression froze. A million things kicked through her mind and by the
time she began to formulate something about a toothache, an extracted wisdom tooth, a sore jaw, she realized it was too late. Her hesitation had undercut
the credibility of whatever she would say next. So she said nothing. A minute or
two passed and she thought maybe he would let it go. Maybe he'd laugh, ha
ha, oh well, can't blame a guy for trying. Maybe he'd feel bad about pressuring
her.

He pried off his sneakers without untying them. He unbuckled his belt,
worked his pants over his hips, and exposed her to the glory of his underwear. Briefs. Of course. The thin cotton already swelled with anticipation.
He kicked the pants onto the floor and then lay back again and closed his
eyes.

A long silence. The vents thrummed. A few voices passed in the hallway.
His legs were thick and blubbery, filigreed with hair. His cock bulging awkwardly against the fabric of his underwear. And his shirt, which he was still
wearing for some reason, was twisted slightly with little gaps strained open
between the buttons, fabric rumpled below the beltline. More time passed.
His breathing evened out. He seemed to be falling asleep, actually, so she
waited a few extra minutes and then quietly began to gather up her share of
the winnings.

His hand came down and took hold of her wrist.

"Ow," she said. "Ow!"

She let go of the chips. She yanked her arm away. On her feet now, she
stood glaring at him, massaging her wrist and ready to head for the exit if he
so much as twitched in her direction. But he didn't. She glanced at the door.
He hadn't even flipped the safety lock. She could leave. Yes. That was clear.
She could leave empty-handed.

"I'm not asking for much," he said. His eyes were open now, gazing
dreamily at the ceiling. A note of self-pity in his voice. "Keep your pants on,
if you want."

Or she could return to Phoenix with enough money to fix her marriage
and her life. So maybe she could do this one ugly chore. Five minutes. Ten at
the most. And if she thought of it like a visit to the dentist, like this thing

happening inside her mouth, then it really wouldn't matter. It wouldn't actually involve her, is what she was thinking.

The elastic hairband was still in her pocket. She pulled it out and used it to tie her hair back. Hair away from the face — that was key. She could do this. She had eaten a live worm when she was ten years old. She went over to the light switch and turned it off. Unbuttoning her blouse, she let her eyes adjust to the brilliant hues coming through the window. The leering carnivalesque twilight. Soft shadows. Colors washing across the furniture and walls. He was watching her, the hard lines of his face visible. Fine. No problem. She could handle it, because as she unfastened her bra she realized the city was going about its business, doing its winning and losing, its buying and selling, its drinking and eating, its construction of rainbows and all the jackpots they contained. She climbed onto the bed and worked her fingers under the waistband of his briefs. The bedspread scratched against her breasts. It didn't matter. It wasn't really happening to her. She lowered her head and took his cock into her mouth. It was small enough for her to do the full sword-swallowing act, which got the expected reaction. She cupped his testicles. His penis leaked. A sour taste in her mouth. It was some other woman doing this. Dallas wasn't even in the room. She was floating above the city, gazing down at the crawling headlights, the lamped houses, the wheeling aberrations of the Strip. She was passing over mountains shaped like half-folded umbrellas staked into the ground. Why hadn't she ever noticed that before? How had she missed such a thing? There was the Air Force base with its hangars and runways angled toward the great wastes of the Mojave, where mushroom clouds had bloomed so many decades ago. She could see it now — the skies full of aircraft shaped like scimitar blades, technology scavenged from alien wreckage, everybody knew it, and he was moaning hoarsely and coming and she was spitting it onto the bedspread, away from the chips, which she couldn't see but was keeping track of, more or less, with her left elbow.

The first thing she did afterward was gather up the chips and cram them into her pockets. Then she started groping for her bra. It wasn't there. It must have fallen to the floor somewhere, lost among the folds of the skewed bedspread. She was pulling up the hem and searching when she realized the guy had raised himself up on an elbow.

"Relax," he said. "My wife won't be here till ten o'clock."

He was so busy laughing at his own joke that he didn't seem to notice she was heaving and tugging at the bedspread. Where was the damn bra?

Then everything stopped. The vents ceased. The light died. She straightened up and glanced outside. The signs stood like dead monoliths in the moonlight. The room was even darker now. She could barely see what was in front of her. And her mouth felt gummy. Her breath stank. She could taste it and smell it and feel it and she needed a shower and she needed her toothbrush more than life itself. To hell with the bra. She grabbed her blouse from the chair and buttoned it as quickly as she could. She went over to the door. He started to say something. He started to move. She opened the door and stepped into the hallway and yanked it shut behind her. Keep the bra as a souvenir, is what she was thinking. She could replace her entire wardrobe now. She blotted her lips on the back of her hand as she headed for the stairwell. A few emergency lights showed her the way. People were emerging from their rooms, asking stupid questions that she ignored. She found the door to the stairwell and started descending. Voices yelling and joking at the bottom. Pinocchio! someone shouted. A woman laughed. By now, she figured, the guy was probably finding his underwear, which she had deliberately tossed under the bedside table. Or maybe he was groping for his pants. She had a fleeting image of people trapped in the elevators and milling around the casino, but it didn't matter to her anymore.

Every casino worth its salt had a backup generator that was supposed to kick in seamlessly, without even a flicker, whenever the power died, so she knew this darkness was basically a gift from God. It wouldn't last. Any second now.

She corkscrewed down a few more floors until she saw the right number and yanked the door open. She shut it. There. He couldn't find her now. The lights came on. Perfect. She strode down the hallway. It was over. It was done. She'd wash him out of her mouth. Her pockets were full of salvation. Let the guy laugh about it if he wanted to, but he had basically spent half a fortune on a blowjob and he'd regret it tomorrow, heading back to his shitty life in some shitty East Coast city with his shitty job and that shitty name Prentis.

chapter 16

It's important to remember that stars collapse. Keris knew this. In her lectures covering post-main-sequence stellar evolution, she described how our sun, with its intermediate mass and average spending habits, would burn for another 5 billion years before expanding into a red giant and finally contracting into a white dwarf. Far more prevalent in the universe at large, however, are the high-mass stars that last for only 100 million years before their hydrogen supplies run low, their nuclear reactions dwindle, and their inner layers contract, triggering large-scale conversions of helium into carbon, carbon into oxygen, oxygen into silicon, and silicon into iron. Iron is the final stage. Its fusion absorbs rather than releases energy, and with nothing left to resist the compression of the heavier elements, the outer layers rush inward at 45,000 miles per second. The core collapses. A few tenths of a second later the strong nuclear force, finally overcoming gravity, sends out a shock wave with one hundred times more energy than the star has emitted during its entire lifetime. It's called a supernova. Keris knew this.

And she knew that the same thing could happen, more or less, to the human heart at certain stages of its existence — the collapse, the shock wave, the aftermath of scattered elements combining with stray protons and neutrons to form cobalt, copper, gold, uranium, and some others she couldn't recall at the moment because she was too disoriented in the darkness. Logan's body against hers. The kiss. The warmth of his hands on her face. They were standing apart now, their fingers interlaced. How had it happened? She didn't care. A door opened and admitted a faint light into the room, leavening everything into existence again with only the barest hints of his features available to her, but it was enough. She began leading him through the crowd. They reached the corridor where other people were spilling from the stairwells and other conference rooms. They made their way toward the lobby. Twilight shone through the atrium glass. Potted trees and shrubs and humpbacked couches arranged like the miniature world inside a terrarium.

She guided Logan outside, into the warm evening. The fountain was dead. The sky was slate-colored, a few stars charging up for their nightly appearance.

He looked at her. "I want —"

"No," she said. "Don't say anything."

She led him through a grove of tangled cactus, past a swimming pool, and then up a set of stairs that thudded softly beneath their feet. She unlocked the door to her room. Dead air. Without the cooling system there was no point in keeping the windows closed anymore, so she walked over to the sliding doors and parted them. A sound of released suction. A sound like a kiss. Her balcony overlooked the golf course — a fairway, a putting green, a sandtrap lurking near it like a black hole in space. The horizon was fringed with willows, branches veined in the final radiation of the day. There was a musk of damp grass. But the sprinklers, like everything else now, were silent.

She turned. He was standing in the middle of the room. She took off her glasses and set them down on the table. Maybe he didn't love her. Maybe he was a person who simply wandered away from his wife occasionally for some guilty exploration, some confidence-building, before returning to her with renewed faith. Maybe he was a person who always took one step over the edge and then stepped back again. It didn't matter anymore. He would reject her as soon as he discovered she was pregnant. But she loved him unconditionally. This was the last, great, necessary thing for her. All this time she had prided herself on giving unconditional love when it was really unconditional sex. She knew this.

She didn't want any mistake or misunderstanding about what was going to happen next, so she went over and wrapped her arms around his neck and kissed him. For a moment it was mechanical — lip pressure, head angle, the movement of mouth on mouth — but then he seemed to soften and mold himself against her. A tremor inside him. His armor began to drop. OK, here he was. This was him. She could feel his shapes and colors. It was like slipping into a hot bath. She eased down his neck, her lips grazing a pulsing artery. Yes. This was him. She could feel his fingers at the back of her head, threading themselves into her hair, his body humming as if he had been struck with a tuning fork.

An exploding star sends out a shock wave that collides with interstellar gas and heats it until it glows. The resulting nebula, enlarged and spectrally enhanced through observatory telescopes, displays burning shawls of indigo and magenta, filigrees of corn-colored light. At the core of it — the heart, let's say — are the remnants of the original star. A neutron star. Imagine our sun squashed into an object with a ten-mile radius, spinning at thirty revolutions per second and emitting pulses of radiation. It is rich and powerful and strange.

She slipped her hands inside his sportcoat and eased it off his shoulders. She unbuttoned his shirt. Working her way down, she untucked the shirt from his pants, then took hold of his wrists and freed them from the cuffs. She tugged gently on the sleeves. His shirt fell to the floor. Placing a palm on his bare chest, she felt his heart. It was nearly volcanic. She smiled. He smiled back. She lowered her hand to his belt and unbuckled it. But when his pants dropped she realized, too late, that the shoe-barrier was still intact. Whoops. They both laughed.

He reached down and removed everything — the shoes, the socks, the bunched-up pants — and straightened up wearing only his boxers. She took hold of the waistband and eased it gently over his erection. She cupped her hands around his erection and brought herself up against his bare body and kissed him again. His hands were on her shoulders. She became conscious of voices passing on the walkway below the open window. The scent of bare earth. The room was nearly dark now, the surfaces around them dissolved into watery depth and essence.

She was still fully clothed. She took his hands and guided them to the zipper at the back of her neck. He did the rest. Her dress opened and fell away. The bra came unfastened, the underwear slid down her legs. He was kneeling on the floor now, kissing her stomach right where the baby was. A flash of guilt. She tried to let it go. She gasped as he worked his way down. Then a clumsy moment as she turned and pulled back the sheets. They lay down together. He was there. This was him. Kissing the inside of her thighs. Finding his way into her with his tongue, parting the folds until he reached her inner pulp. She rose into the pleasure slowly, taking time to relax, floating and drifting upward, sailing far beyond herself, suddenly shaking and jerking and banging her knuckles against the padded headboard when she flung her arms back. By the time it subsided she realized he was next to her, holding her. She kissed him. She eased her way down his body and tasted him. Then she crawled up again and rolled onto her back.

He hesitated.

Yes, she said.

He moved on top of her. She took his erection and guided it into her, and then she cupped his shoulders, the smoothly knotted muscle in her palms. The density and warmth and pressure. Corona. Chromosphere. Photosphere. Interior. He was adjusting and touching different parts of her, pleasure flaring out and rising and expanding until he finally lowered himself and pressed his face into her neck, and she gripped the broad planes of his back and felt his erection pulsing and then coming. And then she came. She clenched him. She held him.

She released. She nearly started crying. There were crickets now. Sandals rasping on the pavement outside. The mild glare of a flashlight passed across the ceiling as the world returned to its steady state. His skin was hot. He seemed to be layered over her, his cheek touching hers, his mouth at her ear. They remained that way for a while, finding their way back to themselves, unmixing themselves until they finally separated, almost reversing positions as he rolled onto his back and she turned onto her stomach and laid her head against his chest, listening to the heavy thud of his heart. There was a long, beautiful silence. Crickets pulsing. The gently throbbing night.

The phone rang. It erupted like an air-raid siren. The power, obviously, was still out. The phones, obviously, were working just fine. She felt an urge to swat the thing like an alarm clock, but she knew the only person who had the hotel number, so she picked it up instead. And then she dropped it. It slipped from her fingers like a bar of wet soap. Her fingers, her limbs, her body — they seemed to be out of phase with each other, refusing to cooperate with her thoughts. She lifted the receiver by its cord and managed to hang on to it this time.

"Charlotte's stuck!" Sophie cried from the earpiece. "We're here alone!"

"Wait a minute. Calm down. Charlotte is stuck where?"

"At work! In the elevator! A security man called and said they're trying to get her out, but there's something wrong with the — the *thing* that opens the door."

It took a moment for Keris to pick up the thread. Charlotte. Work. Her law firm was on the eighteenth floor of a high-rise in downtown Phoenix, and today was Friday, so the —

"Are you there?" Sophie asked.

"Yes," she said. "I'm here. I'm really here." She realized this didn't make sense. She hauled herself up and scrunched a pillow behind her back. "Did you lose power?"

"Duh! Why do you think Charlotte is stuck?"

"Do not," Keris said, "take that tone with me."

"Sorry."

"Is Katie there?"

"Yes."

"And Chow?"

"Yes."

"Chow will protect you."

Sophie snorted into the phone. "We're not scared, Mom. We're hungry. There's no food in the house."

Keris squeezed her eyes shut. Duh! She tried to offer some suggestions: The neighbors. Delivery from a sandwich shop. Sandwich shop? Sophie repeated incredulously, as if Keris had suggested hailing a cab in their suburban neighborhood. And anyway, there was no money in the house, either. At this point Keris was still fumbling for a solution—and trying not to resent Charlotte for failing to stock the cupboards—when Logan spoke up.

"Is that your daughter?"

She nodded.

"What's going on?"

She covered the mouthpiece and told him.

"Call her back in five minutes," he said. "I have an idea."

It was a good idea. Easy. Reasonable. And moreover, Sophie and Katie would like it. Logan called his house and spoke to Erin and told her the situation, then passed the phone over to Keris, who gave directions to Charlotte's house. Then Keris called Sophie again and relayed Logan's description of Erin so they would recognize her when she arrived to pick them up. Keris told Sophie to leave a note for Charlotte explaining the situation when she came home. *If* Charlotte came home. Keris had a feeling she was sleeping in the elevator tonight.

"We're planning to leave here first thing tomorrow morning," she told Sophie. "So I'll pick you up early afternoon. Don't forget to bring Chow's dog food with you."

A mild snort at the other end.

"I know. Duh. But make sure you feed him."

She hung up. She flopped back onto the mattress. Then she looked over at Logan. He was lying on his back with his eyes fixed on the ceiling. Faint signs of withdrawal.

She rolled onto him, resting her chin on his chest. "Hello again," she said.

"Oh, it's you. What a pleasant surprise."

She heard his stomach grumble.

"Wow. That sounded like it hurt."

He didn't say anything. She picked up the phone again and dialed room service. A woman on the other end said they could make sandwiches and salads. Keris relayed the information to Logan and he answered it with a single nod. She placed the order. She hung up.

"This phone work is exhausting," she said.

He stood up and went into the bathroom. When he came back he was wearing one of the hotel-issue robes. He walked right past the bed and stepped out onto the balcony. This she did not like. But she found the other robe and followed him out there. Cool air. Mingled smells of earth and vegetation and concrete. Sky gleaming overhead with twenty-four-carat stars — their facets untarnished, for once, by terrestrial light. He was gripping the railing with one foot wedged between the bars, like he was going to climb over. She came up next to him.

"What is it?"

A long silence. She steadied herself for whatever he was going to say next. He hadn't seemed like the kind of man to downgrade her after sex — to resent her for giving him what he wanted — but she had been blindsided by stranger things. Like her ex-husband's affair. It occurred to her that she wanted to tell Logan she loved him, and that she should have said it the moment they were alone in this room.

"She's gone," he finally said. "Dallas. And she took everything with her. The money, I mean."

A cascade of relief. And then pain — second-hand pain — as he told her about the phone call he had received before the presentation.

"You think you know someone, and then . . ." He shook his head slowly. It was happening now. His voice was breaking up and he was starting to cry. She wrapped her arms around him. There was no way to avoid the trauma, the internal bleeding that came from this kind of injury. She had been through a divorce. She had been betrayed. We all have. She knew this.

The same highway. The same lanes. The same burning distance to the Colorado River and the same bridge over it. But the journey was in the other direction this time, and the car belonged to Keris. Logan sat in the passenger seat, watching everything pass. He empathized with the ransacked towns even more deeply now. He knew how they felt: Laissez-faire. Let it happen. Let the fast-food and convenience stores pile up on the main drag, let the paint peel, let the palm trees slouch and the topsoil burn off. This is the natural conclusion. This is what we are.

The rest of the night had passed strangely. Out on the balcony, he had sobbed like a five-year-old and then surprised himself by devouring a sandwich as soon as the waiter set down the tray. Then he had eaten the rest of

Keris's sandwich, which she had barely touched. Sitting back from the bread crusts and smeared remains of his appetite, he had looked over at Keris and told her everything he felt about her. He had tried to talk about their future, but slid helplessly back to his failed marriage and his lost money and his doomed job. He had paced up and down the balcony, his robe flapping open, chastising himself for his stupidity and his mistakes. She had listened to it. And then she had said enough already. She had felt the same way about her divorce until finally accepting the paradox that she had needed to make certain mistakes in order to become the kind of person who would regret them. Did this make sense to Logan? It did. But it was also easier said than done. To which she had said, fair enough.

They had gone back to bed. They had slept—or at least Keris had slept, with a low-grade snore Logan had envied. He had spent most of the night re-acting to memories transformed in light of what Dallas had done. So that's what she meant. That's what she was thinking. That's how she pulled it off. Even the most tender moments detonated like landmines when he stepped on them. The hardest task ahead of him, he realized, would be learning how to live with his own thoughts in the middle of the night.

In the early hours of the morning Keris had rolled over and put her hand on his chest and told him that she loved him. Just like that. He hadn't even realized she was awake. He had said the words back to her. And then elec-tricity had returned—a soft thump in the walls, a subtle life-force returning. The flashing digits of the clock. Then she had fallen back asleep. With great effort, he had managed to rouse her for breakfast, followed by a brief return to their rooms for showers and packing. And now the road. The tires hum-ming steadily beneath him. Mild music on the stereo. A guitar twanging, drums beating half-time. They talked now and then, but mostly she left him to his thoughts. There was still the issue of what he was actually going to do once he got home. He could call Dallas's mother to see if she knew any-thing. And then? Call the police? Hire a lawyer?

He closed his eyes. Last night he had tried to follow Dallas's betrayal back to its source, but it was like traveling upriver in an undiscovered coun-try, searching for a legendary wellspring that simply didn't exist. There were too many tributaries and sidestreams, too many rapids foaming with her one-night stands, the eddies of her previous boyfriends. Farther up, deeper into the interior, there were the narrow bends of her adolescence, the vines hanging low, slopes trickling with the snowmelt of her parents' marriage. The air was heavier here. The sky swollen with rainclouds. The current thin but surprisingly strong. Eventually it tapered off among the brush and saplings, the headwaters of her personality burbling up from some aquifer whose depths and pressures he couldn't measure. He asked her about it, because she was standing next to him now, eyeing him suspiciously with that lowered chin of hers, but she turned and walked away. He followed her and repeated the question, dogging her through the forest until they reached the lobby of the Economics building and began climbing the stairs, his voice clogged, out of breath as he asked her over and over again why she had done it, his elephant feet growing heavier by the moment. When he reached the top he found Deck and Dr. No moving the furniture out of his office.

He jerked upright. The highway. The sunlight. The humming car. His neck was sore. A sense came to him, retroactively, of his head drifting and weaving with the motion of the road.

"Do you want to lie down?" Keris asked.

He looked over at her. "Is there a first-class section I don't know about?"

"Behind you."

"If I lie down, I won't be able to wear the seat belt."

"I'm a careful driver."

He gestured at a large van, gargling black smoke as it overtook them in the passing lane. "You're not the one I'm worried about."

She nodded. "Fair enough."

"How about you? You look exhausted. Want me to drive?"

"I'm fine, thanks."

The music shifted to something more lush and complex. Horns, keyboards, backup singers. There was something else he needed to ask. It had occurred to him last night, a minor act in the carnival of worries, but it seemed more important today.

"I know," he said, "that it's bad form to ask this question. Especially after the fact."

She raised her eyebrows. "Yes?"

"I didn't have any condoms with me. And you probably didn't either."

"I didn't want a piece of latex between us. I trust you."

He took this in. She trusted him. OK. But it was like having an alcoholic approve of his drinking habits.

"Was I correct in doing so?" she asked.

He nodded.

A moment passed. She took her eyes away from the road and shot him a look. "But that's not what you're worried about. Correct?"

"Well," he said.

"Go ahead. Please."

"I've been with the same woman for a couple of years now. But you aren't married. And . . . I understand that you probably . . ."

"Yes?"

"That sometimes you might . . ."

"Yes?"

"That you might see other men."

"Yes. And I have sex with them. I'm still waiting for the question, Logan, and I'd like you to ask it in the most straightforward and clinical way possible. Please."

"Do you use condoms with other men?"

"Yes."

"With all of them?"

"Yes."

"Including Deck?"

This last comment struck her hard. She closed her eyes. Her fingers tightened around the steering wheel. Logan glanced at the road ahead, devoid of traffic, but with the landscape ripping toward them at highway speed, and he raised his hands toward the dash protectively. When he looked at Keris again her shoulders were shaking. Then her mouth burst open and she laughed. She laughed hard.

"What—," he started to ask, but he was drowned out. He looked at the road again. "Slow down," he said. "Pull over."

To his relief, she eased the car into the breakdown lane and brought it to a halt. She slumped against the wheel for a minute, then removed her glasses and set them on the dash. She gushed laughter. She held her stomach like it hurt. When it finally subsided she rummaged through her tote bag and pulled out a tissue.

"I don't understand," he said.

"Neither do I. Why am I laughing?" She dabbed at her eyes. "Oh, I'm sorry about this. I suppose I should be mortified that he's telling stories about me. 'An excellent fuck. Five stars.'" She caught herself. "I assume he gave me a positive review?" She kicked back against the seat and started roaring again.

Logan waited. The music continued playing on the stereo, rising, dropping, leveling off with a chorus. A car thudded past, rocking them with displaced air. His annoyance was just giving way to a what-the-hell feeling—a sense that if she was laughing this way, he didn't have anything to worry about— when he realized that her laughter had merged seamlessly into tears and she was crying. She put both hands over her face, her shoulders heaving. He didn't know what to do.

"What is it?"

She shook her head. The radio reared up with a new song and he reached over and turned it off. The only sound now was her sobbing. Another car passed. He waited.

"There's something I need to tell you," she said, wiping her tears with the back of her hand. "Something I should have told you earlier. Before last night."

"More truth? Don't tell me now. I can't take it."

She faced him with red and swollen eyes. "I have to."

"Tell me something else first. Prepare me for it. Lead into it slowly."

She faced forward and pressed her palms against the steering wheel in frustration. She blew out a breath. "All right," she finally said. "You know the universe is expanding. But you probably don't know that the expansion is accelerating. The best theory to explain this phenomenon is known as Inflation, which posits the existence of dark energy propelling galaxies away from each other until they reach the speed of light and effectively disappear."

"When is this going to happen?"

"Thirty billion years from now, give or take."

"Forgive me if I don't seem worried."

"Listen to you. You sound like Dr. No. As if the time-frame disproves the point. This is a growth model on the cosmological scale. Endless expansion. Exactly the kind of thing you've been arguing against. But it's real. It's natural. Everything is moving farther apart and becoming more disconnected." She turned to face him again, her glasses still on the dashboard. She seemed more naked to him now than she had been in the hotel room the previous night. "If the universe is behaving this way, what makes you think people are any different?"

This was the first pessimistic note he had ever heard from her. "What are you saying?"

"I love you," she said. "Despite everything, I love you. But I made a mistake two months ago. During the conference in Tempe."

"You and Deck. I know."

"And something else that affects us."

He took a breath. "OK," he said. "Tell me."

She told him. There was a long silence afterward. A few more cars passed. Logan gazed beyond the windshield, at the day throbbing in golds and dusty blues. A haggard palo verde stood by the side of the road. Guardrails gleaming and wavering, a steady wash of thermals warping the air. He couldn't speak. If someone had offered him all the money in the world he wouldn't have been able to utter a word. The only thing he could do was stare numbly toward the blurry horizon, full of sun and dust.

The engine was still running. Keris sobbed for another minute or so. And then, almost casually, she blew her nose and put on her glasses and put the car into gear.

Erin never knew she had muscles there. She wasn't a biologist or anything, but she knew the logic of her own body, which said no way were there nerves in her upper arms capable of generating that kind of pain. This was supernatural, but it was also totally real. Blame it on the rake and shovel. Blame it on her sudden zeal for yardwork. Blame it on—all right, she admitted it—her lack of exercise. So anyway, here she was with her dead arms, her lower back crooked and stooped like an old lady's, like where's my tapioca pudding. She stood at the kitchen sink, good sport that she was, easing the iron skillet into the water. Talk about hardware. It was the size and weight of a manhole cover. Her arms were pleading for mercy, but a deal was a deal. Ozzy had cooked breakfast, so she was cleaning up the damage.

Ozzy, in fact, had served up about a billion pancakes that morning, complete with powdered sugar and rivers of fake syrup that the girls had consumed like it was their first and last meal. Erin was no psychic, but she sensed strict parents of the no-sweets-no-television type. They were all sprawled in the living room now—Ozzy, Sophie, Katie, cat and dog—watching something with a lot of tinkly music and high squeaky voices. Obviously, a show for young girls. But Ozzy didn't mind. Ozzy would watch anything you put in front of him.

She was rinsing the skillet when she heard the muffled creak and clatter of the garage door through the wall. Logan was home. Early, she thought. Except, wait a minute, didn't he go in someone else's car? Maybe he took the automatic gizmo with him because it was easier than using the key. She thudded the skillet into the dry rack, turned around, and leaned against the counter with the towel slung over her shoulder. Dishpan hands. Drained face. She was thinking up some joke about Housewife of the Year when the door opened and Dallas walked in.

OK. So Erin had seen enough photos on the walls and tabletops to recognize this woman as The Wife. And she had also looked at the photos carefully enough to recognize something about her—a dark hint in the eye, the hot smile—to know this wasn't a person she wanted to meet in the emotional equivalent of a dark alley. But it was happening now. They eyed each other for a few moments before the woman set down her suitcase and unslung the purse from her shoulder.

"Funny," she said, running her eyes down the length of Erin's body, "I thought you'd be much older."

"Huh?"

"Did the conference even happen? Or was that just an excuse to have the weekend together?"

Just then the television gave out a shriek. Dallas cocked an eyebrow and walked over to the archway. Erin followed her. This, she guessed, was a sight most unwelcome to the queen: Ozzy lying on the couch with Puffy curled up and sleeping on his chest. Chow, also asleep, on the second couch. The girls watching TV from the flaps of some kind of tent they had made with afghans and chairs pilfered from the kitchen table. Ozzy raised a hand in casual greeting before letting his attention drift back to the screen.

Dallas turned and looked at Erin like she had sprouted an extra head. "Who the hell are you?"

Erin told her everything, helplessly peppering it with compliments to Dr. Smith for letting them stay at the house this weekend, and during the power failure yesterday he had called and asked them to pick up his friend's daughter and the friend's daughter's friend—oh, and the dog, too—and did she see all the yardwork they had done in only two days?

The woman looked like she was about to erupt. She worked her fingers slowly and deliberately through her hair.

"Oh," Erin added, "and there was this phone call."

The woman nailed Erin with her gaze. "I want this place cleaned up."

"Sure. Obviously. I mean, I was just—"

"And then I want you out of here. This isn't the Salvation Army." She picked up her bags and carried them toward the bedroom.

Erin took a breath. "But Dr. Smith—"

The door slammed.

"—said we could stay."

The door didn't respond. Erin felt venom suddenly balled up in her throat, eyes burning. Where did this woman get off? She took a few steps toward the door, but then stopped with her knuckles raised. The excuse for knocking was going to be, hey, just thought you should know about the phone call from Mr. High Finance—you know, just to continue the impression of semi-adult responsibility, with maybe the hope of a temporary reprieve until Logan came home—but she sensed that a knock would provoke only more agitation. Like something worthy of the Richter scale. Besides, Erin knew herself. She knew that her own anger would slip its noose. Or she'd start crying. Or both. Which seemed to be happening anyway. She turned away. She wiped her eyes. Then she went into the living room to tell Ozzy.

Self-interest. Competition. Supply and demand. These were the forces at work as Dallas stood in the bedroom, unpacking her suitcase. She unfolded, unfurled, unstuffed. She shook out a clean dress—one of her backups—and wedged it into her overpopulated closet. Don't even ask how tired she was. She had crawled out of bed extra early, cashed in her chips, and hit the road with sleep-wrinkles still mapped across the entire western side of her face. No breakfast. No appetite. She had brushed her teeth twice. And somewhere in the open desert she had stopped at a mini-mart for some gas, some candy bars, some cigarettes. She had stayed within sight of her car the entire time. Doors locked, alarm on. Nobody was going to come within sniffing distance of that money, is what she was thinking. And you'd think after all that she could at least return to the serenity of her own home instead of this refugee camp, which in her opinion was an obvious sign that Logan didn't think she mattered anymore.

She filled up her laundry bag and kicked it back into the closet. She heard a commotion through the wall. A dog's bark. A child's protest. Chairs scraping on the floor. She bridged a hand across her forehead and paused for a moment. OK. All right. She knew how to bypass her own pain for the sake of higher goals. This would be beneficial. It would allow her to be The Forgiver, wounded not only by Logan's weekend tryst, but by the violation of their home-space as well. He'd have to compensate for the loss, the damage to her privacy. He'd have to earn her trust again. This was the part where she skipped the review of her own offences. Perfect information? This wasn't Dallas's thought, but it was true just the same: Nobody wants perfect information. It would ruin every life it touched.

She put away her toiletries, brushed her teeth, and then, returning to the shopping bag on the bed, did her final accounting. She dumped it out. She sorted the bills into bundles, stacked the bundles into piles, and arranged the piles into a three-by-three pattern like the squares on a tic-tac-toe board, a configuration pleasing to the eye. This was her way of decompressing and sorting through her thoughts. What to do with the money. There was the repayment of two major loans, of course—one from Logan's investments, the other from her credit cards—but there were also these leftover piles. The surplus.

The noise on the other side of the wall began to gather and concentrate itself at the far end of the house. Soon none of this would matter. The open house, the affair, the tiny paper-cuts he had inflicted on her with every inch of emotional distance he put between them—it all had zero weight, to be perfectly honest. She could forgive him, but she didn't know if he could forgive her, and so she would keep her sins camouflaged until further notice. She lit a cigarette. The smoking, however, wasn't going anywhere. This was part of her. Logan would have to accept it.

She could hear the activity spilling outside now, loosely organized in the street. She peeked out the window. The blonde girl and her boyfriend were loading backpacks into a dented sedan while the two little girls—one brownish, one pale—stood watching, the brown one holding that damn cat in her arms. A thick-maned dog sniffing at the tires. Grocery bags and cardboard boxes everywhere. She receded back into the bedroom and waited, smoking, until she heard the doors smack shut, one by one, and then the cough of the engine, and then the grinding of the gears, and then the chitty-chitty-bang-bang of the car finally disappearing down the street.

She emerged and paced through the empty house, reclaiming it, checking it for damage. Everything seemed fine if you basically ignored the locker-room smell in the guest bedroom. She opened the window. She closed the door. Let it be cleansed by fire. She settled in front of the TV with a drink in one hand, a cigarette in the other, the remote ready to blank the screen as soon as Logan showed up because it would detract from the impression she wanted to make. Which was? Judgment Day. She wanted to see the expression on his face as he came through the door still fresh from seeing the other woman. He'd be cowed. Dallas would be cool.

Some time later she heard the engine thrum in the driveway. A pair of car doors thudding. Keys jingling at the threshold. Every sound amplified in the expectant silence. Television off, attitude on. Hot and humming. She was ready. But the face of her husband, when it appeared in the living room, seemed warpainted and malarial, like a vision of the person he might have been five thousand years ago. And the sight of the other woman only made it worse. Dallas had been expecting a vamp, or a saucy young thing like that student, or maybe even a Miss America contestant—anyone, in other words, with the basic hardware required to lure men away from their wives. But this . . . this short-haired, spectacled professor-type with, all right, maybe a half-decent body . . . *this* was the competition?

Logan stood in the middle of the living room, trying to fix Dallas, it seemed, with the force of his eyes, pegging her to the armchair. Who did he think he was?

She crossed her legs. "How was the conference?"

"How was the baby shower?"

She took a drag from her cigarette and slipped the butt into the empty soda can she had been using as an ashtray, exhaling a jet of smoke. She refused to look at the other woman, as if it would cancel her presence. "Can I kill you now?" Dallas said. "Or do we have to talk first?"

"Let's skip all that and call the police. Let's see . . . theft, forgery. What else? What else have you done that I don't know about?"

She lost what she was going to say next. A heat rose through her, flaring in her armpits.

"Come on," he continued. "I want to hear it. Light up another cigarette and tell me your story." He walked over and, with a theatrical gesture, took her empty glass from the coffee table. "Or do you need another drink, too? That's all you do, isn't it? Smoke, drink, watch TV. Anything except think. That's you."

He was clenching the glass in his hand, like he might throw it at her. She was ready to move. But then he set it down and lifted his hand away from it slowly, fingers spread, as if making sure it would stay there.

She nodded slowly. "Well, thanks. This is the most attention you've given me in the last two years, not counting sex. Which is the only thing, to be perfectly honest, that you've —"

"Excuse me," the other woman said.

Dallas turned toward the woman — what was her name? — Maris, Harris, Paris.

"Excuse me," she said again. "Sorry to interrupt, but where's my daughter?"

Dallas smiled. "I'll tell you what. Let's make a deal. A trade. Your daughter for my husband."

"I don't understand what you —"

She walked toward the woman calmly, like hey, let's talk business. "You see, this isn't my husband. You basically kidnapped the real Logan. And now you're going to tell me where he is." She reached for the woman, wanting her collar, wanting her throat. "You're going to tell me what you did with him."

Logan stepped up and blocked her. She tried to get through him, but no matter how much she scrabbled and leaned and pushed, she couldn't get any closer. His impregnable chest. She tried to slap him. He caught her by the wrist. They struggled for a minute until he finally pushed her back toward the couch. She screamed.

"You're not my husband! I want him back!"

He stood there with his shirt skewed, breath rising and falling hard. "You kicked them out. Didn't you?"

"Me? I'm just a stupid blackjack dealer. I can't put one thought in front of the other. I don't even know my own address." Her cheeks and forehead were burning, an entire furnace trapped in her face.

"They're at your house," he said, turning his head slightly to address the other woman. "It's the only place Erin could take them."

The woman didn't say a word. She retreated into the entryway and then out the door, shutting it gingerly behind her. A minute later her car started up and drove off.

"What a lovely family you have," Dallas said. The words sounded strange. Apparently this was her voice, her mind, her feelings rearing up like shadows in firelight and she hardly recognized them, to be perfectly honest, projected onto the walls of this cave, dark and evil and true. These were her thoughts. This was her. She told him so. She told him what she thought about him. She didn't hold back. She said everything there was to say and he stood there and took it, even nodding occasionally like he agreed. When it was over he waited maybe ten seconds before starting in about some phone call he had received in Palm Springs. The investments. OK, she thought. Here we go.

"That? It's nothing. I did it to help you, actually." She dropped into the armchair and lit another cigarette, calmly telling another lie. Why not? She was already neck-deep in deception, so what did it matter if she continued? A friend had warned her, she said, that the broker was actually an embezzler and so she took the initiative to divest because otherwise Logan would have wavered and waffled forever until the money disappeared to Venezuela or something, just like his parents' money. And since he didn't seem to . . . she stopped when she saw the expression on his face—the lines, the brittle surfaces. She blushed terribly, like a child telling the teacher the Loch Ness Monster ate her homework. She took a breath. All right. He wanted the truth? Here it was. She told him about the gambling, the debts, her plan to win it all back at the craps table in Vegas. This was the new and improved version of events that didn't include Felix and, it should be noted, this was the best truth Logan would ever get from her.

"And?" he asked.

"And what?"

He opened his arms grandly, sarcastically. "Did you rake it in? Are we rich?"

She exhaled smoke. The space and angles of the living room were palpable to her now. The empty kitchen with its humming fridge. The guest room Logan had slowly claimed as his study and the backyard beyond it, torn up like an eternal construction site. Just like their bedroom. She could admit it now. She had tried to make it work. She had really tried. They had made love in that room — in every one of these rooms, as a matter of fact — baptizing each section of the house. Ours, ours, ours. But everything was either his or hers, and it would be sorted out accordingly, no matter what she said next. And that was the spic-and-span truth. She took a breath.

"I lost it," she said. "I lost it all. Every dime. I gambled it away while you were fucking that woman in Palm Springs." She glanced down. Her cigarette was finished. Her gin and tonic was finished. She dropped the butt into the glass. "This is the part where we kill each other."

He sank onto the couch and covered his face with his hands. "I think we've already done that. Get out of here. I'll send some papers to your mother's house. Sign them."

"I'm not signing anything that I don't—"

"I keep the house and the furniture. You keep your precious car. It's more than fair. You know that."

She didn't reply. She headed straight for the bedroom and retrieved the shopping bag from under the bed and packed it into the bottom of her largest suitcase, covering it over with a few blouses before Logan came into the room — to watch her, basically. To supervise. There seemed to be springs tightening inside her, electrical wires in her stomach. This was her. This was him. Jackpot and bust. She was all sevens. He was oranges and lemons. They had never lined up correctly no matter how many bets she had placed. But look at the slots vertically instead of horizontally and see how close together the signs really are. This was the hardest part to take. How little space separated everything from nothing. It wasn't her fault. It wasn't anyone's fault. She inserted the coins, she pulled the lever, she watched the wheels. The alignment was too miraculous to happen in real life, like a perfect conjunction of the stars.

They said goodbye with ten feet of air between them, and then the freeway welcomed her, like it always did, with signs listing all the places she

could go. She drove with the pedal vibrating against her foot, engine screaming, her throat burning as she sang and cried with lyrics on the stereo. She
had the necessities: the car, the clothing, the shopping bag full of severance
pay. She'd stop at Mom's for a few days to catch her breath. But she wouldn't
stay. She was done with Vegas. She was done with everything familiar, everything that reminded her of her old life. She wanted to start over. She wanted
the territory ahead. She wanted square dealing and fair chances. She wanted
the blacklist replaced with a blank slate. She wanted to navigate her life
by the stars. Don't deny it anymore. This is who you are.

chapter 17

Logan avoided therapy. Always thinking well of people who sought professional help, he also thought, nevertheless, that it was something he'd never do himself. You know the type. Great for everyone except him. He secretly prided himself on having the intelligence and strength to fix his own problems. This was a key ingredient in the Male Autonomy Soufflé — a special WASP version of the recipe, Keris informed him, that had been handed down through the generations. Just don't sneeze while it's cooking, or the thing will collapse.

But let's stick to the facts. After Dallas left, Logan sat in the living room for a while, staring at the empty soda can she had used as an ashtray. Then Erin and Ozzy returned to drop off Puffy, arriving just as a truckload of xeriscape rocks pulled into the driveway — a delivery he had scheduled several weeks earlier but forgotten about — so he put on his rattiest clothing and grabbed a shovel before the trauma could get hold of him. He spent several days finishing the backyard. Erin and Ozzy helped. He paid them. He fed them. At night he watched the movies they rented from the video store — stylish, off-centered, music-synched testaments to today's misunderstood youth that Erin and Ozzy praised as "getting it right." In other words, he was making his best effort to avoid thinking. But then the backyard was restored, Erin and Ozzy were gone, and the house confronted him with its accusations of space and silence. Sure, it would have been silly to rip through the rooms right away and toss out the Blues Festival poster she had hung in the bathroom or the rickety chair she had purchased at an overpriced boutique, but the real question is why he didn't try to make it easier on himself by packing up the rest of her belongings or at least playing the stereo once in a while to replace the sound of her voice. And the real answer is that he was clinging to the evidence. He wanted to understand how they had loved each other.

One morning he filled a backpack with water bottles and energy bars and biked all the way out to the casino where she had worked. Here was the dusty border of the Indian reservation. Here was the municipal grid dissolving into plainsong. As he crossed the parking lot he glanced at the sign throbbing weakly with its electric fever, its faint pulse in the day's full glare. He locked his bike to a railing. He approached one of the tinted glass doors. And when he opened it the smell of ground-in cigarettes hit him like an ogre's breath. The sullen darkness. The bells and whistles. The bright plumage of the games. He wandered up and down the aisles, remembering not only Vegas but the video arcades he had frequented as a boy, his precious quarters devoured by aliens and asteroids. He finally settled at a machine in the corner because it seemed like the one she would have liked. Bet. Deal. Hold, hit. He kept reversing the values of keys and accidentally keeping the cards he wanted to throw away and vice versa, although his luck didn't seem to improve after he straightened it out.

When his money ran out he stared at the screen. He tried to picture her continuing after this, perched on the stool, chin lowered, eyes fixed, seeking new values in every hand. He tried to imagine her coming back for more. What did she see in it? What did it do for her? He placed his palms against the machine as if the answer lurked somewhere inside, burning in the circuitry. Then he looked past the hunched backs of the other players. Here was the smoke, here were the mirrors, here was the repulsive symmetry of the aisles. The tinted doors in the distance, masking the light of day. He didn't understand why someone would choose to be here. He didn't understand her desires.

He slid off the stool. He walked outside. He stood in the sun for a minute before he finally went over and unlocked his bike. The only thing left for him to do was to go home.

And the only thing left to do, once he got there, was to continue working on his article and develop it into a full-length book. He did it in six days. Admittedly, not much shaving or bathing took place that week, and the prose was a mess, but the basic structure was in place. Furthermore, he had managed to feed Puffy and ease the allergy by washing his hands after he patted him and making the bedroom a cat-free zone. He had even paid a few bills. He seemed to be holding it together.

OK, then. It was Thursday night or something. He drank the last beer in the fridge and paced the house in a stupor as his printer spat out three hundred pages of raw text. When he reached the living room it occurred to him that he couldn't have done this with Dallas in the house. She wouldn't have tolerated his obsessive state of mind, his distraction, his general air of neglect. This was the double-edged sword of her absence. He could leave the toilet seat up and feed Puffy in the kitchen and wear the same clothing three days in a row because she wasn't there. But she wasn't there. So he went to bed alone. And he lay there for hours with memories returning to him — the magnetic resonance of those first few months they had spent together. Her old bedroom in Vegas. Her legs wrapped around his waist. Her shoes on the kitchen floor and her voice in the shower and her favorite restaurants where they had eaten off each other's plates.

The next morning he awoke to stark sunlight, heat bleeding through the walls, no vehicle, no food in the house, and a cat who, with the instincts of a former stray, had gnawed a hole through his fifty-pound sack of cat food and was now drinking out of the toilet. There was, in short, no reason for Logan to haul his ass off the mattress until late August. And that suited him just fine.

Keris called. They had spoken several times over the phone, but he had avoided seeing her because — well, let's be honest here — she was a significant factor in his depression. Carrying Deck's child. Maybe she could bear it, but Logan couldn't.

A few minutes into the conversation he made the mistake of mentioning that he was in bed.

"What's this?" she said. "You're still horizontal this time of day? I thought that was *my* job."

The phone was resting on the pillow next to his ear, his arm draped over his eyes. "I already pruned the tree in the backyard and went for a bike ride this morning. Early. Before the heat set in. I'm just having a little siesta."

A long pause on the other end of the line. "For real?"

"Oh," he said. "You're asking about *reality*. Well."

"Well?"

"Don't worry about me. I'm top-shelf. I'm ready for consumption."

"What does that mean?"

"I don't know. I got it from a movie." He rolled onto his side and balanced the phone against his head so he wouldn't have to hold it. "How's Lamaze class?"

"*Lamaze?* Please, Logan. The birth process would go more smoothly if I squatted on the floor and quacked like a duck."

"I'd pay money to see that."

"Lamaze is a pacifier designed by the medical establishment to give a woman the illusion of control while her baby is removed like a faulty appendix."

"So what's the alternative?"

"A birthing center. A real one. Independently owned. Unaffiliated with hospitals and their assembly-line profit margins."

"You sound like you've done your homework."

"You would too, if you . . ."

"If I what?"

There was a long pause. "I'd like to give you a name and phone number. This is a woman I know. A therapist. Her name is Maria."

"Wait a minute."

"She combines verbal counseling with holistic naturopathic techniques. Reiki, shiatsu, herbal therapy. This is simply a number for you to have. You know, like the little box on the wall that says 'Break in case of fire.'"

"You're changing the subject."

"Maria is a healer in the truest sense of the word."

"You think I need help."

"I don't know what you need right now, Logan. My marketing team is stumped. I'm simply providing this number as a resource that you may use or disregard as you see fit."

He sighed. "You know what this means, don't you? It means I have to find a pen and paper. It means I have to get up."

"No, you don't."

"What are you going to do, come over here and write it down for me?"

"I'll call back and leave it on your answering machine."

"Should I hang up now?"

"Hang up now."

He pressed the disconnect button. He let the receiver roll away from his hand. His arms and legs were outstretched, dead-ended, like outlying districts no longer required to report in. The phone rang. The machine clicked. Her voice echoed in the kitchen, and as she recited the name and number it occurred to him that she could read the entire phone directory and he would listen, her voice humming warmly in his ear.

"Logan," she said at the end. "I'm here. Call me if you really want to see me. You know what I mean. I miss you. I love you."

He listened to the click, the dial tone, the silence afterward in which the house reverted to its quiet rhythms. Blood and pulse. Aqualung humming through the slatted vents. He stared at some glints in the ceiling, diamond-flecks ignited by the wash of daylight coming through the window, trying to make them into constellations. He closed his eyes. The world exhausted itself a little bit more. Animals died, forests shrank, atmospheres thickened. Oceans became more tarnished. Five more minutes of damage and loss.

Puffy meowed, announcing his trespass into the bedroom. Logan felt the plop of the cat's body on the bed, his little steps poking across the mattress, and then his soft weight as he scaled Logan's chest and finally settled there, purring, in sphinx-pose.

Logan's eyes began to itch. "All right," he said. "All right, all right, all right."

He rose from his slab. He sneezed. He carried Puffy into the kitchen, filled his bowl properly, and stroked him as he listened to the message again. Then he sat down on the floor and cried. When he was finished he called the therapist. She worked, she said, in half-day sessions, with a free space that had just opened up that afternoon. Was he available? Logan said he could probably clear his schedule. And when he hung up the phone he laughed. He wiped his eyes and laughed.

A week later he decided to go to his office and see what was waiting for him there. What else was he going to do? It was too soon to go back to the book. Therapy was digging into his very foundations and exposing all his faulty joists and supports, but he was tired of loitering at home all day. At least on campus he could pretend to be normal.

He biked through the June blaze. The sun. The dust. The roads thundering with traffic. The campus bikepaths were clear, the walkways nearly deserted. Summer session. No stress, he thought, as he locked his bike outside the Econ building. But then a great chill hit him in the lobby. A polar bite to the air. The secretaries in the main office were wearing sweaters because, they told him as he picked up his mail, something was wrong with the climate control and soon they would be cryogenically frozen with their fingers poised over their keyboards and would he please inform their next of kin. He laughed and continued on, climbing the stairs until, well, there it was: His office. Intact. His nameplate still on the door. He unlocked it. He dropped into his chair and looked around, at the papers and books stacked on every available surface like dirty dishes after a banquet. He sorted through the mail. Junk, junk, junk. Except this: A copy of the Fall Supplement, which listed corrections and additions to the course schedule, and a memo from Dr. No announcing the first administrative meeting of the Economics Institute, at which time the restructuring of the curriculum would be announced. Logan nodded. Of course. Now that his position had been clarified in Palm Springs, the resources of the department—or, to be accurate, the Institute—would be reallocated accordingly. All requests to teach his favorite material would be denied, ostensibly due to lack of demand, while his drudge-work on various committees and standard-issue courses would increase until he either quit or surrendered.

With a slow sweep of his arm, he cleared the mail off his desk and into a wastebasket that was already too full to accommodate it. The Fall Supplement spilled off the top. He reached over and was about to stuff it back in when he found an envelope protruding from the pages. This happened sometimes. The secretaries crammed all these things into his mailbox so that if he didn't grab each magazine or catalog by the spine and shake it . . . He opened the envelope and read the note inside. Then he read it again. It had to be a joke. But there was a phone number scrawled next to the signature, so he went over to his desk and dialed it.

"Hey," a man said on the other end. "You finally got my note. Where are you?" His voice was mild and calm. A Pacific-island cadence.

"On campus."

"That's perfect. I'm at the address on the letterhead. Come on down, man. Check this place out."

Logan packed up his bookbag, locked up his office, and descended the stairs. At the bottom there was an elevator with the doors jammed open and someone stooped over a couple of cardboard boxes. The person stood up. It was Deck. Logan halted in mid-stride and was about to retreat when Deck saw him.

"Well, if it isn't the Invisible Man," Deck said.

"The debate was over when I left."

"It certainly was."

Logan thought of replying to that, but instead looked him over. Shorts, T-shirt, reversed baseball cap. He glanced at the boxes on the floor.

"Moving in," Deck said, as if answering a question.

"I thought your contract didn't start until August."

"It doesn't. Novak pulled some strings for me." A smug edge to his voice.

"For you, or attached to you? You know," Logan said, holding out his hand like he was playing with a marionette.

"Laugh, clown, laugh."

Logan headed for the door. So this was how it would be. No final words or settlements, no ultimate vindications. Just the constant exchange of small-arms fire. When he reached the bike rack outside he noticed a payphone next to it. He went over and dialed Keris's number.

"*Him?*" he said when she answered. "You had sex with *him?*"

"You've been seeing Maria."

"I'm trying to figure this out. You and Deck. Yes, I've been seeing Maria."

"I can hear it in your voice."

"Please give me some kind of answer."

"Have you ever bitten into a chocolate only to discover some awful-tasting goo in the center?"

He sighed. "All right, all right. For Christ's sake."

"Look on the bright side. I could have answered by saying, 'Think about who you married, Logan. It undercuts your credibility in these matters.'"

"You just did."

"I know. I'm sorry. I love you."

The voltage rose in his chest. How could he say the words back to her when he doubted their value? He said goodbye and hung up softly, sweating already, and then went over to his bike and nearly burned his hand when he touched it, the metal irradiated with painful sunlight.

The neglected streets off Mill Avenue. The dirt lots. The broken sidewalks. The Mexican restaurant where he and Keris had eaten their first meal together. Logan leaned his bike against an old adobe house and stepped inside. The doors and windows were open, the hallway littered with wires, conduits, toolboxes, drop cloths, paint cans. Electricians in one room, painters in another. They pointed Logan toward the kitchen, where he found the person he was looking for.

"Hey," the guy said, looking up from some plans spread on the counter. He shook Logan's hand. "Donny Hilo. Good to finally meet you. Like I said in the note, I wanted to talk to you in Palm Springs, but I was happy just to find my way out of there without a seeing-eye dog."

"What's on your mind?"

"I'm here to tempt you with lower pay and longer working hours."

"Headhunter, huh?"

"Bottom feeder."

"Ouch. Flattery will get you nowhere."

Donny laughed. He had broom-bristle hair, a round face, a thick upper body that came from bone structure rather than exercise. He was wearing jeans and a collared shirt despite the heat.

"You know the deal with the Puritans, right?" Donny asked. "They spent years scrounging for, you know, nuts and berries and whatever game birds they could find, while the whole time there was this bay full of lobsters right in front of them. Yuck, they said. Scavengers. Those things live on the bottom of the ocean."

Logan nodded. "Not bad. That's the best bail-out I've heard in quite a while."

"You've heard of Soltrans?"

"To be honest, I haven't."

Donny wiped the sweat off his forehead. His skin was glistening. The room smelled of primer, burnt metal, dust. "Exactly," he said. "That's my point. We're based in San Francisco. And most of the time, you know, it feels like we're changing the world. But whenever I leave the Bay Area it's like waking up the morning after a party. Nobody's heard of us out here."

"Who's 'us'? What kind of organization is this?"

"A not-for-profit group promoting sustainability and responsible economics." He went over to a briefcase on the far end of the counter and pulled out a folder. "This is us," he said, handing the folder to Logan. "Take it home. Peruse. The most recent newsletter announces our new office, right here."

"Here?"

"Here. Belly of the beast. The world isn't San Francisco. It's Phoenix. It's Kansas City. It's Atlanta."

"Actually, the world is Nairobi and Bangkok and Mexico City."

Donny pointed at him. "Right. I stand corrected. This is the problem. Provincialism. Tunnel vision."

Logan asked a few more questions about the organization. Donny took him through the house, through the heat, through the paint fumes, shouting over the electricians drilling in the living room. They sat on the front steps outside, shaded by a large pine that had escaped the clearcuts of local construction.

"Palm Springs," Donny said. "That was just a whim, you know. My brother-in-law works at the hotel and he told me about it, so I drove all the way out there. I'm looking for an enlightened economist. One who can write. Is that you?"

Logan took a breath. "Maybe. Keep talking."

"It would be the two of us, for the most part, running this office. We'd be laying the groundwork for a mass movement. Campaigns. And I don't mean the simple, knee-jerk protest stuff you see all the time. You know, people just reacting to sweatshops and oil spills. We'd be a proactive force, proposing changes in government and individual behavior. The underlying stuff. We'd stimulate people into higher awareness. We'd seduce the local politicians and the chambers of commerce and other business organizations."

"Sounds exhausting."

"Come on, man," he said, making an expansive gesture. "You want to change the world or not?"

Logan stood up. He shook Donny's hand. Then he went over to his bike and put the folder in the bookbag hanging from the handlebars. "I'll think it over. By the way, you've conspicuously neglected to mention the salary."

Donny smiled. "If you ask me now, you're a brave man."

"What's the salary?"

Donny told him.

"I'll call you," Logan said, mounting his bike.

"Don't look at the salary. Look at the flexible hours, the health insurance. It's all in the folder."

It was all in the folder. The mission statement. The description of past and future projects. The community activities. The newsletters, the citizen-action pamphlets, the reviews of two books published by people who worked at the organization's headquarters in San Francisco. He read it all sitting on the couch with his feet propped on the coffee table, high-tempo jazz playing on the stereo. There was a copy of an article identifying Soltrans as a sign of a new trend—which is how magazines pegged everything—called New Consumerism. Logan had to smile at that one. The vote-with-your-dollars myth. As if choosing the lesser of evils solved the problem. But this was the magazine, not the organization. The organization, it seemed to him, was clearly ready to make the jump from local to national importance, and the job description included not only what Donny had mentioned, but also the broader task of forging ties between public and private interest in order to overhaul the economic system itself. In other words, it was exactly what Logan wanted to accomplish. But when he saw the goal stated explicitly on paper, its impossibility overwhelmed him. And what about teaching? Could he live without the classroom?

He tossed the folder onto the coffee table. Maybe he wouldn't have much choice in a couple of months. Dr. No's memo had already made it clear that he was shifting the goalposts and redrawing the territory around Logan, effectively cutting him out of the game. Speaking of which . . . Logan reached into his bookbag and pulled out the Fall Supplement. Might as well get it over with. Deck would probably be listed for a sleek new course, while Logan, by contrast, would be lucky if his own Intro to Macro class hadn't been relegated to a broom closet in the football stadium. But what he found in the Economics section brought him to his feet instead. Classical Theory and Modern Practice, taught by Dr. Smith. The course he had proposed last December, and which the administration had supposedly rejected.

Just then the phone rang. He went into the kitchen and answered it.

"I know I'm a major pest for calling you at home," Erin said, "but I just heard about that course you're teaching."

"So did I. I think it was listed by mistake."

"Does that mean it's dust already?"

"Not necessarily." He walked back into the living room and lowered the music, then stretched out on the couch. "If a miracle happens and the class fills up, then Dr. . . . then it can't be canceled, because the only valid excuse would be a lack of enrollment. But you know how it goes with the Supplement. By the time it comes out, everyone is either gone for the summer or registered for other courses."

"Give me the scoop on this thing."

He described it. As he talked he could hear a clicking sound on her end, the unmistakable sound of someone typing at a computer keyboard.

"That's heavy metal," she said. "I mean, really heavy metal."

"Are you typing?"

"Reporting."

"Oh God."

"At ease, soldier. I'm not Lois Lane. I'm just notifying the group."

"I wish I knew what you were talking about."

"A few of us started an e-mail list during your class. Sort of like, I don't know, color commentary. But anyway people kept forwarding it and adding more names to the list and it ended up being pretty big. So I'm sending this out and telling everyone to spread the word."

Logan put a hand to his forehead. He shut his eyes and felt all the gratitude come cracking through his voice. "Thank you, Erin."

She said it was the least she could do. He thanked her again before he hung up. Then he mulled it over. If he played dumb until August, the course just might fill up. But that didn't answer the question of how it had appeared in the first place. Course proposals didn't approve themselves. They didn't pass through the administrative gears and sorting systems on their own power, collecting stamps and signatures. So who was the culprit? Who was the ghost in the machine?

Deep in the Bradshaw Mountains, beyond the logging scars and burns sanctioned by the U.S. Forest Service, there was still a place where you could walk with a sense of eternity in the air. The ponderosa pines. The scrub oak. The manzanita crouched low with their slim maroon branches. Whenever Max Silverson had visitors, he enjoyed pointing out the alligator junipers, named for the texture of their bark, and the prickly pear in the exposed sections marking the continuity of low to high desert. He breathed in the robust scent of the earth. The pine needles and leaves. The wind, the sun, the silence. He was there now, climbing a trail toward his favorite lookout spot—a crag near an abandoned mineshaft. But don't worry. It was perfectly safe. In fact, the only reason his wife, Jeanine, wasn't with him at the moment was because she was nursing a sore ankle back at the cabin. He walked slowly, steadily, with a smile on his face courtesy of that pure blue heaven known as retirement.

Or maybe the smile was due to something else. Long before he had reached his golden age, for example, he had anticipated—in a purely physical sense, the way your mouth waters up for that first bite of food—that he would do something subversive before he left the office. Now, don't misunderstand this. He always pictured it as a sort of prank rather than an act of real consequence. Something that would say, in essence, I'm not exactly the person you thought I was. The role is not the man. And while we're on the subject, it should be mentioned that he had had his differences with Dr. Novak in the past—minor things not worth going into here, except to say that an agreement in ideology does not imply one in methodology.

Logan's presentation at the conference had seemed, at first, like a load of preposterous nonsense. After all, Silverson had spent his career among general equilibrium models and competition policy and the aggregation of consumer demand. But after the rush of events was over, and as he was driving back to Phoenix alone and in utter silence—because this was how Silverson liked to drive, his car a moving meditation cell—he was struck by an odd thought. And the odd thought was this: What if Logan is right?

He stopped for a moment and looked back over his route. The sloping flanks of the mountains. The forest pulsing in high-altitude sunlight. He took off his hat and wiped the sweat from his forehead. These were supposed to be the twilight years. These were supposed to be the years when his life was solved, his beliefs confirmed, the furniture set firmly in place. These were supposed to be years he spent with his grandchildren in bittersweet surrender to a falling demand. He wasn't supposed to want another seventy years or, even better, another century or so. He wasn't supposed to doubt he would ever tire of these mountains, these trees, the expressions on his wife's face. And he certainly wasn't supposed to want it with such passion in his old bones.

He set his hat back on his head. Classical Theory and Modern Practice. So be it. He turned and continued walking.

Logan agonized over the choice between working at Soltrans or continuing to teach at the university—the opportunity costs involved with each one—until he sat up in bed with the realization that they didn't have to be mutually exclusive. He called Donny the next morning and asked if he could work on a freelance basis. An occasional project here and there. An article or two. He could attend some meetings, talk to government and corporate officials who needed convincing of economic points. But he simply couldn't give up the classroom.

There was a brief silence at the other end of the line. "I had a hunch you were going to pitch something like that," Donny said.

"I know you can't pay me much."

Donny chuckled. "You're a tough negotiator. We'll have to work on that before you start talking to these business organizations."

"It's a deal, then?"

"Yeah, it's a deal. In fact, I might have something for you next week. I'll call you when I have the details."

Logan hung up feeling an odd mixture of excitement and relief. He couldn't quite understand it, so he brought it up in therapy later that day, apologizing to Maria for changing the subject.

"Well, you're not really changing the subject," she said. She sat in an armchair across from Logan. Plants surrounded them. They were both drinking iced tea.

"But we were talking about the way I loved Dallas. How I treated her and probably hurt her sometimes without realizing it."

"Uh-huh."

Logan thought for a minute. "Are you suggesting," he said slowly, "that my decision to combine these two jobs is connected to all these other personal issues?"

"Why would I suggest such a thing?"

"I hate it when you do that. But OK. All right. I'm getting it. This is going to be a lot harder—I mean, I'll be doing extra work above and beyond what I'm already doing at the university. But it's also a way to unlearn one kind of love and replace it with a new one."

Her eyes widened. "Uh-huh."

"And by doing both jobs, I'll be teaching other people how to do the same thing, but in an economic sense."

Maria didn't reply. She let his own words occupy the silence.

Logan sat back in his chair and looked away. Was that it? He tried the idea on for size: One activity is a natural extension of the other. Life out there is inseparable from life in here. Go out to the freeways and shopping malls, the sidewalks, the parks, the offices and construction sites. Look at the withering planet from a space capsule. We need to do this differently. We need to learn how to live all over again.

He stood. Maria stood. This was the strange part of the process — the non-verbal part of the process, and therefore the part he had the most difficulty accepting. But he did it anyway. He lay down on the massage table and closed his eyes.

Two hours later he biked home. He opened the fridge. He chugged a fluorescent sports drink and then, before he knew what he was doing, went back out and climbed onto his bicycle again and pedaled all the way to Keris's house. He rang the doorbell. He could a hear a vacuum cleaner running. He rang it again. He pounded on the door.

The noise ceased. The door opened. She stood there in an oversized T-shirt and a pair of her ex-husband's boxers, her glasses slightly lopsided on her face. She didn't look pregnant. No, wait. He stepped inside. He held her and felt a thickness in her mid-section. It was really happening.

She reached down and patted his waist. "You're losing weight," she said.

"And you're gaining it."

He was here because it felt like the thing to do and so he was doing it. He needed to be more this way. He knew this. He didn't resist it anymore. He didn't resist the urge to kiss her, to remove her glasses, to hold her face in his hands, to tell her that he loved her. Soon they were on the couch with the curtains hastily drawn, daylight brimming at the edges. Chow barked in the backyard as he sensed the commotion. They were naked. Keris wrapped her legs around him. He buried his face in her clumped hair. When it was over she began to sob quietly. They lay there for a long time. They hardly spoke. There was a garbage truck guttering some distance away, and then it arrived in the alley behind the house, setting off Chow again. The whine of a hydraulic arm. An avalanche of trash. The thud of the bin before the truck moved on.

Logan squirmed. The upholstery itched against his bare skin. The vacuum cleaner sat a few feet away, squat and brutish, its swan's neck coiled on the floor. He looked around the room. Pictures and odd objects. The ordinary air of a Thursday afternoon.

"Sophie will be home soon," Keris said.

Logan rose from the couch and began to get dressed. "I'd like to meet her."

"Are you sure?"

"Yes, I'm sure." He sat in a chair across the room to put on his sneakers. "Look at me."

She was lying on her side, her belly slightly swollen, her hips enlarged. He realized he had been avoiding this—looking at her completely, directly—since she had removed her clothes.

"No virgin territory," she said. "Is this OK with you? Is this something you can accept?"

A few minutes later he stepped into the heat. He was losing weight, he was gaining color, he was biking through the dust and pollution and exhausted traffic. He passed shopping carts in the canal. He passed agave and shrubs with trash tangled in the branches, broken furniture stabbing the soil. He tasted death in the air. You could spend your life searching the world until you found a place that hasn't been ruined, and then you would be the one ruining it.

He put his bike in the garage. He picked up the mail and brought it into the kitchen. The catalogs. The credit card offers addressed to Dallas. The electricity bill. He ripped it open and stared at the numbers for a minute. Then he went over to the thermostat and turned it off. The house fell silent. Puffy came over and rubbed against his leg.

"You want to go outside?"

Logan walked over to the sliding doors and parted them wide open. He felt the heat wash over him. He felt the weight of the sun. Puffy strolled outside, pausing, sniffing, tail flicking with the promise of every new scent. Logan took a deep breath. It caught in his lungs like mustard gas. He coughed. He laughed. He stood in the middle of the renovated yard with tears in his eyes. This is what he wanted: The rock. The cacti full of thorns. The citrus trees he had adopted even though they didn't belong there. A cat that made him sneeze. And Keris. Pregnant with Deck's child.

"OK," he said, nodding. "OK."

This was him. Here he was: A person who loved the ruined world. Did that make him foolish? Did that make him dumb?

Try it. Love the dying things. Love this universe without grace, without salvation in the stars. Love the solitude of the human race. Love confronting the mistakes and flaws that have made you what you are. Love your partner's old bedrooms. Love the harm you've been done. Love strangers more than flowers in your vase, more than the extra car in your garage.

Can it be that simple? Can the beggar weigh more than the coin, the gambler more than the bet? This is humanity on the aggregate scale. This is what you want, this is what you get.

acknowledgments

I would like to thank the people who have assisted and supported the writing of this book, among them Ron Carlson, Melissa Pritchard, Jay Boyer, and Alberto Ríos for their top-notch instruction; Katherine Tarbox for lighting the original fire; Bernardo Aguilar for introducing me to the field of ecological economics; Jim Lydanne and two of his associates, whose names have long since been lost to me, for providing insights into the world of casinos and gambling; Kristin Herron for submitting to a vital interview; Adam Campbell and Mick Jackson for their savoir-faire; Zoë Waldie for her matchless skill and conviction; Richard Beswick and Reagan Arthur for their editorial magnificence; and, above all, Allyson Stack, for her contributions too vast and essential to name.

THOMAS LEGENDRE was born in Maine and studied at the University of New Hampshire and the University of Delaware before getting his MFA in creative writing from Arizona State University. He now lives in Edinburgh with his wife and their daughter.